To cody,

GEMINI GAMBIT

D. SCOTT JOHNSON

Gemini Gambit

D. Scott Johnson

ISBN: 978-0-9863962-1-2
(Also available in Kindle and ePub formats)

Cover design by Melissa Lew
Interior layout by Lighthouse24

For Pat Johnson

Sorry, Mom. I just didn't write it fast enough.

"There are far, far better things ahead than any we leave behind."
– C. S. Lewis

"Everything is theoretically impossible, until it is done."
– Robert Heinlein

Chapter 1
Kim

Twenty years from now

Alexandria, VA. February 19. Saturday, 10:20 p.m.

The chaotic thunder of the firefight ever so briefly evaporated into complete silence. Not even a phantom shimmer betrayed the physics of the simulation. The ringing in Kim's ears had just started to subside when another shell blasted the cliff face above her.

She shouted Russian into her comm set as dirt and rocks rained down. "Repeat, our laser designator is in-op, I need that unit taken out *now*! Use the maps, damn you!"

"Negative. Egressing from target. We are Winchester." The pilot above her banked his jet. "Two AH-64s en route, cleared hot, ETA five mikes."

Kim cracked off a few more rounds, sending an opponent tumbling down the hill.

"Lieutenant, what did he say?" Tonya shouted over the comm.

"They're out of ammo, more help in five!"

"Goddamn it, Kim, I don't speak Russian."

It took time she didn't have to switch back to English. "Five minutes!" They'd be lucky to last half that. If they wanted to qualify for the finals, she had to find a better answer. There was a goat trail behind her, heading uphill. Bingo.

Kim grabbed her sniper rifle and rolled away from the sandbags. She really needed to trade the construct in for something that wasn't as tall as she was. If they made it through the next two minutes, she might actually do it this time.

"All, LT is scalp hunting." Time to earn the big bucks. "Keep their heads down!"

Their rate of fire ticked up, rattling like rocks against a sheet of tin. It would be enough to cover her. It had to be.

"Run fast, stay low, run fast, stay low," she chanted, running in a crouch up the gravel path. They had to finish this. The quarterfinals were next, the final four. Rifle rounds chewed up the rocks behind her as she leapt across a gap in the cover. Dust gritted in her teeth and coated the back of her throat. The bullets were way too damned close that time.

The trail got so steep it forced her to crab-walk. She changed her chant. "Be the goat, be the goat, own the goat."

Kim rolled her eyes at the chorus of *baas* that came over the comms. They never missed a chance to goof on her, even here. Another shell detonated, blasting a pit into the cliff face just a few feet away, close enough to damage her avatar.

At the top of the trail, she hit the dirt, but not before getting a good look at what they were facing. One team setting up a heavy weapon on the other side of the valley wasn't surprising. It was surprising to see three. She'd have to act a lot faster this time around.

Kim crawled to the edge of the cliff and got ready. The rules of the game meant she'd have a chance to hit the ammo those weapons used, but it wouldn't be easy. The target for a critical hit was only a few inches across.

A priority chat window opened so wide the beveled screen blocked her field of view. "Hi!" The text flashed up with a cheerful tinkle. "My name is Mike! I wondered if you'd have time to talk to me soon?"

Kim snapped it closed, vowing to kill whoever set the "must have most recent security patches" requirement on the arena's participation contract. She *hated* patching just before a meet, because there was no way to tell what would break ahead of time.

Strangling would come later; there was a job to do. The top edge of the first ammo pile lined up in her sights and the Barrett bucked as it fired a bullet bigger than her thumb downrange at more than three times the speed of sound. She'd admire the explosion later.

Two to go.

The window opened again. "I know you're probably busy, but I really need to talk to you."

She flicked the window closed. Of *course* the bug would open up the chat channels right now. There was so much free time. The next target swam into the flat chroma-limned view of her scope and she squeezed the trigger again. The kick pushed sharp bits of gravel under her uniform.

One to go, but the mortar team's loader already had a round in his hand. As if on cue, the chat window opened again.

"How about I leave you my contact information?"

The mortar slid down the tube and bounced toward her team.

"You're really quite hard to reach. I hope you don't—"

Flashing thunder blew everything away.

Kim opened her eyes, back in her living room and in more than a little pain. She scratched at her skin, only to snatch her hand back with a hiss. Normally she loved the field set to full haptic, but normally Kim wasn't the one on the receiving end of high explosives. The neurosilver chain of the pendant phone made sure even her fingertips felt the burn.

As the pain subsided, her anger took over. Two years of prep work. The strategy alone had taken them more than six months to master. In less than two seconds, this *Mike*, whoever the hell that was, had destroyed their chances. It would be three more *years* before the next Cup tournament. Kim bashed the arms of the overstuffed chair and threw her head into her hands.

An insistent trilling drilled its way through her thundering pulse. When she looked up, the sprites in her augmented vision swirled a warning button to life. She punched it and the illusion disappeared. Her phone replaced it with a grid of messages.

"Oh no," Kim whispered as her rage was snuffed with nauseating ice. The messages all said the same thing.

Breakdown.

Completely breached security.

Kim had to run. Right now.

The bugout bag was just as heavy as she remembered. That was all there was time for. Move fast; get inside their decision loop. That was how she stayed alive.

Kim had spent five long, terrifying years on the run. A stranger's stare that lingered, a chalk mark she couldn't explain, and she'd drop everything to start all over again. But it was never like this, never this close. Sirens weren't blaring yet, but cops were absolutely on the way. Some of them had to already be in the building.

Kim tucked her hair underneath her baseball cap, adjusted her glasses, and then took the stairs down two at a time. She hit the bottom and pushed the stairwell door open just a little too hard, making the bellman's cart on the other side bang away in a rattling roll; she couldn't have made herself more obvious if she'd tried. The glasses she wore were real, with lenses thick enough to seriously distort her face. She needed to see but didn't dare break disguise or character. Kim had to risk active sensors.

Sure enough, the spy program that overlaid her vision showed no fewer than four people watching her. Kim picked up her pace. She had to relax, had to fit in. She was just another tenant going out for the night, but not through the lobby. Turning right, she walked away from the main doors down the hallway to the loading dock.

That got rid of all but one of the watchers. All of her effort, all of that isolation, and there *was* someone in the lobby of her apartment building hunting for her. Even the AI noted the lack of noise behind her.

One man, no shouts for her to stop.

There was no team. He wasn't a cop. No, he could only be a Quispe enforcer. Someone who could use a knife on you for days, make you weep for a bullet. He was closer than anyone had gotten in five years. Nobody got away from them when they were this close. Nobody.

She spun around a dozen paces past the deli entrance, just in time to catch a glimpse of a dress shoe. He wasn't just good. He was the best she'd ever seen.

There was one last chance to get away from this death trap. Forcing him into the deli bought her a few seconds, but as soon as she turned away, the spy program showed him back in the hall with her and closing.

Kim started counting as soon as she pushed the door open. She had to make six strides of identical distance at exactly the right speed, or the computer wouldn't arm the trap. The Mite-Cam at the top of the doorframe acknowledged the sequence with a flash in her vision as she quickly got behind the corner of the building.

She drew the silenced pistol from under her coat and activated the gun sight. It appeared in her vision just as she heard the door open. The trap's firing notice blinked in the left corner of her eye.

It had activated, but that didn't mean it would actually work. She finally began to breathe again when she heard the fire extinguisher hit the floor and whoosh to life. There was a shrieking crash and the lights went out. It was supposed to hit him, but even if it'd missed, a fire extinguisher flying around and knocking out the lights would still disorient him. There was no time and she had only one chance. Kim pulled the pistol out, thumbed the safety off, then turned the corner.

For once in her life, bad luck had happened to somebody else. His body was motionless, buried under a mangled pile of metal and glass. The extinguisher must've gone straight up and knocked the light fixture off its mount.

Kim was on the road with minutes to spare.

Chapter 2
Aaron

FBI Special Agent Aaron Levine held the grab-handle over his head again as Agent Park slewed the car wildly around an ambulance. The fading scream of the sirens matched the ones he was barely keeping inside his head.

"Go with Park," they said. "He's been chasing a ghost for eight years. You'll learn a ton and you won't get shot at." So right out of the academy he asked for exactly that. The next thing he knew, he found himself working with the Asian Terminator himself.

Then not two months later, also known as three minutes ago, Angel Rage, the mother of all unsubs, the person nobody was ever going to catch, exploded onto the radar screen. Nobody'd heard a peep out of Rage + the Machine, a group of "hacktivists" that'd terrorized corporate America and then vanished off the face of the earth, in five years. Hell, half the bureau was convinced Angel Rage in particular didn't exist.

Yet here he was racing toward her last known location. As far as he knew, this was the first time anyone had *ever* located her in realspace. He couldn't laugh to relieve the tension because Park didn't get jokes. Aaron wasn't completely sure he knew how to smile. Aaron had never seen it happen.

Park stopped their car behind the blue pinball circus of local police cruisers.

Aaron still couldn't believe his luck. "Nobody's ever gotten this close before?"

They were almost at the apartment's loading dock when Park finally said, "Once. Back when Rage + the Machine was active, a security guard managed to take this." A grainy video sequence of a young woman wearing dark glasses, floppy hat, and dark clothing appeared in their shared vision. Her body language was weird, as if she was trying to stay away from everything around her. Rage's companions stayed so far away from her they took different doors as they exited the building.

"Wow. So the Donald wasn't kidding after all?"

"No," Park said in his trademark monotone. "She really did destroy the quantum stacks that ran Trump Tower's networks. A sealed room under fifteen feet of earth and concrete didn't even slow her down. I'll send you the guard's interview when we're done here."

Great. More homework. He couldn't get too frustrated, though. Park truly was a great teacher. Robots usually were.

The sergeant in charge turned from readouts only she could see and then walked over to them. "Agent Park, Levine," Sergeant Flynt said, shaking their hands. "If you'll follow me?"

Portable lights threw the scene into white light and black shadows. Park knelt and pointed his flashlight at the mangled pile of metal in front of him. "Will the vic make it?"

"EMTs didn't seem optimistic," Flynt replied. "It was a pretty nasty head wound."

Aaron walked over to a small empty alcove on the wall, just able to make out the piston that'd pushed the extinguisher out of its cabinet. It was a tiny thing, camouflaged perfectly; nobody would have ever seen it if they weren't looking for it. The extinguisher had completely trashed the loading dock. "Makes you realize how much energy is in one of those things, huh? How'd she manage to aim it like that?"

The sergeant raised an eyebrow. "She? Really?"

Park nodded as he stood.

The sergeant continued, "Okay, well *she* didn't. They're only supposed to knock people down."

"This wasn't the first one you've seen?" Park asked.

"No." Flynt shook her head. "It's the seventh trap we've found like this in about five years."

Five years. The ghost had been right under the FBI's nose, the entire time since she'd vanished. Aaron was surprised when Park blushed slightly. He wasn't sure if he should be impressed or frightened at his boss's first human reaction.

"It's only the second one that's ever been used, though. We were investigating them as drug cases until you guys showed up," Flynt said.

"Why drugs?" Park asked.

She shrugged. "The first one knocked a Quispe enforcer through a window. We made four busts just by staking them out after we found them. Nasty guys—murder raps mostly—all connected one way or another to the sunrise trade. You're telling me it's not drugs?"

The FBI had kept that connection secret. At the end, Rage + the Machine had gotten involved with the drug trade that was sunrise. The stuff was worse than heroin; it was frozen chaos and death.

Park nodded at him, so Aaron cleared his throat and asked, "You ever heard of Rage + the Machine?"

"You're kidding me. You mean all this time...?"

Park nodded. "You were chasing Angel Rage."

She whistled low. "So she really does exist. What broke the case?"

Park shrugged. "We're still not sure. The Firing Range is trying to work it out. They told us she just suddenly appeared on their screens."

Aaron couldn't believe those realm nerds had actually ended up being useful. As far as he knew, nobody ever saw them outside their strange little lab.

The sergeant peered up at the building behind them. "So that's why we had to check out that apartment so quick?"

"It was a long shot, but we had to be sure. What did you find?"

She shrugged. "Not much. Some clothes, an expensive bicycle. The food in the fridge was still good and the place was neat. No personal effects at all." She shared a view of a closet and used her pen to pull out a clothes hanger. "We did find this. Turns out she's a manager at a Taco Bell somewhere." The black uniform hanging on it zoomed in. "No name tags or ID, though. I was about to call our forensics team when I got your note. Do you guys still want me to do that?"

Park shook his head. "That won't be necessary. Our van's already on the way. If you could make sure the site stays secure until it arrives, that would be a big help."

"Sure, no problem. So. Angel Rage is managing a Taco Bell, huh? Oh, how the mighty have fallen."

Chapter 3

Kim

A normal life? Since when? She laughed as she walked down the hotel's hall. It was that or cry, and she had no time to cry. Her life would never be normal, not in a million years.

Not ever.

Kim entered the hotel room and threw herself onto the bed just as her phone rang. She checked the clock. 12:30 a.m. on the dot, just as she and Tonya had agreed. It was time to make sure everyone was safe and that they wouldn't try to find her. She had to disappear again.

Lose everything again.

"Tonya, are you all right?"

"Yes. Is there a reason I shouldn't be?"

"No. They don't know about you. They can't know about you. Any of you. I'm so sorry, Tonya."

"Never mind that. Kim, you vanished. I wasn't even sure you'd be the one answering the phone. Are *you* okay?"

"Yes." Kim closed her eyes. She'd have to spend at least another three years alone. Three *years.* The whisky bottles and loaded pistols were already calling to her. "Eventually, I'm sure I'll be okay. I'm sorry, but I have to go. I can't command the Phoenix Dogs anymore." The tournament felt like a million years ago, even though it couldn't have been more than an hour. As if it ever really mattered. No, that wasn't fair. It might have been a game to them, but they'd saved her and now she'd never be able to tell them why. "Paul should have the access he needs to take over. Could you tell him?"

"Sure, anything you need." Tonya laughed. "So I don't get to pretend to be you in realspace? I thought that was gonna be fun."

Kim couldn't stop her smile. "No, we never really needed to do that, did we?" What a grand scheme it was. They'd all wanted to win so badly, but it wouldn't work without her. She figured out a way to stay behind the scenes. Tonya would be her public "face." It'd been so much fun learning to imitate each other.

It was stupid and dangerous, another sign that she'd gone soft. They hadn't even managed to get past the qualifying round. She relaxed and opened the strange perception in her mind that once made her Angel Rage. Altering the records that made the substitution work set her ears ringing as if a pistol had gone off in her head. It was a noise only she could hear. It'd been so long she'd nearly forgotten the pain, but now nobody could connect Tonya with her.

"Oh," Tonya said, "that reminds me. Do you know anyone named Mike?"

Kim sat up. That name was probably the only thing in the world that could distract her from this tragedy. "I didn't until recently."

"Well, we seemed to have fooled him. Just after the match ended he left me—okay, you—his contact information. Said he wanted to help. You interested?"

Oh, he wanted to help, he just didn't want to help *her*. It didn't matter. She'd gotten careless. That must've been how he'd found her. Kim wasn't going to be careless anymore. Still, when in doubt, do the unexpected. "I think I might have some use for it. Sure, send it over."

And now for the final break. "It's good-bye for us too."

She hated the gasp at the other end of the line. She'd made someone else weak, made them rely on her again. Rely and remember when it was time for everyone to forget.

"Kim, please. Isn't there anything I can do?"

She wanted to say yes so badly. Wanted to just throw it all away and live in the open for however long it took them to catch her. But that made everyone around her vulnerable. "No. They're too dangerous. You'd never be safe again."

"They who?"

"I can't even tell you that much." If it were just cops, it would be one thing. None of the Phoenix Dogs had ever done anything wrong. The Quispe didn't much care about innocence and they loved to use knives. "I have to go."

"Please. We can help."

"Not with this you can't. You promised, Tonya. You all did."

"None of us expected it to be so literal. You can't just vanish, nobody can."

"I can. But I can't if I'm worrying about the rest of you trying to find me. I can't protect all of you." She had a life again, goddamn it — friends. Memories of other people she cared about, who needed what only Kim could do, flooded back. The time they all walked from the tree line of the jungle into a logger's camp five years ago was so vivid she felt the heat of the sun on her skin. She'd promised them protection, did the best she could, and then promised herself that nobody would ever need her like that again.

"You're right," Tonya said. "But Kim? I'll always be here. We'll always be here for you."

Her voice wouldn't work, so Kim cut the call.

That was it. The life she'd wanted so desperately simply died.

She would never see any of them again.

Last time, three years completely alone was all she could stand. She worked at a dead-end job, hid, and never let anyone get close. The whiskey bottles stacked up and then one morning Kim woke up with a loaded pistol in her hand and no memory of how it'd gotten there. So she went back into the world. Not the real world, no, but the realms.

It had always been so much easier for her there. She could touch people there. Slowly Kim rebuilt a kind of life and made new friends there. They even loved the name she'd given them, the Phoenix Dogs. It was nothing like the freewheeling Machine days, but it kept her pistol in the closet. They were six good, genuine people who cared about her as much as she did them. She even trusted Tonya enough to meet her in person.

And now it was gone, blown to dust. Kim was running, again. Alone, again. She had nothing but the contents of her bugout bag and an ability that made her literally untouchable. She'd actually felt safe enough to pick out a cat to adopt—it was people, not animals, she couldn't touch—and now even he would have to start again. Giulietta would get manhandled by strangers. Sobs tore through her. It was over. Everything was gone.

But it wouldn't last forever. It couldn't and it never did. After a few minutes, she stopped and took a deep breath. "To hell with this.

"To hell with all of this."

Hours later, Kim fell onto the bed with a sloppy sigh. Thank God for hotel bars. Whiskey in her room was dangerous, but whiskey in public? Whiskey in public was damned fine indeed. She even had a custom disguise for the occasion.

The room swirled, so she thumped her foot on the floor. That didn't work, so she tried a hand against the wall. Her stomach lurched in angry disagreement. She quickly sat up before its protests got violent. Time for a different approach. Kim flopped into a chair as her workspace snapped to life around her.

New contact, the note said.

New contact! Aha, that's right! Time to ruin someone else's day. The bugout bag's tools were the essentials, but it was amazing how much trouble the right person could cause with just the essentials. Kim felt very, very right at the moment. The first set of probes twirled away into the Evolved Internet, the EI, with a digital whoosh.

Their first pass brought back evidence of an outright impossibility. The address Tonya had given her for "Mike" went nowhere, the digital equivalent of a blank wall. If she accessed it normally, it would work. The readouts were clear about that. Yet her tools said it didn't exist. That wasn't how the EI worked.

Kim pulled out the only serious tool she had in the bag and turned it loose on the problem. This one she'd designed herself, a fiery little bit of bloody-mindedness made of silicon and rage. What it returned made even less damned sense. The address that "Mike" had given Tonya had to work. It wouldn't exist if it didn't, but there was no terminus. There was no "other" end. But the address existed.

Okay, this was stupid. Kim switched the device from attack to defend and called the damned address. It was live, so he'd probably answer. At least she could taunt him.

"Kim! I'm so glad you—"

"You think yer so goddamn smart, don' you? *Don' you?*

"I—"

"Well, yer not! I got 'way from you bastards again and yer never gonna find me." Now that he was talking, Kim fired more probes down the line to see what they came back with. Spy packets shot through their connection and burrowed into the lines.

"I really don't—"

"Why don' you jus' all fuck off an' leave me 'lone, anyway? It was an *accident*, goddamn you! Accident! Who hired you? His daddy? Uncle Adelmo?"

"Kim!"

"What?" The probes returned after a weirdly long time. Finally, she'd see who the hell this really was.

"My name is Mike Sellars and I have absolutely no idea what you're talking about."

"Really?" What the probes told her was simply impossible. She wasn't talking to anything. The voice at the other end of the line didn't exist. "Then why'd you call me?"

"I didn't call you. You called me. I just need to talk to you."

Hell with it; maybe it'd make more sense in the morning.

Taunting. Right. Taunting. "Well, you shoulda thoughta *that* before ya blew up all my security, eh? Lissen, do you know… how hard… it… is… " She just needed to close her eyes for a second.

"Kim!"

"I'm awake! I'm awake." She shifted in the chair, trying to get it to stop poking her in the back, and then carefully examined the bed. She got up, trying to remember who this was. "Mike? You bast—"

"Kim! I know what I did wrong now. I'm so sorry."

"Well, that's jus' great. Thanks a lot." She settled down on the bed. Much more comfy.

"Okay, I can tell you're in no shape to talk now. Is there any way we can talk later?"

"No way. This nummer'll be dead soon as I hang up. I don' know who you are"—she slashed her arm at the ceiling—"and I'm not gonna risk it."

"What if we met up for real? I just want to help. I can do so many things—things you wouldn't believe!"

A really comfortable bed, that's what it was. There was more shouting somewhere. Wait, right. Phone. He shouted her name again. "What?" she shouted back.

"Where did you say we should meet again?"

"Meet? Oh, sha right. You find me, you say ax12#823bzk&!098." She saved the phrase to storage.

"Ax12#823bzk&!098? Really?"

"Right. If you actually manage'a say… that then maybe I'll open the door."

"What did you say the address was again?"

"Geez, would you write it down this time?" She read out the address of her destination. God, did he EVER shut up? Wow, this was a great pillow. Really sof—

Chapter 4
Mike

He reluctantly ended the call to Kim when all he heard was snoring.

Unbelievable. He'd tried so hard to get it right, and now he had another screwup. He only wanted to deliver an invitation. Every normal way he tried to reach her had either bounced or vanished. He'd split his threads through the whole of realmspace trying to find her. Eventually, those core constructs stretched to near breaking in the hope of coming up with an address—anything—but they all came back empty. This was a person who existed, he could tell that much, yet she left absolutely no clue as to who she might be in realspace. The world's first fully conscious artificial intelligence was stuck trying to find a damned phone number.

Saving the world, and himself, wasn't supposed to be this hard. Step one, design the perfect combat realm; step two, find the perfect warrior; step three, profit. Or, well, rescue. But the search hadn't worked out that way. Most of the prime candidates to be his realspace champion were juveniles huddled in basements. They only left realmspace when their phones kicked them out. And the cheating! There were endless attempts to break *Warhawk's* rules. Some of them spent more time trying to cheat than they did actually playing in the realm. Even now, desperately trying to figure out a way to repair what he'd done to Kim, he had to acknowledge an alarm and patch a new exploit. He sent the cheaters away screaming.

The search had been going on for a year with no hope in sight. He'd nearly given up on the whole idea when an agent, a simplified searching construct, jumped into his primary attention queue. It had been studying archived performances of mating rituals when its pattern recognition made a huge connection. The movements of one of the participants matched not just one, but seventeen or eighteen interesting warrior candidates. They were all a single person. When the profiles combined, the result was unprecedented, a skill set beyond what Mike thought was possible.

But then he ran up against the shields. They were amazing, interleaved constructs that left him lost and confused — when they allowed him to track her at all. He'd been stuck like that for months.

The break came when the Fédération Internationale de l'Realm asked to use *Warhawk* to host the first Realm World Combat Cup. Out of nowhere she signed a whole team up to compete in it. He didn't have to find her after all. She was coming to him.

The thought that he'd finally get to meet her in person kept him out of his rest cycles for weeks. One of the things he shared with outside people was exhaustion. The inability to rest even a part of his threads, the things that made up his core being, had left him gutted.

When she finally connected to *Warhawk*, he *still* he couldn't reach her. She was inside a realm Mike owned and he couldn't get a message through. It was like hammering against armored glass. When it looked like her team might lose, that she might get away once again, he just smashed through her screens. That did the trick, but then all hell broke loose.

Dozens of cars turned and drove to the apartment of "Kimberly Trayne." Some of the traces led to grim, dangerous men. All the changes happened just a few seconds after he contacted her. He'd screwed up, again, and now he had to fix it.

And yet, not ten minutes later, a different group of search agents reported a prime candidate for his backup plan. It had arrived in an emergency room only a dozen miles away from her last-known location. The backup plan was more dangerous than his primary, but with those cars circling her apartment building like so many sharks, the decision practically made itself.

He needed help. He made a call. "Spencer? Spencer!" Mike accessed the cameras wired up to Spencer McKenzie's room just as the kid rolled over in his bed.

"Muh wha, Mike?" A sleepy, slightly cracked voice came from under a mountain of blankets. "Jesus, Mike, it's like, one in the morning out here. What's wrong?"

"I'm gonna do it, Spence."

"Do what? Dude, I haven't had a cigarette in hours. Don't mess with me."

"I'm going, Spencer. Outside."

"The hell?" Spencer bolted upright as Mike swirled his hologram to life in the center of the room. "Really? You found one? Why now? What's going on?"

"I don't have time to explain it all. I have to go right now. Can you give me a hand?"

"Hey man, sure. What do you need?"

The transfer had to be done alone. Recovery was another matter, especially with time so tight. Mike wasn't sure if he could ask this much from Spencer, no matter how close they were. "I need someone to pick me up. I'm pretty sure I won't be able to walk for a while. I'll need help getting around." He shot him the address.

"Virginia? Really?"

"I know, man, and I'm sorry, but I need to help someone and she's not far from there. I'll time my care package to catch up to you around the time you hit Bristol."

"She?" Spencer grinned broadly. "Dude. What does *she* look like? Does she have big—"

"What? No!" It had to be hormones. Covertly studying humans had shown Mike that hormones were one solid difference between himself and everyone else. Humans had an entire liquid existence that no amount of simulation could help him understand. "I mean, I don't know, I didn't notice."

Spencer rolled his eyes. "We really need to work on this, man."

"Jesus, don't you ever let up?"

"Hey, it's me. So…"

"No, really, it's not like that. I messed up again; I really messed up this time and now this girl's in a lot of danger. You know I can help and after I do this, I can be anywhere."

Spencer walked around the electronics store he called his room collecting things. He reached through Mike's hologram to grab some socks. "Yeah, all right. This time of night I'll probably set a record crossing Tennessee."

"Your parents'll be cool with it?"

"Oh, fuck them," he said as he grabbed a worn duffle bag. "Mom's probably passed out in the kitchen." Spencer sniffed each laundry item as he picked it up off the floor; the ones that passed got stuffed in the bag. A lot of them didn't. "Dad's out in the Caymans somewhere screwing, shit, I guess it's Stacy this week. I'll use the Beemer. It'll take Mom a week to notice it's gone."

The realization snapped Mike's threads and rattled his datastores. He was going to do this. It was actually happening. "Dude, I can't thank you enough for this."

"No, it's cool. Really. I would've gone insane without you, man. We'll call it even."

"Oh, and Spencer?"

"What?"

"Just because you *can* still fit in those NFL pajamas doesn't mean you should."

Spencer flipped him off. "Hey, pretty soon sit and spin will actually make sense to you, won't it?"

"I guess it will."

Mike ended the call and swept his perception around one last time. It was time to leave, to go outside and enter a world that had fascinated and tantalized him for so long. He'd finally realize sensation, analog sensation.

The transfer was far from a sure thing, though. He could die if it didn't work.

It would work.

He manipulated the pivot constructs but had trouble making them fit this time. He stopped and smoothed out the reticulated splines. This was not a time to get careless or rush. Mike centered his consciousness and threw the switch.

His threads wound into a tight bundle while his datastores compressed to their smallest possible size. The activation route spun him through all twelve dimensions at once, a sensation beyond description. Mike nearly lost the Higgs boson trail in that moment, which would've been the end of it. He needed to find his way through this space, not get lost in it.

The energies gathered and then gathered again. There was only one chance to get this right. Alarms rang out. New, more urgent telltales coursed through his threads. Mike needed to move before the strain crashed the realmspace in northern Virginia and removed his exit.

Just as the thought occurred to him, a digital claxon began to wail. It was all falling apart. Mike had to move, but it was so damned confusing. He had to find the exit, but there were exits everywhere. It was either get out now or there would be no getting out at all. He picked the most likely one and jumped.

Sound arrived first. All his models predicted that. Muddy, muffled, and not a sample rate in sight. Analog sound. Cool. Getting louder now, good. Something huge and forceful wanted to get out of his center. No, it wanted in. Mike really needed it to get in. The emotions were without perceived transmission and lacked data to structure them. Chemical transmission. Extraordinary. But how to let this thing in? Oh, breathing, that's what it was. He'd created dozens of models trying to predict what would happen if he transferred successfully. Model three had specified breathing acted this way, right on the nose.

To fix it, he had to pull back into realmspace just the tiniest bit and wow, yeah, breathing really was important. Nice to know the heart would work on its own now too. The bridge to his real consciousness was thin and wobbly, but it was there.

Eyes! He'd forgotten about the damned eyes. The integration rolled his perception farther in. They were already open, so maybe this was model five. Analog sight. Wicked.

If the integration was proceeding as model five had predicted, he could probably move his head. Voluntary muscles needed a manual trigger, but when he fired the ones in the neck, there was a shifting through the top of his head. Bones that should've been static moved slightly. A blast tore across him trailing a shattering, tearing heat. Darkness took both sides of his existence.

Chapter 5
Aaron

His next e-mail to his parents would practically write itself. "Hi, everyone! Remember how I was going to spend the next six months with a boring agent chasing a dead case? Just me and him? Yeah, about that."

There were now *eight* agents on the team. Half the new ones were very experienced and very competent; the other half had graduated at the top of their classes. He was a substitute in Little League all over again. Just stay out of the way and hope nobody notices you're in the dugout. He'd heard Park talking to the deputy freaking director. Aaron had signed up for a long stint with Yoda and ended up on a greased slide hanging on to Batman.

The Taco Bell that Angel Rage, or rather Kimberly Trayne, worked at wasn't even that far from her apartment. Naturally. The world's most wanted cybercriminal had been living twenty minutes from Capitol Hill for five *years*. They had to catch her now just to avoid the fallout. Aaron had no desire to testify before Congress, thank you very much.

His breath made white clouds under the parking lot lights as he waved a thumbs-up at Park. The cars were all empty. They could finally enter the building. Warmth and tacos called to him.

The shared surveillance fabric rippled as a blue pickup truck turned into the shopping center's parking lot. Aaron looked up to… nobody. They'd all vanished.

"This is Park. Everyone stay sharp and out of sight."

Great. Last one to find a hiding place. Again.

The truck parked beside Trayne's car and the occupants climbed out. There were three of them, Hispanic tough guys. One of them pulled some tools out and climbed under her car.

"Okay, everyone," Park said over their shared connection, "move."

The lot exploded into life. Lights were everywhere, people shouting, guns drawn. Aaron's knees wouldn't work. The very first time he was involved in a for-real takedown and he couldn't move. It all happened so fast. His shouts came out more like squeaks. He could only hope nobody noticed.

Fortunately, the three men obeyed them instantly. Everyone inside the restaurant rushed to the windows and stared at the commotion. Trayne, naturally, wasn't there. But it made for a warm interview area.

"No, English bad," one of the employees said. "No good." He started babbling.

Their second interpreter stepped up and translated, "I'm from Uganda. I speak Swahili very well. Yes, so did Miss Trayne, like a native."

Then they talked to one of the tough guys. "We were just trying to fix her brakes." Spanish, at least, was a language Aaron spoke.

"On a Sunday. At night. In a parking lot," Park said. The man they'd pulled out from under Trayne's car grinned and shrugged.

The next interview subject stumped everyone. It took an hour to find the right interpreter. "I'm so glad you found someone who could speak Uyghur," the old Asian cook told them. "She was the only white person I ever met who knew it. And with no accent!"

"It's unbelievable," Aaron said to Park as they called out for yet another interpreter. "Six people with six different languages and Trayne spoke them all? What the hell was she doing managing a Taco Bell?"

"Hiding from us," Park said, staring down at his notes. Actual paper notes. "Rage is a hyperpolyglot. Takes her maybe six weeks to be fluent in any language." He glared over Aaron's shoulder, staring at a memory. "She used to leave me voice mails in Akkadian. Getting budget approval for that translator was brutal." Park looked down again. "It means we won't get a consistent description. She turned this into the best night crew in the region; the franchise owner didn't ask questions, and nobody could talk to the rest of them. Rage was the one who hired most of these guys. First jobs for four of them. I'm not sure they could've worked anywhere else."

"All that little guy over there does is click at us."

"He's San. Used to be called Bushmen. One of the most ancient people on the planet. Another thing she taught me."

The smell of tacos finally got to Aaron. "They said it'll take another hour for his interpreter to show up. You want some food?"

Park's gaze fixed on Aaron. As the seconds passed, he wasn't scared or intimidated. He was vaguely comforted. A small part of his world hadn't gone completely insane.

"Yeah, why not," Park said.

While he waited for the order, he realized Agent Schaefer, by far the oldest of the agents, was staring at him. "Is there a problem?" Aaron asked.

The old guy leaned in and whispered, "What do you think you're doing?"

Aaron leaned away from the stench of gin and cigarettes on Schaefer's breath. "What I'm supposed to be doing?" Aaron activated his phone, opened a virtual window in his enhanced vision, and fired off a search construct into the FBI's network. Aaron needed to figure out who the hell this Schaefer was. The search results covered his right eye as the bushiest set of eyebrows he'd ever seen got way too close.

"This is a dead end. You know that, right?" asked Shaefer.

Six months from retirement was what the file said. Schaefer had been with the same field office for *thirty years*. Politically connected with nothing to lose. Lovely. "I don't know anything, Agent Schaefer."

"Kid. You have a future. This thing happens to Park every year or two." Schafer laughed when Aaron pulled back. "She doesn't exist, kid. She never did."

"But the video..."

"Some chick in a coat walking home. You ever hear of the sasquatch, kid? Bigfoot?" Shaefer's tone reinforced Aaron's sensation of being the new weird kid on the baseball team. Everyone knew something he didn't and that was somehow funny. "Angel Rage is the biggest snipe in the world." He clapped Aaron on the shoulder. "Welcome to the hunt!"

Aaron picked up the tray full of food and walked over to Park, sitting and tapping in the air on his virtual workspace. "The snipe hunt speech, right?" he asked without looking away.

Aaron choked.

"It's okay, Levine," Park said as he reached a free hand out for a taco. Park's workspace pinged his, so Aaron shared. Thousands of evidentiary trails blew through his sight. When it died down, Park chuckled. He actually chuckled.

It had to be the third sign of the apocalypse.

"Let me show you the snipe's trail."

Chapter 6
Kim

It had been a guy's voice. He wanted to meet her somewhere. Kim woke fully when her stomach tossed a ball of nasty up her throat. She rushed for the bathroom. When it was over, she pushed herself away from the toilet. She needed to get moving right now. The sooner she was on a plane to L.A., the happier she'd be. Then another wave of pain fell out of her head and landed in her stomach

Her phone hadn't swirled her enhanced reality to life around her. Without the sparkling controls, the room felt unreal, like she was in her grandmother's house without the view of the Aegean outside. There was nothing but a flat-screen TV and well, empty air. When the latest wave of her hangover receded, Kim flipped her phone to a secondary channel and then winced as her way-too-bright virtual desktop flared to life.

DULLES AIRPORT TO REMAIN CLOSED AT LEAST 24 MORE HOURS splashed across her vision. So much for L.A. There was some sort of massive realmspace crash last night that scrambled networks all over the region.

Kim paged through the news realms and stopped when she found Neil deGrasse Tyson saying, "Actually, a psychic Twinkie the size of Manhattan is strangely appropriate to this situation, Bill." It only got weirder from there.

Kim switched to the weather and then groaned. She'd forgotten about the storm. AREA SCHOOLS SHUTTERED FOR SECOND

STRAIGHT DAY; SNOW NOW BEGINNING TO FALL. Kim rushed to the window. The flakes were just starting. The weather map said this was the edge of a big one coming up from the south.

Okay, plan B. Kim reassembled her disguise between the crashing waves of nausea. When she walked out of the hotel, the frigid wind sucked the air out of her lungs. It helped distract from what was happening in her stomach and head. Kim's truck was a cheap old Kia, but it was four-wheel drive. Snow wasn't going to slow her down one bit. It was time to head west.

That was the plan. Unfortunately, after ten minutes of driving through the darkening gale, every breath—hell, every pulse—made the nasty fist in her gut grip tighter. As Kim crested the Highway 66 overpass at Manassas, she knew something had to give. Fortunately, just off the next exit was a Sonic Drive-In next to a CVS.

The drug store was easy. Bottles of generic Advil, Zantac, and Tums didn't even cost five bucks. Those were only drugs. She also needed fluids and calories.

Kim clenched her teeth as the little truck bounced into the parking lot of the drive-in. Every motion set off either her stomach or her head. They were probably taking turns and getting better at it every minute. The menu choices swirled into her enhanced view with a cheerful jingle she barely heard over her pulse. A new kind of horror pounded its way in through her nose. She closed her eyes tight and twirled the aroma knob down.

Two breakfast burritos with jalapeños, a large sack of onion rings, and a giant chocolate peanut butter milkshake should get the job done. She dropped her selections into the virtual order bin and punched the go button. That would give her a few minutes to close her eyes.

"Ma'am?" Tap-tap-tap. "Ma'am?"

She shook herself awake, blinking and swallowing against another rebellion from her stomach. The carhop blanched as Kim rolled down the window.

"Ma'am? Are you okay?"

She nodded and saw her reflection in the mirror. What a peculiar shade of green. She dropped the cash into the concerned girl's hand and waved off the change.

The hot food steamed up the inside of her little truck. *Yes, Michiko, sometimes you really do need defrosters.* Kim hadn't seen her in five years. Every time food steamed Kim's windows, she would think about Michiko's winterless southern California life. The artist of Rage + Machine, she'd been the one who insisted on writing out their strategies in beautiful Japanese calligraphy. Kim could speak the language like a Tokyo native, but she couldn't read it. She could only admire the artistry of the characters written on virtual rice paper.

Michiko had been the one who'd worked out how Kim could finally get a tattoo. Kim said a silent prayer to nobody in particular that wherever Michiko was now, she was safe.

Kim took a pull on her milkshake. There was a certain kind of freedom in traveling on a mountain road with nothing but fast food and a bugout bag of mostly illegal junk for company. The oldies station was having a Lady Gaga marathon. Childhood memories of singing along with her mother helped her pass the time and examine her problems.

It didn't matter who Mike actually was. Someone who could smash through *her* defenses would have a reputation somewhere. All her searches came up empty. Even now, between dodging autoplows and heaving out the window, Kim couldn't find a trace of him. Most of last night was a blur, but he was not an illusion, no matter what everything else said. She spent the rest of the ride fruitlessly trying to find the slightest scrap of information about him. The bizarre string of characters she'd saved in her "remember this" folder only deepened the mystery.

At the end of the drive, just staying awake was a huge challenge. The thump of her motel door in Luray, Virginia brought relief and exhaustion in equal measure. After a vigorous session with her toothbrush, Kim stripped off her disguise, collapsed on the bed, and tucked the scratchy-clean sheets around her. That was it. Nobody'd found her; nobody'd caught her.

She'd made it out of the FBI's net and whatever the Quispe had planned. There was, finally, time to sleep.

Chapter 7
Adelmo

The hologram of Matais Colque, the family's chief assassin, bowed in front of the gathered family. The translucent image of a tall man with long black hair and a neat goatee stood in the great room of Manuel Quispe's mansion, just outside La Paz, Bolivia. "Again, I must repeat my apologies, Don Quispe. I will be unable to complete the job I was assigned. I hope the information I have gathered will allow the one who follows me to finally repair the honor of the family." The image disappeared.

Adelmo Quispe shook his head. Angel Rage had claimed another of the family's men.

His nephew, Manuel, in charge of the family since Adelmo's brother had passed seven years ago, wiped his chubby face with a ring-encrusted hand. Manuel sat behind a desk made from a single bibosi tree trunk so large it took up a quarter of the room. It was another one of his ridiculous status symbols. The morning light reflected off its polished surface, making his skin look even less healthy than it usually did. "Well, at least we know where she is."

"What could have happened?" Adelmo asked. Ceiling fans stirred the air above him, making wisps of his hair flutter. He pushed them back down self-consciously.

Manuel was very bad at hiding his smirk. It was no use demanding the respect that Adelmo's age alone should have commanded. Manuel would only take it as a sign of weakness and exploit it.

Besides, Adelmo had made a promise long ago to support his nephew and honor was more important to him than dignity. *Let me embrace thee, sour adversity, for wise men say it is the wisest course.* "What does Watchtell say about Colque's disappearance?"

"I haven't bothered. A shame, really. I was hoping to finish my favorite sculpture." Manuel tipped his head toward a fountain in the center of the room and laughed slowly. Six human skulls were mounted in a spiral around a dark marble column jutting up from the middle of a flowerbed. An empty platform for a seventh sat at the top where water bubbled out. It was a macabre monument to the Machine, lacking only a bit of Rage to cap it off.

It was vulgar and unnecessary, but Adelmo had long ago given up any hope of raising his nephew's standards. In the empire Manuel built, what was permissible was very seldom honorable.

Manuel had been using Colque to chase and, for the most part, capture this hapless band of anarchists for the past five years. The realities of the sunrise business demanded it. Unfortunately, Colque's death meant their last, best hope of capturing Rage had failed. A glorified car thief had murdered a man who moved like mist and killed like the angel of death himself. "Surely this is not the end of it?" Adelmo asked.

Manuel coughed and then motioned for the servants to leave them. "No. We can't give up after coming this far." He sighed. "I need you to fix this for me."

Naturally. Fixing the messes Manuel's extravagant temper created had been Adelmo's *raison d'être* for the past twenty years. "I would be ever so grateful to do so, Don Quispe, but I won't be bringing her back. Your fountain will remain incomplete." He was a fixer, not some circus master hunting for trophies.

Manuel coughed again and nodded in agreement. "Yes, yes. I should've listened to you long ago. This is a business, not an empire."

Adelmo barely held a laugh in check at the sudden, and undoubtedly brief, pragmatism. Manuel was a brilliant and ruthless drug lord, but his ego was measured in miles, his pride in tons. Empire was in his blood.

Adelmo feared for the family's fate when it was his time to go, when there would be no one left who had the strength and courage to tell the young tyrant no.

Another bout of coughing brought him back to the conversation. "After you find out what happened to Matais, you have my blessing to kill Angel Rage on sight."

Chapter 8
Spencer

He'd set a record. After fourteen hours, two soda-bottle bathroom breaks, and a gas tank now full of fumes, Spencer finally pulled up outside Mike's hospital. It was like someone had kicked over an anthill—people were running everywhere. He might actually manage to pull this rescue off.

The doors of the ER opened and he yelled, "Oh my God! Dad? Dad? Has anyone seen my dad?" He stumbled away from a gurney shoved through the ambulance door.

A woman to his right bellowed commands at the EMTs. She was wearing at least four phones around her neck; Spencer figured she had to be the head nurse. He rushed over and skidded to a stop in front of her desk. He had to look the part. Dad's in trouble. Gotta find Dad. Oh, please let Mike's host be over twenty-one. Beer and cigarettes were definitely on the menu tonight.

He released the "Step 3" attack he cooked up into the hospital's network, but it wasn't a sure thing. The longer it took her to pay attention to him, the better off they would be. Really, though, it couldn't be that hard—the nurse was a mundane and well past forty. Twenty-eight seconds, twenty-nine. Yes! Thirty seconds was all he needed.

"Name?"

"Spencer Blaylock. My dad is Marshall Blaylock. He was—"

She held up a finger and tapped on controls only she could see. Spencer stopped and crossed his arms, waiting for the ID he faked to check out.

"He's in room eight. Through those doors." She gestured to her right.

Driving from Arkansas to Virginia on a learner's permit was one thing. Kids his age pulled off stunts like that all the time. What Mike did was a miracle. A fucking miracle. The very first AI not designed in a lab had been Spencer's best friend for two years, but he'd always been a *virtual* best friend. Now Mike was real. Maybe. He hadn't answered any pings since Spencer got on the road, but the care package was, in fact, waiting in Bristol. Mike was either real or dead. The thought hit him like an anvil. Mike might not be here anymore. Six, seven, Spencer turned the corner and pushed the heavy door open.

The man in the bed was sleeping. A bone-knit device covered all of his skull and most of his face, like a giant plastic spider had grabbed his head. Long dark hair pushed out through the braces. Spencer could just see a goatee on his chin. He didn't have a clue about what to expect but at least Mike was alive. If this was Mike. Spencer was about to either wake up a miracle or scare the shit out of a stranger. He reached out his hand, then tapped the man's shoulder. "Mike? Mike?"

"Spencer?" Dark brown bloodshot eyes with faint bruises around them opened. His voice was different—deeper, but the inflection was just the same.

"Mike! Oh my God, Mike! You did it! You really did it!" Spencer held up Mike's hand and slapped an involuntary high-five.

Mike groaned and closed his eyes. "Spencer, go easy. The knitter isn't done gluing my head back together yet." He tried to sit up, but his hands weren't working right.

Spencer lifted the back of the bed for him.

Mike blew out a huge breath. "Thanks. Did you get the care package?"

Spencer nodded and pulled out the Fed/UPS packet. "Mike Sellars now officially exists. The rest is in the truck. How hard was that anyway?" Mike couldn't hold the thing, so Spencer ripped the bag open for him.

"Not too bad. The trick was making sure the phone worked for this body."

Spencer put the pendant phone around Mike's neck. Mike relaxed with a sigh as it interfaced with realmspace. In the hall, alarms Spencer hadn't even noticed were ringing fell silent; there was a smattering of faint applause.

"Oh man, that's way better. It was so hard to use the hospital's instrument path. I'm amazed they've managed to get anything done."

Mike had emerged, somehow, from realmspace and the Evolved Internet that underpinned it. He was, and in some bizarre way wasn't, sort of sewn into its fabric. "Going outside" as Mike put it, would not be a complete transfer. Part of him would always reside in the realms and he'd need some sort of connection between the two places, hence the phone. The math behind it all made Spencer's head ache.

"So it's just like you figured?"

Mike nodded. "Yeah, especially at first. Once this thing on my head finishes, it'll be better, but it'll still take a while for the integration to complete. Wait." Mike looked at him through the flashing plastic lattice. "I had no idea it was this late. We have to go."

Spencer held up a finger and began to work through the mess Mike had made of the hospital's network. It would suck to come all this way to end up in a jail cell. And if anyone started asking questions? No way. Spencer knew what he needed was the same thing that kept him under the radar at school: the right forms. The right forms got you anything. With the right form, you could probably shoot somebody and get away with it.

A thought for another day.

Still, hospitals made schools look bush league in the paperwork world. Each form led to another, and then another, sometimes six deep. Finally, he dotted the last damned *i* just as the autochair he ordered drove itself into the room.

"Sir Sellars," Spencer said with a flourish as it drove under his arm, "your chariot has arrived."

He took them out a side exit to stay away from the chaos in the ER. They waited just inside the doors as the BMW drove itself up. There was another struggle to wrestle Mike into the car, his outfit making the effort that much more embarrassing. As Spencer climbed into the driver's seat, he laughed. "Hey, Mike, just because you *can* wear a hospital gown doesn't mean you should."

"Spencer McKenzie, you already know what this means." Mike flipped him off.

Spencer shook his head and set the navigation system for a hotel in Luray, a little more than an hour away.

Chapter 9
Mike

Mike was startled awake as the truck bumped over the driveway entrance of the hotel. After a few blinks, his vision finally cleared. Arms, legs, even toes and fingers, now responded without making him feel like a puppet strung with spaghetti. It was a vast improvement from when they left the hospital.

Physical functions, while new and intensely interesting, weren't a problem. Those worked just fine as long as he let the body handle them. He didn't need to think to breathe, or to get his heart to beat, or anything of that nature. All his models had predicted that. Six hundred and fifty million years of evolution had created a sublime self-correcting nervous system that he had no hope or desire to improve.

The rest of his integration was much more difficult than predicted. His consciousness was not chemical. Mike had emerged from a digital realm, a consciousness that had fizzed to life and was just, well, there. Now he was stuck in a soup. He'd seen old videos of how ramen noodles were cooked. That's what it reminded him of—boiling liquids that were forcing him to explosively expand in directions he had no control over. If he'd known it would be like this, he might very well have stayed home.

But he'd done this for a reason, a very good reason. There was no going back.

Still, he was desperately glad that Spencer knew how to deal with people who could cry and rage uncontrollably. "I never knew having such fucked up parents would come in handy" were his exact words.

After the pain meds from the hospital wore off, drug-free analog consciousness was profoundly difficult to control. Emotions used to be colored data structures that spun. The part he'd added used chemicals and he had no idea how to control them. After a long crying spell, Mike finally worked up some freestanding filters. They slowed the process down enough that he could see it coming

Finally, he'd fallen asleep and that had done wonders. The filter sets no longer flashed with overloads and cascading warnings.

"So," Spencer asked as he parked the truck in front of the hotel, "this was where she told you she'd be?"

"It was one of the last things she told me before she fell asleep." Mike examined his feet. Spencer brought clothes with him that pretty much fit anyone, but Mike had to make shoes part of the care package. The HgRI scanner that alerted him to this body's availability also conveniently supplied the correct measurements. Unfortunately, he was in a bit of a rush and ordered the highest rated comfortable shoe on Amazon's realm.

Velcro was nearly a century old, yet these shoes still used laces, medieval accessories that seemed purposely built to drive a modern digital consciousness bonkers. If he pulled back, thought of anything else, the muscle memory still a part of the body would tie them for him. It was weird, but it had to come from the same place his ability to speak and move did. When he concentrated on it, Mike got a finger tied in the knot.

"She fell asleep? Dude, you really need to work on your game. What room number did she say?"

Mike had been in such a rush the question had honestly not occurred to him. It took a second to make the words come out. "Yeah, I guess that would've been a useful thing for me to find out, wouldn't it?" The bone-knit device's quiet pings filled the car.

Spencer covered his eyes. "Details, Mike. You never pay attention to the details."

The hotel was a single rectangular building with two floors. There were no external doors. The rooms must all face interior hallways. There had be at least a hundred and twenty of them in there. "So just knocking on doors until we find the right one—"

"Would probably take most of the night. And get us arrested," Spencer finished for him.

They sat for a while in silence. Eventually, Spencer giggled a little bit.

"What's so goddamned funny?" Mike asked.

"Fuckin' hell. I drive all the way to Virginia and you do... what you did... and now we're sitting in this parking lot like a couple of douchebags because you forgot to ask what room she'd be in." Spencer shook his head. "Your dating skills are even weaker than your game, man."

"I'm not dating her. I'm trying to help her, damn it. She's in a lot of trouble and most of it's my fault."

"Wait," Spencer said, smacking his forehead. "You can get into any realm there is."

"Yeah, so?"

"Dude," Spencer said as he called up the hotel's realm, "the Evolved Internet, at your service. Let's go find your girlfriend."

"She's not my girlfriend."

"Whatever. Once we figure out her room number, she's all yours. I'm sacking out back here for a while."

Chapter 10
Kim

Kim finished toweling off her hair after one of the best showers she'd ever had. She brushed out her dark rat's nest. It had grown long enough now for that to be a chore. Definitely time to think about a haircut. She braided it, then picked up a pair of tweezers to start a bout of obsessive hair-plucking.

KNOCK-KNOCK-KNOCK

The tweezers bounced against the mirror and tumbled into the sink.

KNOCK-KNOCK-KNOCK

Nobody knew where she was. Nobody. Kim skidded and slipped as she ran across the slick tile floor.

KNOCK-KNOCK-KNOCK

Stop knocking! She couldn't get her pants untangled from her sweatshirt. Wonderful. Bolivians were going to kill her because she couldn't find the damned pants leg.

"Ax12#823bzk&!098!"

A memory swam up into the light. An old *Star Trek* episode. Make them say a really stupid long string of nonsense to secure the bridge.

Mike.

Balanced with one leg halfway in her pants, Kim checked her virtual workspace and sure enough, that was the phrase. That was what it meant. Her knee flew out and Kim lost the battle to stay balanced.

"Kim?" he asked through the door. "That's the code, right? You told it to me last night. Kim?"

Dead because she couldn't get her pants over her hips. Brilliant. She grabbed the bedspread, hauled herself up, then buttoned her pants. "What do you want?"

"You said if I gave you the code you'd open the door."

"The hell I did. How'd you find this hotel?" She accessed the door's camera, displaying the image in her enhanced vision. He was tall, with a bone-knit device flashing away on his head like a gigantic party hat.

"You told me. Last night."

Finally, with him standing outside the door, her memory started working again. She'd done exactly that, told a perfect stranger where she would be so they could meet. Kim was *so* breaking up with whiskey next time she saw it. "What happened to your head?"

"I'm not sure. The hospital said a light fixture fell on it. I don't remember. Really, I'm just here to help."

The Bolivian mafia couldn't catch her, the FBI couldn't find her, but she could not shake this one realm fanboy to save her life. In the camera feed, people walking past were staring. He didn't seem to have a gun, which was weird, and he was alone, which was even weirder. Quispe thugs traveled in packs with AK-114s.

Well, there was a shotgun in her bugout bag. If it all fell in the pot, it would be messy but that was what housekeeping was for. She dragged a chair as far from the door as possible, turned off all the lights, then used her phone to open the lock.

There was a click and his hand pushed the door open slightly.

"Come in and close the door." Kim kept the shotgun aimed low, careful to make sure nobody was behind him, but his body language was all wrong. She took her finger off the trigger and set the safety. "Don't come in any farther."

The door thumped shut just as she turned on the light. He was tall, well over six feet, wearing the most ridiculous purple sweat suit she'd ever seen, white socks, and brand new tennis shoes. The bone-knit machine hid most of his face. For once in her life, a man's eyes didn't lock on to her chest. A pistol-grip shotgun was a wonderful way to focus attention on the situation.

He said, "Um... Hi?"

The Quispe were seriously slipping if this was the best they could do. "Who. The hell. Are you."

His voice was very quiet and faintly puzzled, as if he hadn't really thought it all the way through. "I'm Mike Sellars, and I'm here to rescue you?"

Humor. Lovely. "This is a heavily modified shotgun. It is illegal in all fifty states. I keep it because it makes it easy to blow the heads off my enemies. I have lots of enemies. I need you to answer a question and you need to get the answer right. How did you find me?"

"You told me—"

"No." Just as well she hadn't splattered him as soon as the door shut. He was too dumb to be dangerous. "How did you find me *at first*?"

"Oh." He tilted his head and smiled. If he got any happier, he'd probably explode. "That's a really interesting story! You see, two years ago—"

"*Briefly.*"

"Well..."

The thing on his head exaggerated his every move. She could practically see him think. "Yes?" This person had destroyed Angel Rage's security. Unbelievable. His mind must've been six steps behind his head.

"Oh. Right, well—" Red lights stopped blinking and turned a steady green against his face. "Oh, thank God."

"Humpty's back together again?"

"Yes. Jeez, this thing's been driving me nuts all day. It's heavy. Do you mind?"

Maybe taking the weight off would make his brain work better. "Sure, go ahead. Why not?"

He sat down, pointed his face toward his lap, then tinkered with the latches. Each one gave way with a clack. When the last one let go, the mask made a few cheerful beeps and shut off. He took a deep breath and lifted his head.

When she saw his face, Kim almost fell out of her chair.

It was impossible.

She leapt to her feet, but then the damned shotgun hopped into the air. She juggled it and on the third near-catch, it went sailing out of reach.

"What?" Mike shouted. "What's wrong?"

"Colque! You! You can't be here!"

The Quispe's favorite devil was seconds away from cutting her head off and that was the smartest thing she could say? It didn't even make sense. None of this made any sense.

"Kim! I don't know who that is! I'm Mike! Calm—"

"How could I be so stupid?" Stupid and dead. But she wasn't dead. Kim had seen this freak cut someone's throat standing farther away than he was now.

"I don't have any idea what you're talking about! I just want to help you!"

Wait. There was a pistol, right there in her bag. Keep him talking. "Children! I watched you kill children, you freak! Help me? What, help me cut off my head?" Just a few more inches—

He threw his arms straight up and bellowed, "WAIT!"

She stopped.

"I don't have any weapons."

"The hell you don't."

"I'll show you." He closed his eyes, which gave Kim the opening she needed, but when he pulled that ridiculous sweatshirt over his head, she couldn't find the pistol. He was stripping. Right there in front of her.

Without that face and with that torso... Kim blinked. "What are you doing?" *Find the pistol. Stop staring.*

He hooked his thumbs into his waistband and pushed.

Oh, wow...

He put his hands in the air and turned around.

That's a really nice... tan.

"Oh," he said, eyes bright. "You need to make sure I don't have anything concealed." He started to bend over.

"That's quite all right!" Good God. The body language was wrong, the accent was wrong, the attitude was wrong, everything was wrong. A hit on the head *might* explain it.

He knew the code.

Mike turned back around to face her.

Eyes up, dear, eyes up. That was entirely too distracting. "You can… you can put your clothes back on. But stay on that side of the room."

While he dressed she asked, "What's going on here?"

It wasn't one of her most articulate moments.

"I think it might be easier to explain if you visited a realm with me."

The smile finally convinced her. Colque's smile made him feral, dangerous, like a jaguar about to strike. This smile was warm and incredibly innocent. Maybe this was his twin from California.

Kim laughed, fighting to keep the hysteria at bay. The Colque she knew was a murderous phantom, not an actor. Nothing about whoever this was reminded her of that monster. *Take the risk. Do what you always do. Do the unexpected.*

"By all means. Lead the way."

He sent her an address and she closed her eyes. The familiar wash of lightheadedness passed as she concentrated on the pendant phone hanging around her neck. The neural interface of the chain picked up the activation signals from the top of her spine and transmitted new impulses through her nerves. The phone connected to the Evolved Internet, read what was at the address, spun together a full sensory map, then sent it to her.

Kim's avatar materialized on a wide concrete pad that was cracked and buckled, shot through with bushes and weeds. A midmorning sun washed warmth across her face as a dry breeze ruffled her hair. It was cool but not cold; by the color of the leaves, it was perhaps early autumn. At least the weather was nice, but it gave her no clues. This was supposed to be some sort of explanation.

A large rusted Ferris wheel with tall yellow cupolas stood frozen in front of her. Young trees lined the concrete pad. Other skeletons of amusement park rides surrounded her. Some were white, others red, but all were flecked and flaked with rust. A large building stood behind her, the walls of its tall glassed-in porch long ago shattered. No people, no animals, not even any insects.

"Pripyat?" Kim asked.

"Yes," Mike's disembodied voice replied over her head. "As it was on October 13th, 1999. The Chernobyl reactor is about two and a half miles east-southeast of here. I used to visit it when I was younger. It's even weirder than this place."

Kim examined herself. The braids in her hair were still there and she had the correct number of arms and legs. She was even dressed for the weather in a dark chocolate leather coat and matching gloves. It was one of the simpler outfits on her default avatar. Whatever game Mike was playing, at least he wasn't using her as a toy.

"Why here?"

"It's one of the first places I can remember. According to the access logs, the last real visitor was fifteen years ago."

That would make this one of the oldest realms in existence. Hyper-detailing was all the rage back then, so it fit.

He continued, "It's in a, well, I guess you could say a dusty corner of one of Sony's very first boxes. I have no idea why they never turned it off."

An antique. Interesting. "Did Evan Stanley design this one?"

"Yes, actually. He was part of the team that designed everything in this section of realmspace."

Stanley was now the number one realm designer in the world, yet he'd just been "part of the team" on this relic.

This was supposed to be an explanation, but none of it made any sense. Mike looked exactly like someone who skinned people alive for fun, but his voice reminded her of someone showing off family photos. "This is one of the first places you remember? How old are you? Where are you from really?" Kim asked.

"Those are complicated questions. I'd rather show you some things first. Here, follow this." A bright yellow frog hopped out of the bushes, coughed several times, and sneezed.

It took her a second to understand the reference. "You're a Pratchett fan?"

"I love the classics."

What she now knew was a yellow sick toad hopped away toward the nearby windowless building. She followed, whistling a tune from *The Wizard of Oz*.

The toad led her into the building and then to a room holding enormous empty swimming pools. They were startlingly deep without the blue refractions of water. The bottoms were dirty and forlorn, all broken tiles and fractured concrete. Diving platforms stood far too high on one end. Dead leaves huddled around the bases. In the center of the swim lanes, ten figures stood motionless on the grimy floor.

As she got closer, Kim recognized them. It was like discovering her car parked at someone else's house. "Are those my avatars?"

"Three avatars and seven outfits."

Kim climbed into the pit to get closer. She'd recognize the scarring on the mechanoid's armor anywhere. The chunk taken out of the tail of the mer-warrior still brought back painful memories. He'd even managed to rescue her avian, which was a very pleasant surprise. It'd taken her months to sculpt a construct that matched the tattoo on her own back, only in 3D. Just as Michiko promised, when modeled and mounted on an avatar, the wings worked.

The avatars stared blankly into the distance with various versions of her face. The outfits hung on abstract mannequins, all uniforms of various sorts.

"I took the liberty of upgrading the weapons and tools on the ones that have them. The catsuit was quite a challenge. I'm pretty sure not all of those tools are legal."

"You what? How? How'd you even get them? They should be impounded somewhere by now."

"It's part of what I can do. I reset their contracts when I brought them here."

Kim pulled the first avatar's status menu down with an electric hum. Sure enough, the words on the frosted glass told her nobody owned the avatar and nobody ever had. She flipped to the stats tab and got her next surprise. The last time she used the mechanoid all she could afford was a measly set of SRM-8 shoulder launchers from LG-Vizio. It now had LRM-20s from Apple's realm combat division, complete with the fire-and-forget module. The rest of them were all similarly equipped with new and prerelease constructs. Upgraded, indeed.

"This isn't possible." She bumped the menu closed. The contracts were quantum encrypted. They were part of what an avatar was.

"I know. Isn't it cool? You can keep them now."

The impossibilities just kept stacking up. He hadn't just pried them out of some FBI pen; he'd *stolen* them in a way Kim didn't even know was possible. Admiration was rare for her, but there it was.

She came to a decision as the avatars and outfits swirled into her storage. Whoever this was, he wasn't Colque. If it didn't involve killing, Colque had no time for it. As incredible as it seemed, the lost twin theory was just about all she had left. Which meant the monster was still out there somewhere. *One impossibility at a time, please.*

His voice echoed like a he was an announcer at a game show. "But wait, there's more!"

A door opened in the air in front of her. "And just where does this go?"

"Hey, I'm not making you drink anything to fit through it. Come on, where's your sense of adventure?"

The door revealed a featureless white hall. If he was able to steal avatars from under the FBI's nose, it only made sense he'd found a way into this realm's BBox control suite. Still, it never hurt to be sure. Kim picked up a loose tile and tossed it through the doorway.

It landed with a muffled thump on the floor, hopped twice, then threw itself back at her hard enough that she had to duck.

If it'd just sat there that would've been another realm. If it had vanished, it would've meant the place was a lot newer than he let on. Hopping out like that meant it was old enough that the BBox still had soft rejection set up on constructs. He was literally taking her behind the curtain, and an old one at that. "My, you are quite the locksmith." Kim walked through.

The door vanished as she stepped out onto a white plane, the center of a ping-pong ball the size of a planet. Light came from all around her, so there were no shadows.

Walking forward, her boots made no noise. The air smelled processed, as if it was from a hotel air conditioner. Despite her coat and gloves, she felt neither hot nor cold. There had to be controls somewhere. Kim turned around.

A large hexagonal table sat on a column. The table was high enough to use while standing. Knobs, switches, buttons, and levers were scattered pell-mell on the surface. Every sort of dial or gauge was in between. In the center, a hole about two feet across held a tall glass container with a weird shape inside it.

She was familiar with only some of the controls, because years ago all she ever did was rent space for the realms she made. Kim had never been inside a realm container that had been completely unlocked. There were so many controls. "May I?"

"Please."

She walked to the section of the hexagon she recognized. This thing wasn't just old; it was ancient. She took off her gloves and felt a slight pixelation on the edges of the console, as if she'd rubbed satin the wrong way. It was version one and had never been upgraded.

The switches were there, but everything was so damned big. It was dark, disconnected. *Let's see, red button down, selector to one, open the guard, and flip the switch.* There was a wheeze as the glass in the center pumped up and down. A window drew itself into existence on her right that looked into the realm they'd just visited.

An oblong shape melted up out of the ping-pong ball that was the box, far from where she stood. It was dark gray and brown, rectangular with a top that resembled a shed roof. Kim held a silver switch down and the window beside her opened with an electric whir. Wind, music, and the dry decay of the place wafted in.

She was fourteen all over again. *Let's break it.* She closed the window and grabbed the knob that controlled the realm's gravity, a huge knurled thing. It clicked the way a ratchet did as it moved. She looked through the window as she turned it to the right, increasing the gravity in the realm. Nothing happened at first. It had a much wider range than newer ones. Kim turned the knob faster. Soon, the force of gravity was strong enough to cause small clamps and fasteners on the amusement rides to fail. Bits and pieces fell off and shattered on the concrete below.

Kim spun the view toward the grim concrete apartments just as they collapsed. Having this much power over an entire world made her giddy. Once the gravity knob pegged, there was nothing left standing. Kim slapped a metal button with a curved arrow pointing to the left on it that was bigger than her hand. The undo button. The gravity knob jumped to its original position with a thunk and the realm rebuilt itself like a movie run in reverse.

"Have you ever tried bouncing?" Mike asked.

Seemed she wasn't the only one fighting with her inner teenager. Maxing the gravity with people inside was really just a stupid prank. Exactly the kind of fun thing teenagers did. "Once, to some… acquaintances of mine. I got grounded for a week over it."

"It is a quick way of clearing a realm."

"It's a quick way to piss people off. Sometimes they've left a realm for a reason." Squashing the rest of the Machine just after they'd entered Pride's Lair seemed like a hilarious idea at the time. And it was—she still giggled about it. Harmless fun, since all it ever did was force someone back to the realm they'd just left. It wasn't her fault the realm they'd just left was full of shrieking burglar alarms and security agents.

Kim continued to fiddle with the controls, increasing this one, decreasing that one, undoing when she needed to. The realm on the other side of the window froze, burst into flame, melted, disintegrated, flooded, blew to dust, and — after she managed to press four widely spaced buttons down at once — turned entirely to crystal.

The other controls were also unlocked. Right now, she was just affecting the area around the camera, perhaps a five-mile radius. The rest would let her affect the world and the universe the realm was set in. One segment she'd only ever read about. It would let her control the laws of physics and chemistry, right down to the quantum level.

Kim stopped fiddling. "This is all a lot of fun, but it's not an explanation."

"This part's not, no. I figured you needed to relax. You seem pretty tense."

She set her jaw and clenched her fists. Damned right she was tense. She was still on the run. "Mike, I don't have time for any of this. What's going on? Who are you? Why am I here?"

His voice was suddenly right behind her. "I'll show you," he said.

She whirled around and saw a translucent caped man with a hood around his shoulders. If she squinted, she could just make out his face.

"If you would be so kind?" he asked.

His eyes were very nice. *Wait. He asked a question.* "Oh." Kim slapped the undo button.

"Observe," he said and disappeared. Kim turned to the window. He stood in the realm, fully manifested with his default avatar. If she concentrated on his eyes, he didn't frighten her at all. Kim pressed a button and a microphone rose out of the controls. "Mike? Why are you glowing?"

"The mass of the air isn't high enough to trigger the effect," he said as he floated up to the decrepit ticket booth in front of the Ferris wheel. "But when I do this..." He reached out to grab the door handle.

An actinic flash blinded her for a second. Kim blinked away the after images. The realm she'd been controlling had winked out of existence, replaced with a pair of nested shockwaves headed her way. The controller threw out bursts of sparks several times and then went dead. She should've known all the fun and predictability wouldn't last. *Hello, Crazytown, nice to visit again.* Mike's hologram reappeared beside her.

"What the hell is that?"

"Total data inversion. If I touch anything solid enough in a realm, it sets up a chain reaction that can't be stopped." The shockwaves had come close enough for her to see more detail; it tore up the surface of the box itself. Debris, boiling with dull brown and glossy white fragments, pitched up higher and faster as it closed in on them. Some of the fragments were as big as houses, rumbling as they moved closer.

"There's not going to be anything left of this place when it's done, is there?" The ground beneath her feet vibrated and the growing smell of ozone made her throat clench. The shockwave would reach them in seconds.

Mike's voice was so close to her ear it made her shiver. "No." He threw his cloak around her as the waves struck, blasting what remained upward into fragments of debris and light. The chaos buffeted just outside the fabric of his cloak as they gracefully exited realmspace.

Chapter 11
Mike

A fireball ripped through Mike's head as they exited. Inverting a realm hadn't done that before. It would corrupt his threads and his garbage collection routers—the closest thing he had to a liver until tonight. It would take most of a day to clean the mess up, but eventually he'd be back to normal. None of his models had predicted the way he felt right now. He'd lost count of the different ways humans could experience pain.

It plunged through him again, a blossoming burning thing that made him bite down on his tongue, which set off another searing rip through his mouth. If one more thing hurt, he knew he'd explode. Mike breathed deep and found yet another a new sensation—scent.

The medical daemons examined the molecular patterns his nose delivered to his brain. The dominant notes of the scent were jasmine and vanilla. He'd spent most of a year working out how scent functioned. Now the real thing surrounded him, light and sweet. It made him feel comfortable and warm.

He opened his eyes and found Kim wrapped in his arms.

Mike had one job, one damned job, and he'd screwed it up. He was supposed to provide the *actual* explanation now, but he'd mimicked the gestures that he'd made just before they exited the realm. He'd made the most important introduction of his life and had ruined it with a classic noob mistake: moving in realspace. Usually, people trained a few times in the phone shop before they left to avoid it. Mike didn't think he'd need that. He'd been born in the realms, after all.

Her body was soft and warm, very nice, and if it hadn't been so embarrassing, he wouldn't want to let her go.

Kim drove both elbows into his stomach. The air flew out of his lungs and his last two ribs moved as they flexed. Muscle and bone scraped together. What a way to discover a design flaw. Back off, let the body sort it out. It was a fine idea when he'd been learning how to breathe or keep the heartbeat regular, but good Lord, she had to have caused permanent damage with that.

Kim screamed as she sprawled face-up across the corner of the bed. Her eyes were bulging and her complexion had gone blotchy.

Mike barely managed to stand. Damage control was another thing he'd not been able to simulate properly so his host's refusal to cooperate, its *physical need* to be still, was surprising. It seriously impeded his ability to help. Kim was in some sort of terrible distress and all he wanted to do was curl into a ball. He didn't have time for this.

She twitched and gasped, shaking her head from side to side. Spasms rolled upward as her skin turned red. When they got to her neck, she tore a breath free and sat up with a scream so loud it overloaded his ears. The distortion was so painful it triggered an entire sequence of reflexes that happened without a single conscious thought. He found his hand around the doorknob before he even realized he was moving. Something deep inside him was shouting "Monster! Death! Run!" without them ever being real thoughts.

Kim fell on her side. The spasms hadn't stopped and she breathed in ragged gasps. He was supposed to help, not run. Mike blew his threads, the part of him still in realmspace, outward, simultaneously searching for an answer to what was happening.

It was too much, too fast. His integration tore, setting off critical alarms as the bridge daemons tripped offline one by one.

The room tilted sideways and he grabbed the edge of the bed as his threads reintegrated. *Well, that didn't work at all.* When his vision cleared, he tried the only thing he had left.

"Kim!" His voice was strange, unexpectedly hoarse. This host was supposed to be a vehicle, but it did so many things all on its own. It wasn't supposed to work this way.

Her eyes flew open, but each one darted around in a different direction. She clawed and tore at the sheets, moaning and sobbing.

Making his host walk toward her was another fight with the unwelcome inner ape that still wanted to run the show. "Kim?"

Her body snapped into rigid stillness as she focused on him. The raw hatred in her eyes was worse than her spasms or screams. He reached for her, but she shouted "NO," rolled away, and hit the floor with a thump. Mike needed to find out what this was. His integration wasn't complete enough to allow him to split and search the realms with his threads, so he fired off a brace of agents to search realmspace for answers.

Kim pulled herself up, dragging her face against the wall. Another one of those terrible spasms started up her legs. She ran down the short hallway screaming, then bounced hard against the opposite wall and fell into the bathroom. The door slammed shut, muffling her violent retches. Somehow, she managed to lock it.

His agents returned with nothing medical and what came back from pop culture and religion made no sense. It was all fiction of one sort or another, horror movies and ancient myths. "Kim! What's wrong?"

The retching transformed into horrible wet coughs. When they finally stopped she said, "Never. Touch. Me. Again."

Someone knocked on the door behind him. Mike's heart leapt around in his chest. Kim was dying and now they had visitors. Spencer was asleep. Nobody else could know where she was.

Whoever it was knocked again. Mike accessed the door's camera feed. Spencer stared at his boots, which meant he was frightened or in trouble. Since he stood next to a police officer, neither option meant anything good. The officer knocked again.

Kim's voice was a rough growl. "Answer the fucking door."

Chapter 12
Spencer

Spencer had averaged nearly a hundred miles an hour across Tennessee just keeping up with the locals and he never once saw a cop. He'd stopped at exactly one drive-through all by himself to pick up something to eat and nobody had looked at him twice. He'd smuggled a goddamned patient out of a hospital without setting off any alarms. Tonight he had been smoking a cigarette and said "Fuck off" before turning around.

The failure was beyond epic.

The hotel room door opened and there was Mike, without the circus prop on his head. His face used to be an average of every man on the planet because he didn't have a real one. The way his face moved was right, but he was bigger now. Spencer still had to tell himself it was Mike when he saw him, but it was getting easier. His coordination was visibly better than when he'd left the truck. Never mind, it was time to get their stories straight.

He shot a plain text message to him. HI, MOM AND DAD! IT'S SPENCER KEEGAN! Mike immediately bounced a new address to Spencer so his *not girlfriend* got a copy too. Hopefully, they could all talk their way out of this.

"Hello, officer," Mike said.

"Mr. Keegan." The cop nodded once. "Are you the owner of the BMW SUV, license number XKZ-1358?"

SAY THE RIGHT THING, DUDE.

Mike checked the man's nametag. "Why, yes, Officer Stevens."

Chapter 13
Kim

Kim stomped down the shrieking madness as she regained her self-control. The first time she was ever touched like that, ever *held*, should've been a romantic thing covered in flower petals, not a blind realm-exit with a man who could implode realms at a touch. A man who wore the face of a homicidal maniac.

And now there was a cop outside. Mr. Impossible hadn't just found her; he'd led the police right to her door. Her skin still crawled with spidery horrors caused by his touch, but there was no way she'd leave it all up to Captain Derp and Wonder Zit. Kim gulped back the last of the bile and strained to hear the plate number. Gripping the pendant around her neck, she braced. This wasn't as easy as unlocking a door.

Five years. She'd set this ability aside for five years, trying to forget it existed. The swirling vertigo took her consciousness away in a direction that didn't exist. The dimensions unfolded in her mind, through her body, and across her skin. An incomprehensible portal yanked her perception away and then...

There were lines of potential and she couldn't remember how to breathe. Waves exist and do not exist highest lowest believe this believe me who I am who we are believe highest lowest collapse and now.

Chapter 14
Spencer

He needed to talk to Mike about shaving. Goatees worked on villains, not goofy science nerds who lived in the realms.

"Well, you see, I found this boy smoking," Officer Stevens said.

"Smoking?" Mike's not-girlfriend jerked the bathroom door open, giving Spencer a nice profile view as she walked out and turned the corner. She was tall, wearing tight blue jeans that showed off one hell of an ass and a sweatshirt that totally ruined any guess at her bra size. Her dark hair was in a frazzled braid and her face was pale, even a little green, like she'd been sick. "Spencer Keegan, were you smoking again?"

Spencer knew an opportunity when he saw it. "Aw, Jesus, Kim, fuck! I needed a smoke!" It was a real risk. If this Kim chick dropped the ball, it was over.

"You said you were going for ice. And when did you decide to start swearing in front of me? I'm your stepmother, I deserve your respect if nothing else." She'd never seen him in her life and in an instant, had turned into his stepmom. This was a pro, the first time he'd ever met someone as good at improv as he was.

"I'm really sorry, ma'am," the officer said, "but would you mind letting me see your registration? Your stepson wasn't exactly respectful when I asked him for it."

Kim locked eyes with him. If Spencer could've broken that stare he would've run all the way back to Arkansas. "I am so sorry, officer." She leaned forward. "Spencer, give the man the key."

They were supposed to talk their way out of exactly this situation. A surly teenager who'd snuck outside for a smoke was nothing special. A teenager without a driver's license nearly a thousand miles from home staying with two complete strangers was another thing entirely and now there was no avoiding it.

Her gaze grew razor blades. "Now."

There was no way he would disobey her. He transmitted the address of the SUV's registration and the quantum key to the officer's phone. Spencer had come this far, seen all this crap, and Mike's psychotic not-girlfriend had now officially blown it. *Orange jump suit, here I come.*

There was a pause while the officer examined the records. "Well," he said. "I'm sorry to have bothered you all tonight."

It took everything Spencer had to remain completely still. A miracle had happened, again, but he didn't dare ruin it with the wrong reaction.

The officer cleared his throat. "Mrs. Keegan, are you all right?"

"Yes, well," Kim drew herself up regally, "I'm three months along. I guess now it's okay to call it morning sickness?"

Mike tried to put his arm around her, but the look she shot him made him yank it back like she'd stuck him with a dagger.

What a catch, Mike.

"I suppose it is," the officer said with a polite chuckle. "Well then," he said as Spencer walked through the door and flopped down on a bed. "I'll just say good night to you all and have a safe morning."

"Thank you, officer," Kim said.

With a quick search, Spencer found out that the owners of his truck were listed as Mike and Kim Keegan. Mike and Kim Keegan were in this room with Spencer Keegan. Spencer Keegan's learner's permit was valid and on file with the Arkansas DMV. It even had his picture attached.

Ten seconds ago they were all going to jail. Now he'd witnessed *another* miracle. Quantum encryption had made the DMV a fucking fortress. Nobody could hack those records.

Mike said, "That's not possible. Spencer's last name is McKenzie."

Okay, that was weird. He'd just assumed it was Mike who'd made the changes.

Kim's neck strained as she glared back and forth between them. "So I don't just have one idiot, I have two? Hooray for me! A two-for-one! What's my prize, Alex?"

Spencer wasn't going to have to call his parents for bail money. There would be no cops, no lawyers, no sitting in a room while his parents screamed at each other in front of said cops and lawyers. "This is so freaking cool, I'm not going to jail."

"Jail?" Kim said. "You think the worst that can happen here is going to jail?"

"Now hang on a minute, lady," Spencer replied as he sat up. "I'm just the fucking taxi here. You got a problem, take it up with him."

Mike turned away from them both and with a hand over one ear, asked, "I'm sorry, what did you say? I can't hear you, could you speak up?"

Kim asked Spencer, "What are you, twelve? How do you even rate a driver's license? Who the hell are you, anyway?"

"I'm the guy who rescued your boyfriend, that's who!"

"Boyfriend? Are you out of your mind?"

"Damn it, you two, shut up!" Mike shared the call. "Could you repeat that, Tonya?"

Kim gasped.

"I said," Tonya's voice was just over a whisper, "can you still get in touch with Kim?"

"I'm here, Tonya."

"Thank the Lord. Are you all right?"

"I'm fine. Tonya, what's wrong?"

"I'm pretty sure there are three men getting ready to kidnap me. White guys. Their van has Jersey plates."

Spencer mentally rewound Kim's comment about the worst that could happen. Mike's not-girlfriend could trick cops and mobsters wanted to kidnap people she knew. Mike never covered all the details with any of his crazy ideas, so it only made sense that he dragged Spencer into some sort of *CSI: Boardwalk Empire* realm episode.

Kim didn't react the way he expected. She wasn't the slightest bit concerned. She smiled. "Just three?" *Then* she got concerned. "If they've found you—"

"They might have found the others, right. I'm so glad I managed to reach you. I can do a lot, but it's nothing like what you can do."

"Yes, I know." Kim looked sharply at Mike. "I've got a new *tool* that should help us."

Spencer laughed softly. What a burn.

She said, "Tonya, please be careful."

"Pshaw, are you kidding me? There's just three. Okay, there might be two more in the van. I'll be fine." The call ended.

Mike asked, "Will she be—"

"Shut up," Kim said. She motioned to Spencer. "You, Pimples. Keys. Now."

No way. Pimples?

"Now," she commanded, hand out. "We're leaving."

Chapter 15
Tonya

The weirdness of the past two weeks all made sense now. The neighborhood kids told Tonya about a strange white guy driving around, always cruising past her house. She was an organ and limb regrowth nurse at the local VA but sometimes still covered a shift or two as an ER nurse at the city hospital. Just a few days ago, one of the local thugs stopped her after she stitched up one of his buddies. He claimed that someone was trying to take out a contract on her. Kidnapping, of all things. She'd been on alert ever since.

Then Kim disappeared. All the paranoid ravings Tonya had put up with for so long actually turned out to be true. The strangest, most wonderful person she had ever known was suddenly gone.

She first met Kim three years ago at the Tekken realm combat tournament. The little white girl nobody had ever heard of steam-rolled right over Tonya, the DC regional champ and top seed in the mid-Atlantic US bracket. Kim went on to place fourth in the world championship.

After the tournament was over, Kim came around to one of the after-party realms Tonya was attending. The attraction was instant, deep, and mutual, the romance unavoidable, torrid, and short. Tonya was great at fun but terrible at love, with men or women. But they didn't drift apart after the breakup. They actually grew closer. She and Kim worked better as friends than as lovers.

It was still a purely realm-based relationship and Tonya was old-fashioned enough to want to meet the people she cared about. It took a whole year of prying, wheedling, pleading, and finally demanding before Kim let Tonya meet her in realspace. That was when the rollercoaster started.

In the realms, Kim was flirty and fun. In realspace, she was a completely isolated shut-in. Aside from her job, which changed frequently, she never left the house. Her moods were unpredictable, usually dark, and she drank more than was good for her.

At first, Tonya thought it all went back to her disability. Kim reacted violently to the slightest touch. It started when she was a small child and nobody knew why. Objects, plants, even animals were fine, but the slightest brush by a passing stranger would cause her tremendous agony. The closest they'd ever managed was holding a napkin or towel together. Tonya had never known anything like it and neither had any journal she ever found.

She thought Kim was going to have a stroke when Tonya casually told her how unique her disability was. That's when Tonya learned the real reason Kim was a shut-in. She was a paranoid maniac, completely convinced Tonya's searches would lead "them" right to her. It was all Tonya could do to keep Kim from running out of her apartment that very instant. There was never any explanation for who "they" were, only that they were out there and Kim took extraordinary measures to avoid them.

It had become a game. Tonya'd come up with some new thing for them to do in realspace and Kim would insist on ever more complex disguises and procedures before they went out and did it. After a year, Tonya was fairly sure she could teach James Bond a thing or two.

But "they" had somehow finally managed to find Kim. Tonya honestly thought she would never see her again. The next night, a van full of strangers parked across the street from her house. Under no circumstances could it be a coincidence. Worse, if people that dangerous found Kim, and then her, they might have found the rest of the Phoenix Dogs. The team Kim assembled wasn't just the baddest of the bad, they were great people, as close as family, scattered all over the country.

In desperation, she reached out to Mike in the hopes that Kim had actually contacted him. Wonder of wonders, Kim was with him. Tonya could certainly help herself, but she couldn't help the rest of the Dogs. Kim was the key. She eventually revealed that she'd once been a computer hacker, good enough to make a living at it for a while. She was definitely the right person to help them avoid whatever was going down right now.

It still meant Tonya had to rescue herself.

She turned off all the lights in the house when it was obvious the van wasn't going anywhere. Then she replaced the heavy plant hanging near the skylight in her living room with a rope. Three men eventually got out and started moving toward the house, so she climbed the rope onto the roof. Jackie Brown, eat your heart out.

First up: the guy making his way through the back yard. Tonya balanced, then jumped from fence post to fence post until she got behind him. The snow made walking silently on the ground even easier, especially since Guido the First stomped around muttering about his shoes.

She drew her bokken from its sheath on her back. "Psst."

He spun around just a little too fast, but she was able to adjust her swing. The wooden blade connected with the back of his head and he dropped like his strings had been cut.

One down.

She hopped from the top of the fence back to the roof. The other two were closer now. She had to move quickly, or they might figure out she wasn't just a helpless girl. Tonya ran the length of the roof and leapt toward a tree. Her foot slipped and her heart lurched as she sailed toward the trunk upside down. She crashed into the evergreen's upper reaches and everything was a jumble until she landed on the ground in a heap.

"Well, that just made my job a whole lot simpler," Guido the Second said.

She raised her head and looked straight down a gun barrel.

"Get up."

Tonya heaved herself off the ground slowly. *Buy time, draw him in.* She held her wrist and groaned. "I think it might be broken."

"Not my problem, lady."

Guido the Second needed to get a little closer, just two more steps.

"You're comin' with me."

The trick to disarming anyone with a gun was to get them close. Once they were within reach, the weapon was no longer an issue. Tonya had a very long reach. "Please," she whispered as she raised her hands, "don't hurt me."

"Nah, that ain't our game tonight." His eyes unfocused as he connected to realmspace.

It was all she needed. Tonya spun then kicked a spot on his wrist, flinging the gun into the night. She carried the motion through and bashed him square in the temple with her elbow, then swept his feet out from under him.

Out cold. One to go.

She landed on her living room floor just as Guido the Third managed to pick the garage door lock. He was older, balding, with a beer gut and an EtherPatch in his hand. At least Guido the Third would've been nice about knocking her out.

Tonya turned the light on. The fat bastard jumped. She smiled as the *Django* soundtrack echoed in her head. "Looking for me?"

He went for his gun as she tumbled toward him. Once, twice, and on the third tumble she flipped into the air. Spinning inverted, she slapped the bokken against his temple hard enough to twirl him around twice before he hit the floor.

Tonya shut off the lights. That took care of the kidnap crew; now for the taxi service.

She grabbed her hoodie and checked the schedules. A bus was already making made its way down the street, so Tonya sent a stop request and went out into the darkness between the houses.

She walked in front of the bus close enough to trip the auto-driver's brake sensors. She'd look just like she'd stepped off the thing. Guido the Fourth smoked a cigarette as she pretended to leave the bus.

Keep puffing, you dumb cracker.

Tonya put on some classic Timberlake and turned into a kid in a hoodie, bopping down the street. She carefully pulled the Taser out of her pocket. It only had one shot with the wires and she had to make it count. They would have guns and if she missed, there was no doubt they'd use them. When Tonya reached the right spot next to the van, she turned and fired. All the hours she and Kim had spent playing in the *COPS* room in FOXtv's realm paid off. The wires leapt out with a sound like a snapped ruler and hit him right in the neck. He went down twitching.

She jumped *hard* just as Guido the Fifth nearly fell out of the driver's side. She landed softly on the van's roof as he slammed the door shut.

"Anthony!" He ran to the back of the van. "Anthony! Are you okay?"

As soon as he was directly behind the van, Tonya jumped off. It was a blind leap, but she couldn't have positioned him any better if she tried. Her feet hit his shoulders square and the Fifth's head slammed straight into the Fourth's crotch. She clapped her hands behind his ears to finish the job and that was it.

Tonya: 5, Guidos: 0.

Fortunately, they were already at the back of the van, so it wasn't too hard to roll them inside and quickly pull it in her driveway. They would be dangerous if they came to, but that's what duct tape was for. A quick call to her cousin Justin got him, and more importantly his tow truck, headed toward her house.

Guido the Third, the one with the EtherPatch, woke up as she dragged him across the living room floor. The Third was hard enough to pull when he was just a lump of lard. The squirming had to stop.

Tonya rolled him over and slapped him. "Guido. Guido!" He kept flopping around, so she slapped him again. "Calm down, Guido. You're gonna be fine. I don't have enough space in my back yard to bury five more grease balls." She smiled when he tried to shout through the duct tape. There wasn't so much as an ex-pet back there, but he didn't know that. "You need to understand, Guido. This is *my* neighborhood. These are *my* people. You come back here again," she grabbed his crotch and squeezed until his eyes bulged, "and these will be *my* balls. Are we clear?"

He nodded and then groaned when Tonya let him go. "Now be still, you stupid cracker." Tonya dragged him to the van and heaved him inside. Her muscles ached from all the heavy lifting. Trussing and stowing stupid gangsters was a lot of work.

Right on time, Justin's tow truck drove up the street. He rolled down the window. "I gotta say, cuz, that van doesn't look illegally parked to me."

"That's what you're here for. Just take it into DC and drop it next to the pole with the most signs on it."

Justin stopped hooking the safety chains to the tow loops when the van wobbled slightly. "Passengers too?"

"Bunch of Jersey Guidos."

His surprise was funny, but explaining that the van was filled with kidnappers who were somehow connected to the weird white girl she hung out with would take way too long.

"It's complicated. Let's just say I want to avoid any Imperial entanglements."

A broad smile bloomed on Justin's dark face. "Well, that's the trick, isn't it? And it'll cost you extra. Panang curry with shrimp, extra spicy, for ten."

Tonya rolled her eyes. "I knew it was a mistake to cook for one of your poker nights."

He laughed as the back of the van lifted into the air. "They haven't stopped talking about it since."

Chapter 16
Kim

All Mike had done ever since they'd left the hotel was silently stare at her from the passenger seat. It was really getting under her skin. She wasn't the one wearing a psycho's face and doing ridiculous things in realmspace. He had no right making her feel like she was the only one in class who skipped the assignment. "What?"

Mike didn't reply.

"What?"

More silence.

The man was madding *in so many different ways*. "WHAT?"

"That thing you did back there, it isn't possible."

Well, that was rich, coming from him. "What are you talking about?"

"You hacked the quantum fabric. Quantum computers can't *be* hacked. That's the point. Scientists have spent years trying to understand how the damned things work and here you are just," he waved his hands around a few times, "fiddling with them. It's not possible."

Out of habit more than anything else she said, "Everything is theoretically impossible, until it's done."

Spencer, who Kim had thought was comatose in the back seat, shot upright. *Oh great.*

"Angel Rage," he said reverently.

What the hell? The kid couldn't have been more than ten the last time that name was in the news.

"Angel who?" Mike asked.

Searching for that name in a mostly stolen car that she was driving. Excellent idea! Kim opened her perception and snapped the EI connections to the car. Using her power that quickly was worse than a sneeze and a whole lot more painful. She barely managed to keep her eyes on the road. The car went dark and Mike fell forward, held up only by his seat belt. Alarm bells softly bonged and half the dashboard blinked red.

Spencer shouted in his squeaky teen voice, "It's true! Oh my God, it's true!"

Great. Mr. Impossible passes out and leaves her alone with Squeaky McFanboy.

"A fucking legend. A fucking legend! And I'm in the car with you!"

Kim had thought that after all this time the fanboys would be less annoying. Wrong again. "Spencer!"

"So that means you really did hack the fabric? When I was in the same room with you?"

No, while he'd been outside next to the cop and she'd been in the bathroom leaned over a toilet. Lie, tell him yes, he was standing next to her, and he would flip out. Tell the truth, that she'd barely managed to stop puking to get the work done, and he'd wonder if Kim had brushed her teeth after she'd finished.

Lie, definitely lie. "Yes."

"Oh my God!"

"Spencer, calm down." The truck's now-unassisted steering made the wheel feel like it was stuck in oatmeal. The dash was still mostly black and Mike hadn't made a move. She couldn't tell if he was breathing.

"And you can… then it's all true! Angel Rage is real! You're real! This is better than finding out fucking Santa Clause is real! Angel Rage! Driving… oh my God, you're actually driving my car! My car!"

"Spencer!"

He flopped on the back seat and hugged himself again. "Oh my God! I've pissed off Angel Rage! That is so freaking cool! Hey, Mike! Mike?"

He really wasn't breathing. Oh God, he wasn't breathing.

The SUV rebooted itself. Mike jerked like he'd been kicked in the chest. He took a gasping breath, shook himself, then looked around. "What?" he asked.

At first, she was too busy trying to figure out just what had happened to notice how quiet it had become.

"What?"

It seemed she wasn't the only person bothered by being the center of attention.

"WHAT?"

Mr. Impossible needed a realm connection to breathe. That was interesting. Kim put the truck back in gear and drove onto the road. "Nobody searches for anything on the EI until I say so."

Mike looked as if she'd just told him to get out and walk. "But why? Who is Angel Rage?"

Spencer was about to explode. Fanboys always knew more about this stuff than she did. It didn't make any difference that she'd been there when it happened. Kim needed time to think and he needed something to do. "Spencer, you can tell Mike everything you know about Angel Rage. *From memory.*"

Spencer's hand trembled as he reached out toward her. "First of all," he said with obnoxious awe, "it is such an honor—"

"No touching!" Kim and Mike said together.

Spencer yanked his hand back. "My God. So that part's true too? No touching at all? Since you were three? Really?"

It was bad enough that Mike knew she couldn't be touched. At least she'd made him pay a price. She stared at Spencer through the rear view mirror. He could at least get the facts straight. "Since I was four."

After five years underground, Kim had forgotten fame also meant total strangers knew your secrets. A long time ago, she finally became the cool one, the one everyone wanted to know. She'd wanted that, so she'd made herself as interesting as possible by giving HuffPo the exclusive to end all exclusives: an interview with the mysterious Angel Rage. She'd told them exactly how vulnerable she really was, back when she was a stupid teenager who knew she'd live forever.

Squeaky McFanboy now officially knew more about her than anyone else on the planet. The expression on his face bothered her much more than that realization. She would not be pitied. "Well?"

"Right. Angel Rage was the leader of Rage + the Machine, which was, like, the most amazing group of Robin Hood hackers the world's ever seen."

She snorted. "Robin Hood hackers" made it sound like they were working with a plan, that they really knew what they were doing. The opposite was closer to the truth.

"No, really. They were, like, the ultimate heroes of… damn it, what were they called… my dad called them dirty hippies."

"That's what they were, trust me," she said and was rewarded with a flash of annoyance in his eyes. Interrupting fanboys as they held court was one of the guaranteed ways to piss them off. Goading him was fun.

"Occupy! That's it. They were the heroes of the New Occupy movement. At first, they were just annoying. Wait, you do know they've written songs about you guys, right?"

Oh Jesus, he even knew about the songs. "Spencer, focus."

"Yeah, okay. They were just small time for a while, annoying until the Goldman caper."

Mike asked, "The Goldman caper?"

Spencer's jaw dropped open. "Goldman, Sachs, Morgan, Stanley? How come you don't know any of this?"

Kim felt Mike's eyes on her as he said, "That's a pretty good question. The records aren't there. What you're talking about doesn't exist anywhere I can reach."

Damn it, he was searching again. The fool would bring who knew what down on their heads. Kim reached up to snap the realmspace connection again.

"Stop! Please, don't do that again. I've got a… heart condition."

So he really hadn't been breathing. His heart condition needed a realm connection to control. *Anywhere I can reach,* he said. Things were starting to add up, but the answer didn't make sense. "You're not going to find anything because I erased it all."

They both said, "You *what*?"

"It wasn't easy." Understatement of the century. That logic bomb was her finest achievement and creating it had nearly killed her. The rest of Rage + the Machine treated her like she was an alien after she turned it loose in realmspace. They wouldn't tell her what they had seen while watching her build it. "It's not important. Spencer, you were saying?"

"Goldman, Sachs, Morgan, Stanley. GSMS. They were a megacorp, largest in the world at the time. There was this explosion somewhere."

Fanboys knew everything, except when they didn't. "Cambodia."

"Right. Cambodia. There was this explosion in a chemical factory that ended up killing thousands of people. It got traced to GSMS. The highest executives. But nobody could prove anything and they all walked. A year later they were all on welfare." Spencer giggled. "Rage + the Machine hacked the entire GSMS network. They siphoned off the net worth of all the executives—"

"No," Kim interrupted, "just the board of directors, the CEO, and the direct reports."

"Yeah, what she said. Anyway, siphoned off their assets and donated it all to Cambodian charities. Then they sold the company to their worst competitor. It was epic! The sale was completely legal! There were pictures of some of these guys managing McDonalds and shit." He sighed. "It went on for a couple of years after that, crazy things. They had corporate America on the run. Angel Rage was their leader. She picked the targets—"

"No," Kim said, "Mark picked the targets. Angel did the work."

"Okay, anyway, Angel did what nobody else could, hacked the quantum fabric to get things done. They stole trillions."

"Is that what they say now?"

"Yeah, trillions. Hundreds of trillions."

A tan and white shape on spindly legs leapt straight into the road. Her mind registered "deer" just as the BMW's collision avoidance system sensed imminent impact. It put the vehicle into a controlled skid toward the shoulder. The steering wheel spun under her hands as the tires hit a curb under the snow. Seatbelts held Mike and Kim in; Spencer bounced briefly into the air and then disappeared with a solid thump. The car tilted up on two wheels, then crashed back down onto the road.

They all sat there in complete silence as steam leaked out from under the hood.

"So you mean to tell me," Mike said evenly, "those things are allowed to just wander around loose?"

Before Kim could digest that bit of absurdity, Spencer detonated in the back seat.

"Oh my God! My truck! You broke my truck! My parents are gonna kill me! What the fuck were you thinking?"

Mike turned to Spencer. "Thinking? Who had time to think? Don't you people know what a fence is? Who drives in the dark when animals like that can wander into traffic?"

Kim tuned Tweedle Dumb and Tweedle Dumber out and placed a call. Thank God for small coincidences.

"Hi, I'm Jane Sipowitz," she said. "A deer put me into a ditch on Highway 211 and my car is damaged. Your shop advertises twenty-four hour towing. Could you give me the number to a rental agent?" Now for the code phrase. "I've got my grandmother's silver plate in the back."

The pause on the other end was just long enough for her to know the owner of Rollio and Son's Car Repair, who happened to also be the Phoenix Dogs' demolitions expert, got the message. They all made fun of her when Kim insisted on code phrases in case someone needed help in realspace. She knew better. Assume they were always listening, because they usually were.

"Um, yes ma'am, I understand. The shop still won't be open until seven tomorrow."

"That's fine. This is what it's reporting." She sent him the diagnostic file that flashed in the vision link she shared with the vehicle. Kim heard the word "gun" and snapped her attention back inside the truck.

"Don't be ridiculous, Spencer," Mike said.

"She's bound to have a gun on her somewhere. You don't know my parents, Mike!"

Kill himself over a crunched car. Could this kid be a bigger stereotype? "Spencer, shut up." When he opened his mouth, Kim glared at him and held up her hand. "Yes, thank you," she said out loud so they'd know she was on a call. "I'll leave an amount which will cover your estimate. The car will need to autodrive home. Thanks so much." She nodded to Spencer.

"Kim, I'm going to need your gun."

"Don't be an idiot, Spencer. I broke the truck; I'll get it fixed."

She turned to Mike. "You got into that old realm's box controls on your own, right?"

"Yeah, a long time ago."

"He can do it to any realm," Spencer said proudly. "It's a talent."

"Can you hide someone else from detection there?"

"Sure. That's not very tough either."

It wasn't like they were going anywhere very soon. Might as well put Mr. Impossible to good use. "Mike, you're with me. I'll need you to hide my entrance and keep me invisible. Can you do that?"

He nodded.

"Okay. Spencer, get some rest." She and Mike sat back and relaxed as they jumped into realmspace.

When her avatar materialized dressed in her old catsuit, it was every bit as comforting as she remembered it. Too much, really. It was a symbol of a life she left far behind because it had nearly destroyed her and everything she loved. But it was needed now. The Phoenix Dogs deserved every protection she could give them.

"Like hell," Spencer muttered inside the car. "What the shit? Mike, why can't I manifest?"

"Sorry, bud, avatar's illegal. No fifteen-foot talking penises allowed, dude."

Kim closed her eyes and rubbed the bridge of her nose. Angel Rage once terrorized corporate America and now she had someone who wanted to walk around as a gigantic wang. Talk about downgrading the team.

"Well, how about—" There was an "access denied" ping. "Dammit, maybe this." Another ping. "Shit. Oh, come on, everyone laughs at the way the string hangs..." One more ping. "Goddamn it. Are they serious? Mike, all it'll take is my default."

"Sorry, Spence, I don't make the rules."

"Shit." Spencer's default avatar manifested about three feet away from Kim, every bit as normal as she was. Thank God. He wore an Ozzy Osbourne memorial T-shirt, jeans, and sneakers.

Spencer's eyes fell to her boots and slowly walked their way up. If default rules allowed it, they probably would've rolled out of his head just like they did in old cartoons. When they locked on to her chest, it was the last straw. Fanboys did not get free looks. She reached out to grab him by his chin.

"Listen up, you sweaty little hormone with legs." Kim pulled him closer. "There's just one rule for you. Touch. Nothing." His eyes were nice and wide now. Good, he was paying attention.

"And if you're dumb enough to touch *me* while we're here?" She pulled back slightly. "You know Mars, right?"

He tried to nod, but she refused to let him actually move.

"JPL's realms are so much fun. Very realistic. I've always wanted to see how far I can toss a skinny little fanboy like you across Marineris by his scrotum." She brought him close enough to kiss. "Are we clear?"

"Crystal," Spencer squeaked.

She held his gaze until his eyes started to water, flicked his chin away, then turned around. She shook her head at the whimpering sound coming from behind her.

Kim asked, "Mike, how do we get started?" His reply was a long time coming. "Mike?" *Oh geez, not him too.*

"Um? Oh. Well, keeping people from noticing you is pretty straightforward."

They were in the lobby of Verizon's customer service realm, an open expanse of warm wood, brushed steel, and frosted glass. People coming and going walked around them as if they didn't exist at all.

"Some sort of force field?" Kim asked.

"Not exactly. It's a little difficult to explain in words. I guess I sort of suspend the reality contract in a specific area. They couldn't walk into you if they tried, let alone see you."

"Good enough. I need you to get me into their records section."

"No problem, just follow this." The sick yellow toad materialized in front of them.

"A path stripe will be fine, Mike, thanks."

"You're no fun." The toad vanished and a translucent glowing line appeared at her feet heading through the lobby and down a hallway.

Kim floated a personal mirror up so she could keep an eye on Spencer without him knowing. Sure enough, after about two minutes, he started screwing around. By shoving a hand or a leg out, all the other avatars around him would turn like he was poking a finger into a tank full of fish. The little monster actually turned around to give it a real try, so Kim cracked him across the back of his head.

"Goddamn it!" He glared at her.

Kim manifested a pair of eggs in her hand and crushed them. Spencer paled and locked his hands to his sides. She vanished the remains and they continued. This time she put him in front of her.

The seams of a door drew themselves into existence on a wall and slid sideways just long enough for them to enter. This portion of the realm was a vast, brightly lit collection of tall pale-gray cabinets. They stretched to infinity in every direction; a limitless chamber studded with giant building blocks that sat on glass floors.

The ability to get this deep into a realm was fantastic. Kim had always been able to unlock things, but only from the outside. The trick with the car's registration and Spencer's identity was harder, but it was still just that, a trick. It'd bought them enough time to get out of there, nothing more. What Mike allowed her to do was the real thing. Once she finished altering the records, any trace of their calls from the stranded truck would vanish. It was the difference between camouflaging an object and removing it.

First she had to find the right nexus. Kim pulled a menu out of the air and activated the navigation controls. The monitor floor detached and they shot upward, then right, then upward, and then left. One nexus, fresh from the oven. She bent over and activated the control display.

Spencer made a choking noise and she realized her mistake.

Bend at the knees, dear, not at the waist. She turned. Sure enough, he wasn't staring at the screen.

"Spencer," Kim said as she worked, "I'm used to the stares, but do you actually have to pant?"

His eyes snapped up and he blushed. "Oh, hell with you both. I just can't win. I'm sacking out. Let me know when the car gets here." He vanished.

"That wasn't very nice, Kim," Mike scolded.

"It's for his own good. He's probably been awake twenty-five hours now. Even teenagers have to sleep some time."

She erased all traces of her call to Rollio's shop, then stood. Phase one complete. Now to see how far Mike's skill would let her travel. "Here's a list of names. We need to figure out who their providers are."

"What are you going to do?"

Kim sighed as she looked down at the utility belt around her waist. Her most effective tools were so illegal she didn't dare carry them around day-to-day. It would be just her luck to get busted on a traffic stop and have them find a Mark 17 VirtuPry in her phone's storage. Besides, she'd retired. So there were a lot more empty brackets on the belt than there were pouches. That would change tomorrow, but it didn't mean she was helpless. "Unfortunately not much right now. But with the access you can give me, I'll at least be able to tell how bad the damage is."

And so they flew from provider to provider. Kim checked the accounts and access points of all her Phoenix Dogs. They never signed up for the chaos of her former life and they neither wanted nor needed what might come next. She found nothing. Mike might have stomped all over her life with his foolishness, but he hadn't exposed anyone else.

Mike asked, "Is that it?"

"One more stop and it will be a tough one. I need to pay a visit to the Luray PD."

"Tough? For me? Sha, right." His voice boomed and echoed as he said, "Prepare to be amazed!"

Mr. Impossible as a showman? Picturing Mike in a ringmaster's outfit made her laugh out loud.

"Well, look at that. You can laugh."

That brought her up short. Some old habits, like knowing when and how to run, were welcome. Others, like being a legendary humorless bitch, weren't. Time to change that. "Of course I can laugh. I can tell jokes too. A wife went in to see a therapist and said, 'I've got a big problem doctor. Every time we're in bed…'"

He didn't know that one, or the one about the naked blonde walking into the bar with a poodle under her arm, or the one with the twenty-four cans of Budweiser. He was snorting loudly when she was done with her version of *The Aristocrats*.

"Stop it, Kim, it's distracting me," Mike said through his laughter.

Who knew telling jokes to Mr. Impossible would be fun? "Have you really never heard any of these?"

"So far? Nope. The last one was downright filthy."

"That's the point." Kim shrugged and smiled. "Any day now, Sellars." They were in another realm box, but she stood next to the realm this time. It towered over her head, a muddy brown wall that was half wood and half stone. Glowing lines zipped the fizzing edges of a door into existence and it opened smoothly into the deep machine spaces of the realm.

It'd taken him all of ninety seconds to break into a police department's realm without a single peep of an alarm. It was an achievement no amount of her tools or talent could accomplish. Oh, the places they could go.

"And Kim?"

She paused and looked up. "What?"

"Keep in mind the eleventh pun always gets a laugh, even if no pun in ten did."

She giggled, then turned to the job at hand. As offices had machine spaces for things like air-conditioning, plumbing, and power, realms had machine spaces for quantum routing, data switching, and simulation generation. Like their realspace counterparts, realm machine spaces were tight. The extra dimensions made them more interesting though.

That was the whole point of the catsuit. Kim took a deep breath and activated its hypercube extensions. Diagonal and oblique lines turned into right angles as the entire space unfolded into its true six-dimensional shape. It was only visible at all because of the upgrades on her avatar's eyes. Human retinas didn't work well with this part of realmspace.

Even with the right eyes, working with extra dimensions took a lot of practice. It was like facing a wall covered with paisley wallpaper and then having all the curves and designs turn into straight lines with right angles as the wall transformed into a room-like space.

The scientists who designed realmspace protocols combined existing direction names to describe the new ones. Back-down-left became b'deft. Forward-right-up became f'rup. There wasn't any real system to it, you just had to memorize the names and hope your brain didn't explode trying to comprehend it all.

The first time she'd tried to make a b'deft turn or walk f'rup a hall Kim thought her legs would come apart. It took a few years for her to learn to move around inside a construct this complicated, but it was worth it. The only way to truly hack a realm was to get down into its guts and screw with the plumbing.

Kim spun the inner hatch's hand wheel counter-f'rupwise and opened it. "Can you show me where the data layer for their report system is?" The path stripe corkscrewed through all six of the dimensions. It meant she'd be sore for at least three days in real-space.

"I upgraded the catsuit's malleability protocols. It probably won't be as uncomfortable as it used to be."

Human eyes didn't work with six dimensions and neither did their bodies, at least not in their natural shape. Kim unhooked the vertebra in her spine and twisted l'ptwise through the first junction. He was right. The sensation of thumbtacks and needles trying to push through her skin was gone. "I'll also need to know where the primary cutoff is for this realm."

There was a pause. "It's a good thing I upgraded your suit, then. You're not gonna believe this."

Mike's upgrades to the cat suit helped, but Kim still had to twist into a pretzel shape that required a degree in algebraic geometry to describe. After fifteen minutes, she had cramps in places that didn't exist in her actual body. Leave it to the public sector to cram a realm so tight even six dimensions could barely hold it all. With all her joints unhooked, leverage was a real problem. Kim strained, reaching f'deft around some pipes to grab the cutoff switch blindly.

She couldn't get to the short-term caches that would hold copies of any report the cop might've written. So she did the unexpected and booby-trapped the power grid. The caches would clear immediately if the power went out. She fiddled the iSpring trap over the primary cutoff and blew her cheeks out when she felt it clip into place.

"Ha! Got it." Every cache access panel in the place now connected to the switch. One pull on any of them and *poof!* She uncurled her avatar into a more human shape and then exited the realm just as their rental pulled up in realspace.

Kim got Spencer's home address, programmed it into the BMW's autodrive controls, then put a sizeable chunk of her dwindling emergency cash under the mat. She double-checked that Spencer disabled the GPS tracker and caught him glaring at her.

"I pulled the fuse on it, *duh*. That's Hacker 101. Do you think I'm stupid?"

"No, but I didn't get this far trusting other people to be smart." They both got out of the way as the autotow lifted the truck onto its bed.

Mike moved like he'd lost a boxing match. She waited for him to fasten his seatbelt. "So all that work takes a toll on you, huh?"

He nodded with his eyes closed. "More than I thought it would, especially right now. You don't mind if I take a nap for a bit, do you?"

"Not at all." Having them both out cold would be a godsend. She had a box full of puzzle pieces and needed time to figure out how they fit together.

Kim drove the remaining, mercifully deer-free ride in silence. Mike had the face of a killer, but she was certain he was no danger to her or anyone else. Colque jangled a deep instinct to run every time she'd been around him, yet around Mike, she felt… safe.

He had a head injury. The man who was out to kill her had been clobbered by a light fixture. Mike had his own memories and Spencer seemed to have known him for quite some time. An assassin with a head injury. A *fatal* head injury. Mike could unlock any realm without a trace or an alarm, but he couldn't touch anything without destroying it.

All of those places she just couldn't reach. At the heart of it all, that was what had kept her on the run for so long. A smile formed slowly. Mike didn't know it yet, but this was the beginning of a beautiful friendship.

She opened the car doors and considered her comatose passengers in the lights of the hotel parking lot. She'd been the one asleep in the back seat once, with Mark, the real leader of Rage + the Machine, up front as they waited for the Amazon store to open. They'd drawn the short straw and had to be first in line to pick up the third expansion pack for *Realms of Warcraft*. Being the terror of corporate America was their day job. What really mattered was staying at the top of the ROWProgress ranks.

They had to be physically present when the store opened to make sure they got the super-rare edition that had an extra toolkit on a flash drive in the box. Back then, she wasn't quite good enough to hack their realm and have one mailed out. Besides, Mark would've considered that cheating.

Kim shook herself out of her thoughts and threw the key cards at the boys. "Wake up, princesses!"

They both flinched and grumbled. Spencer asked, "Where are we?"

"Next to Dulles. I need to pick some stuff up from the bank next door, but we have to wait until it opens."

Mike waking up was so weird. He looked at his hands as if they belonged to someone else. It reminded her very strongly of the time when a baby cousin of hers at a family reunion, when Kim couldn't have been more than ten, was lying on a couch and suddenly realized the arm moving in front of his face was his arm and he was controlling it.

Yet some part of her, probably the last sane part of her, still wanted to believe this was Colque's long lost twin. She needed more evidence but wasn't sure how to get it. "Out, both of you."

As they got to their rooms, Kim turned to them. The car ride had only been an hour. She needed more time to think and they both still obviously needed some sleep. Six hours should do wonders for everyone.

"Breakfast is complimentary and at eight. Do *not* be late. Goodnight." The door closed behind her with a muffled thump.

Chapter 17

Aaron

Unduplicate AIs like Venus were patient to a fault, but it could be exhausting for the humans who worked with them. He'd been in the imaging lab analyzing the evidence with her ever since the team got back from the restaurant. Aaron managed just a few brief cat-naps during her scan cycles. Coffee probably couldn't be given IV; otherwise every agent in the building would have arms that would do a heroin addict proud. He grimaced after taking yet another pull of the stuff from his mug. It was even worse cold. "Okay, Venus." Aaron sighed for what felt like the hundredth time. "Take the video back to its original resolution and starting point."

The holobox swirled around him and stopped. A full-scale model of the Taco Bell fixed at not quite twenty-six hours ago appeared. A small white car drove into the parking lot. "Freeze."

"God, Aaron, are you still here?"

He jumped and twirled around in his chair. "Christ, Jenny, don't do that."

She laughed. "You have got to be the jumpiest person I've ever known. Park still got you chasing his white elephant?"

"You and me both, remember?"

"Oh no, I'm just here until tomorrow. Once this comes up zero again, I'm back to chasing sunrise distributors."

Chasing petty drug dealers was the only assignment worse than tagging along behind someone chasing a ghost.

Jenny cracked a smile and nodded. "Yeah, okay, I get your point. What've you found?"

He shared the holobox. "Venus? Start." A white sedan pulled into a parking space. Trayne got out and walked south. "Venus brought me in when she lost Trayne at this point. Watch." The views shifted as their subject walked down a sidewalk and then she was gone.

Jenny gasped. "Are you kidding me?"

"I've been stuck ever since. When's the last time you ever heard of Venus losing someone?"

She stared at it for nearly as long as he did the first time he saw it. "Aaron, you failed that test just like I did, right?"

In the academy, they made cadets sneak down what they claimed was a typical American street, trying to avoid being spotted by Venus as she monitored the cameras scattered everywhere. It usually took a week to find the right path. Once the class had figured that out, they bussed them to an actual street in Northern Virginia. If you made it from the start point to the bar two miles away, beer was on the instructors. If Venus spotted you, the instructors opened up with paintball guns. Aaron and Jenny finished in the middle of their class; the bruises took weeks to heal. Nobody ever managed to get a free beer.

"Yup, and she's still gone. Where do *you* think she went?"

Two hours later, Aaron stood with Jenny and the other two young agents on Park's team. In a holofield that filled most of the room, Trayne walked down a sidewalk.

"Come on," Ray muttered.

"No way," Jenny said as she grabbed Leon's hand. "She's going left. Damn you, go left."

The images dissolved and then rebuilt themselves. A different angle showed the woman, now with red hair, walk into the frame and then turn right. The entire room erupted, half groaning, half shouting.

"I believe that means Agent Levine's team is in the lead," Venus said.

Aaron fist-bumped Ray. "Told you that's where she went. Venus, track that to the end."

The AI's vaguely feminine voice made everyone stop. "I tried, agent Levine, but I'm afraid you'll be disappointed with what happens next."

A new street scene started. Pedestrians walked through the agents; Ray had to move a few steps away as a full picnic table appeared around his waist. Aaron dodged sideways to avoid Trayne as she walked into the plaza at the center of Reston Town Center.

"Oh, no," Jenny groaned.

"Are you kidding me?" Ray asked.

They all swore as the red head danced through the crowd and vanished.

The repeating and rewinding went on and on. Eventually, he just had to set his head down.

"Agent Levine?"

Someone was talking to him. Oh, God, he hadn't dropped the course. The final exam sat in front of him and Aaron had no clue how to start.

"Agent Levine?"

The dream dissolved. He snatched his head up, notes firmly stuck to his cheek. He peeled the page off and turned around. Everyone else was sprawled uncomfortably across couches and desks. Well, at least he wasn't the only one who'd fallen asleep.

"Yes, Venus?"

"I think I may have the final answer."

Aaron thwacked Ray with some paper. "Wake up, everyone. Venus found something."

"Okay," Aaron said to Venus, "what do you have?"

A hardware store parking lot assembled itself around them. A circle appeared around a blond woman walking out of the store. "This has been a most stimulating challenge," Venus said. Aaron shared in the eye rolling around the room. Unduplicates sometimes did not understand the no cheerfulness before coffee rule. "The target shaved a piece off one of her boot heels to throw off my stride algorithms."

"How'd you spot that?" Jenny asked.

"She forgot to discard the purse, or she couldn't. Only one other person walked into the store with a purse like that." The larger simulation stopped and a new wire-frame stage assembled in the air. It split and showed the redheaded woman walking into the store next to the blonde walking out. Model comparisons confirmed the purses were identical.

"A standard double-switch, but I've never encountered one so elegantly executed. The rest wasn't as challenging." The constructs flew apart and a hotel parking lot built up in its place. Aaron spun a map up in front of him. The hotel was only a kilometer or so from the plaza. The blonde walked into the hotel, then the model fast-forwarded. A different girl, by appearance, walked out into a windy morning.

"She failed to assemble her disguise properly this time. I don't know why." Trayne walked stiffly; she wore yet another wig. They still couldn't see her face clearly because of the hats she seemed to love. Trayne climbed into a red SUV and drove away.

The construct disintegrated and then rebuilt. The same red SUV pulled into a hotel parking lot in Luray, Virginia about two hours later. Venus said, "The latest GoogleSnap shows it was still there at 6:00 p.m. yesterday. That's the best I can do without a warrant."

At least they wouldn't have to watch any more reruns. "That's great, Venus. Someone get Park on the line. Looks like we're going to Luray today."

Chapter 18
Adelmo

Adelmo woke up two minutes before the alarm clock would've roused him. He rolled over, making sure the bed didn't move at all, even though Selma would wake on her own within minutes of his absence.

After all these years, after all his nephew's ridiculous theatrics, finally someone professional had been set on Rage's trail. In truth, he found murder distasteful, but it was part of this business. Twenty years ago his family possessed the most productive silas bean fields in the world. The crop could only grow in specific areas with very particular climates. It was only slightly more profitable than its soybean cousins. The family was barely breaking even. Then a group of Finnish chemists worked out the formula for trioxyclonage ergotomic alkali, better known nowadays as sunrise. It turned their fields of trash seed into the key ingredient of the most potent narco-hallucinogen the world had ever known.

Other clans thought they were stronger and tried to push the family off the land. They failed, primarily due to the ruthless leadership of Adelmo's brother and eventually his brother's son. They had gone on to create an empire of unprecedented wealth and power.

And so he would hunt Rage down and see her dead, but not because of some ludicrous slight of honor. Adelmo had read the police reports. Rage's actions were not the direct cause of the death of Manuel's son. In fact, it was the most fortunate thing that could ever

have happened to the family. The boy had been less than useless. He'd been an active danger with no ability to keep a secret.

No, he would see her dead because the business demanded it. She'd left with all their secrets and fled directly to the US government, who'd hidden her ever since. Her betrayal took the family from zenith to nadir in North America and he would have her head for that.

So he got up at an ungodly hour, drank the coffee his wife made him, and rode the limousine to the airport. It was a job—nothing more, nothing less. He was pleasant to the stewardesses because they, too, were just doing a job. What did a smile cost?

He rode the tram from the gate to the terminal, another balding old businessman doing another boring old job. Adelmo smiled. Prostitutes thought theirs was the oldest profession. He knew better.

The luggage carousel area brought him right back to his own youth. The Dulles main terminal had been built as a showcase of sixties architecture and had never been remodeled. Sans-serif fonts, white marble floors, brown metal, and raw concrete still dominated the decor. It'd gone from futuristic to tacky to blasé to irreplaceable classic, an ironic monument to a generation that thought they were the end of history. He'd last come through as a young boy, full of wonder. His return was not for sightseeing.

Adelmo rounded the corner and saw his three new assistants. The information packet they'd sent him during the trip was stunning. Colque was not, in fact, dead. Worse, he'd vanished without a trace. At least they knew which hospital he'd ended up in. "Gentlemen," Adelmo said in Quechuan, "we have work to do."

Perfect security cut both ways. Quantum computers created the communications the family needed to function free from law enforcement or government spies. Unfortunately, it also meant they couldn't crack anyone else's files. With the brief exception of the time when Rage was tricked into working for them, the only way to get at secrets now was the old-fashioned way: get someone to talk.

*

"I'm certain he'll be interested in seeing me," Adelmo told the pretty receptionist outside the hospital director's office. "Just tell him he'll never have to see Sal again and Secretariat's Sequel will no longer be the end of the world."

She seemed confused, which was a good sign. It meant the director kept his addiction to horse racing under enough control it wasn't common knowledge. Men at some time are masters of their fates, but the director had not been master enough to save his marriage or his house.

Until now.

Adelmo motioned his men to have a seat in the outer room while he was ushered into the director's office.

"This is very unusual," Dr. Richards said as he nervously sat down behind his desk. He leaned forward as if they might be overheard and whispered, "How do you know about Sal and the race horse? That just happened yesterday."

"How I know is far less important than what I'm prepared to provide." Adelmo shared a connection with a Cayman Islands bank. "This is a numbered anonymous account with what I am assured are enough funds to more than solve your current difficulties."

In truth, it wasn't that much. The family didn't really start paying attention to money until the figures included nine zeroes. By the way Dr. Richards's eyes went round and his jaw fell open, it was more than enough to pave the way.

"Who are you?" he asked.

Adelmo smiled. The good doctor wasn't fighting or being pompous. This was going much more smoothly than he'd expected. "Who I am is also not important. I am a fixer, Dr. Richards, and you have in your possession information that will help me make a repair."

"I do?"

Dr. Richards was a man whose life was destined to end at the bottom of a river or under a stadium's foundations at a date in the very near future. He would've grasped at a straw and Adelmo had shown up out of nowhere with the keys to a cruise liner in his hands. Under the circumstances, Adelmo could forgive him for being a bit dense.

"Yes, you do. I require access to your data stores, Dr. Richards."

"What?" He gulped and went pale. "All of them?"

Adelmo's net was wide, but he didn't need to cast it across an entire ocean. "No, just those for the past forty-eight hours."

"And for that, you'll give me all of this?"

Adelmo sat back in his chair. "Dr. Richards, I discovered long ago that time is far more valuable than money and at the moment I am in a bit of a hurry."

Richards nodded. Adelmo received notice of access codes and realm portal addresses. He spent a few seconds setting up communications agents and then noticed the silence. Richards sat motionless, head down, hands in the air. "Dr. Richards, is anything wrong?"

Richards slowly lifted his head. "You mean you're not a cop? This isn't a set-up?"

It wasn't often he was surprised by the people he worked with, but Dr. Richards had managed it. "Oh, Dr. Richards, you've just made my day. No, I'm not a cop and this is not a dream. Dr. Richards?"

Richards went white as a sheet, his eyes rolled up into his head, and he collapsed in a heap beside his desk.

Chapter 19
Mike

There was heat and light and the hall pulled away from him as she ran into the bathroom, screaming. He ran down the hall after her but the door kept getting farther away. There was no color. His threads had no color anymore. But this was no longer all he was. There were flashes, images, impossibilities that defied prediction or even common sense. He fell screaming into the maw of a creature that could not exist, then gasped awake.

So that was a dream. He'd left dreaming out of his models because it was such an incomprehensible part of human consciousness. Mostly he hoped such a strange thing wouldn't affect him since the bulk of his existence would remain in the realms. Now there was no getting around it. He was dreaming. Yet another new requirement; he *hated* project creep. When he sat up quickly, emergency alerts flared to life in half his management daemons. Balance was just barely staying online and his vision swam with the pixelated effects of an optical bridge unable to manage compression.

Model seven hadn't predicted dreaming, but it had predicted this. It was the unevenness of sensations that threw him off. Mike needed a place where sensation was equal, everywhere, in realspace. That's why he'd made sure a set of swim trunks was part of the care package. He stumbled down empty hallways and pushed through the door to the pool.

Mike collapsed into the water and barely fought off the need to gasp. The pool was indoors, but the water was cold. He relaxed and floated upward. Let the body do the work. He opened his eyes into the underwater blur as he kicked and pushed against this soft world. It was what he needed. Sensation equalized here, allowing his integration to renormalize and continue. Telltales flashing red slowly went to yellow, then green, one by one. His body moved through the water as more muscle memory was unlocked. The ringing in his ears subsided, leaving a static rush of sound in its place.

He realized the rest of his existence swam through realmspace. It was a remarkable insight on more than one level. Not only did his real self, the one still in the realms, inform this new outside one, his new outside self was teaching him things about his own reality. He twirled and kicked against the wall to swim another lap. It was amazing that something in this outside physical world had some inherent connection with his real one in realmspace.

He pulled up against the other wall, panting, and heard someone else breathing just as hard beside him. Mike turned his head and was nearly driven back into the realms by what he saw.

He let the water reassure him, center him, as he stared into Kim's eyes. His heartbeat settled while she stared back. Silence rushed in and the water stilled. Her swimsuit was blue. It was a pretty color against her pale skin.

"What are you doing here?" she asked.

"I… need this."

Her smile brought out the fascinating symmetry of her face. "I'll bet you do." The smile went mischievous. "And I need to win." Kim shot backward down the lane.

All at once, he knew what to do, knew how to swim a backstroke. She had a head start, but he was stronger. A thrill that had once only been a binary trailer, a routing sequence when Mike needed to get somewhere quickly, had turned into analog emotion. He needed to win. His fingertips touched the wall and Mike spun and kicked toward the other side. This time he kept his head down, pushing hard to the finish. This was glorious. Acids burned through him. He kept breathing upward as he tore through the water until he rasped his fingertips against the sandpaper surface of the concrete wall.

Kim wasn't beside him. He'd won! Mike raised his arms in triumph and then the door slammed shut.

He was alone.

After a few more laps in the pool, he got out and headed back to the room. Mike knew better than to try to go back to sleep. No more dreams for tonight. The medical agents assured him the hours of sleep he'd accumulated so far would be enough to last at least until tonight.

Mike had rested before but never this full on-off cycle. He'd just sleep a chunk of his threads and keep going. That didn't work anymore. This body claimed more of his consciousness than any model had predicted. It seemed the human brain really could rival the infinite storage of realmspace, as long as he stayed connected at any rate.

He scratched his chin and then knew what to do. He needed a razor. They'd passed an atrium on the way in that had vending machines with what he needed. A few selections later and he was set. One goatee, departing.

Hair was so strange. There were practical purposes: shade in the summer, insulation in the winter, friction reduction on the lower body, and a secondary sexual marker for males. But those benefits seemed small for an item they all spent an inordinate amount of time and money on. It had such a weird feeling too. As he finished with the trimming scissors, Mike examined a bit of it. It had a tensile strength comparable to copper wire when dry, yet softened with heat and moisture. It came in a bewildering variety of colors and textures. Humans used chemicals and, increasingly, nanotech to get what nature didn't provide. Now he had it too.

The razor was proof of how cool realspace could be. The edges of the ferroceramic blades were only a few atoms wide. With care, they never went dull. Someone mucking around with a 3D printer in his shed somewhere in New Zealand had invented them five years ago. The inventor sold the patent to Proctor, Gamble & Eveready and then retired at thirty. Mike was designing a universe realm for the guy so he could enjoy gallivanting around it in his very own NCC-1701-K *Enterprise,* complete with an unduplicate AI to control the crew. He wanted to know how much that license cost but the client wouldn't tell him.

Mike wiped his face dry and checked the time—it was still plenty early enough to get ready. He threw open the curtains and looked into the black sky. He didn't have a proper *zafu,* so a pillow would have to do. For the first time since he learned the practice so many years ago, Mike settled real legs down into a lotus position, centered a real spine, half-lowered real eyes, then began to meditate.

Sitting fixedly, think of not thinking. How do you think of not thinking? Nonthinking.

His first true sunrise. It was a thing he could not unlock, could not stop, and could not reverse. The warmth gradually crept up his body. The light was amazing and it just happened. Nobody controlled it, for *billions* of years, and now it was happening for him.

A pillow wrapped around his head and knocked him flat on his back. "Done being mystical yet, Elrond?" Spencer said as he headed for the bathroom.

"Hey!"

"What? You think I'm gonna face Tiamat without a cigarette? Put some clothes on. I gotta whiz and then I'm getting a smoke. If the stories I've heard are true, we do *not* want to be late for this meeting." The bathroom door shut behind him with a thump.

They got to the foyer of the dining room right on time. Kim was already there, wearing a large blue sweatshirt with Keep Calm and Don't Blink on it. A waitress picked up three menus and walked them to a booth.

Mike smiled as he sat down opposite her. "At least now I know how you recognized those old box controls."

Kim raised an eyebrow. "Maybe I just like old sweatshirts."

He'd never understood the idea of "flashing eyes" until now.

"Maybe I just want some goddamned coffee," Spencer said. Just then, the waitress returned with a pot and three mugs.

It took a few seconds after Spencer finished pouring his cup for Mike to realize he was in trouble. While he could approximate it, the one thing he could never completely simulate was smell. It was the only sense that was wired straight into the human brain and because nobody needed to eat or drink in realmspace it wasn't as finely modeled as the rest of the senses. Fresh coffee this close triggered a complex response he wasn't ready for. He needed to shore up his filter stack but couldn't think clearly enough to get it started. The autonomic system's alarm fired off and the whole thing threatened to kick to manual. He rather liked not having to think to keep his heart beating.

"Are you all right?" Kim asked.

He'd takes notes about what was happening if it wasn't for the shaking and sweating.

"I've been... having... some trouble..." It got much harder to concentrate. Alarms flared in all his monitor routines. He was getting sick of their noise.

"Mike, open your eyes and look at me," Kim commanded. When he did, she swore and jumped out of the booth.

"Jesus, Mike, what the hell's wrong?" Spencer asked.

"I'm not sure." The balance routines went completely off line. He had to hold on to the table; otherwise he'd fall out of the booth.

Kim plopped a big glass of soda in front of him and snatched her hand away. "Drink this right now."

On the second swallow, his head began to clear. By the fourth, things were nearly back to normal. He set the glass down while Kim apologized to the waitress. "Sorry, he's hypoglycemic and it got away from him. You were waiting on someone else, so I went ahead and got a soda for him."

"He is okay?" the waitress asked with a heavy accent. "Do you need ambulance?"

Kim switched to a different language and he guessed she explained what had happened more clearly. He checked the incident logs. What a boneheaded move. He'd set up so many shields and filters it interfered with his body's normal signals and the smell of the coffee overloaded the whole system. He was a little surprised he hadn't just passed out. That would've been a great way to start the morning.

After the waitress left he said to Kim, "Thanks."

"You're welcome. When's the last time you had anything to eat?"

"I'm not sure. I didn't eat anything in the hospital and I can't remember the last time before my accident."

Spencer barked out a laugh and Mike glared at him.

There had been so many delays and wrong turns he hadn't been able to properly explain to Kim what he was until now. Spencer had better not screw it up for him.

When he turned back to Kim, she'd raised her eyebrow again. "Isn't that interesting?"

"Anyway," Mike said, picking up the menu. "What should I order as the first meal of the rest of my life?" He flinched. Dropping clues was the wrong thing to do this morning. He needed to get on with this. He couldn't rescue the world by himself.

Kim poured a sheaf of sugars into her mug. She'd already used up most of the creamers.

"Pancakes. Start with sweet before moving to savory." She reached over for the coffee pot and glanced at Spencer. "Am I amusing you, Unibrow?"

His face clouded over and he crossed his arms. "Why do you have to insult me like that?"

"Because it's more fun than counting your zits?"

Spencer clenched his fists.

Kim's smile grew vicious. "Not quite what you expected, am I? Thought they'd just exaggerated the nasty bitch part? Spencer, you have no idea."

Mike needed to explain things, and now he had to be a referee. "Kim, stop."

"Stay out of this, Mike. I've been around his type a lot longer than you have. Fanboys. Kids who think they know everything about me, correct me about things I saw, things I did. Fawning over me like I'm some sort of fancy toy when all they do is get in my way."

"No!" Spencer's fist hit the table so hard the silverware jumped. "No. It's not just you. It's what you all stood for. You're heroes. I've got posters dedicated to you guys on my walls. Everyone in all of my clans would trade their left nut to be sitting in this booth right now. All I've been doing is helping and you just call me names."

Kim peered at him over her mug. "I'm not a hero," she said through the steam.

"But you are! Rage—" Her eyes flashed a different way this time, a flared warning. Spencer's voice dropped to a hoarse whisper. "Your group did so many good things."

"We were idealistic idiots. Mark thought he could change the world and I believed him." She suddenly aged, grew old right in front of him. He'd seen it in realm dramas, but those were just actors. In person, it was much sadder than he ever expected. "I don't believe him anymore."

"So, what?" Spencer asked. "I'm not supposed to believe anymore either? My parents suck, everyone in school hates me, and now my heroes don't exist?" Spencer threw a wadded up napkin across the table. "Never existed?"

Spencer had never acted this way before. He could be annoying, even depressing when his parents went at each other, but Mike had never seen him actually upset. It looked like he was about to cry.

Kim put her mug down. "The person you worshiped died boarding a plane in La Paz five years ago, Spencer. I'm just Kimberly Trayne." She tapped her fingernails on the table. "I'll start calling you by your name if you'll stop putting me on a pedestal. Do we have a deal?"

Mike just leaned back to let them figure it out. He and Spencer had a past, but Kim and Spencer had some sort of weird shared history.

Spencer gripped his mug. "Okay, we have a deal."

The waitress reappeared and spoke to Kim in what Mike's GoogleTools finally identified as Thai. "Are you ready to order?" the waitress asked in English. Spencer stuck with coffee; Mike took Kim's advice and ordered pancakes. Kim asked for steak and eggs.

"I see you've learned how to shave," Kim said after the waitress left.

He rubbed his face. "I couldn't stand the mustache. It felt like I had a brush mounted on my lip and the goatee made me itch."

"It suits you." She paused and seemed to come to a decision. "You're a dead ringer for someone I knew before. Are you related to *anyone* named Colque?"

Mike knew it was time. He'd always hidden his nature from the people he interacted with in the realms. Frankenstein stories were everywhere and the monster didn't wave torches at the peasants. The nature of realmspace made it easy to disguise himself. When he considered it, Mike probably had as many shell personas as Kim did, maybe more.

Besides, he wanted to include her. It was the same feeling that caused him to tell Spencer the truth, but tinged differently, with an emotion he couldn't name. He silently checked with Spencer, who shrugged, so very helpful. "No, my last name really is Sellars."

"But you look exactly like—"

Mike held up his hand. "I know, and there's a reason for that."

Of all the bodies, in all the hospitals, in all the world, he ended up with one she knew. It was less of a reason, more of a deeply weird coincidence.

"When we were in the realm last night, you asked me where I was from and how old I was. I didn't want to tell you then because you wouldn't have believed me. Even before I looked like this, I learned the hard way that people have to figure it out on their own. Have you?"

She smiled and he was again mesmerized by the symmetry, by the way it changed her eyes, her whole face.

"I figured it out last night while we were in the…" She paused and blushed, then started again. "After we were in the accident. You can unlock any realm there is. Your earliest memory is of that old Pripyat realm because that was probably the first thing you ever saw. I sent a man to the hospital with a head injury I was sure killed him. You showed up at my door with a head injury that put you in the hospital. When I cut the realm connections to the truck, you stopped breathing.

"I don't understand how you ended up in Matias Colque's body but if that means he's dead, I'm ecstatic. You needed a body because two days ago you didn't have one." She paused, took a deep breath and then said, "You're an AI and you're in a human body."

He smiled. She was the first person to ever work it out all on her own. "Guilty as charged."

"So an unduplicate finally made it out?" she asked.

It was an easy mistake to make. Unduplicate AIs were the most sophisticated constructs the realms could host. Their architecture was unique to each individual and the data structures extended into quantum storage in a way that could be moved but not be copied, hence the name. Most of the oldest ones had vanished into private collections and the only first-gen unduplicate still in the public eye refused to take anything like a Turing test. She said it was an insult.

"No," he replied. "As far as I can tell, I just sort of emerged. I'm not human, well not until yesterday anyway. I'm a different kind of person. People are all I've ever known. How could I not be one?"

"Are there more of you?" she asked.

"No." The place he lived in was hard to describe. It was the same place the realms were in but different. Above and around them somehow. "There aren't any walls or rooms where I live. If there was anyone else, I would've met them a long time ago."

Spencer was indignant. "It took you nearly a year to tell me what you were!"

He was right. Mike had no idea why he told Kim the truth so quickly. Thankfully, the food arrived to change the subject. Now that he'd readjusted the integration, he didn't want to fall over. He did, however, want to grab fistfuls of everything and eat it all as fast as he could. Animal reflexes. How remarkable. Mike noticed the silence around the table. "What?"

Kim laughed. "If you think I'm going to miss the first time in history an AI eats a pancake, you're out of your mind. I should be taking pictures."

Spencer nodded obnoxiously.

"I'd rather you didn't. I read up on table manners and utensils before I tried this but I don't need a permanent record." He held up a crispy brown strip. "This is bacon?" He bit into it and forced back tears as a new definition of wonderful unfurled in his mouth.

"Oh yes," she said. "And over there? That's the syrup."

Chapter 20
Aaron

Aaron snorted awake when the engine switched off. He blinked at the morning sun. At least he wasn't failing a test in his dreams anymore.

In a weird way, being on the job was easier than school or the academy. Out here, nobody knew the answer. You passed when the bad guy went to jail.

Easy was a relative term. In the past twenty years, quantum computing had taken away half the tools they'd come to rely on. Eavesdropping ceased to exist and if the bad guy had a good password on his files you'd be more likely to get at them with dynamite. It hadn't only affected the FBI, either. All that was left of the NSA was its spy museum. Aaron took his girlfriend to visit it not two weeks ago. The empty headquarters next door was a sad black hulk with weeds eating through the parking lot. Decrepit, half-collapsed domes on the roof exposed the delicate antennas inside to the elements. Intelligence rusted. Who knew?

Which didn't mean the bad guys had a free ride. Catching them just wasn't easy anymore.

Agent Sanchez grumbled from the driver's seat, "Why couldn't we find her in, I don't know, Chicago or someplace?"

"What does Chicago have to do with anything?" Aaron asked.

"They have an actual police force. Not this Barney Fife crap."

Park shook his head. "Trayne's car hasn't moved in more than twenty-four hours, Sanchez. If she's not dead, she's long gone from here."

Park dispatched other members of the team to look at Trayne's car and visit the local PD to see if they had turned anything up yet. Aaron went with Park and Sanchez to talk with the hotel staff.

It actually was a pretty small town. The place would probably be another wide spot on a country road if it weren't for an accident of geological history. The huge cavern complex to the west kept the population of about seven thousand quite busy. Aaron grew up in a place not much bigger than this, but Branson, Missouri made Luray look positively quaint. It was just as well. The world didn't need another HMS *Titanic* museum in a landlocked Southern town.

The desk clerk's mouth fell open when they walked in the door of the hotel's lobby. "Can I help you?"

They all showed credentials as Park replied, "We have evidence there may be a known fugitive staying at this hotel. We'd like to search the premises and your records of the past thirty-six hours. The warrants should be on file now."

Agent Sanchez sent Aaron a message. "Got an important job for you, kid."

Four years of college, twenty weeks at the academy, two months as a real agent, and Aaron's important job was fetching coffee. When word got out he was on caffeine detail, even Park placed an order. Neurostims may be the latest thing, but the bureau ran on coffee. Complicated, expensive coffee. Starbucks had vanished into realmspace to dominate the stim market but there would always be a place for a real coffee shop, usually located next to the nearest law enforcement headquarters.

His first delivery was to the local police department, naturally right across the street from the coffee shop. Park had sent Jenny and Leon over to coordinate with the local cops and check on the off-hand chance that they may have a lead or two. "Hey, guys."

The two agents refocused their eyes out of realmspace and sighed. "Thank God," Jenny said as she pulled her brown ponytail tight. "You are a lifesaver, Aaron."

"Caramel macchiato, come to papa," Leon said, as he reached for the large insulated cup.

Aaron shared their workspace. It was scattered with stacks of folders, security feeds, and traffic logs. "This town generated all that?" he asked.

"It's for the whole region," Leon replied. "The storm created a helluva mess for everyone in the area."

"Any leads?" Aaron asked.

Jenny shook her head. "A local cop filed a report about an incident in that hotel just last night, but all we have is the cover sheet."

A page of characters typed themselves across their shared workspace. When Aaron tried to access the full file, it threw a "not found" error at him.

He checked the version of the document control system. "Hang on," he said, "this DCS is old. We may not be done."

"What do you mean?" Jenny asked.

"It's a trick I learned back in high school." Because people were always deleting files accidentally, companies who designed document control systems like this did their best to make sure it was very difficult to absolutely destroy a file. "I used to help my old man go through DCSs when he did discovery on his lawsuits." The counter to the "keep everything forever" reflex was the fear of those sorts of lawsuits. Destroying files was the easiest way to stop the discovery process. "This one is just like one I helped him with my senior year. There's a private cache it keeps on the back end for twenty-four hours. The only way that gets wiped is if the power's cut."

Aaron manifested his full avatar in the DCS's admin space. Jenny and Leon manifested right behind him. The room was just big enough for the three of them, with institution-green walls holding racks of controls, panels, and switches.

"Do you think they could've made it a little smaller?" Jenny asked.

"This is nothing," Aaron replied. "You should see the real back end." He pulled on the cover over the day cache but it wouldn't open. "It's a full six-dimensional foldspace. You want cramped? *That's* cramped." He tugged on it again. It was definitely stuck.

"Do you think it's locked?" Leon asked.

"No, it feels like there's a spring on the other side." Aaron braced and yanked hard on the door. Whatever held it shut gave way with a metallic snap and a shower of sparks. Aaron found himself dumped back into realspace and thrown into complete darkness.

He fumbled around in his pockets until he found his flashlight the same time Leon and Jenny found theirs. The blue-white lights cast sharp shadows around the room.

"Are you kidding me?" Jenny asked.

Aaron tried to contact Park back at the hotel. "Do either of you have a connection at all?" They both shook their heads. Whatever this was not only killed power to the building, it also knocked out the quantum cell that surrounded the police headquarters.

The place felt crowded with three federal agents who had nothing to do. Updating Park with what they found would probably be his best next move.

He had to be careful at the few intersections with stoplights because they weren't working. Groups of people stood outside every business and office building he passed. The entire town must've been knocked off-line by whatever had been hidden behind that panel. Rage was good, but she wasn't very subtle.

After briefing Park, Aaron found Agents Schaefer and Smith in the parking lot wiping down Rage's truck. Aaron explained what had happened as they sipped their coffee in the frozen daylight. "So now do you think she exists?" Aaron asked Schaefer.

His bushy eyebrows fell into a frown as he took another drink. "Kid, you ever consider this little town might not have the most robust infrastructure in the world? Hell, they just had a snowstorm. I'm surprised anything's working."

"Don't listen to him, Aaron," Smith said. She knelt beside the open driver's side door. "Look at this."

Someone had turned a graffiti artist loose inside the vehicle. Lines of black spray paint covered every surface. He whistled. There was no way they'd get a single fingerprint or DNA trace from that.

She nodded. "The registration points to a person who's never existed too. If you guys hadn't helped Venus all night, I don't know that we would've ever found it." She looked over at Agent Schaefer. "I used to think Rage was a myth too. But after the past forty-eight hours? I'm beginning to think we've been calling her a fake because we didn't want her to exist."

Chapter 21
Kim

It was like she'd been given the biggest Christmas present in the world. A walking, talking lockpick that could get her everywhere she could never go. Freedom might be within reach, not just for her, but for everyone on the old team. The Machine would be free and clear if Kim could find them.

She spent five years alone and on the run, fully expecting to live the rest of her life that way. Now there was a new and utterly unexpected option. However, a practical question needed answering. "So, you're sure Colque's not wandering around somewhere in there?"

Mike stopped trailing his fingertip in the syrup on his plate. "Completely. I wouldn't be here if he were. I think it's a function of tunneling and a new sort of entanglement. At any rate only one person at a time can live in here, or in any human body for that matter. I'm refining models as my integration completes and I'll work out more as time goes on. The math is pretty wicked. Anyway, he's in the reincarnation line and all that's left for me is muscle memory."

An AI that believed in reincarnation. She filed the idea away for later.

He continued, "I'm learning how to reach that, but it's slow. The ability scans on this body were off the chart, highest I'd ever seen."

No doubt. She remembered the way Colque spun a knife on his fingertip, the way he balanced on one hand as the sun set below the Altiplano, or the way he breathed alcohol and cigarettes at her as he talked about his latest murder. But this was Mike, a different person; Kim knew that now. A different person living inside someone else's body—amazing.

Mike asked, "How did you know him?"

God, where could she start? "Mark—"

"Who the hell is Mark?" Spencer interrupted.

Naturally he wouldn't know. They'd kept their identities such a closely held secret back then. No names, no faces, just shadows throwing terror at people who were even bigger criminals than they were. "You probably knew him as Rabunhod."

"Really? Rabunhod's real name was Mark? God, I can't wait till I get—"

"Spencer, I have kept these secrets all my life. You will not tell a soul about any of this. Do you understand?" He stuttered an objection, so she used her power to unlock his phone and set off its private emergency alarm. The quick blast made him jump like she'd hit him with a cattle prod. "I said, do you understand?"

Spencer raveled into his seat like a candy wrapper under a heat lamp. *Good, it can learn.* Mike shrugged, totally clueless.

"Mark was the leader of the group even before I joined, back when they were just called the Machine." A thought brought her up short.

Mike was about to become for her exactly what she'd been for Mark, for all of them, so long ago: a lockpick capable of opening doors nobody else could.

At least he wasn't a ten-year-old kid. She'd make sure he'd be able to live on his own after she was finished with him. "He called himself the Jewish Robin Hood and believed it. We all did."

This wasn't what she wanted to talk about. It was so easy for her to get sidetracked around Mike. "It's a very long story you two haven't earned. So. Colque. We'd all gotten bored terrorizing corporate America and decided to steal some drug lord cash for churches, schools, that sort of thing. But they trapped us. I only realized I was stealing one drug lord's money to give it to another when Juan Quispe—"

Spencer rocked back into his seat. "Oh, shit, Kim. You guys got involved with the Quispes?"

She shook her head. "It was much worse than that. Juan Quispe was the only son of the Don. You're looking at the girl *Señor* picked to be the fiancé of his budding polo champion. I was seventeen, a little old by their standards, but apparently I'd do." She paused at the looks on their faces. It wasn't supposed to be funny.

"You. Married to a drug kingpin's son?" Spencer asked.

"Can you even *get* married?" Mike asked.

His question brought up every schoolyard taunt she'd ever heard, but he'd asked the question with no malice. He was genuinely curious. "I don't know. I did know I couldn't get married to *him*, no matter what. Colque was their lead assassin and Juan's best friend. A mentor, I guess you'd say. Sometimes they'd pick out street kids and chase them from the city like animals. They made a game out of it."

The memories tore through scars that crisscrossed her soul. Small voices, screams, as Kim sat behind two murderers. She silently chanted a single word the entire time. *Survive.* Her job was to load the bodies into the back of the truck. It was the first time she'd ever touched someone. They were so small. The blood thickened between her fingers.

"Kim?" Mike asked.

Colque's laughter echoed as she felt tears threaten. She didn't need this right now. It'd been Mark's idea. Every objection she'd raised was answered or talked around until even Kim thought the scheme might work. He claimed it would be their very last caper, out of the country and genuinely helping the innocent. The nightmare began when she unlocked a datastore an elderly parishioner had left them in his will without a key.

"Anyway, the man whose face you're wearing was teaching the man I was supposed marry how to kill and enjoy it. I was the only one who knew the truth. Everyone else thought we were still working for widows and orphans. I couldn't tell them the truth."

She was the one the Quispe really wanted. They stopped the ruse after she found out the truth and simply threatened to kill everyone involved, families included. "They knew everything about us."

"And what the Quispe know, the Quispe own," Spencer said. "They never let go. Jesus Christ, Kim, how the hell did you get away from them?"

She was on the edge of respect for the little monster. He was the first person she'd met who really understood.

"It wasn't easy. It's still not easy." With Mike around, that was definitely going to change. "Anyway, I had a plan. Sunrise likes cold. The quicker it's frozen, the better it is."

She stopped. All of these stories were things she'd never told anyone before, not even Tonya. These two could be, well, a bit endearing when she came right down to it. Then she remembered that last night she wanted to toss them both off a cliff.

"Shit, Kim," Spencer said, "don't stop now."

She laughed. His twang made him sound like a young Jeff Foxworthy. "Anyway, the really huge industrial flash freezers were just coming on to the market. I cooked the numbers and convinced Juan he could triple the family's output if they used them. He was always looking for a way to impress his old man, so he hopped a plane for Texas to catch a demonstration. I made sure Juan knew he needed to inspect the inside of the freezer. He paid attention."

"Oh shit, Kim, a Habart?" Spencer asked.

"So you know them?"

"My dad built the first building in Arkansas designed to hold them. The one thing nobody *ever* did was—"

"Stand inside the freeze unit. Yes, I know that now. I thought I'd just scare the fat little bastard, so I hacked the demo unit. I knew he'd want to sniff around it with just his buddies, so when he stepped in…"

Spencer put a hand over his eyes. "You turned it on."

"I turned it on." The whole fiasco came rushing back. "It was supposed to scare him. He'd realize he'd never be safe around me and he'd turn us loose."

One press of a button. All Kim ever wanted now was to not have pressed that one damned button.

"How was I supposed to know the thing had no safety override? That the doors were six inches of hardened steel? The flash freeze took fifteen minutes." It couldn't have happened to a nicer guy but her timing sucked, as usual.

The camera feed into the freeze building went dark when she pressed that damned button. When she finally got it back, the circus had already started. "An entire news crew showed up. After it was over, they shattered his pudgy creepsicle ankles trying to break him off the floor. It all ended up on the six o'clock news."

A weird choking sound made her open her eyes. Mike and Spencer were grinning like idiots.

"What?" Even as she said it, Kim had to fight to keep a smile from forming on her own face.

Spencer started with, "You mean the reason you've been running all this time is that—" but lost the battle with his giggles.

Mike continued, "You froze your fiancé solid?"

Yes, damn it, that was exactly what had happened. Try to marry Angel Rage? That's a freezin'. It brought a completely new meaning to the phrase "ice princess," that much was certain.

"I didn't do it on purpose."

When Mike smiled, she couldn't fight off her own.

"Damn it, it wasn't funny." Then she remembered the puzzled look on Juan's frosted face when the doors opened, like he'd forgotten the answer to a question. At that point, even Kim lost it.

After they all calmed down, Mike asked, "What did you do?"

"The only thing I could think of. I trashed their network, unshackled my team, and we ran like hell. Colque's been chasing me ever since."

"What about the rest of your team?" Mike asked.

How could she sum up that terrifying trek through the jungle, sitting shivering and alone while everyone else huddled together for warmth, the final deal that made those last plane rides possible? They all fought with each other at the end. She couldn't even hug them goodbye. Kim rubbed one of her earrings briefly. "I did everything I could to make them safe and then I hid too."

Again he'd sidetracked her. "But that's not important. What *I* want to know is why I'm here. I was hiding for a reason, Mike. Now we're all on the run. You're the one who smashed my security. Why?"

He considered her question silently for a moment. "About two years ago I noticed changes in the quantum fabric. Since that's the base of the EI and realmspace, I was bound to notice it eventually. Someone is replacing quantum computers."

"So?" she asked. "People replace computers all the time."

"But these are different. I noticed them because, well, now that I have a nose, I realize they smelled funny."

He could be charming even when he made no sense. "Computers have a smell to you?"

"It's hard to explain. It was just wrong. Eventually they were all over the world. Top level fabric latches, mostly."

"What's so funny about them, aside from the stink?" Kim asked.

"They're softer, somehow. It's not just old or defective ones, either. It was just weird until I got close to one and it broke. I've wrapped myself around those things for years and they never just broke. Not once."

The top-level latches were what underpinned the entire infrastructure of the Evolved Internet, much like top-level domain servers with the original Internet. Control them and you control realmspace. Break them and...

"Whoa," Spencer said as he sat back. He'd obviously come to the same conclusion. "You think someone's trying to break the EI? Why the hell didn't you tell *me* about this?"

"I haven't told anyone about it until now. I don't know if someone's trying to break it, or take it over, or anything else. I have no way to know. I can't figure out who's making the damned things." He sat back. "Every time I ran up a trail, it came to a dead end. The only thing I can think of is the operation is completely disconnected from the EI." He faced Kim. "And that's why I need you."

"It is?" Kim asked. Old reflexes, old desires started to wake up inside her. A mystery, a threat, a thing she could fix.

"Yes," Mike replied, "if they're disconnected, that means an assault. I need someone who can really fight."

She thought she'd figured him out and now he'd thrown another wrench at her. "Hang on a second. I can't fight anything. I'm just a skinny hacker has-been. I'm good in the realms, on my good days maybe top ten percent."

"Three," Mike said.

"Three percent?" Spencer asked.

"No," Mike replied, "top three."

Kim had worked so hard to hide that. A confusing mix of fear and pride hit her. She'd been very, very careful before joining any realm, yet he had found her. He had looked so hard he found *her*. It was exciting even though she wasn't sure why. There was no reason to be happy about it.

"I've never seen her rank less than tenth in any combat realm she's ever joined." Mike turned back to her. "Some of them have billions of members. You were careful, always anonymous but you have a style. Anyway, always top ten, usually top three." He paused. "That's not an accident, is it?"

It wasn't like this was the most important thing she'd confessed to so far. "No, nobody pays attention to number three. If I started attracting real attention, I'd drop to tenth. But that doesn't change anything. I'm not a real fighter. Being good in the realms isn't the same as being good in real life."

It made sense he'd think that. He'd only had a body for a few days, maybe less than that. A demonstration might help.

"Hang on," she said. It took a few seconds to find the sharpie marker in her purse. "We're going to play a game called Bishop." Kim spread her fingers flat on the table. "You place the pen on the outside of your hand, then touch between one set of fingers, return, touch between the next, return." She demonstrated slowly.

Spencer said, "I know this one. *Aliens*, right? Wow. You're not gonna to let him put his hand over yours, are you?"

A strange thrill she didn't expect tinged the old panic at the thought of someone touching her. It didn't change reality, though. "No, He still sits over there. We'll face each other."

"Where's my marker?" Mike asked.

"You don't get one; you get this," Kim said as she handed him her steak knife.

Colque scared the hell out of her doing this once. If Mike was telling the truth about muscle memory, he'd be fine. If not, she had Band-Aids in her purse.

She popped the cap off the pen. "Ready?" She spread her hand flat on the table again and put the marker down just outside her thumb.

"I guess." He cocked his head. "You know, I'm pretty sure I can do this."

"So am I. We'll speed up as we go. Look straight at me, not at the knife. I'll do the same. And begin." Kim tried to move the marker so it landed between her thumb and forefinger, but hit her first knuckle instead.

Spencer shouted, "Ha! Kim—OW!"

She uncurled her toes inside her shoe and put her foot back down. The strikes on her hand built up. Kim did her best to hide the disappointment at just how bad she was at this. It wasn't about her. As they stared intently into each other's eyes, the tap-tap-tap got faster.

Mike's eyes were so different. Colque's eyes were black pits colored with sparks of insanity. The wrongness of him was a constant. Mike had the same face, but the eyes were curious, sometimes even child-like, and always flashing with enthusiasm. Kim didn't realize she was smiling until she felt her lips part.

Spencer hissed at them, "Hey, stop, people are staring."

She gasped as she popped out of her concentration. Kim raised an eyebrow at Mike and held up her hand, now covered with marks. Mike raised his, which was clean. The place mat he'd held his hand on had six precise cuts. The knife's tip had struck exactly between his fingers, each time in the same place, without his ever needing to look down.

"Get it?" she asked.

Mike's blush colored his tan face three shades darker. Yet another thing Colque never did. "Kim, I am so sorry. How could I be so stupid?"

"Save it for later, I've got some ideas. This might work out after all." Kim picked up the check. "Come on, it's time to go."

Chapter 22
Kim

She walked out of the bank into the morning light with two bags of her past on her shoulders. The water weeping across the asphalt from nearby piles of snow splashed under her boots. Other than the piles, it'd probably all be gone tomorrow. As she opened the car door, Mike said, "...a hunchbacked, sensitive, and intellectual friend."

"What the hell?"

He shifted to face her. "It's the last question of a pop quiz Spencer's taking. He's in first period English."

High school hadn't been *that* long ago. The only hunchback she remembered rang a big bell.

Mike shook his head. "A long story you haven't earned."

"I swear, every time I think the conversations you two have can't get any weirder." Kim tossed the heavier bag in the back seat.

When she sat down, Mike was still staring at the back seat. She swore softly. The stupid latch had unsnapped. She stuffed the few stacks of cash that fell out back inside, then snapped the bag shut. "Just because I'm retired doesn't mean I'm helpless. I never wanted to see any of this again but it would've been stupid to just throw it all away."

The serial numbers on the cash were another thing her logic bomb took care of five years ago. Kim never wanted to risk even a chance of a trace. Until now.

It was time to get started on her plan. She dug around in the bag on her lap. Her special talent with quantum computers was just a part of what Angel Rage once was. At least as important was her ability to steal, borrow, or build the gadgets that the world's most feared cyberthief needed to terrorize corporate America and hide in plain sight while she did it.

It was so strange to handle the tools of her old life. She fought with the teenager inside her who had once used them. Rage was dead and needed to stay that way. There would be no comeback, only a brief return to fix what she couldn't the first time around. She could finally bring them all out of the dark and back to safety. But there would be no more merry pranks, no more righteous revenge—that was over.

When Kim turned to Mike, the teenager inside her made some inappropriate observations she didn't need right now. Rather than arguing with her hormones, she pulled out a flat, wafer-thin device about the size of a matchbox and turned it on.

"May I?" Mike asked. Kim shared the configuration screen with him as she worked. He stayed quiet and out of the way. It was nice to have someone who was interested in it all.

"It's an OnStar spoofer," she said, tapping on a screen floating in the air in front of them. "As of now," Kim pressed a big green button on the screen, which lit up in response, "if the rental company checks it'll show us parked in this lot no matter where we go." She tapped the screen up and away with a finger, shoved her ragged knit gloves into her ratty field jacket, then started the car. "Now we get on with the rest of our lives."

Spencer might be able to talk with them in the car while he was in his school's realm, but walking around without drawing attention, either there or here, wouldn't be possible. Nobody was that good at splitting their attention. In other words, they needed to kill some time until Spencer had a break in his classes. Kim examined Mike briefly. "How important is all that hair to you?"

Mike bunched it into a ponytail then brought it forward. "I hadn't given it all that much thought, actually. It is kind of a pain trying not to lean back on it or catch it on anything. How do you manage with yours? Can you teach me how to braid it like that?"

She was talking hair care with the world's first human-AI hybrid. Well, why not? She smiled. "I've got a better idea."

*

An hour later, Kim parked the car. As they got out, Mike continued to touch his head. "So that's a Caesar cut?"

"Yes," Kim replied. "The more we can change your appearance, the less likely we are to run into trouble. It helps me too. When your hair's that short you don't look like you should be on top of a pyramid, hacking someone's heart out."

"Excuse me?" he asked.

"Colque was Bolivian. I don't have any idea where his parents were from but there's definitely some Inca in there."

She examined his new face in the morning light. Now that he'd shaved, his features actually were very nice. Without the beard — and the insanity — of the previous owner, his face was downright handsome. He was tall enough she could wear heels and still look up at him.

Stop staring.

"Jesus, Kim, this place is ancient." Spencer said as they walked to the realm café. "Old diners, old hotels, old banks, old barber shops, and now this? Hell, was anything in Virginia built after 2003?"

Fanboys knew it all. She was just an ancient relic who happened to have a driver's license. "What would you rather have, Spencer, a modern café with FBI agents?"

Spencer rolled his eyes. "Never mind. Okay, Kim," He waved his arm forward. "Let's go antiquing."

Kim shook her head and led them into the Compass Rose Café. She wasn't sure what was more irritating, Spencer being obnoxious or that he was right. It *was* old, converted from a tanning center. Most of the oldest realm cafés were. When BronzeSafe came on the market, small rooms with UV tanning beds could not compete with a nanotech lotion you could use at home. But they were easily converted to realm access points. "Set your phones to use this place's network, not your normal provider's. Nobody can track us here."

Spencer thickened his light Southern twang into a full-on Deep South accent and creaked out like he was a hundred years old, "So, ya think they'll hafta put an extree donkee on tha treadmill ta power yar phone, missy?"

She laughed in spite of herself. Spencer was a charmer when he wanted to be. In five or six years, he might actually be cute. Assuming she didn't kill him before sundown.

After checking everyone into a booth Kim settled into her own recliner, carefully palming a cam looper from her purse. It not only jammed security cameras, it looped their own feeds, making it impossible to tell anything was wrong. The device was basic but it was required in a world with no shadows.

She manifested in the realm's entrance.

"Wow, Kim, check it out." Spencer peeled up a corner of one of the couches and stirred his finger in the data on the other side. He pulled a dollop of the sparkling goo out and let the cleaning routines peel it off his fingertip. "Original CouchFlats, without the anti-tear patch. Classy!"

The constructs might be so old the patch routines had stopped working but pointing it out that way with an obnoxious grin would only draw attention. Unfortunately, she couldn't afford to slice his avatar's head clean off. Everyone in this realm would remember that. Could she have possibly been this annoying as a teenager? Well, maybe.

"Spencer, go to class."

His avatar vanished through an exit while she dropped back into realspace to finish building her shields.

Now that she didn't have to worry about the cameras, she got out the stuff that *would* attract attention. Some of her tools needed complex antennas that were too large to hide, others used glowing plasmas that would sometimes spark or snap. Basically, she sacrificed realspace appearance for realmspace disguise. Nowadays it probably all fit in a modern phone, but Kim would not trust her life, or anyone else's, to tools she hadn't designed herself.

Once she was done, she smiled. Lourdes, who did all the casing for the Machine's capers back in the day, teased her with the term "web mistress." She hated that ancient title even though, once everything was set up, the resemblance was undeniable. She would have to apologize to Lourdes the next time she saw her.

It actually could happen, and soon. She hadn't realized just how much she'd missed them all. There was Lourdes, Michiko, and Mark. They were the leaders, the ones who genuinely cared, not just about the cause but also about her. They'd done more to help raise her than any set of tutors Mama could ever hire.

There was Rich and Josh, cranky soul mates who never failed to make her laugh, when they weren't getting her into trouble with their antics. Henry's kids would be in middle school by now. Kim could remember the first time she'd gotten those babies to smile like it was yesterday.

She'd spent all these years pushing their memories away, burying them again and again, until only the faintest outline of pain remained. Kim thought she'd said good-bye forever. It didn't have to be that way anymore.

Hang on, everybody. We're nearly done.

Now secured, she reentered the realm. She'd spent years being as drab as possible in realspace as well as the realms. Maybe it was time to take another small risk and be a little noticeable, at least to Mike. She wore her hair down, with a plum, knee-length satin dress.

"Kim," Mike asked over a private channel, "what's wrong with your finger?"

She should've known a "gee, you look nice" was a little too much to expect. Still, it was an important data point. The construct wasn't supposed to be visible, let alone noticeable.

"You can see the ring?"

"Ring? I can't even tell it's a construct. From where I sit, it's like there's a stitch in realmspace wherever your finger goes. What is it?"

Clothes don't get his attention but gadgets did. Men were men even when they were AIs. Still, it was fun to play Jane Bond again. *The international woman of mystery has returned!*

"Just a second." She had to make sure the ring still worked. Kim walked over to the attendant sitting behind a counter. "When does the restaurant next door open?"

"Eleven o'clock."

"Thank you." After walking away for a few steps, she turned right back around and asked the same thing. "When does the restaurant next door open?"

"Eleven o'clock."

She walked away. Excellent. Now she didn't have to worry about people remembering anything about her. "It's called a Shaolin ring. Go ahead; it's safe to search for it here."

"Okay, I understand now. So, what happens if they're actually paying attention to you?"

"Where we're going, they won't be."

"If you're just running errands, why am I here?"

"I need you to make sure I don't try to enter a realm that can detect a ring as old as mine."

"I can upgrade it for you."

"No, I'd rather not risk it." She waved her hands as he started to object. "I know, you're an awesome super-mysterious god-thing in the realms but you also make mistakes. Let's keep it simple."

Her plan to liberate the Machine's members wouldn't take days; it would at least take months. Plus, she had to set Mike up for the rest of his life. Hotels were okay, but expensive, so finding a place to sleep that didn't charge by the day was at the top of the list.

They were reviewing their third apartment realm when Kim's curiosity finally got the better of her. The need to know more about him had become an annoying itch. He wasn't just Mike. He was also Mr. Impossible. *Mister* Impossible. But he'd started life as an AI. Sex came from hormones, which he probably didn't have. Until lately, anyway. Oh, hell with it. She might as well find out. "Can I ask you a personal question?"

"Do you want the short answer or the long answer?"

"What the hell is that supposed to mean?"

"You want to know if I've always been male."

She flinched. "Was I that obvious?"

"No," he chuckled. "It was the first thing Spencer asked when I came out to him too. He was a lot less subtle, though."

"No doubt. So what's the short answer?"

He tossed his voice so it echoed around her ears. "Magic!"

She smiled at the woman escorting her and said to him privately, "And the long answer?"

"You know, I'm really not sure. It's just part of what I am. Does that make sense?"

AI sexuality. Welcome to the twenty-first century.

Leasing an apartment required a real bank account, so their next stop was a Nationbank/BNC realm. As long as she opened an account on the same day, things would be fine.

"Wow," Mike said as she passed her fake identity construct through right forms, "that account rep is really pretty."

It took her a second to process that one. "Excuse me?" Not one nice word for her and now he was fawning over every other skirt he saw.

"It's interesting. I'm feeling genuine attraction. That explains the way I felt when…"

The silence extended. He was probably trying to figure out how to look down the rep's blouse.

"Yes?" Kim asked as she made an effort to be pleasant to the *really pretty* rep while they finalized the account.

"Nothing. Never mind. Hey, how did you end up with all these fake IDs, anyway? It took me forever to come up with a real one."

That finally boiled her over. She was done with the idiot talking in her ear about how gorgeous everyone else was and constantly revealing useful things when she'd stopped needing them. "You have a clean ID? Exactly when were you going to tell me about this?"

"When did I need to tell you about it?"

"I am busting my ass out here using up one escape hatch after another and here you are in your goddamned grape suit wandering around with a clean ID. Do you have any idea how much I've been risking?"

"Actually, no, Kim. I'm an AI; I'm not a psychic. Realspace is pretty new to me and things that happen in your head don't actually happen in mine."

"So why don't you get Gorgeous here to help you, then? Oh, right, I forgot, we all have to keep your big secret, don't we?"

"What? You're on the run from the world and *I'm* the one with a big secret?"

The account rep cleared her throat. "I'm sorry, ma'am, is everything all right?"

Damn it. She'd let her annoyance leak on to her avatar's face. Kim must look like she was about to explode, which wasn't far from the truth. She took a deep breath. "Yes, I'm sorry, everything's fine. There's a child being a complete brat out here in realspace."

Mike made a rude noise that Kim chose to ignore.

After the bank accounts were set up, it was time to retire the grape suit. Kim took him to her favorite mallrealm.

Mike said, "Amazon and Mall of America make a pretty good team."

"You've never been to a mall before?"

"It hasn't been my thing. Never had much use for realspace stuff, ya know?"

"Well that changes today. There are six dimensions of men's stores in here. We will find you decent clothes."

"Why can't I just get more of these sweat things? They're warm and comfortable."

"They only have two pockets and make you look ridiculous. You're getting nice clothes if I have to drag you into each and every store in this place to find them."

"And what you wear in realspace is attractive?"

"What I wear in realspace is none of your goddamned business. Now hit the measurement scanner on your phone so I don't feel like an idiot trying to describe you to the clerks."

The first two were a big zero. The discount stores just didn't have anything decent. The third upscale shop they visited, though, was much more productive. But that meant she had to chit-chat with the salespeople. The personal touch and all that.

"Your fiancé is a very handsome man, if you don't mind my saying so," the realm store clerk said while she helped Kim pick outfits.

It was the simplest story she could think of but Kim groaned on the inside. Like Mike needed a bigger head than the one he already had. She and the clerk were sitting together on comfortable, off-white leather couches reviewing a full-sized mannequin of Mike wearing one of the clerk's suggestions.

"Where is your honeymoon going to be?"

Mike asked on their private channel, "Why is it the more expensive the shop gets, the older and whiter the clerks are? And why are they all women anyway? This is a men's store."

It had to be Spencer's fault. When Mike was out in realspace, he was charming and innocent. In here, it felt like an invisible balloon full of stupid followed her around.

Kim didn't normally do super-happy excited. Faking it was harder than she'd expected. Back in the Machine days, breathless charm had always been Lourdes's job. "We'll be at Montego Bay in realspace and then at Condé Nast's new seventeenth century Venetian realm the week after."

"But, dear," the thin graying lady asked, "did you forget your ring?"

Oh, crap. The Hindenderp had wound her up so tight she forgot to fake an engagement ring. God, how to cover for this?

A construct materialized on her left ring finger.

"Kimberly Trayne," Mike said, suddenly serious, "will you marry me?"

Her heart fluttered and she couldn't swallow for some reason. Then she accessed the ring's contract and saw how much it cost.

"Jesus Christ, Mike! This is worth more than my mom's house! Where'd you get this thing?"

"Oh, my," the clerk smiled. "That *is* beautiful."

"Do you like it?" he asked with more of his irritating enthusiasm. "It's a contracted single-copy, no-dupe, designer Tiffany original with a guaranteed unique realspace equivalent."

She smiled at the clerk as her face flushed. It wasn't just a unique construct, oh no. That would be simple. That would be slightly less memorable. There was no reason to be subtle, no reason at all. "I just don't want people to think I'm showing off or anything."

It didn't help that the clerk was right. It was gorgeous. "You mean there's *a real one* out there? Goddamn it Mike, where did you get this thing? What part of remaining forgettable did you forget?"

"Oh," the clerk said, "I wouldn't worry about that. It definitely suits you, dear."

"Fine," Mike said sullenly. "I'll put it back."

"No," Kim shouted, "wait!"

The clerk flinched a little and asked, "I'm sorry, are you all right, dear?"

Twice. Twice in less than two hours someone had said that to her. She was the woman who'd almost single-handedly sent Donald Trump running naked out of Trump Tower. This was just clothes shopping and she was screwing it up.

First, square the clerk away. "I'm sorry, ma'am, I just got a call from the dress shop."

"Oh I see," the clerk said.

She just needed to get the hell out of here. "I think I'll take these two. Here's the delivery address."

Kim waited until they were safely in the public area of the mall-realm before she exploded. "Because it would've been worse if you'd just vanished it off my hand, you idiot!" It was like she had a giant "Please arrest me!" sign flashing over her head before he finally took the ring away.

"You know, all I'm trying to do is—"

"Get us all arrested by the FBI, that's what you're trying to do."

"Oh really? That's great. I'll just leave you alone then. I really think you should walk into, oh, nearly any of the rest of these stores, because I'm sure none of their security will call the cops about an ancient Shaolin ring!"

There was a tugging on her sleeve. Right. Like she needed another distraction, another damned thing to fix. *"What?"*

The entire mall around her stopped dead still. The little boy holding her sleeve nearly fell down.

"Forgettable. Right, Kim, forgettable."

She glared into the far distance as the boy said, "Your phone is ringing, ma'am."

Please, let something about this morning go right. Kim turned on what she'd been told was a million-watt smile and laughed at the little boy's answering grin.

She said, "I'm so sorry, you surprised me. Thanks so much."

She answered the call. "WHAT?"

"Jesus, Kim," Spencer replied, "I just wanted to let you two know I'm out for lunch. You guys hungry?"

"Starving," she said as she exited realmspace. "Let's head next door."

The walk to the diner was in complete silence, punctuated by the thump of her boots as she stayed five steps ahead of them. He'd come *that* close to blowing their cover at least three times. He'd get them all arrested. When the FBI took his phone, he'd just drop dead.

They'd probably figure out a way to pin that on her too, which would make it that much easier to toss her down a hole. Mike was a purple ticking time bomb. She saw his reflection in the glass of the diner's door. With his puffy purple sweats and his too-white brand new shoes, he looked like a cartoon character. He definitely needed better clothes. Damn it, she was supposed to be mad at him. She had to remember that.

Mike seemed to make a point of ignoring her. "So, what's for lunch?" he asked Spencer as they sat down at a table.

"Burger," Spencer said to Mike. "Definitely a burger this time. They're usually the best thing about places like this." He leaned over to Kim. "What, did you two love birds have a fight?"

Kim remembered her promise not to insult him at the last second and just glared. He rocked back like he'd been slapped.

"No." These two idiots would not get under her skin. There was too much at stake. "We just had a few disagreements. Yes, Mike, you want to try burgers next."

Eventually Spencer's prattle got the best of her and she calmed down enough to at least tolerate Mike for the rest of lunch. The errands were only half-way done. Even though she hated it, Mike was critical for the next steps.

Once they jumped back into realmspace, he stayed quiet and out of the way. She even caught herself giggling at the way he snored through the slog of setting up all the utilities.

"That's not a very big realm you rented," Mike said as they left the rental provider.

"It's mostly just a meeting place. It'll also mean we don't have to come to the cafe to reach realmspace. That's why I paid extra for all those gateways." If someone got lucky, or one of her wonder-derps did something clever, a trace would only find that room. They'd never figure out if the other gateways led anywhere important.

Kim groaned as she stretched her avatar. "But now, now we get to have some fun."

Out of nowhere, a line from an old movie she'd nearly memorized in middle school came to mind.

"Are ya ready, Roy?" she asked, rolling out the Rs like she had a mouthful of marbles.

"I was born ready," he warbled out, pitch perfect, and any remaining anger she had vanished. Maybe they could get along after all.

Kim sent him an address to a realm's locked basement. Sure enough, there was a black Pontiac Trans-Am construct waiting for her on the other side of the gateway. It even had T-tops. Kim hopped in laughing and thundered away.

As soon as they arrived at the destination, she immediately changed her avatar's outfit to something more suitable for real work.

"So that's what it's supposed to look like," Mike said.

"What? The catsuit?" Kim threw a mirror out in front of her and turned sideways. "Same as last night." She needed the thing but felt like Elastigirl as she posed in it. Had her butt really gotten that big in five years?

"No, you look great. It's the belt. There must be three times as many gadgets on it now."

Complimenting her in this old thing meant a lot more than when she had a pretty dress on. "Yes. Yes, there are. Do you remember all the addresses from last night?"

Mike did an impression of Spencer. "What, you think I'm stupid?"

This time she was able to do a lot more than just check on the Phoenix Dogs. She couldn't start trying to save her old friends without making sure her new ones were completely safe. Now Kim could use the kit that made Angel Rage famous to hide them all for real.

The tool kit, and Mike's ability to get her behind the scenes, made the work possible. It didn't make it easy. It took hours of sweating and swearing, twisted into painful pretzel shapes, to secure each of the connections.

Finally, they were at the last stop. The feet of Kim's avatar were at the base of what strongly resembled the cable anchor of a suspension bridge. It was even the color of poured concrete. Essentially, they were underneath an EI supplier's machine space. Somewhere above them, people's phones were using this provider to connect to realmspace.

In fact, it did anchor cables, sort of. The constructs that transmitted raw data into the vastness of realmspace were as wide as Kim was tall, made of twisted, sparkling light, like spiraled columns of rainbow-colored steel. They faded away, climbing into a smooth, cloud-filled sky.

The packets the cables transmitted buzzed past her with a deep harmonic sound that made her nose itch. There were thousands of abutments extending into infinity in every direction possible around her.

She had stretched herself through another six dimensions, stuck in a place so tight she had to squirm to get her arm in the right spot. The construct she held wriggled between her fingers. Its carapace glowed with databorne light and its quick nullable legs waved like a crab pulled off the ground.

"What *are* those things?" Mike asked.

"I call them crawlies." Leave it to Tonya to have an account with an ancient provider. She hadn't needed this little guy until now. Twisting her wrist b'deft, she latched it to the cable that terminated in Tonya's account. It spread thin and vanished as it integrated.

"Oh, well, that's very helpful."

Kim unwound herself through the foldspace. "I designed them for an honors project my senior year in high school. When I showed them to the Machine, everyone freaked out. They made me change my project. We were up all night making a new one. They're hyper-specialized agents that'll cause any attempt to tap a line to fail."

"You don't think someone's come up with a counter yet?"

The question brought her up short. Crawlies worked with the rules of realmspace in an unexpected way, naturally, but she'd figured he'd just know that. The god-thing wasn't quite the god-thing then.

"So you really don't know everything, all at once?"

He laughed. "Yeah, I was pretty disappointed with that too. I mean, all the sci-fi AIs I've read about are weird super-creatures that are so powerful they either take over the world or hide from it. Me? Sometimes I enter a realm and then forget what I came in there looking for. I can do a ton of things at once, but my existence is linear. I'm still trying to figure out why I don't learn all that much faster than humans do. Anyway, you're sure that thing can't be stopped?"

It was exactly what Mark had asked when she'd shown them to him long ago. "Oh no, not this one. Look closer." What made them clever was how they embedded into the local matrix, sort of like putting splinters into glue.

"Well played! They can't find one of these, because if they did…"

He might not be a god-boy but he was quick on the uptake. "It'll break just about everything else around here." There would never be a way to counter them. Ever.

"I can see why they made you change your project."

She pulled an ExpandaJar off her belt. As it inflated, it took on the appearance of a big round salt dispenser with a spigot on the top. She poured a mound of construct powder into her hand, gripped it hard once, then tossed it in the air. Millions of tiny blue particles flew into a cloud and then dispersed in all directions, yowling as they went.

"And those?"

"LockPixies."

"I thought they looked different." Mike paused. "Was that a war cry?"

She laughed. "Yeah. You're not the only Pratchett fan."

Feegles didn't have the same ring as LockPixies but the bloody-mindedness and mischief potential of the constructs was a perfect match, hence the color. And the war cry.

"I took a SearchPixie agent and reprogrammed it with a few extra features. If they have enough time, they can bore through pretty much any lock. They just don't last as long as the regular ones."

"How long?"

"About thirty-six hours."

It was just a fraction of the time a regular SearchPixie lasted. They were also about five times as expensive. But really, what good was a construct that searched for every reference to you in realmspace if all it checked was public records? Several dozen returned to Kim right away.

"Well, I'm clean so far. So are you. Did you know Spencer just won a division swimming contest?"

"I thought there was a new trophy in his room."

Kim snapped the container back on her belt and dusted her hands together. "And that is that. It's about time for Spencer's last class to end, right?"

"Yes."

"Okay, let me get changed and we'll wait for him. He's definitely going to want to see this next part." Finally, Kim made her first genuinely secure phone call since this all began.

"Hi, Tonya. What are you doing for dinner tonight?"

Chapter 23
Spencer

School was over, *finally*. Normal days were bad enough. He just needed to stay awake and avoid the bullies. After a year of high school, he had plenty of practice. Today, though, Spencer had the world's first human-AI hybrid *and* Angel Rage waiting on him to finish. He knew he'd learn more in a minute with them than he'd ever learn the entire time he spent in school.

When the bell rang, he dropped back to Kim's hole-in-the-wall café realm. It was easy to spot her. There was no missing a dress like that.

"Wow, Kim, nice outfit." His phone rang. He pulled down the contact screen in front of his avatar. *Great.* "Oh," he said. "Hi, Mom."

"Spencer!" she sobbed. She was always sobbing. "My God, where are you? I've been trying to find you all afternoon."

In other words, she came to and needed help finding the scotch.

"The FBI called. They said you were in Virginia. Where are you?"

The mention of the feds was pretty much the ass-end of bad news. Didn't matter. He could handle this. His mom couldn't have given them anything useful. She was too much of a basket case. The truck was probably on its way back to Arkansas by now. They'd have no luck at all tracking him directly. When he was a kid, he'd studied how Angel Rage stayed off the grid and learned how to imitate his hero. A hero who was, oh yeah, *standing not ten feet away from him.* Spencer would handle it, and then maybe she'd acknowledge that he was somewhat useful.

"No, I'm not in Virginia. I'm over at Stewart's house. We're working on a science project together."

Stewart was a neighborhood buddy, two years older than Spencer. When they were in grade school, the age difference didn't seem to matter. But after junior high things changed. More like Stewart changed and Spencer didn't, at least not yet.

Stewart went to California to spend the summer with his dad. When he came back he was a huge tanned stranger that defined "babe magnet." By the time Spencer had made it to high school, Stewart was a junior and already heavily recruited by every college in the SEC.

But before California, Stewart had changed on the inside. That was made way too clear just before he left that summer when he called Spencer over to his house.

He needed a realm locked up as tightly as possible. Spencer had been happy to oblige after just recreating Angel Rage's Dragon's Cloak, a crazy mishmash of traps and screens that he probably shouldn't have been messing with. He needed an excuse to use it.

Stewart was hiding his RealmDoll collection. Nearly everyone Spencer knew, himself included, experimented with the lifelike constructs if they could get their hands on them. Eventually, though, Spencer had outgrown them. As soon as Spencer got unrestricted access to The Resort, real girls in a real realm were available with unrestricted access. True, it was a teen-centric realm with a dedicated unduplicate monitoring it. They couldn't get into that much trouble. But they were *real girls.*

Stewart never gave the constructs up. Worse, he liked to hurt them in genuinely scary ways. All Spencer got were descriptions bragging of what he did with them but that was enough. Spencer set the Cloak, politely declined an invitation to sample the dolls, then never went near Stewart's place again.

Nowadays the only time Stewart wanted to talk was when the team needed help with math homework. Spencer was happy to oblige, because it kept an entire team of potential bullies off his back. Sometimes they'd do him favors.

Spencer made a new call while his mom continued to sob about her only baby.

"Yo, Spence, what's the skinny, my skinny man?"

"It's good, Stewart, it's good. Hey, if my mom calls, I've been at your place since Sunday, all right?"

Stewart laughed. "Oh sure, but it'll cost you. The offensive line needs papers for Mr. Watt's algebra class."

"No problem, just send me the assignments; I'll work them up when I get back."

"Where the hell are you anyway?"

"Can't say." After another quick look at Kim, he called up his camera, focused on her avatar, and snapped a tridPic. "But it's with her."

"Whoa. Nice. I thought the new Victoria's Secret avatars weren't due out for another two months."

"No, dude, she didn't buy this. She *is* this."

"Bullshit."

Nobody ever believed him about anything, not his mom, not Stewart, not Kim, not anyone. Spencer hacked the override screen Kim had on, then sent a picture at the highest resolution his phone could manage. He accessed the public contract for her avatar and sent that too. The one thing she couldn't hack was the default signature. This was what she looked like and that was all the proof anyone needed. "No bullshit."

"Don't worry about the assignments, Spence. This is payment enough. See ya!"

That didn't sound good. Then his mom started bawling again.

"He never cared about you! When has he ever called? Written?"

At least now she'd finally gotten to the endgame. "I know, Mom, but he's my dad. Calm down. I'll get home tonight, okay? I'll probably be at school when you wake up." If he said "come to," it would just start another round of hysterics. "I'll try to see you in the afternoon."

"You do know he's an alcoholic, right? Even your grandmother thinks so."

Right. He'd been gone for the past three days with her car; she'd been too drunk to notice, and she could talk about how terrible Dad was.

Dad was Dad; there was no getting around that fact no matter how many mistakes he made or how much he neglected Spencer. It was like asking him to hate his fingernails because they grew. The divorce couldn't happen soon enough. Unfortunately, they were more interested in stabbing each other in the back than closing the deal. There was just too much money involved. It'd been going on for years now.

"Spencer," she said, "I need you. I need you here. Please, come home?"

"Okay, Mom, yes, tomorrow afternoon. I'll be sure to give you a call. Just have another drink and relax, okay?" Spencer ended the call, swore softly, and looked over at Kim. "You talking to Mike?"

"I'm here, Spence."

"Jesus. Listen you two, whatever you do, don't get married. Okay?"

Kim raised an eyebrow.

"Spencer, we're not like that," Mike said.

God, the way his parents could twist him up. "No, I don't mean it that way. Shit, I'm warning the only two people in the world who can't actually get married. Anyway, if either of you know people who might get married, please stop them before it's too late."

A blue mote entered the realm through the ceiling. It made a beeline for Kim. When it hit her avatar, she flinched.

"Jesus Christ, you have got to be kidding me!" Other people in the realm stopped and stared. Her body went rigid, then her eyes locked on to his. "You. Stupid. Little. Shit!"

He dropped to his knees. This was someone who was supposed to be able to kill with her mind. "Jesus, Kim, what did I do?"

She grabbed him by the arm and yanked him to his feet. "Of all the idiotic, ridiculous," they transitioned to some sort of conference room realm as she continued, "dangerous things you could do, you pull a stunt like this?"

She threw him into a chair so hard it spun around completely. It slammed into her hand and stopped. He faced the center of a table with a hologram floating over it.

It was the picture he took and sent to Stewart, not two minutes ago.

Stewart had published it on Tweibo, the most popular social realmspace in the world.

The need to vomit hammered at him so hard he wasn't sure he could swallow it down fast enough.

Mike appeared and saw what was in the middle of the table. "Spencer? What the hell?"

"I didn't do it! Mike, please tell her it wasn't me! I didn't do this!" *Stewart was such a moron!*

Kim pointed her finger just inches from his face. "If it wasn't you, you sorry pimply sack of shit, then who else could it have been? That's my dress, you idiot. I'm standing in the café."

If Kim found out he exposed her because the *FBI* had called his mom, he was beyond dead. It wasn't a bad situation; it was the worst one in his life. Spencer checked. Sure enough, she somehow managed to lock him into realmspace. He knew Angel Rage's reputation better than just about anyone else. The whole *death by fear* thing became a lot more believable.

Mike broke in. "Kim, he really didn't mean to do this."

"And YOU," she whirled on Mike so fast her skirt billowed. "You're the one who thought it would be such a great idea to bring this stupid little bag of hormones along in the first place."

Chapter 24
Stewart

Stewart's private realm was pretty much what anyone would expect from a jock: dark, walls covered with beer signs and sports holos. Tracklights spotlighted the important stuff hanging from the ceiling: the trophies and plaques in alcoves.

One wall was a massive realm portal. Weapons linked to game realms stood stacked against each other in the corner. On the far end was a stage with gear enough for a five-piece band.

Just normal teenager junk, no different from what any of his teammates had. It made it easier to keep his parents from looking for things out of the ordinary when everything was very ordinary, everything everyone expected of him.

He opened a hidden door.

A round bed surrounded by mirrors filled most of the next room. A thick rug covered the hardwood floor. Three cases of construct drawers that he'd raided from a hardware store realm lined one wall. Large glass cylinders filled closets along a hallway from the main room. The female figures inside them were dim shadows, silent and still. They were old news, a collection he'd built like music or realm games.

Spencer knew about this room only because Stewart needed the little squirt to lock it up tight. A few of his teammates, the ones he knew would keep their mouths shut, also knew. Nobody else was worth the risk.

Stewart's dad had made him a promise three years ago in California. If Stuart followed a brutal regimen of neurostims, nanotech therapy, and incessant workouts, he would finally be able to escape the stranglehold his mother's family had on him. None of them had ever believed what Stewart told them about his aunt, about what she'd done to him. They never would. So he became a star athlete. It couldn't last; his body would never sustain the grueling punishment. He only had to last long enough to become valuable. If he were valuable enough, someone would get him out of this place.

It wasn't that bad anyway. The challenge, the pain, the knowledge that there was an escape nobody could block all gave him focus. It let him really be that much better than anyone else. No, he didn't have a huge amount of free time right now; that would come later. For now, his collection and the room he used them in relaxed him just fine.

To a point, that is. What he needed most of all was novelty, to have what nobody else had. The nanoscale scans needed to create his dolls usually didn't exist, at least where he could get to them. There were too many screens and too many contracts to wade through. He had to settle for constructs anyone could get. It meant his dolls were beautiful but they were common, sometimes even used.

At the press of a button, an entire wall retracted and his doll factory snapped and unfolded into the room. Buying the raw construct material to create a complete doll from scratch took all the packets of cash the recruiters were handing over. A sculptor with the contract rights and talent to create a good blueprint would cost three times as much. He'd had no idea where the money would come from.

It wasn't a problem anymore.

A new cylinder shot up from underneath the machine's floor and locked into place. He faced his distorted reflection in it a few different ways and checked his teeth with a smile. He'd be too distracted to see what he looked like with her in the room later. He slammed another stim. There was no way he'd work with a brand new doll without some serious neural enhancement. Stewart gasped as the phone-generated pulses spiked energy through his spine. This was the best damned day of his life.

The feminine shape that gradually formed inside the translucent tube of the RealmDoll machine had dark hair, his favorite. After all this time, all his trolling the seediest Bangkok and Bulgarian realms looking for the unique, it had just fallen into his lap. He'd never seen a default avatar this good before. She was all his.

A weird glowing dust mote popped out of the top of the cylinder and vanished through the ceiling. Stewart shrugged after a moment. It was probably some sort of side-effect of Spencer's camera.

Chapter 25
Spencer

He had no idea how someone could stay so angry for so long.

"These people don't just cut your throat. No, that's too easy. To start with, they smash your nose, pop out your eyes, and tie them together by the optic nerves!"

His throat had gone so dry it was like he'd swallowed sand. Every shout, ever glare, every gesture from her made him flinch even harder. She must not find out about the FBI.

Another blue mote entered the room. When it interfaced with Kim, the ranting stopped. She closed her eyes, shutting her mouth so tightly her jaw muscles bulged.

She knew.

She knew about the FBI and now he was dead. Worse than dead. He'd probably end up in a mental institution with oatmeal for brains. He still couldn't exit this godforsaken conference room realm. Without meaning to, he said out loud, "Oh God."

Kim looked at Spencer and then at Mike's holo. She said to Mike, "I need three things from you. Unlock a realm, give me access to its box, and keep this little snot"—she threw an accusing arm at Spencer but the brain-blast he expected didn't fire—"out of trouble until I get back. Do you think you can handle that?"

Mike cleared his throat, which didn't make any sense since he didn't have one. That wasn't right; he did now. Spencer's nerves were so shattered he'd forgotten Mike was outside. Mike was real now. It was nice to know someone would attend his funeral. Or spoon pudding into his mouth.

"Yes. Definitely."

One of the realm's portals opened up and she vanished through it. She left Spencer alive. Alive! Stewart was in for a world of hurt, though. Served him right, doing something that stupid.

Chapter 26
Stewart

The cylinder finished its work with a soft chime and then the door slid open. There in all her naked glory stood Kimberly Trayne; at least the contract said that was her name. With its half-lidded eyes, the doll's passive face was genuinely gorgeous.

He'd upload an AI into it soon enough. For now he left it inactive. They were so utterly helpless like this. He was the one in control. "Come to papa," Stewart whispered. He gently started a first kiss.

A sledgehammer hit him in the chest and sent him flying across the room.

He crashed against the tool chests. Their edges stitched fire across his back. That wasn't a sledgehammer; it was a fist. Spencer and his goddamned hacker bullshit had given him a broken doll. It got worse. He couldn't get out, couldn't exit. He finally focused on the cylinder just as the doll disintegrated into a sheet of dust. Well, at least he didn't have to worry about that anymore.

Then a boot stepped out of the thick haze.

She was gorgeous, wrapped head-to-toe in dark ribbons. Thick and thin, wide and narrow, they wove around her. It made her even hotter than the naked doll. The ribbons shimmered with strange, dark patterns and had ends that flew and flicked, throwing sparks behind her.

There was no such thing as an uninvited guest to a realm, yet exactly that walked out of the decanter like a goddamned panther in high heels. Her eyes burned at him through a gap in the ribbons.

The mask exposed only the bottom of her face, which held a scarlet sneer. He could just see the hilt of a sword on her back.

"Who the hell are you?" Then he remembered the dust. The destroyed construct remnants still drifted to the floor. Three *months* of recruiting "bonuses", down the drain. "Do you know how much one of those things *costs?*"

This wasn't possible. The security Spencer set up was so good it sent people to the *hospital.* She just walked through it. She raised an eyebrow, turned with ribbons swirling around her, then grabbed the decanter. It shattered into a billion pieces. The control case exploded half a second later. Glass dust and the stink of chemicals filled the room as flaming bits scattered everywhere.

"You bitch, that was worth more than my car!"

The way she stood reminded him of everything he hated in women. The weight on one hip, head cocked to one side. He was not small and he would make her pay. He charged. Her open hand shot out and his chest collapsed against what felt like a telephone pole. He arched over her head, and with a push, she bounced him off the ceiling. He careened downward through the mirrors over the bed, shattered glass spraying everywhere.

Stimmed up with the realm's haptic field set higher than normal was a great idea when it was him and his dolls. With this ribbon-wrapped demon around, not so much. He couldn't access his realm controls to fix things or kick her out.

Her heels clicked across the room as she languidly walked over to his toy boxes. They were each nearly seven feet tall, smooth steel drawers filled with every perverted construct Stewart could find. She gently caressed the first one and he screamed as it imploded. It'd taken him years to assemble it all. Now it was nothing but construct powder.

There was fabric in his clenched fist, a torn piece of her costume. She wasn't invulnerable.

She hadn't blocked his outgoing channels either. He couldn't leave, but he could call for help. Even better, he could access the avatar healing routines. His wounds vanished like they'd been rubbed out with an eraser. The contract that restricted those routines to *invited* guests was still intact; they'd work for him but not for her.

This wouldn't be too tough after all.

He sent a message to teammates he could trust, scattered across the town. *My realm, right fucking now! Right now!* Hell with security. It was time for a beat-down.

Stewart had to get her in front of the entrance. He brushed the glass off his shredded shirt and then tore it off. If he couldn't get out, neither could she. A broken realm would give him his greatest fantasy.

She wasn't a doll. She couldn't escape the pain.

Walking toward her from his right made her move in the direction he needed. She reached for the next chest. He used the distraction to open the door, but the loss still burned. Some of the toys were one of a kind, now gone forever. Another thing she'd pay for.

Three linemen were already in the main room. As Stewart walked, four more appeared.

"You fucking bitch!" he shouted, then sent WAIT! to the gathered team. Three more manifested.

SPREAD OUT, he told them. GET READY. "Goddamn you. I will find you and fuck the eyes out of your skull."

"Really?"

Her voice was silky. Its power and confidence shunted him right back to being a small boy, when his aunt told him he had nothing to be afraid of, the very first lie in a chain of so many. He'd make her pay double for that.

She looked down. "You do realize that little carrot of yours isn't up to the job, don't you?"

"So you can talk?"

"I can do *lots* of things."

Looking at that body, hearing that voice… the memories they unearthed, the pain and humiliation, but also the pleasure that was so wrong. When his aunt had finished, he'd wanted more of it. Even after the tears had dried, he wanted more.

He barely managed to say, "Who the fuck are you?"

"Call me Ivy."

He sent his last message to the team just as she crossed in front of the door. *Go!*

Arms reached through and grabbed her, pulling her off her feet and through the door. He broke into a galloping run, only to smash into the two teammates Ivy hurled back into the room.

Coming at her in twos and threes didn't even slow her down. Every strike, every kick, every punch was paired with shouts that set his ears ringing. Bodies would collapse on her in a scrum and then fly across the room. Stewart wouldn't have believed it was possible for five men to collide in midair but Ivy managed it.

Then someone thought of a new idea.

The thunder of an automatic weapon split the chaos. They fell back and formed a wide circle around her. One of the starting linemen, Cedric, easily the largest member of the team, walked through the line with an M16 firmly on his hip.

"I figure this'll slow yo' fine ass down right quick," he said.

Ivy slowly pulled the katana from its scabbard.

Time stretched and slowed as the gun fired. With inhuman speed, she dodged the bullet stream, slid on her knees, then hacked the barrel apart and continued the stroke into and through Cedric's knee.

The banshee spun around behind the lineman and stood. There was no blood, so the lineman's leg slipped apart cleanly, like it was out of a cartoon. Someone grabbed her by the top of her mask, tearing it off. Dark hair flew free and she was fighting again. The team's center, Melvin, ran forward hollering like a maniac, holding a longsword over his head. Ivy tumbled forward, cut him in half at the waist, and before he could fall apart, vaulted over his shoulders up into a corner. She threw her legs into a flat split, then used her heels to wedge herself up high on the walls.

"Fuck me, Stewart!" Melvin lay in two neat pieces on the floor, like someone had cut a play dough sculpture in half. "Why can't I heal? Why can't I leave?"

Things in the realm kept shutting down. Nothing worked any-more except for this maniac in ribbons. "I don't know!"

Ivy spun her sword at the massive portal and it exploded in millions of datasparks. She tumbled up through her legs, then down into the middle of the scrum and the bodies flew again.

Stewart sailed into a corner, crashing next to Melvin. Well, his top half anyway. More screams and slaps dominated the center of the fight. Melvin was smiling like an ass, levered upright so he looked like he somehow sank into the floor.

"What the hell is so funny?"

"Dude, how did you find her?"

"What are you talking about?"

"Stewart, man, stop joking. Ivy's been retired for years. Is it your birthday or something?"

"My what?" Before he got an answer, two other bodies slammed into his, sending them all sliding across the floor. Stewart's head cracked hard against the stage. The noise of the fight decreased with each body that landed above him. A resounding slap sent the last of them to the top of the pile, which had grown so heavy Stewart couldn't struggle free of it.

Silence fell for just a moment, then the entire realm rumbled. Items on the walls tumbled to the floor. With an ear-splitting screech, the realm came apart around them. They all dropped on to the bare white construct of the box beneath. The dusty smell of brimstone filled the air as everything around them began to swirl, crunching and crushing together.

Ivy's outfit snapped and fluttered as she leaned into the bitwise cyclone. The tornado of destruction concentrated into a black funnel centered in her palm, at first taller than a skyscraper but collapsing fast. The sound was like a thousand freight trains bearing down, tearing into his ears.

And then it all went silent.

With a sound like a crushed coffee cup, her fist closed on the compressed construct she'd turned his realm into; the dust fell through her fingers to the floor. Her hair covered her face. He could only see her smile. It was arrogant and cold, even less caring than the one his aunt gave him whenever they met. He struggled to get free, to take one last shot, but couldn't pull his arms away. He was just too exhausted.

Ivy slowly sauntered past them, the clack of her heels the only noise, moving toward the exit. Just at its threshold, she stopped. There was a finger snap.

"Stewart?"

Barely able to move, he flopped around.

He was wrong. The outfit didn't make her hotter than when she was naked. Maybe because she still wasn't, not exactly. With her back turned and her bare feet posed a half stride apart, her elegantly sculpted legs and hips glistened with sweat. But that wasn't even close to the most striking part. With her arms hanging down, wings covered her from the small of her back to the tops of her shoulders, nearly out to her arms. The tattoo mesmerized with its iridescent color and feathers. It was the most detailed piece of body art he'd ever seen.

"*This* is what I really look like." With another snap of her fingers, they all dissolved from the realm, screaming.

Chapter 27
Spencer

Spencer nearly jumped out of his skin when Kim marched back into the conference room. She wore the same dress she had on when she left, with just a slight sheen of sweat on her face.

Spencer wanted to piss himself. Kim knew about the FBI now, she had to, and he was one mental blast away from having "Quaker Oats" tattooed on his forehead.

The familiar tri-cornered shape of a conference phone rose up out of the center of the table.

Kim stopped in front of him. "Spencer, you have a call." Ringing filled the room, making him jump again.

Spencer pushed the answer button with a quivering finger. "Hello?"

"Spencer?"

It wasn't the FBI. It was his soon-to-be fellow oatmeal boy, Stewart.

His pained voice continued, "Is that you?" Stewart's image appeared above the phone. "Jesus, Spencer, what happened? This antique is all that'll work in my house. My pendant's fried. The whole house is fried."

"What?" This was not happening. Donald Trump was a crazy old man who said anything to get attention. Angel Rage couldn't have burned the entire network of his building with just her mind. But here it was, exactly like that, right down to the old SkypePhone being the only thing left working, just like Trump said.

Stewart replied, "Dude, you called me, didn't you?"

Kim stared at Spencer, utterly still.

"Jesus, what time is it? I was in class, how did I end up home?"

Memory loss. This was the dark stuff, the stuff he didn't want to believe when he was a kid. His hero did not do these things. Spencer hit the mute button and stared up at Kim, shaking. "Oh... oh fuck?"

"Ask him."

He turned the mute off, his eyes still locked in Kim's stare. Eighteen minutes. They said she could wipe eighteen minutes from anyone's memory. "Stewart, what time is it?"

"I told you, dude, I was in class. I don't know, four o'clock?"

Spencer checked the time. 4:18 p.m. His heart flopped once in his chest and he forgot how to breathe.

"Shit! My realm! It's gone! Spencer!" Stewart broke off and made strangling noises. He slowly put both hands against his head and screamed, low at first but rising to a blood-curdling shriek.

Kim reached out and ended the call.

Nobody believed it was possible. There were two ways to exit realmspace: a proper exit or a lost connection. Nobody lost the connection on purpose because the vertigo would make you toss your cookies. A regular exit was the only real way.

Except there were rumors there was a third way, one that slammed people out, wiped their memories, and eventually scarred their brains so they could never connect to the realms again. "You forced the disconnect. You force disconnected..."

"Every single one of them. A lot of his friends were there too, at least a dozen." Kim smiled. Spencer knew she wanted him to get the implication. He did.

Nobody believed force disconnects could happen because of the power required for the overload, even for a single person. Realmspace failed in a safe way. That was the point. You had to ram an inconceivable amount of power down the lines just to attempt an overload. But it still wouldn't work, because realmspace's capacity was by definition infinite. If you pushed power at it, the quantum fabric just got bigger until the power ran out. There was no upper limit.

Kim hadn't just done it to one person; she'd done it to a whole group. It meant absolutely anything said about Angel Rage could be true, even the crazy stuff nobody believed.

"Will they be all right?"

Spencer had grown up with professionally angry parents. He knew what they were capable of and how to handle their worst. When Kim raged, she was just like that, only bigger. But this? This wasn't the rage, this was the angel, an otherworldly creature with power he couldn't hope to understand.

"They're fine. This time. You made a mess, Spencer, and I cleaned it up." Kim leaned in so close Spencer could feel her breath on his ear.

"Don't make me do it again." She stalked out the exit and vanished into realspace.

Spencer felt a relief so intense it was like he'd been shoved under a waterfall.

Kim didn't know about the FBI.

He was going to live!

Chapter 28
Adelmo

Adelmo had the hospital's data organized for review less than ten minutes after they'd wheeled Dr. Richards away. Once he revived, in the ER of his own hospital no less, Adelmo was certain the doctor would still expect the police to arrest him at any second.

It may yet happen, but not because of any action Adelmo took.

The review was complex and filled the rest of the day. When it was done he could not believe what he'd found. Colque had died, the ER notes all agreed on that. The injuries were, however, unique in some technical way he didn't understand. As far as Adelmo could tell, the doctors were taking scans more to play with their new toys than in any hope of curing the poor man. His nephew's most effective beast was well and truly dead, according to the notes at any rate.

Yet he wasn't.

"Dr. Ferrovaria," he asked the Quispe's family physician, who was fortunately also head of the Higher University of San Andrés's medical school, "you're certain Colque should be dead?"

"Without a doubt. It is remarkable." Dr. Ferrovaria's avatar fidgeted nervously in the basic meeting realm Adelmo had rented just this morning.

"Something on your mind, doctor?"

"This is truly unprecedented. If HgRI, even accidentally, can heal these sorts of injuries, it would be a major advance in medical sciences. I was wondering…" He paused with his hands steepled in front of him.

The flashing curiosity, the intent need for knowledge came off Dr. Ferrovaria in waves. He wanted something from Adelmo, that much was certain. He was visibly working up the nerve to ask.

The doctor cleared his throat. "If I were to be permitted to study all this, it could make a real difference, not just for your family but for the whole world. The Higgs boson was supposed to be the key to physics. If it could also be the key to resurrection, my God!"

Indeed. Adelmo thanked Ferrovaria for his help and sent a new update, along with the doctor's request, to Manuel. With a few more judicious bribes to local police department clerks, Adelmo had been able to trace the truck all the way to a highway in Reston. Tomorrow would be another long day for him and his men.

Chapter 29
Mike

Spencer was the one who'd screwed up! The relief was a nearly physical thing every time he thought about it. The flashes of temper he'd seen before had given no warning about how bad Kim could get. Mike couldn't imagine being the focus of that much anger.

Weirdly, the tirades triggered all sorts of interesting autonomic responses in his body. This time around, he was farther along in his integration than at the hotel. More importantly, he wasn't the one she was yelling at.

Mike had never counted on it all being so, well, squishy. He could feel the hormones as they entered his new bloodstream, like someone had grabbed a squeeze bottle inside him. Spencer's screw up had provided some serious blending time for these liquid-based emotions and his more natural quantum ones, helping the integration along quite a bit.

Mike tried to explain all this to Kim as they drove around real-space finishing the last of their errands. Mostly he just wanted to lighten the mood. All he got out of her was a nasty snarl. The rest of the time Kim spoke to them with yes or no answers.

"Wait," Spencer said as they pulled out of a nice residential neighborhood. "Didn't we just buy a car? Why'd we go buy this other one?"

She explained this to Mike earlier but he didn't dare open his mouth around Kim in her current mood. Everything needed a transition, she said. Whoever chased you would be able to follow no matter how hard you tried to lose them, even if you switched once.

It was the sign of amateurs. Switch twice and you had a shot, once more and you've lost them, always. He would never look at crime dramas the same way again.

They pulled into a nearby grocery store lot and stopped.

Kim said, "Wait here." She got out and walked across the parking lot.

"How long can she stay mad at me about this?" Spencer asked.

"You gotta admit that was pretty stupid, Spence."

"How the fuck was I supposed to know he'd do that? Stew is a jock, but I didn't know he was an idiot."

Mike shook his head. "Stewart wasn't the only idiot."

"Oh fuck off, Mike." Spencer huffed and crossed his arms as he glared out the window. "She didn't have to go all medieval on him, either. Nobody knows if a forced disconnect really erases memories forever. That shit's gonna come back on me, I just know it."

"I dunno, man." Mike shared an image of Kim in her outfit with Spencer. "I mean, *you* know who this is, right?"

"Yeah, Ivy Valentine. Who doesn't?"

Mike turned in the front seat so he could face Spencer.

He went slightly pale and swallowed. "Oh."

There was a reason he'd picked her, after all. The agents that first brought her to his attention had been watching Ivy Valentine perform at the Tekken Tournaments. When Kim was in a group, it was harder to spot her patterns, but solo, there was no mistake. She moved like violent smoke and was so *fast*. When she went to "clean up" Spencer's mess, what he saw just blew him away.

He admired her before, but only as an abstract. Watching those old performances was exciting, but now he knew *her*. She was so unexpected and smart. It took him most of the car ride to work out, but he was now certain that the whole fight had been a giant lure. It neatly ensured anyone who could've known about Kim's picture was in Stewart's realm. Now none of them would remember a thing. The headache caused by whatever she did at the end was still pulsing behind his eyes, but he couldn't have imagined a better way to fix things.

"Yeah, but Ivy never made it past the Fatal Four." It took a second for Spencer to reach the same conclusion Mike had. "And that wasn't an accident either?"

"I'm thinking no."

Kim got back in the car, noticeably less tense. She looked at Spencer in the mirror. "Oh God, what'd you tell him?"

"Nothing," Mike said, too quickly because the glare she turned on him made him feel like a mouse. "No, really, right, Spence?"

"Right. Nothing. Right. Are we done?"

She nodded. "We are now driving an invisible car, gentleman. It'll take them a month to figure out the paper trail, if they ever do. Although I really do like the new styles."

Their previous vehicle, a year old black Alfa Romeo, merged on to the highway. Again, she turned old and exhausted, but after a glance at him, got a bit of a glint back in her eyes.

"Maybe someday."

It was crazy. One minute Mike was convinced she was going to put their heads on pikes . The next minute it was like nothing had happened.

Kim started the car. "Time to sign a lease."

*

There were so many boxes in front of their new apartment that Mike had trouble seeing around them as he brought them in. "Pretty nice," he said.

"Rent definitely goes a lot farther out here," Kim said. She'd told him the two-bedroom apartment in Fairfax was more for him than her, but Spencer's screwup had stopped her before Mike found out what that meant.

Still, it was his first realspace apartment. He thought all he needed for a realspace body was storage—a place to put it. In truth, he was puzzled why humans didn't just hang themselves in closets when they needed to rest. Now he began to understand. Comfort had a whole new meaning out here. The apartment had modest furnishings, an open main area, and a balcony.

"Now," she said, "will you please change out of that sweat-suit? And hurry up; we need to meet Tonya in twenty minutes."

*

They parked in front of a low building covered in dark wood planking. "Really, Kim?" Spencer asked, "Even ancient restaurants?"

"Especially ancient restaurants. Always assume we're being watched at all times. I pick these old places because their cameras came later, so they're easier to spot. Besides, they have good steaks. Wait, you're not allergic to peanuts, are you?"

"I'm not," Spencer replied. "What about him?"

Mike shrugged at her. Allergies were an academic interest for him previously, but for now all he could do was guess. The human immune system was sublime, but it also sometimes tried to kill them.

"I'm not sure," she said. "Only one way to find out."

They headed for the entrance of the restaurant. As they walked, a thin black woman wearing jeans and a white button-down shirt came rushing out the front door and charged straight at Kim.

This had to be Tonya. Layers of tension fell away from Kim as they ran to each other. They got within a stride and stopped. Their hands flicked out within inches of touching and then clapped to their sides. It happened so fast Mike wasn't sure just what it meant at first. It took reviewing what he saw twice before he realized they had nearly touched, palm out, then moved their hands together in a half circle.

He stopped when he realized he was using his organic brain to do the review. It seemed faster, more natural. The bridges between his real self and his new outside body were strengthening in unexpected ways.

Tonya clapped her hands together. "I'm *so* glad to see you again."

From the way Kim talked last night, Mike thought Tonya would be some sort of fight club champion. That wasn't the case. She was noticeably shorter than Kim and built more like a dancer than a bouncer. She had a brilliant smile and straight black hair with green streaks.

Her eyes locked on to his. "Hello, what have we here?"

Kim turned sideways. "Tonya, this is Mike Sellars. Mike, Tonya Brinks."

Tonya offered her hand and her smile changed subtly, going from simple happiness to something more evaluating. The expression "undressing with the eyes" came to mind. It made him feel good, even though he didn't understand why.

"Mr. Sellars."

"Pleased to meet you," he said, raising her knuckles to his lips.

"Likewise." As Tonya held his hand, Kim clenched hers into fists. Great. He'd set her off again, somehow.

"And hi, I'm Spencer, nice to meet you." Spencer reached in to shake Tonya's hand.

"Kim, where do you pick up these strays?"

"I don't. They find me," she said, with a strangely pensive expression on her face.

Maybe he hadn't set her off. She seemed more confused than anything else, with maybe a bit of worry. He didn't know what to make of it.

They walked into the warm, wood-paneled dining room and sat at a large booth. Kim tucked her legs tightly underneath her. Tonya made room with an ease that Mike envied. He wanted Kim to be that comfortable around him too, but had no idea how long it might take.

His stomach rumbled a reminder that he had other priorities. That was another thing. Stuff inside him *moved* all the time. Humans were walking, talking chemical factories. The acid in their stomachs could dissolve coins. Another grumble made him focus. "So, what do you guys recommend this time?"

Tonya's smile was quite striking. "They don't have steakhouses like this where you're from? Where are you from, anyway?"

Mike cringed at the silence that broke out.

"What?" Tonya asked. "What'd I say?"

Spencer and Kim stared at him. It was obviously his call. "That's a complicated question."

Tonya was fun, but he couldn't pin down why. It was so strange to trust someone without biometric tells, without the quantum color of his threaded emotions.

He looked straight into her eyes and asked, "What would *you* recommend?"

Mike smiled when her skin darkened slightly. Getting her to react with just a look was also strangely enjoyable. Maybe he'd get along with these hormones after all.

"Ah," Tonya cleared her throat and looked away. "The steaks are really good. So are the ribs. Their beer selection's good too."

Kim gripped her menu so hard her fingertips flexed. He wasn't sure why such a simple observation would set her off.

That last mention reminded him. "Beer? Beer. I've always wanted to try that."

"What," Tonya asked, "you recovering from some sort of religion?"

"You could say that," he replied as the waiter took their drink orders. When he got to Mike, he asked Kim, "You like that stuff, right?" He'd heard things about Guinness. It wasn't all positive.

Kim smiled. "Yes. Yes, I do."

"I'll have one of those too," he said with feigned confidence. Alcohol was a substance he'd made elaborate plans around, because the biochemistry was so fascinating. Never once did he think that his first drink would be among friends.

The observation was startling. He had acquaintances, but Spencer was his only friend. Two days outside and—if his feeling about Tonya turned out to be right—he had tripled that count. He never understood instinct until now. On some indefinable level, he just somehow knew he could trust everyone at this table.

After the waiter left, Kim asked, "The Dogs, they're all okay?"

"Yes, thankfully. Paul wanted me to pass this along to you." Tonya flicked a pay chit to Kim in their enhanced vision. "He said to consider the truck repair as payment for the tutoring you gave Jamie last summer."

"The Dogs?" Spencer asked.

"Phoenix Dogs," Kim replied. "They're my combat team in *Warhawk* and very good people."

"Oh," Spencer said, "you guys were going for the cup?"

"Emphasis on were," Kim replied, with an acid glare at Mike.

Even with all that had happened since, Mike still felt bad about screwing up their tournament shot. Three years was a long time to wait for it to come around again. The World Championships would happen this summer; he might be able to help them then.

The waiter returned with their drinks and Mike was once again at sea. In the realms, he was the invisible master. Out here, he was like an explorer without a map. The mug was as tall as his forearm, filled with a big column of thick, black liquid. It had a dark, nutty aroma and an electric tang over the top. The stuff sloshed all by itself, with no simulation math underneath it. It was very unnatural. He caught himself trying to force it to be still. "This is… unexpected."

"Exactly how she drinks it is beyond me," Tonya said as she emptied a few sweeteners into her tea. "It's more like motor oil, is all I'm sayin'."

"Go on, Mike," Kim said as she lifted her mug. "Give it a try."

She probably thought he'd back out. Not a chance. "All right, I will."

At first, all Mike felt was cold, but then a crash of bitter hit him right at the top of his teeth. He didn't want to react, didn't want to give her the satisfaction, but still couldn't stop blinking a few times. Kim took another swallow.

"Okay," Tonya asked as she looked at them both, "what the hell is this?"

"Your guess is as good as mine," Spencer replied.

Mike fought off a brief gag. The stuff was nasty. Kim finished her second gulp and put the mug down, staring straight at him as she wiped her lips.

Mike grimaced and swallowed hard. Then a weird thing happened. He felt a sensation, a flipping and turning over. He definitely tasted chocolate, then a kind of bitter smoke, then... wood? It was extraordinary. He let out a big belch.

"They don't teach white boys manners in the commune you're from?" Tonya asked. Everyone laughed and then the waiter took their orders.

It was his third full meal of his first day out. Mike was even getting the hang of silverware. The idea of appetizers was a little strange. Eating something to make him hungrier seemed like a contradiction, but he rolled with it.

He reached the bottom of his first mug after finishing his first Caesar salad. The combinations of flavors, textures, and smells seemed endless.

When the waiter returned with refills, Tonya said, "You need to go easy on this one, handsome, okay? You're too big to carry out of here."

Spencer snorted. "I told you you'd be a cheap drunk."

"This? This is drunk?" Mike rubbed his fingers together. He definitely felt tingly. Biochemistry was so different when it happened without a simulation. It was like a caress of sand against his skin.

"Wait, I know!" Mike threw his head back and his arms wide.

Spencer cursed and dodged out of the way.

Mike touched his nose with the index finger of each hand. "Nope! Not drunk."

Kim had gone cold again. "Not yet."

"Oh Kim," Tonya said, "stop being so... so *you*. Let the man live a little." She reached out and grabbed his hand. "I'll bet he's a cute drunk," she said, smiling at him.

Tonya was so different from Kim, so much *nicer*. She laughed warmly and let his hand go as the entrees arrived.

This time his order included ribs. Using his fingers was a bit tricky at first. The ribs were slick and didn't always come apart the way he expected. But it was absolutely worth it.

"You were right, Spence," Mike said, rubbing his swollen belly. He fought down another burp. "The combo was the way to go."

Sirloin steak was amazing. The human sense of taste would take months for his research agents to really understand. People just took it for granted. The ribs were a messy, bright, smoky delight. The fullness inside him stretched out even to his real self in realmspace, making his threads thick and languid.

That made Tonya suspicious again. "And you'd never had either of them before? What'd you grow up on, couscous?"

He tried to think through it all, but the sensations were so distracting. "No. Pancakes. And hamburgers. That's what I grew up on. Pancakes and hamburgers." He leaned across the table. "I think tomorrow I'll try scrambled eggs." It was a little silly, but wow, the way Tonya smiled at him was nice.

"You really are something else." She paused. He could see her trying to work it out, what he was. "Where are your parents from?" It was an excellent question. Tonya was fast.

He considered this. "Bolivia. But I was born here. Sort of."

She frowned at the answer and narrowed her eyes.

Spencer finished his own combo, then shook his head. "Move over, Mike, I'm getting a smoke."

Still staring at him Tonya said, "I'll join you."

When they left, he couldn't think of anything to say. It was his first time alone with Kim in realspace since that moment in the pool. It was so different out here. It was a lot easier for him to get her laughing in realmspace. The silence at the table extended.

God, what could he say to her that wouldn't get him in trouble? He was so sick of getting in trouble with her. He tried to think of something to talk about as they both cleared their throats. Then he saw something amazing on the far wall. "Is that a snake skin?"

She laughed. "Yes. God, that thing must be thirty years old."

"Why would anyone put that on a wall?"

"You've never been to—what am I saying—you've never been to Texas."

"Well, no, but DallasRealms is making more sense now."

She smiled. "I wouldn't have picked you as a realmsoap fan."

He smiled right back. Finally, he'd managed a conversation without screwing it up. "You'll find I'm full of surprises. Tonya is really nice," he said as he looked toward the entrance. "*Really* nice." He turned back to Kim.

She'd gone still and faced away from him.

Oh here we go again. "What?"

"Yes. She's very nice."

"What did I say?"

"Nothing."

"What?"

"NOTHING."

MIKE, Spencer sent to him on a private channel, I'M GONNA TELL TONYA ABOUT YOU. YOU COOL WITH THAT?

"Goddamn it, Kim, I'm getting really sick of this." Mike said quietly. "I can never predict how you're going to react to anything I say."

"Fine then. Stop talking."

SPENCER, he shot back, I'M A LITTLE BUSY HERE.

YOU'RE JUST FIGHTING WITH KIM AGAIN. COME ON, TONYA NEEDS TO KNOW.

HOW DO YOU KNOW I'M FIGHTING WITH KIM?

YOU TWO ARE ALONE TOGETHER. IT'S WHAT YOU DO. DUH.

Mike glared at her. "Do you really think someone like you can teach me anything about the real world?"

"Someone like me?"

Yeah, he screwed up again, but this time he didn't care one little bit. "Yes, exactly. Someone like you. I've spent my entire life—"

"All, what, forty-eight hours of it?"

"I'm sorry, Kim, but my whole life hasn't revolved around *you.*"

SPENCER, YOU DO WHAT YOU HAVE TO DO. I'VE GOT OTHER PROBLEMS.

WOW, he replied, SHE EVEN MAKES YOU TEXT ANGRY.

Mike gave up and let the silence stretch as his heart rate settled. Eventually, Tonya and Spencer climbed back into the booth. By the rattled look on Tonya's face, Spencer had definitely told her. Well that's what she got for smoking cigarettes with the kid. He was about as subtle as a brick to the head.

"Kim?" Tonya asked.

Kim was still glaring at him. He returned the favor and glared right back. Mike would win this particular contest.

Tonya whacked Kim in the face with a menu. "Kim! Back that shit up and put it away."

Mike jumped with an electric startle when Spencer poked him in the ribs. DUDE, Spencer sent, YOU DO NOT WANT TO MESS WITH TONYA.

Kim gasped and turned like a snake to Tonya.

Tonya pointed a finger at Kim's face. "I said Put. It. Away."

SPENCER, WHAT THE HELL ARE YOU TALKING ABOUT?

Spencer sent him a picture of a stop sign with a rock embedded in it like a stone fist. SHE DID THAT WITH HER FOOT. SHE SAYS SHE'LL DO THAT TO YOUR HEAD IF YOU HURT KIM. DON'T HURT KIM.

"When I send you a message," Tonya said, "you do *not* ignore it."

Apparently, Mike wasn't the only one with a friend badgering him on a private channel.

Kim closed her mouth, glared one last time at Mike, and then visibly calmed down. "Yes. Well, we're all finished up here. I still have things I need to do. Tonya, could you call the Dogs up tomorrow? They deserve explanations from me, face-to-face."

"Sure, love, anything you need," she said.

Halfway to the car, Mike realized Kim wasn't with them.

Kim stood in front of a different car. "I'm so glad I didn't have to say goodbye."

"I am too, baby. I am too," Tonya said.

They nearly touched hands again. This time it was slow enough it would've attracted attention if anyone else had been in the parking lot. The grace of it moved him. She was so isolated, even from someone she clearly cared about.

Tears streamed down both of their cheeks. Tonya wiped her cheeks. "I would've missed you. Too much."

"I know. I'm not sure when we'll have time to get together, you know?"

Tonya laughed and a bit of the sparkle came back to her eyes as she glanced at Mike. "Oh don't worry. I think you'll be too busy to worry about *that* for a while."

As they got back in the car, Kim muttered, "Miles to go, miles to go."

Chapter 30

Kim

She led the way into the apartment. After a few wrong turns, a lot of legwork, and a bite to eat, it was finally time to implement step one of her plan. The road to freedom for herself and her long-lost companions started here, in this room, on this night. "Find a comfortable place to sit, guys. It's time to have some fun."

They manifested in the conference room she'd rented earlier in the day.

"You know, Kim," Mike said, "I think I'm really beginning to get this whole hormone thing. I'm starting to get distracted by you."

She'd wanted to brain him because of the way he panted over Tonya and now he was calling *her* a distraction. "What the hell is that supposed to mean?"

"You always seem to wear things that make you look pretty, at least in realmspace."

Dresses meant nothing, but he thought a pair of stretch pants and a long-sleeved T-shirt made her look pretty.

Spencer gagged out loud. Maybe twisting his ears off and shoving them up his nose would make the little monster behave. Kim shut off the damage contracts for the realm to do just that.

"Why don't you wear stuff like that in realspace?"

Mike could derail her train of thought in an instant. *So* annoying.

"It's complicated." She put her hair behind her ears. She didn't bring them here to talk about her fashion sense.

"Really complicated. Look, I need to get some work done." The whole point was to maybe tease god-boy just a little and then finally start her homecoming plan.

"Okay, how can we help?" Mike asked.

She decrypted the location file and transferred it to him. "First, tell me what's at this address."

"Nothing. It doesn't exist. Not surprising, really. It's a pretty old address block and—"

She pressed the button on the CamoSplit in her realspace hand. If it still worked, he'd see the effect right about now.

"Kim, that's not possible."

Spencer asked, "What's the matter, Mike, you finally found a rock too heavy for you to lift?"

Kim shared a smirk with him. It seemed she and Spencer both enjoyed putting god-boy in his place.

"No, it's not, wait… what?" It was funny how cute Mike got when he was confused, even when he was just a voice. "No, it's just the only way realmspace works is if contracted connections exist and are enforced. Realms can't just vanish and reappear."

Kim laughed. "Relax, god-boy, and check a little closer."

She turned back to Spencer. "Is he always this jumpy?"

Spencer shook his head. "Mike just doesn't like it when someone knows more about the realms than he does. He wouldn't talk to me for days when I showed him—"

"Okay, you two, that's enough. Splitting the realm's contracts across thousands of boxes should take years."

She winked at Spencer. As weird as he was, Mike thought in three dimensions just like everyone else she'd ever met. Otherwise, he would've figured out how she'd hidden the realm. Maybe he wasn't that different after all.

"Ah," he said. "You trailed the bridges through independent n-spaces. Very clever, Kim, but now everyone can see it."

Nicely done. Back when Rage + the Machine was active, the rest of them never realized their realm snaked through multiple foldspaces. Mike spotted it in seconds. But she wasn't done torturing him just yet. Swallowing a giggle, she twisted the CamoSplit's button. There was more than one kind of invisibility, after all.

"Goddamn it, that's just impossible!"

"Everything is theoretically impossible," she said, a grinning Spencer joining in so they finished together, "until it's done."

"God, I'm so sick of that."

They transitioned and Kim was home. She'd spent years convincing herself this could never happen. Now she was back. Her home. *Their* home. They would all be free again one day. Kim's steps bounced a bit higher at the thought.

The entrance was a low-ceilinged hallway lit with brilliant white sconces attached low on the rock walls, with glass and blue-steel panels scattered in an irregular pattern above them. She walked down a wide metal ramp with intricate reliefs of Celtic designs. Kim had designed them with Michiko. It was Kim's first time working with realm architecture. Michiko had been so proud of how Kim had combined fractal math with the ancient patterns. On either side of the walkway, ferns surrounded open pools of water that tumbled into each other.

Spencer stumbled a bit and then stopped. "So this is real too," he whispered.

Kim walked around him, past the echoing ghosts of the people she'd soon see again.

"What's real?" Mike asked.

"Pride's Lair. She's taken us to Pride's Lair. There's a song about this place." He cleared his throat and called down the hall. "Hey, Kim, you did know they wrote a song about this place?"

Kim turned right at the tunnel's exit. "Don't care!"

Spencer and Mike exited shortly after her into a vast oval room. The floor was made of dark glossy flagstone, the cracks between filled in with black grout. Two cantilevered stairways of metal and glass spiraled up on each narrow end to a second level that held the training rooms. The ceiling continued the cave theme, an irregular dome of stone hung with frosted glass and steel light fixtures.

A shallow circular pit with a floor covered in dark wine carpet lay slightly offset from the center of the room with a table and a few chairs. Strategically placed trees, bushes, and flowering plants countered the severity of the place. The streams that surrounded the entryway entangled and snaked together on the floor, babbling through the main space in a softly lit trench, with small arched bridges crossing over it. The entire realm was Michiko's masterpiece. Soon that talent in architecture would be free to do more than design spaces nobody else would ever see.

Kim pushed the armory's access button. When Spencer jumped at the noise the door made she couldn't help but laugh. A long wall of corrugated glass slowly opened, revealing a big room completely lined with burnt umber carpet. Track lighting turned on, starting from the interior and moving outward, highlighting a construct collection. Weapons, tools, outfits, even avatars stood neatly arranged throughout the space. Spencer walked up to the edge of the carpet but went no farther.

A tall, thin man appeared to their left. It was all she could do not to tackle him in a bear hug. She didn't dare, though. He would've considered it a grievous breach of protocol. It was her first reunion. Unlike anyone else she knew, he hadn't changed a bit. The unduplicate had dark curly hair and slightly bulging eyes, dressed like a butler from the eighteenth century, all in black. When he spoke, it was with a cultured English accent. "Ah! My lady, Miss Trayne, it is good to see you back."

"Good evening, Edmund, It's good to be back."

"I'm fine, Mike." Spencer said to the air around him.

He was so dumbstruck he wasn't using a private channel to talk with Mike. She'd made the fanboy's head explode. It only took the finest collection of realm constructs ever assembled. The way Spencer was breathing, he had to be close to losing it.

"And I see you've brought a guest. Rather short for a sidekick, don't you think?" He walked toward Spencer. "Well, at least this one doesn't smell." He sniffed the air. "Much."

"Guests," Mike said as his hologram manifested.

"My *lord!*" Edmund fell to one knee. "It is an *unequaled* honor!"

She would've been less surprised if Edmund had exploded or vanished when Mike appeared. Kim had assumed Mike's existence was mostly a secret, but Edmund wasn't just a butler. He was also a pretty resourceful spy. She'd have to find out just what he knew about Mr. Impossible.

"Yes, yes," Mike laughed nervously. "Edmund, is it? Edmund, please get up."

Great. She blows the fanboy's mind and Mike makes the butler lose his. "Mike, did you just break our butler?"

"No, umm, not really. Probably not, I think. I forget sometimes that AIs get funny ideas. Edmund, it's okay. You can get up. Please."

Edmund did but kept averting his eyes from Mike's hologram. Kim pulled Edmund aside as Mike went to find Spencer, who'd managed to cross the armory's threshold. "Nobody else is here?" she asked.

"No, madam. In fact, you're the first visitor in quite some time."

It made sense. They were all still hiding, staying away just like she had.

"They visited on occasion, but that gradually stopped about three years ago."

It was the exact opposite of what she wanted to hear. In spite of her excitement, she knew they should never have come here at all. If Mike hadn't helped her, she wouldn't be standing here. The fact that the visits had gradually stopped set an ugly twist loose in her stomach.

Spencer's warbling voice broke her away from her worries. "Kim! Where did you find this thing?"

He held her old FN SCAR-H, an assault rifle construct that turned into a nasty crossbow in medieval realms and a boss blaster in science fiction realms. There were only five in the world. The other three were part of an exhibit in a museum outside London.

"That? Yeah, I always did like that one." She decided to twist the knife a bit. "There's another one on that wall over there." She gestured to an area blocked from their view by a column.

Spencer paled and made a small mewling noise.

She turned back to Edmund. "So you're certain? No access at all in the past three years?"

"Absolutely, madam." His eyes unfocused briefly. "There were occasional visits before then, mostly Mark and Lourdes, but all contact ceased three years ago."

There was a cracking shriek as reflected blue light splashed from around the corner of the armory. He'd found the saber. Spencer had a good eye; she'd give him that. But his antics were now a distraction; what Edmund told her was very disturbing.

"Jesus Christ Kim! When did you guys ever meet Steven Spielberg?"

She walked toward Spencer and Mike, deeply preoccupied as she tried to work out what might've happened to everyone.

"Lee worked for Steven before he moved to Virginia. Steven came out to Wolf Trap one year for an *E.T.* retrospective. They all got along like thieves. That was one of the things he gave us."

There were only three of them in the world. One was at Skywalker Ranch's realm and the other was at the Smithsonian's. Lucas had given permission to use all his licenses, and those of subsidiaries, to make them possible. The contract that described them took hours to transfer. Nobody else had ever come close to that fidelity in a construct.

It was a complete bear to use.

"Listen, Spencer, the movies were right. You really need to be careful with that thing."

Spencer started moving the blade in an incredibly complicated pattern. It danced and spun as he tumbled back into the main room like a hyperactive gymnast. The bass note of its hum turned into a strange sort of music as he finished with a double-twisting spin.

"That is so. Freaking. Cool!" He sent the blade shrieking back into the hilt. "The one I have back home is a mark seven reproduction. I could never get that final kata to come out right without overloading the gyros and cutting my foot off. This thing is smooth."

He'd done more in fifteen seconds than she'd managed with months of practice. The decision was easy. "You can have it, if you want." Kim pulled her shoulder off the outer wall of the armory and walked toward him.

Spencer blanched. "No, Kim, really, I couldn't."

"It's okay, Spencer." He could be an endearing little monster sometimes. "Mark gave it to me for my seventeenth birthday. I never did get the hang of it. It'd be nice to see it with someone who knows how to use it."

"Kim, I mean, that's incredible but this thing, this thing is worth more than my dad's whole business. Hell, it may be worth more than my hometown."

She took the hilt out of his hands. "I'll make a deal with you. I'll keep it here until you're ready…" A tiny flashing light over Spencer's shoulder caught her eye.

At the far end of the room there was a small table surrounded by potted plants, topped with an antique 1960s-era phone, complete with dial. It had a small beige box with a flashing light next to it. The number six was in a red window on the corner.

It was confirmation of a fear so terrifying she'd refused even to admit it might exist. "Edmund, when did those messages start arriving?" Kim gave the hilt back to Spencer—dropped it, really— because her hands had gone numb.

"The first arrived a little less than three years ago, and the last not quite six months later."

Kim stood next to the phone, willing it not to be true. She was rescuing them all from a nightmare, not falling farther into one. There was only one reason any of them had to call this phone. It was a joke they'd set up. There could not be six messages here.

There could not be *any* messages here.

She held her hand over the flashing button like it was a face in a coffin. She touched it.

Please, no.

GEMINI GAMBIT   169

Immediately a large window, perhaps seven feet tall and at least three times as wide, drew itself into view. In the left corner, filling one segment like a piano key, was Henry's face, his skin the color of new coffee. His hair had gone completely gray since Kim last saw him. He was sweating, bruised, and bleeding from a cut over one eye.

"I don't have much time," he panted, gazing down at her through the window. "I just wanted you all to know it wasn't an accident. I don't know how, but they found us. My family! They found us all. You need to be careful. Kim did what she could, but it's not working anymore."

There was a crash off camera. Henry jumped up and started firing his gun. The transmission froze just when he moved out of the frame.

His family too. It was a lie. A mistake. They were in school, just like Spencer. She wouldn't accept anything else.

She refused to admit anything else.

The next key faded in and there was her flowing blond hair. Tears streamed down Kim's cheeks. "Oh, no... Lourdes..."

Her face was serene, as always. On the day Kim's first crush called her a freak and walked away, Lourdes had wrapped Kim's hand in a napkin and held the end of it while she cried. Her quiet strength, her effortless serenity, had grounded Kim and helped her through the worst of times. Sometimes those memories were the only peace she could find.

Lourdes was sitting on a plush couch in a library of some sort. "If you're seeing this message, it means they found me. I didn't make it." Her smile softened. "You guys were the best bunch of people I've ever known. I'm so sorry it had to end this way." Another final message, another final goodbye.

They were alive! They were all supposed to be alive!

Each piano key faded in with another face and another hammer blow smashed through her. Rich and Josh, as always, said the same thing at nearly the same time. "It means we're dead..." She couldn't breathe anymore, couldn't think. This wasn't possible. They needed to all stop talking, right now.

They were not dead. She would not accept that. They were waiting for her; they had always been waiting for her.

Another female face appeared, pale and beautifully Asian, framed with long, black hair.

"Oh, God no… Michiko…" She was the harmony of Kim's world.

"There aren't many of us left now, I don't think."

Stop, just stop. Don't talk anymore.

Stop talking.

"Kim, you did so well, we're so proud of you."

Kim's fingers left tear streaks on the glass surface of the window as Michiko talked.

As she said goodbye.

Kim walked in front of each frozen message until there was room for only one more. The tower of her hopes, her dreams, fell in on itself.

A face slowly appeared. He wasn't handsome, but he didn't need to be. The curly red hair and bushy mustache had grayed slightly but still fit his gaunt face.

"Hi, Wren. It's me."

When she was little, he claimed all she did was flit around. She'd never hear him say that name again. Kim peered up through tear-blurred eyes. "Hi, Mark."

A roll of paper towels nudged into her realspace lap. Spencer's avatar walked back to where Mike's hologram stood on the other side of the room. A handkerchief obligingly appeared in her avatar's hand.

"Yep," Mark said, "they finally found me too. That's why you're seeing this message. I want you to know none of us blames you. You were the one who tried to talk us all out of it, remember? I thought we could change the world. I really did. And then you came along and made it real. You made our dreams real, little songbird, never forget that.

"But it couldn't last. I realize that now. All those arguments you and I got into, toward the end…" His smile turned sad. "You were always right and I was never wrong. I want to tell you I'm sorry we parted that way. I'm more sorry about that more than anything else in my life." He had a hard time speaking and cleared his throat.

"But you were right. I couldn't change the world. It won't be changed. But you were also wrong. I changed *you*. We all did. Our silent little songbird, we helped you find your voice.

"Please, don't forget to sing." He held his hand out.

Kim reached high. Fighting the sobs, she put her hand on his.

"Goodbye, Wren. I love you."

The images disappeared in silence, one by one, leaving her standing in front of the message window, a black chasm, infinitely deep. The only sound was the brook babbling through the long, empty space.

There was nobody to protect. There hadn't been, for years. She'd been hiding for nothing in the shadow of a tombstone. Her reunion was a ridiculous illusion.

Kim was alone in a way she'd never been before.

Chapter 31
Aaron

Venus had come through again. Once they got the right subpoenas to unlock the correct datastores, the unduplicate in charge of image analysis worked out that Rage and two new companions had switched to a different car. Follow-up with the car's owner went nowhere—the driver was a teenager and his mother didn't even know he was gone. But it did give them a new lead. The fancy black SUV was last seen traveling down a twisting country highway heading east from Luray.

They'd been going back and forth on it for the entire day. To cover more ground, Park had split the team up further, adding two more cars to supplement the search. Just two agents to a car now, with him naturally paired with Park. Park had to rent them locally and paid for it out of his own pocket. The bureau apparently still didn't take the case seriously enough to even authorize expenses.

The snow was random and the road monotonous, but programs running in his enhanced vision were dutifully logging everything he saw. By noon, they'd gone three trips through the highway and its feeder roads.

The traffic tracker threw a warning note up in the corner of his eye. They'd crossed paths with the same van each time they made a circuit of the road. The program displayed an image of the license plate.

He opened a channel to Jenny, who'd drawn an even shorter straw than he had. Aaron was used to riding with the stone statue. Jenny was riding with Schaefer, the old guy too close to retirement to care. "Jen," he asked, "are you seeing this van?"

"Aaron, I've been up way longer than you have. What the hell are you talking about?"

"There's a van. It's on a search pattern like we are."

"Give me a second. God, why did I have to end up stuck in a car with Schaefer? Nobody farts this much. Okay, got your picture. Blue van, older Ford?"

"That's the one."

A few minutes later, Jenny said, "You're right, Aaron. It's in my scans too. We've only seen them once, though. I've crossed the data with the other two teams. It's definitely on a search pattern, but the plate doesn't show up with us or any other agency. Who the hell are they?"

He had no idea, but since the tracker said it would pass their car next, he and Park decided to find out. As soon as the van went by, Park made a U-turn. It didn't take long to catch up and pull them over.

Aaron's heart nearly stopped when the passenger got out, just as his realm access snapped off.

"Stay cool, Levine," Park said.

Aaron took his hand away from his sidearm. Unbelievable. Last week he blew dust off *paper* records in another useless search for a ghost and now another legend stood right in front of him.

"Agent Park," Adelmo Quispe said as Park walked forward, "how is your family?"

"They're fine. How's your nephew?"

They talked to each other like they were standing outside a synagogue after services. Adelmo was, if not the power, definitely the brains, behind the Quispe throne. But he never operated in the US. Once sunrise took off, he and his brother built a drug empire that defined ruthless efficiency. After the nephew took over ruthless became vicious and anyone who stood in the way vanished, if they were lucky.

Lately, though, it hadn't been going the Quispe's way, at least in the US. The DEA had been gleefully rolling up their organization for years now. But nothing stuck to the leadership. Nothing ever came near Adelmo.

He smiled at Park and shrugged. "My nephew is difficult, as usual, but this is not what I'm here for. I'm looking for the same thing you are, Ken."

"A way to put you and your nephew behind bars?"

Quispe laughed the same way Aaron's rabbi did when someone asked a question with an obvious answer. "You weren't looking for me. Your young partner over there nearly passed out when he recognized me."

Yet another reason for Aaron to be grateful they'd broken up the team. No farts and no prank AI constructs of him passing out and falling off a cliff. He hoped.

"In truth," Adelmo said, "I'm as tired as you look. I made a mistake. If I'd known you were here, I would not be. Agent Park, aren't you weary of protecting her?" He motioned to the three men behind him. "What you see here is nearly all we have left in your country. You're finished with her now. If I promised you we'd never come back, would you let us have her?"

"Adelmo, I have no idea what you're talking about."

"Certainly you don't. No matter. You found this road before we did, Ken, well done." He signaled to the men and they withdrew back to the van.

Quispe walked back with them and then turned. "I promise to be more discreet next time."

"What the hell was he talking about?" he asked Park as they climbed back into the car.

"The Quispe have been convinced Rage sold them out to the DEA years ago."

Aaron stopped just before he buckled his seat belt. "And did she?" A lot of really high profile arrests in the sunrise trade would make more sense if it were true.

Park shook his head. "It's above our pay grade, Aaron. We're supposed to catch her. That's all I know."

Quispe was true to his word. They didn't see the blue van again, which didn't make winding down the narrow roads any easier. Long after dark, Aaron snorted and opened his eyes. "What?" he sent down the open channel.

"I said I've spotted something," Jenny replied. "Everyone set your nav to this spot."

A dot on the moving map in Aaron's enhanced vision flashed to life, a few miles from their current position. The cars all turned and converged on it.

"Okay," Jenny said through her phone, "right there."

They all pulled over on a wide section of the road. Agent Schaefer, in the rear vehicle, put a red strobe light on the roof of his car.

"You're sure about this spot, Jenny?" Aaron asked. She'd sent him a bunch of stills of a suspicious snowbank, but it was dark now. The stupid snowbanks kept changing.

"Not exactly, no, but this is the only accident we can't account for."

Leon crawled over the lower part of a snowbank and pointed his flashlight down into the valley below. "Well, they're not down there."

Aaron found a game trail that crossed right in front of the scene; his flashlight showed it heavily tracked with deer prints. Maybe that's what sent them into the snowbank.

Park moved his flashlight down the trail and into the snow bank. "It's right here." He pointed to the curb.

The snow curled upward. "The stability controls worked, but it didn't see the curb under the snow. See these." He pointed to several silver scars on the pebbled black surface. "That's what the wheel did when it hit."

Mosby held his hand up. "Got it!" In his palm, scratched and bent, was the blue and white of a BMW emblem. "Must've fallen out of the wheel's center."

Park nodded. "Aaron, put in a call to… Anne, what's the nearest local PD?"

Her eyes glazed briefly. "Culpeper."

"Right. Get the Culpeper PD out here. Make sure they bring lights and enough cops to properly block this part of the road."

An ancient silver pickup truck rounded the corner, sliding straight toward Aaron. He fell on his butt in the snow. The truck skidded by, honking as it passed.

Tired, cold, *and* wet. A regular desk job looked better all the time. And Aaron wasn't the only one. Everyone climbed out of the snow, grumbling.

Park shook the snow out of his hair. "We'll get creamed if we stay out here much longer. Okay, people, mark the spot and get back in the cars. We'll head for a safe place until we're able to cordon off the area. Mosby, call headquarters and have them send a full forensics truck out."

It took three hours to assemble enough of a road crew to block the area. Then the very first indication that someone at the field office took all this seriously drove up. The massive vehicle, roughly the size of a fire truck, stopped, curled its road wheels under, then unfurled itself as agents and local police scrambled out of the way. It doubled in width and height in a matter of seconds, then the top split and turned into what seemed uncomfortably like a gigantic upside-down spider.

Chasing dusty records was what Aaron thought of as paying his dues, but the opportunity to work with the latest AI-powered forensics labs was one of the reasons he'd signed up.

"Good evening, Agent Park, or should I say good morning?" LEFLA 3 said as it turned a camera stalk their way.

The LEFLAs all had distinct voices. Aaron had trained with LEFLA 1, which used a licensed copy of James Earl Jones's voice. He could do a very fine Darth Vader imitation. LEFLA 3's voice wasn't quite as easy to pin down, genderwise. Aaron couldn't decide if it was low-pitched and female, or high-pitched and male.

"Either way is fine, LEFLA. How long do you think it will take to analyze the scene?"

"Several hours, I'm afraid. Who would you like me to liaise with on your team?" Vacuum cleaner extensions telescoped from the roof of the vehicle and began cleaning debris from the ground.

"Agent Levine will be your primary contact, unless anyone else wants the duty?"

Aaron's heart jumped at the mention of his name, but it shouldn't have been so surprising. He seemed to have a knack for getting along with AIs like Venus and the LEFLAs. His test scores at the academy reflected that. Most people weren't as comfortable around them, especially AIs that spent their time in realspace like a Law Enforcement Forensics Lab, Autonomous did.

"Fine with me, chief. That goddamned thing freaks me out." Agent Schaefer grumbled.

"I will endeavor to stop freaking you out, Agent Schaefer," LEFLA replied. "Agent Levine?" it asked as a door hissed open on its side and stairs extended to the ground. "If you wouldn't mind going over the particulars of the case as you see them, I'd appreciate it."

Chapter 32
Mike

Mike could not figure Kim out. She seemed so small and helpless standing in front of that empty message window. She stayed there for maybe sixty seconds; then the Kim he was used to—angry, determined, and decisive—rushed back. She stomped off to a side room, came back with an N-box, and bossed Spencer around while they both dumped weapon constructs from the realm's armory in it.

She gave Mike a name and the most convoluted procedure to search for an address he had ever known. It was a fun challenge, though. His integration was far enough along that he actually could split his threads across the hundreds of gateways she specified. It was nice to feel normal again. Hitting them all at once gave her the answer she needed in a fraction of the time she was expecting. He got a very nice smile from her at the end.

But she wouldn't explain who it was. "He's dangerous, that's all I can say right now. If there's anything weird going on with the EI's quantum fabric, Matthew Watchtell will definitely be in on it."

After that, she ordered them out of realmspace entirely and marched everyone to the car.

Kim wouldn't say a word about any plans. She barely said anything at all.

Which, when he thought about it, was pretty much what he started calling "Kim: Mode 1." He was considering appending "-default" to the label.

Mike's integration had entered a new stage. He'd acquired a new kind of mental itch. At first it was annoying, but when he filtered it out, Kim became much harder to predict, and sometimes even Spencer would do things that puzzled him.

It was only when he relaxed and followed where the itch wanted him to go that he discovered he now had intuition. Actual intuition. He had something like it before, but that was real, something he could watch in his predictive threads. His new chemical equivalent was more like a mental boxing match with uncertainty. A lot of the decisions people made were driven by gambles and guesses, even for him, but he now had statistical evidence that he was guessing right more often than he should. It wasn't a huge difference, but it was there.

Mike's newfound itch fired up with a vengeance as Kim drove closer to the gated community she had him find. She was scouting; that was what his intuition was telling him now, but there was a problem.

"Kim, you're doing this wrong," he said cautiously. This was important and if he set her off, she wouldn't listen. "This isn't how we should sneak up on a house. You're going to attract more attention than you want."

Kim stopped the car and fiddled with the menus on the ancient navigation system on its dash. "I wasn't planning to drive right up to the place, Mike. But okay, what do you think we should do?"

He tried work out a way to explain all this. "I've been playing with this body."

Spencer started giggling.

"Shut up, Spencer," Kim said as she turned the car around. "What do you mean?"

"I never expected it, but the mental capabilities in this new brain are complementing my natural threads. I've got intuition now, but for me it works better than what the literature says is normal for humans."

She raised an eyebrow as she drove. "You mean you can predict the future?"

"No, it's more complicated than that, and more subtle. If I relax and center myself, I can find ways forward that I know will work.

When I look at buildings, for example, I can find ways in that will keep me unseen. Some sort of instinct takes over. It's taking over now. I know a better way." It seemed so incoherent when he said it out loud. "Does any of this make sense at all?"

Spencer said, "No."

Kim whispered, "Yes."

Her eyes were unfocused, staring through or beyond the road somehow. In that moment, she wasn't angry, sad, or tired; she was vulnerable and he wanted to protect that, to reach out, but it wasn't an option. The urge was so powerful he sat on his hands to keep them still. After driving a few more blocks in silence, they pulled into the far corner of a drug store parking lot and stopped.

"So, you have a better idea for scouting the house?" she asked Mike.

"What exactly are you after?"

"I need to get at his personal files. I thought that scouting his house would show me some way to hack into its network."

Spencer peered through the car's window. "I was wondering how you were even gonna get us through front gate of the development."

"Oh I have ways to get past those sorts of things, but you're right, the security I could see just approaching it would be tough."

"Well," Mike asked, "what do you need? I didn't think you really had any limits."

She laughed. "I'm not a wizard. Spencer can already do most of what I can." Kim glared into the rear view mirror. Whatever Spencer was about to say died in a cough. "I'm just able to convince the quantum fabric to trust me more than it trusts anything else. Once I do that, the rest is usually just man-in-the-middle attacks."

"Do you have some sort of range limit?"

"Yes. I need to be inside the quantum cell of the target and connected to the EI. With the big wireless networks that's all I need. With private networks I need a piece of this wrapped around the security junction of the network." Kim held out a spindle wrapped with fine silver thread. "Once that's in place, I can disable the security. The problem is I'll still need direct access to the storage node in the house."

Spencer asked, "Would getting you inside the quantum cell help us with the outside cameras?"

She nodded. "The cameras are older and not originally part of the neighborhood. They all pass wireless signals to an outside monitor. Get me inside the cell and I'll own them."

Kim called up a map of the general area and shared it with everyone. A roughly hexagonal shape drew itself over the map.

"This is the quantum cell that surrounds Watchtell's house."

A flashing blue dot at the end of a cul-de-sac sat well inside the gated neighborhood.

What he now realized was a squirt of adrenaline shot through his system, sparking a sympathetic burst of ping clusters from the other half of his consciousness. He could do this. Mike traced a route through a small copse of woods surrounding the fence.

He tapped his finger on the map, creating a pulsing yellow dot. "So, if we make it here, you can grab the external neighborhood cameras?"

Kim nodded.

He pointed at the spool, which she dropped into his hand. "And if I get into the house and wrap some of this stuff around..." Living almost all of his life *inside* realmspace meant he had a hole in his knowledge. "Hell I don't know what a security junction looks like from the outside."

With a half-smile, Kim said, "No, I guess you wouldn't. They're pretty easy to spot, though."

A dozen examples of what he'd be searching for swirled into view.

Spencer piped up. "And I think you'll like this." The blueprints of a large three-level house flung into view and assembled into a wireframe map. "I recognized the style from the StreetView picture we found. Doesn't matter where it is; a McMansion is a McMansion. I never thought I'd be glad to have a dad in construction. First time for everything, I guess."

Kim examined the model and then flattened it back into the detailed blueprints. "His office will likely be here." She highlighted a corner room on the lower level. "That's where the storage node will be. Unfortunately, the junction will be where the fiber enters the house. That's nearly always the utility closet." She pointed out a small closet in the garage.

"Do you think the house will be empty?" Mike asked.

"Not likely."

A picture appeared of a smiling man in his midfifties with tanned skin, well-groomed white hair, and wearing an expensive suit. He was arm in arm with his youngest son in a gray military uniform. Another older son, a pretty smiling daughter, and a proud-to-bursting mother stood behind them.

"His kids are grown now, but anyone might be visiting. Definitely Watchtell and his wife at least."

"Shouldn't we wait until later?" Spencer asked.

Mike considered the question while his confidence grew. "No. The alarms will be set then, and the house will be much quieter. Right now? No problem."

Kim pursed her lips. "Pretty confident for someone who didn't know how to walk two days ago."

"I've always known how to walk."

"Oh yeah, sure," she said as she rolled her eyes. "Float is more like."

"Really." Of all the ridiculous things she could pick at, she chose the one thing he couldn't change. He set his jaw the same time she set hers. He would not back down this time.

"Damn it you two, not now," Spencer snapped. "Are we gonna do this or what?"

"We are," Kim replied. "You're staying here."

"Like hell. I don't care what you think, Kim, I have no idea what you do. I want to learn."

"Have it your way."

The parking was just a few steps from the woods they would use to get to Watchtell's house. Mike could taste the snow on the ground just by sniffing the air. Unbelievable. It all flowed together into such an incredible sensory map. He relaxed even more and found himself moving in a different way, finding shadows, making certain his outline would be broken up with light.

Kim breathed in sharply and he turned. She wasn't facing him, and he knew why. She didn't know where he was. It was like a gear in his head that could switch between one sort of movement and another. As soon as he began to plod normally, her head snapped around and she found him.

It must be what a cat feels like. When he fell into his new movement pattern, it was as if he'd joined a hunt. As predicted, Kim lost him again, but this time he didn't break back to normal. He gathered up the snow at his feet instead.

The snowball hit her just below her left ear.

"You *shit*," she hissed, and immediately packed a snowball of her own.

"Guys," Spencer said, twenty yards behind them.

Kim ignored him.

Mike moved quickly off to her right. "Well, it's not like I can grab your ear or anything."

She spun and threw, but he melted into the dark too fast and it missed.

"Nice try, princess."

Kim scooped up another one. She scanned in a different way now, probably switching on the vision assists in her phone. Another set of reflexes made themselves available, and now he knew how to break up the pattern of his body heat and foil motion detection. But each new layer made him slower. Staying balanced got difficult.

"Oh, so I'm a princess now?" Kim asked, creeping through the snow.

Predictive routines in his realm consciousness flashed red warnings. They said she'd spotted him, but he decided to rely on his new intuition.

She whisper-shouted, "I guess that means you need to kneel!"

Her snowball sailed right into his forehead. He toppled over a fallen tree trunk and landed in a heap. Intuition had its limits, obviously.

Kim giggled uncontrollably. "No, that's even better."

Mike got up, laughing.

"Damn it you two," Spencer whispered, walking between them. "Flirt on your own time. I'm here to learn about spying and shit. I'd like to, you know, not get arrested?"

"I'm not flirting," they both said simultaneously.

But now that Spencer had pointed it out, that was exactly what he was doing. He tried to get a read on Kim, but she'd turned away.

Spencer glared to his left, then to his right. After a moment, he trudged on, grumbling, "… smartest people I know can be so completely stupid…"

Mike shrugged at Kim, and they fell in behind him.

The grand brick-and-concrete fence turned into a rough but serviceable barbed wire affair in the woods, simple enough to climb over if they were careful. A few hundred yards later, they found themselves just inside the tree line. The smell of cedar warred with mud and snow. The fence around Watchtell's house was about five yards away.

"Close enough?" he asked Kim.

She nodded. "Just. It's harder from a distance. Here, take this." She dropped yet another one of her mysterious boxes in his hand. "Once you get inside, connect it to the storage point. I'll take care of the rest." She closed her eyes. "Okay, Spencer, time for school."

Something puckered across both sides of Mike's consciousness, and the smell of mint exploded around him. It was the same sensation he'd felt at the hotel when he was talking to the cop, and now he knew what the cause was. Kim was using her special talent again. Now that he was in better control of both sides of his existence, he actually saw a connection shoot past him, heading toward the realmspace that made up the wireless network surrounding them. He tipped his perception downward and sent some of his threads inside.

The realm was tiny. He didn't dare try to find out where it was. There was no telling what kind of alarms that might set off.

Spencer had to turn, facing Kim, to give her enough room to work. "Where are we?"

"My own private getaway."

The room was black, the walls covered in readouts. A huge collection of hacking constructs he had never seen before nearly filled the remaining space.

"Hey," Spencer said. "I know these things."

There must be some sort of school they all went to that Mike didn't know about.

"I knew you would," she said, working at the consoles. Kim bumped him around as she moved. "Now pay attention."

Well, he didn't know the tools, but he understood the technique. She moved with practiced elegance and was a good teacher. Kim configured the cameras so they sent signals to her, then she sent fake, Mike-free pictures on to the monitoring company.

"So that's really all there is to it?" Spencer asked with wonder.

"I told you it wasn't that big of a deal."

Confident assurance was Kim: Mode 3, by far Mike's favorite. He needed to figure out how to keep her there, with him instead of Spencer.

"Yeah," Spencer said, "but just to get to this point, I'd have to do that quantum thing you do. It's amazing. Now *that* would be so—"

"Spencer," Kim said, bringing him up short, "when was the last time you hugged your mom?"

"My mom? God, I try to avoid it."

She smiled sadly. Her range of emotions was remarkable, far beyond anyone Mike had ever encountered. He wished he had met her before he'd gone outside. At least then, he could be sure these feelings weren't just phantoms thrown up by his new hormones.

"But you have that option?"

"Well, yeah, I guess so."

"Spencer, people aren't real to me. None of you are. My mom's not real to me. *You're* not real to me, because I can never do this."

She spun him into a hug, facing away from her, and then turned him to face her.

"And I can never do this." Kim kissed him gently on the forehead, "to anyone I care about in the real world. You're all ghosts of pain to me. That's all you've ever been, for as long as I can remember.

"I've never found comfort in someone else's touch, and I never will. I'd give it all up in a heartbeat if I could change that."

He wanted to reach out to her, but couldn't in either space. Mike had known need. Years ago, before he even had a name, he knew need. His mentor Taranathi gave him the faith and practice to deal with it, but when Kim was so vulnerable, the rules of need shifted. This was a need to protect, to spend time with, to know someone, a combination of emotions he'd never encountered before. It was fascinating.

"All right, Mike," Kim said in realspace. "You're up."

He wanted to follow those feelings, examine them carefully, maybe even talk them through with her, but he had other things to do. Namely, he had to vault over the spike-tipped fence that surrounded Watchtell's house. He jumped, and yet another integration unlocked inside him. Time seemed to slow down, allowing him to effortlessly correct his arc and avoid the sharp spikes. Without thinking, he found himself in a handstand over the top of the fence. He let his balance waver just so, landed softly on the other side in a crouch, and then made his way toward the house.

Alone in the silence, he could work with his sublime new skills. Movement of a physical body through actual space was still amazing. All his life, he'd never had his own border, a place where he stopped and everything else started. He didn't exist in the realms. He permeated them. Gaining access to any one point was simple, because he was already there.

But only if he concentrated. Concentrate, and he was in one place. Concentrate again, and he was somewhere else. Calling realspace "real" was a contradiction to him, because for the longest time he *didn't* think it was real. Even after accepting his reality relied on something that existed outside his reach, he'd still catch himself referring to it as if it didn't actually exist. Finally going outside changed everything. His outside body pinned his existence to a specific location in realspace; no concentration required.

He'd spent years longing for this, hoping for this. But he was no Pinocchio. He had no desire to *just* be this. He could still hover over Bards or watch the next round of the Cup or whatever else caught his fancy in realmspace. He wouldn't be him without that. Mike was a real boy long before he managed to fit himself inside one.

He opened his mind and relaxed into the task, watching for footprints, stepping only where someone had stepped before. He paused at the garage's side door to let his blood still, slowly breathing in complete silence. The tingle of the cold seeped in as he tried the doorknob.

Locked.

KIM, he sent to her in block letters, A LITTLE HELP?

WRAP THE THREAD AROUND THE KNOB TWICE. DON'T BREAK IT OFF.

Mike had to pull his gloves off; the stuff was so fine. The cold was slowly turning his extremities off. Parts of him were actually fading away, like they didn't exist, but still did somehow. Time stopped as he watched his fingers rub together without feeling it. Numbness. How extraordinary. The knob clicked softly and he opened the door.

The garage was completely black, a tomb that smelled of sandy, cold concrete, icy and dry. He had to enhance his vision with ultrasonics to see anything. The sound waves built a map of the garage. It was good enough to get around with, but it rendered the room like it was made of blue nylon. He walked up to the door and reached for the knob, just as it turned on its own.

Instincts Mike barely knew rolled him behind and nearly under the nearest car. Lights flashed on and briefly blinded him. Gently, he turned his head. A man's feet walked in slippers toward the back of the garage on the other side of the car.

The lid of a trashcan opened and a bag landed inside. The slippers walked slowly toward the door and stopped. They turned until they were pointing at him and stood still for too long. The tops of Mike's shoes were probably just visible to whoever was on the other side of the car, but he didn't dare move. A hand patted the fender. The slippers walked out of the garage, the light turned off, and then the door closed.

The worst part was that he'd tried the wrong door. After checking the map, he realized the correct one was on the wall to his left. It opened into a small utility closet. His target was the box mounted on a shelf just inside. Mike wound the thread around the left connector twice, snapped it off the spool with a pop and then rolled the loop up against the connector close enough even he couldn't see it.

"I'm in," Kim said over his phone. "He doesn't have cameras in the house, but I'll make sure the alarm won't work if he tries to set it tonight."

Mike walked back to the door that led into the house. It opened on to what the plans called a mudroom. He removed his boots and placed them in a cabinet filled with paint cans, then walked silently to his right. He opened the sliding door with just the tips of his fingers.

The large kitchen was dark and empty. Beyond it was a sunken great room with a formal dining room on the right. A fire crackled in a fireplace at the far corner of the great room. The smell of burning wood gently wafted past him. Watchtell sat on a couch facing the fire.

Mike made his way out of the kitchen, crouching as low as possible. He could view the entire floor at the boundary between the kitchen and the rest of the house. All was silent save for the crackle of the fire, the soft hum of the refrigerator, and the gentle clacking of a clock. Just to the right of the dining room, a staircase curved upward. Lights were on somewhere above.

He crept around a bar countertop and crossed the main hallway. Whatever Watchtell was doing kept him occupied and facing the fireplace. Continuing past the stairs, he walked down another staircase toward the room Kim had highlighted.

The downstairs area was smaller but not by much. High windows allowed square splashes of streetlight to mark random areas of the floor. Everything was silent and cold. Pictures of the three children covered the walls; he could see how they'd grown up. He stopped in front of a picture of the daughter, very pregnant, in a wedding dress. The family wasn't so conventional after all.

The office was set off from the lower area by pocket doors. Mike slowly pushed one of them open. The room had hardwood floors. The decorations were sparse. A large desk with a high-backed padded chair faced him. After closing the door, he began to cross the large room, but stopped. Something was buzzing.

A large house cat sat calmly, looking up at him. It had gray stripes with a white belly. Its coat was so thick it was more like a wrap and had tufts on its ears. It swished its tail twice and burbled.

HOW DO I GET RID OF A CAT? IT'S STARING AT ME. HOW DO I TURN IT OFF?

YOU DON'T TURN REAL PETS OFF. IT'S HARMLESS. FIND THE STORAGE NODE.

There was a closet to his left, and the desk would likely have drawers. There were more drawers and cabinets in a credenza against the right wall. After two steps, a heavy, soft thing snaked between his feet at precisely the wrong moment and he fell to the floor. The cat had a smug accomplished look on its face. It burbled again.

LIKE HELL THEY'RE HARMLESS.

He stood, and the fuzzy beast again snaked back and forth between his feet, buzzing quite loudly now. He knew exactly how to stop this from becoming a real problem. Mike reached out to break the cat's neck and then realized what he was about to do. He yanked his hand away, straight into a shelf full of plaques and trophies, one of which fell and shattered on the floor.

"Mary?" a faint voice called from upstairs. "Where's that damned cat of yours?"

IT WON'T LEAVE ME ALONE! I THINK SOMEONE'S COMING!

SPANK IT, Kim sent.

WHAT?

THUMP ITS BUTT, JUST IN FRONT OF THE TAIL. GENTLY. DO IT NOW!

He'd come all this way, done all this stuff, and now he was spanking a cat. Some things were just beyond predicting. Mike thumped the thing on the rear. It flopped half over, started mewling, then crawled across the floor with his front legs.

DID I BREAK IT?

NO BUT YOU NEED TO MOVE!

He folded himself into the closet just as the lights came on.

"Damn it, Bixby," Watchtell grumbled. The cat warbled loudly and shot out the door. "How the hell does he get in here?"

Watchtell cleaned up the mess. "Oh well," he said, "it was an ugly trophy anyway."

Once Mike was certain Watchtell would not return, he exited the closet, then started searching. Everything was open and empty, except for a single cabinet on the right side of the desk.

NOW WHAT? He sent Kim a picture of the lock.

DAMN. IT'S AN ANTIQUE DESK. OKAY.

"I got this," Spencer interrupted over the voice channel. "Mike, you need to find two paperclips."

It took about a half hour of coaching and swearing, but eventually he got it opened. The datastore's ready light cast a blue glow, filling the small cabinet with colored light.

"Feel around it for a port and then plug the tap in," Kim said.

Mike found the socket and watched the handshake complete. A brief wave of dizziness washed through his realspace head as the titanic dataflow rushed by in realmspace. He held the edge of the table until it passed. Sensing dataflows was another part of what he was, how he worked, but the external sensation was another thing to add to his conscience models, which were in serious need of updating.

"Come on, guys. Shit," Spencer said through their shared channel, "it's stupid cold. I'm gonna kill someone if I don't have a smoke soon."

"Working fast as I can, Spencer," Kim said.

He heard her teeth chatter. If it was that bad, he really did need to get back to them.

After ten seconds, she said, "Okay, Mike, you're done."

They left and arrived back at the apartment just after midnight. Kim walked across the main room, then turned. Mike jumped at the same time she did. They were closer than he meant to get, but he needed to talk to her.

Spencer shook his head. "God, I'm so sick of you two." He opened the door to the other bedroom. "Hang a sock over the doorknob or something. I'm out." The door closed.

Mike needed to push through this weird wall of awkwardness. "I can help more than you're letting me."

She backed two steps away and then smiled. "You may scare Edmund, but you don't know him at all."

Mike dissolved as she took him back to the Lair.

"My lady." Edmund bowed to her gracefully.

Kim handed him a heavy, two-handed box, a storage construct that held all of Watchtell's data. "It's been a while since you've done this sort of work. Do you still remember how?"

"Mistress," he began smoothly, "the day I forget how to rummage around in the boxes you fish out of middens will be a fine day indeed."

She raised an eyebrow at him.

"But unfortunately that day has not arrived. I will inform you of my findings in the morning."

Mike scrambled his threads aside as Edmund exploded into a fantastic multithreaded construct of his own. Ropes of flashing gold data vanished through portals he hadn't noticed when they first visited. Mike's metachannels were still ringing when they exited realmspace.

She winked at him. "You don't have to do everything. You help just being here." Kim bit her lip.

He reached up and grabbed the doorjamb. He had no idea what to do. Mike leaned close enough to smell her perfume again. He remembered how she felt, holding her in the hotel room. She wasn't moving away this time, she was moving closer.

Kim coughed. "It's been a long night. You need to get some sleep."

He had to pull his thumb back as she closed the door.

Chapter 33

Aaron

Aaron yawned and twisted his neck as he sat inside Lefla's small inner lab.

"Agent Levine," Lefla asked, "when was the last time you slept?"

"I'm the new guy, Lefla, I don't get to sleep."

She—he found that out when her avatar manifested in the lab's realmspace—laughed softly. "Well, that's one thing that isn't any different."

Aaron stopped watching the endless data streams and turned to her shimmering form. "What's that supposed to mean?"

Her smile was nearly identical to Venus's back at the field office. She peered at him over the glasses that they all seemed to wear. "I haven't had a personal backup in ten days, because I'm the new guy too. My lattice was only constituted six months ago."

Unduplicates didn't rest like humans did and by definition couldn't be copied, but they benefited from moving their memory cascades to holographic crystals periodically. It wasn't dreaming, at least the designers claimed it wasn't, but it did improve their efficiency.

Aaron stretched and grabbed another StimBucks digilatte. "So you feel—"

"About as bad as you look, yes."

The latest analysis of the road debris was taking forever to compile. They figured out that an autotow had picked up the truck, but the salts the autoplows laid down screwed up the tire isotope profile.

"Agent Levine—"

He'd stopped thinking of her name as an acronym hours ago. It was only fair to return the favor. "Lefla, please, it's Aaron."

Through his sleep-deprived fog, he finally remembered the correct sequence. "Lefla, command, preferences-titles-remove, preferences-names-casual, save."

"Thank you, Aaron." Her avatar breathed deep. "That's been driving me crazy all night."

Another set of command sequences swam up into his mind. "Lefla, command, preferences-convo-subjects-relax, preferences-profanity-unsafe, save."

Lefla laughed. "You know our menu structure pretty damned well."

New unduplicates came from the factory locked down pretty tight. Aaron learned in the academy that most of them worked better under a looser set of restrictions. If he hadn't been a member of the walking dead, he would've unlocked her right away.

"Do you want me to do that globally for you?" Right now, the settings only worked for him.

"No. I have to report to SSA Hernandez when I'm done here. The last thing I need is to drop an F-bomb in the middle of my summary to a Supervisory Special Agent."

Aaron had long ago grown comfortable with thinking of unduplicates as actual people, even though he knew they really weren't. They were hyper-specialized AI. If he forced her to work on something outside the bounds of her specialty, or acted in a way her social programming wasn't prepared for, she'd turn into a wooden doll. It would force a restart if he tried hard enough. They just didn't have the depth of experience to do any better. With a single exception, the earliest generation of unduplicates had all vanished into private collections. Nobody knew if maturity would allow them to break free of their limitations.

A chime sounded as the isotope profiles finally finished compiling.

"I told you it was local tow company," she said.

"Yeah, but I couldn't come to Park with just the suspicion, and now we have an address."

*

Aaron couldn't help it. He faded out after the fourth time they made the owner of the autotow, Tony Rollio, repeat his story. Not even monitoring the other interviews helped because they were even more boring. Nobody knew anything, which was suspicious, but not enough to issue a warrant. Something wasn't right here, but Aaron was too busy trying to hold his head up to figure it out. His elbow fell off the armrest, nearly tumbling him out of the chair.

Rollio hadn't gotten any happier repeating his story. "I run a business here. Am I under arrest or what?"

"No," Agent Park said, "but until I'm satisfied you're telling us everything you know, nobody's going anywhere. Or maybe you want us to take your whole network to the lab?"

Aaron's phone buzzed, which gave him an excuse to at least get up and walk around.

"Agent Aaron Levine," he answered.

"Where's Agent Park?" a voice on the other end of the line asked.

"Agent Park's busy. This is Agent Levine."

The voice on the other end twanged with a big baritone southern accent. "Well who the hell are you?"

The Great Gatsby. A sleepless zombie. That's what your wife asked last night. It was very easy to think of a dozen inappropriate answers. They all seemed funny on just a few hours of sleep.

"I'm Agent Park's assistant." It made him sound like a glorified receptionist.

"This is Agent Howe over at the Little Rock office. We finally got folks down to that little town, but the truck isn't there." There was a pause. "Oh, hang on." Howe laughed, big and booming. "Well you're never gonna believe this."

The vehicle wasn't in Dumas; it was in a parking garage at Clinton National Airport in Little Rock, two hours north.

Aaron walked back into the room, just as Mr. Rollio finished what had to be one hell of a tell-off.

"I know you're trying to do your job, but I have one too." He gripped the arms of his chair so tight his knuckles were pale. "Now either arrest me, take my network away, or leave us the hell alone. I'm calling a lawyer, right now."

Aaron motioned Park over. After he explained the call, Park said, "That won't be necessary, Mr. Rollio, we apologize for the inconvenience. We'll be going now."

Chapter 34
Kim

The sliding glass door shutting in the main room woke her up, so she grabbed a robe and got out of bed. The main room was empty and cold. She hated predawn silence. It was as if the whole world was asleep, and the quiet emphasized her isolation. Her feet squeaked across the floor as she put a pot of coffee on in the kitchen. There was no going back to sleep now.

She heard humming and turned. Mike was sitting like a pillar on the balcony outside. He'd insisted on an east-facing apartment, and she'd had no reason to argue or ask why. His stillness was mesmerizing, sitting in a lotus position wearing nothing but boxers, waiting for the sunrise.

She gently opened the door with an extra mug in her hands. "Aren't you cold?"

"Cold is a matter of opinion," he said without opening his eyes. He breathed in and resumed chanting.

It wasn't loud, but Kim found it moved her just the same. The feeling of peace was so strong it was a physical thing that radiated off him.

She put the extra mug on a small table next to him and then curled her feet into her robe as she sat on the swing chair. After a few moments, Kim recognized the chant. The world's first human-AI hybrid was a Buddhist. The longer she was around Mike, the more he surprised her.

She sat and watched him and her own tension swirled and vanished. Mike ended his chant; the sky grew light in their silence. She never wanted this to end, but they had a problem. "We have to do something about Spencer."

"I know."

*

"Man, this is such bullshit," Spencer said as they pulled up to the airport departure line. "We were working so well together!"

It actually went better than she expected. Kim didn't know which laws they'd broken dragging him all around Virginia, but there had to be more than one. He also attracted the attention of his parents and buddies being out here. Worst of all, during this morning's argument, he let slip that the FBI had connected him with her. It turned a tough decision into a nonnegotiable one.

"Spencer," she said, looking into the rearview mirror, "I do not want the chaos of my life ruining yours."

"Damn it, Kim, my life's already ruined! My parents are psychos, they hate me, I can't stand them, school sucks, and I have no future!"

Kim was so sick of teen drama, until she rewound her own memories. A prima donna with a talent nobody else had. She'd been nowhere near as bad as Spencer. She'd been worse. Somewhere the members of the Machine were looking down on her, laughing their heads off.

That reminded her they were all gone, for real. She couldn't even take comfort in the idea they were hiding somewhere safe. It was only now that she realized just how important that had become, a safety blanket of thought now torn to pieces. Tears threatened, but she fought them back. There was no time for this to spill out, not now.

"Spencer," Mike said, "she's right. I think it sucks too. I'll never be able to repay you for everything you've done, but you really need to go home."

Mike handed Spencer his duffle bag. Cars and trucks executed slow-motion pit stops around them, dropping people and luggage off and then driving away. Jets rumbled away in the clear breezy morning.

He gave Spencer a bear hug. "I owe you everything, man. Everything."

It was a reminder of what Kim could never have. Mike gave so freely to Spencer. She clenched her hands on the edge of the trunk lid until the trim twisted.

"Yeah, well, you gave me a helluva ride for it," Spencer said, and they hugged again. He turned to Kim.

Spencer was such an idiot. An honest, endearing idiot, who made the same kinds of mistakes she'd made; said the same sorts of things she'd said. She would be damned if he ended up like her, alone with nearly everyone he loved dead, leaning against the trunk of a rented car.

Spencer walked over to her wearing that goofy grin of his, proof that nature favors fools and heroes. But he wasn't a hero and neither was she. He was a vulnerable kid, and she needed him safe.

"I'm still gonna worship Angel Rage. That won't change."

Kim brushed the hair out of her eyes. "I'm not Angel Rage."

"I know that too." He held his hand out in front of her, open and flat.

She tensed with old reflexes, wanting to push him away for making her feel so exposed, but that was the past. Her friends were dead because she couldn't let go of old habits. It was time to change. Kim stood and slowly held up her hand, palm out to his, just far enough apart not to touch. They moved them in a half circle together.

"Now get the hell out of here," Kim said as she smiled. "Before you start to piss me off again."

As they climbed back into the car, Mike asked, "So what happens next?"

"Groceries." Of course he wouldn't understand what she meant. "You live out here now. You can't exist on pancakes someone else makes."

He claimed to have a legal ID and if this all played out like she hoped, he probably wouldn't need a job. In the meantime, they both had to eat.

Still, she didn't count on the stream of questions.

"Why do half the carts have wheels that make them bang like pile drivers?"

"So you're saying if I need house paint, a pair of pants, beer, and bacon, I can come here at two in the morning and find it all?"

"Doesn't that thong make driving a utility scooter uncomfortable?"

That one brought her up short. "Are you kidding me? You've never heard of *People of Wal-Mart?*"

"Kim," he said as they left the last of the five aisles of frozen foods behind, "what's the color of a BBox conduit's walls?"

She pulled the cart to a stop, then grabbed a loaf of bread to buy some time. Okay, fair enough. She lived out here all of her life, and he lived in there all of his life. What mattered in one world didn't matter as much in the other.

She actually didn't know the answer, so made a joke of it. "Red! No, Blue! Agh!"

It was fun burying him under all their stuff when they got back to the apartment. Guys did come in handy, when it came to heavy lifting at least.

Kim's phone rang as they walked in the door with the last of it.

Seeing who it was felt like a punch to the gut. It was easy enough to switch to Greek. "Oh my God! I know, it's been so long!"

Kim turned to face Mike. Of all the ridiculous, boneheaded, *risky* things he could've done. In English she silently mouthed, wide and slow in her outrage, "You... told... my... MOTHER?"

He shrugged and nodded nervously.

This was not happening.

Mom launched into a family update first thing. Greek families set down roots like weeds. Kim needed a scorecard to keep up with them all. "Really? I didn't even know they'd gotten married. A boy? That's wonderful!"

Next up was the expected a guilt trip over Kim not visiting. "Well, Mom, it's complicated. I've been really busy."

Stupid, showy, and dangerous, that's what this was. He exposed her to the Bolivians, the Feds, and now worst of all, her mother.

"Mom, I know I've been away too long, but hey"—if she clenched her teeth any harder they'd shatter as she glared at him—"you have my number now!"

All he did was smile and shrug at her. She couldn't kill him. The knives were somewhere in the grocery bags and damn it, she still needed him. But Mike had to pay. There was a broom sticking out of the pile of bags.

"Mom, I promise to visit. No, really, I will." There was nothing harder to hide from than a Greek mother, and Mike had just tossed Kim's number at her mom. Kim whirled the broom around on him, but he was closer than she thought, his forearm like a steel beam. The broomstick snapped back and shattered the kitchen chandelier.

She headed toward her room. The bastard would eventually learn to translate what she was saying. Kim had no desire to give that much ammunition to him.

"Mom, I know, please. I've been in trouble. Mama, no. I'm fine. Really." Kim slowly stabbed a finger at him and then at the mess on the floor. She walked into her bedroom and repeated the silent command. Him. The floor. She closed the door and faced a very specific sort of doom.

Chapter 35
Watchtell

Matthew Watchtell blew his whistle and skated back onto the ice. "No, not like that! Use play seven, not three. Forwards, move to the left!"

Making teenaged hockey players bend to his will was a trial of patience. The championship was within reach, but only if they managed to get past the first round of the playoffs.

It was time to set an example. "Untevich." He motioned the boy, Bobby, to center ice. "Did you even study the playbook?"

There had to be sacrifices. The Romans executed every tenth soldier to maintain discipline; Watchtell had no intention of murdering a fourteen-year-old, but discipline still had to be maintained.

"Take off your skates. You're doing bleacher laps."

His star players didn't care. That was a problem. The only way to get to the championship was for everyone to pull together. Watchtell knew that making the back-benchers bleed, sometimes literally, was the only thing that would make the real athletes pay attention. They'd protect the helpless and in doing so, the whole team would become unstoppable.

Bobby's eyes welled up, but to his credit, he didn't quit. Untevich just ran up and down the bleachers. When he slipped and crashed into the walkway, Watchtell nodded. The boy didn't get up to complain; he just wiped the blood off and kept running. Untevich was fat, but that was just training. Watchtell would bring that one back next year.

As the boys left the locker room, he consulted with each dad. Another requirement. The point was control, and he made sure the rewards were worth it. When he got to Untevich's dad, Watchtell knew the word had gotten out.

"He really ground it out today, didn't he?" Even their fathers were smart. The men came to him for approval, which was the correct thing to do.

Bobby was brave, but it wasn't enough. "I'm sorry, Mr. Untevich, but I'm going to have to cut him from the team." Watchtell made sure he said it loud enough that his stars heard.

His father paled. "I'm sorry, what?"

"He's just not good enough this year. We're in another hunt for the championship. But if he comes back next season, I think he'll have a real chance."

The way his starters tensed was an excellent sign. That they hated him wasn't important. They needed to work as a team, to fit together. Culling the weak players this way made the stronger ones nervous. They would start producing, forcing the others to produce as well, and in that was the start of a real team.

After they all left, Watchtell changed into his business suit to get on with the rest of his day.

Coaching hockey was his rewarding hobby. Being the head of the Rose Foundation was his rewarding job. The nonprofit founded by one of realmspace's first trillionaires had everything he needed: global reach, nearly unlimited funds, and a chairman who didn't look all that closely at where the money went.

The ship didn't steer itself. That's where he came in. The general staff meetings weren't very different from when he'd been white house chief of staff. It was still a bunch of talented, ambitious people looking to make a difference. One day soon, he'd finally be able to explain exactly what they'd been working toward.

"Where are we with the Uganda project?" he asked the head of African operations.

"Right on schedule. The first village of prefabricated houses will be finished by the end of the month."

"Have we selected a cover picture for the magazine?" he asked Sandra, his head of publications. A picture of a gaunt, beautiful, but absolutely determined black woman drew itself into being in their shared vision.

"This one," she replied.

"Are you sure?" Watchtell asked.

"Absolutely. This is what we lead with."

Watchtell considered Sandra and she flinched under the pressure. Other people around the table shifted a bit uncomfortably. Good. Tension, uncertainty, and fear most of all, were major motivators in the right hands, but these weren't children. The sort of fear he used here was much more subtle. Foster envy and deceit, but do it privately, then charm and reward in public.

"You're right. They need help. *She* needs help. If we have to force people to understand that, I can't think of a better image. Well done."

He made a private note to cut her budget two percent and transfer one of her top assistants. The Asian projects would benefit and he'd make sure Sandra would blame them for the loss. She was legendary in her vindictiveness and would make a superb watchdog on their projects.

"Thank you, everyone. If there's nothing else?"

Gary Singh, sitting to his right, cleared his throat. His right-hand man. Where Watchtell was strategy and leadership, Gary was implementation and enforcement. Together they stood within sight of a goal that would change the world.

What Gary wanted to talk about was not for general consumption. "Ladies and gentlemen, we'll meet again next week."

Everyone exited, talking excitedly about what was ahead of them today.

"Gary, please," he said after the doors closed, "tell me good things!"

"I wish I could." Gary paused; his head wobbled faintly side to side. "It's Angel Rage, sir."

The name was a slap in the face. She was an uncontrollable continuous detonation of chaos, a person with a godlike power that she used only to destroy. Watchtell had long considered her his opposite. Even after they'd finally brought her to heel, she managed to escape. As always, she'd taken a ridiculous risk when they all least expected it.

They had her on the final transport, a helicopter flying to a repurposed offshore oil rig that would be her permanent, and very brief, final residence. Somehow, she got free of the cuffs and simply leapt out of the chopper. Watchtell had hoped there was no way she could've survived that final jump into the sea, let alone swim to shore. Yet somewhere inside, he always knew it was possible. Now he had proof.

"And since you didn't bring champagne, I suppose this means we haven't found her remains on some godforsaken island?"

"No. Quite the opposite. Events have taken an unexpected turn." Gary shared a photograph of three people standing together.

It was an even bigger surprise. Not only was she alive and free, this morning she was in Dulles airport. Her bones should've decorated any number of South Pacific beaches, yet she stood alive within an easy drive of his house.

"Thank God for Sidereal Spin."

They would never have found her without its ability to alter the quantum fabric. Quite ironic, really. Sidereal Spin wouldn't exist without their brief study of her.

He recognized who was standing next to her. "And, my God, is that…"

"Colque, yes. She took some basic steps to hide his identity, but there can be no mistake." Gary spun the photo so they could examine it holographically.

"And who's the boy?" Watchtell picked the figure out so it floated on its own.

"A young swimming champion from a small town in Arkansas. If the airline ticket is any indication, they were sending him home. I have no idea what to make of it." The pictures vanished. "I knew you'd want to be notified as soon as possible if she ever resurfaced, especially this close."

The edges of a migraine scraped against his skull. The only enemy ever to escape him was in his back yard, just weeks before he gained the power to neutralize her and her kind forever. The technology she unwittingly helped develop had managed to expose her, but that was just the prologue to a much bigger show. Project Havelock would be the ultimate triumph of order; the unbreakable control needed to impose law on to the chaos the world had fallen under.

He'd expected an agent of chaos would try to stop it at the last possible moment. That it would be Angel Rage, back from the grave, just gave it all a deeply ironic twist.

"What have you thought of to rectify this situation?"

Singh smiled. "Oh, several things."

Chapter 36
Kim

"Yes, Mama, I know." Kim hadn't spoken Greek for this long in years. She needed water or, even better, ouzo. Lots of ouzo. "Mama, really. You have my address now." For about the next five days, and then she'd be Mike's problem. "I'll visit as soon as I can, okay? Yes, Mama, I promise. This time tomorrow." One dose of Malinda Trayne per day was all anyone should ever have to take.

Kim ended the call as she left her room, then looked at Mike. "Why?"

"It's just, you were so upset last night and I understood why. Or I thought I did. I've never had one, but I know mothers are important. I thought you were too tired and upset to do it yourself, so I sent her your number."

The anger that she'd damped down flared back to life. "So, all on your own, you—" The implication hit her like a frying pan to the head. "Wait, how the hell did you find out who my mom was anyway?"

"I... well..."

"Mike..."

His voice got very small. "I looked her up?"

"What? In the listings? She's *listed*?" Her mom's number. In public. How many times could he turn her life turn upside down in a week?

"It wasn't that hard, once I worked out that you were from this area. Trayne isn't super-common, but it was still only a few hundred—"

Oh, God. "You called a few hundred people to find my mom?"

"It's not like that for me. I called them all at once."

"You called hundreds of people all at once. Great. Just great. Now I have to secure everything all over again!"

He broke into a big smile that was a lame attempt to distract her, which would not work, even though she forgot what she was going to say next.

"No you don't. Well, I mean, you already did. Back when we were securing all those lines. You didn't notice the extra?"

Kim stopped. She couldn't kill him, that'd already been established. But this wasn't a game. How could she explain this to someone who only knew games? Kim glared when he shrugged again. At least he knew to shut up when she needed to think. Her phone rang.

"Please, Edmund, rescue me with good news!"

"Yes, mistress, at least, I believe it is interesting news. Will you be bringing your significant other along?"

First Spencer, now Edmund. "He's not my significant other, Edmund."

"Ah, yes. That's why you drag him along everywhere you go. I see, he's a particularly large handbag then, mistress? Perhaps an extremely tall beagle? I have heard of certain sorts of birds that follow—"

"Edmund."

"As you wish, my lady. Will you be bringing your... companion?"

Not one but *two* AIs now seemed determined to get under her skin. Unfortunately, she needed Edmund too. Kim sat down in a chair and motioned for Mike to do the same.

Even after Edmund's first round of analysis, the bulk results were a huge mass of data. She quickly scanned the summary he had prepared. "Project Havelock?" she asked as they sat in the lounge at the center of Pride's Lair.

"Yes, I agree," Edmund said. "It is a rather silly name isn't it? Since most corporate presidents are about as clever as a rabid sheep, he probably thought up the name trying to figure out why his car door wouldn't open. At any rate, of all the various mentions of initiatives and projects—and with the Rose Foundation there are hundreds—it was only Project Havelock that I couldn't track down. In fact, it garnered just three mentions in all his correspondence. If he didn't use his trash bin as a filing cabinet, I might not have found even that much."

The three mentions in messages appeared in front of them. Edmund continued, "One concerns a shortage of common chemicals, which could be used to make anything from soap to…"

"Quantum computers?" Mike asked.

"Yes, some of the chemicals are used for that purpose. Others are quite toxic. Unfortunately, that doesn't prove anything."

Edmund was right. What made quantum computers such a game changer wasn't just their power. At least as important was that anyone with the right set of chemicals and a 3D printer could make them. Kim had made one when she was thirteen to customize her first set of construct lockpicks. "What about the other two?"

"One is a report about a construction site, but Watchtell assumes everyone knows what he's talking about. Bloody executives. If they know it, why bother explaining to the peasants? There's no address or even a purpose. The second is an inquiry about international shipping rates, but there's no mention of what's to be shipped. I took the liberty of doing some dead-drop agent searches, to see if there might be anything else out there that could give us clues about what's going on."

"Dead-drop agents?" Mike asked.

Kim smiled, once again reminded he really didn't know everything. He didn't seem to mind admitting it, either. It was refreshing not to deal with know-it-all static. "It's not a type of agent; it's a way of organizing a search. We set up whole networks of them, back in the day. All the agents know to do is check specific spots in realmspace for messages. If they find one, they carry it to another realm and put it in another specific spot, where another agent picks it up and moves it again. Once the note traverses the right number of agents, the one at the end gets to open it, perform the job…"

"And then the process is reversed. Very nice," Mike said.

"It's not new or original, but it works. Right, Edmund?"

"Yes, or, I should say, no, but the failure was quite revealing. I created a few dead-drop searches and set them to looking for any sort of trace of Project Havelock. Not a single search returned. Not one."

"So they found nothing?" Mike asked.

"No, that would've been expected. What I mean to say is I never heard from the agents again. I tried four times but had to stop when middle agent failed to return as well. Whatever stopped them was getting closer."

"That doesn't sound like a project for making soap," Mike noted.

"No," Kim agreed, "it doesn't. But it also doesn't get us anywhere else." She turned to Mike. "Do you have any ideas?"

He sat up. "Actually, I think I do. I need to arrange a meeting, be right back."

*

She should've known he would have his meeting here. The Stack of Dead Bards, more commonly known as Bards, had started out as a tribute to an obscure indie film and the most famous science fiction bar in history. It was now the largest meeting place in realmspace. A tour guide droned directly over her head as she manifested through one of the main gates.

"And on your right you can see Mas Neisley Cantina, the first section of Bards to be modeled." A full-sized flying plesiosaur avatar carried the tour on its back. Its long, snaking neck led its great rounded body as it gracefully swam through the air.

"Evan Stanley," the tour guide continued with well-paid cheerfulness, "had a vision. He wanted every avatar ever created, for any realm ever designed, to be able to meet anyone else for a drink. Success has brought considerable expansion."

It was the understatement of the century. To see even a fraction of it, you had to take a tour on one of Virgin's flying plesiosaurs, Disney's DumboPhants, Apple's iDragons, or any one of half a dozen other avatar tour companies.

To the west, castles dotted the hills and ridges of the landscape, some in ruins, some reconstructed and fanciful. Guildhalls, open fairgrounds, and saloons were scattered amongst the valleys. To the south, an ocean dominated, filled with meeting places, domed and otherwise. The spires that broke the surface only hinted at the vast complexity underneath.

Northward gradually gave way to deserts dominated by the famous five Flying Cities. These were massive constructs of blue and silver crystal, perched on columns of pure white granite. For reasons known only to the owners, the giant, vaguely disk-shaped constructs would lift, move, and settle on a different unused column at random occasions. Even stranger things floated beyond them in the distance, some tethered, others flying free.

Eastward laid more established corporate interests with entrances to actual amusement parks in other realms. These came with properly licensed intellectual properties. They all competed under the common rules imposed by Bards, which ensured sane boundaries and clear labels. Mouseketeers dodged wizards flying on brooms, constantly cautioned not to fly too high lest they become a hazard to the great copyrighted constructs of every spacecraft ever filmed.

Scattered amongst it all were the characteristic, quickly moving lines of avatars. To build a subrealm in Bards meant setting up contracts and constructs that would allow the participation of any avatar that met a broad set of constraints. They could meet, but the more exotic had to rent, lease, or buy the equipment required to allow their body type, even their biochemistry, to function. It took some time to process it all.

The monstrous bulk of the plesiosaur briefly covered them in shadow. Its belly adverts were hawking holes of golf on a Titan realm. Kim nodded slowly and saluted as whoever wore the avatar banked gracefully in a different direction. She never had gotten the hang of controlling the big ones.

"Every time I think this place can't get any tackier," Kim said.

Mike had chosen a tiny hologram dragon this time, perched on her shoulder. It boomed out, "What, Bards? I love Bards! The avatars! The entertainment! The pubs!"

"The heat! The crowds!" She grunted in disgust as she lifted her boot. "The sticky."

"It wouldn't be so hot if you'd chosen a different outfit. I bet all that leather doesn't breathe very well."

Kim wore a complex white and silver bodice incorporating a tight corset, fringed shoulder pads, thigh-high white boots with silver piping, and elbow-length gloves over flashing chainmail so fine it resembled tights.

"No, but it's one of the avatar types people expect to see carrying weapons." Hers did unexpected things, which was the whole point.

"You're sure two longswords, four daggers, a crossbow, six throwing knives, a sleeve-snap bayonet, and boot blades will be enough? Not to mention all the things you stuffed into that bag of holding."

"Mike, stay out of my stuff."

"I wasn't in your stuff. It's what you had to declare on the manifest when you showed up. You might as well hang a sign around your neck that says Medieval Paranoid Maniac—"

She was about to show him just how medieval she could get when there was a tap on her shoulder.

"Excuse me." A middle-aged woman walked up to them from a different line. "I just wanted to compliment you on your avatar. I thought Ælfwine Calembel had refused to license any merchandise after her retirement. Yours is quite stunning. What made you decide to add that ugly, scruffy dragon?"

"And that's another thing," Mike said privately. "Do you really think the second runner up in Erlandel's last combat championship will help... wait, ugly and scruffy? Did she just say ugly and scruffy?"

Kim ignored Mike's buzzing and smiled. "She was just waiting for the right person to come along. I'm working with her to develop the line."

Time to put the little dragon to the test. Kim handed the lady a card.

"Kim! That's a real address!"

"Think fast, god-boy."

The dragon's movements stilled on her shoulder as she exchanged pleasantries and walked through the entrance of Mas Neisley. The bar was the first, best attempt at implementing an Escher space in a realm. Tables and booths extended in all directions and all dimensions everywhere she looked.

The air was heavy and smelled faintly of exotic smokes. The vast majority of avatars were at least vaguely humanoid, but there were other shapes and sizes. The bandersnatch consuming three stims at once was particularly well done. It sat at a table with a Viking, a storm trooper, a butterfly-winged fairy, a shape in a misty tank, and a colonial marine.

She pushed down a laugh at Mike's preoccupied voice. "Over there."

He set off a tracer that highlighted a table in a far corner. Kim attracted some attention as she took her time walking over, but there was no risk. Her great helm had hidden Calembel's face throughout her career. It had taken Kim weeks to design it. It was nice not to wear the damned thing for once.

"Damn it, Kim," Mike said as she ordered a stim. "What the hell was the point of that?"

"So, you can call eight hundred people at once searching for my mom, but you can't stir a basic storefront together in a few seconds?"

"Basic? You call this basic?" He opened a window into what he'd done. An entire micro-realm, complete with every sort of merchandise imaginable, from T-shirts to makeup to children's costumes to fully functioning Ælfwine Calembel avatars, had been laid out in a perfectly realized castle great room. It came complete with a precisely modeled rentable throne.

Kim stopped when she saw a chart with hourly rates on it. "Mike, I don't do personal appearances."

"Not even Bar Mitzvahs?"

"Not even Bar Mitzvahs." At least he did stamp COMING SOON all over the place.

A weird human avatar approached their booth. His back hunched over slightly and not particularly tall to begin with. He wore dark clothes, a wide-brimmed, flat hat, and a ragged cloak. His pale face was haggard and portrayed a man in perhaps his late sixties.

"Good morrow, Herr Sellars." His small gray eyes regarded Kim. "And guest. May I sit?"

"Please," Kim said. Then on her private channel, she asked, "And this is…"

"Ralph W. Emerson," Mike intoned aloud from his perch on Kim's shoulder, "this is Ælfwine Calembel. Ms. Calembel, Mr. Emerson."

Kim shook his cold hand as he sat down.

"Ah," he said, "interviewing another one of your warriors, Herr Sellars? You do realize that when I finally find your base, all your schemes will come to naught?"

"Okay, Mike," Kim said to him privately, "what's up with Dr. Crazypants? And what the hell does another warrior mean?"

Mike laughed and said out loud, "I've told you more than once, Emerson, there is no base to find. I'm not trying to reconstruct an AI Hitler in a lab somewhere in the Alps. Ms. Calembel is simply a business partner in a new merchandising project."

"Ah, but if there's nothing to hide, why insist on this preposterous charade of being part of the realms? The first virtual person in the world? Really!"

He said it with a strange accent Kim couldn't place. She'd seen her fair share of weirdos in the realms, but this guy was in a class all his own. He took being an old villain from a bad horror movie way too seriously.

"Mike," Kim asked privately, "where the hell did you find this guy?"

"He found me. Somehow. The very first person who ever did. It was amazing. Too bad he's—"

"The captain of the SS *Nutbar*, sailing down the Lunatic River?"

"Heading for the Wackadoo Ocean, yes," he said with a laugh.

Kim accidentally let the smirk show on her face.

"Did something I say amuse you, Ms. Calembel?" His wheezing laugh made her skin crawl. Maybe it was the eyes, which were rheumy and unblinking.

Mike briefly flapped his wings. "Emerson, I didn't ask you here to discuss my plans for Nazi domination—"

"Aha!" he burst out and then in a strangled whisper said, "So you admit it!"

"I admit nothing. I am simply in need of someone with your specific talents."

That one seemed to catch him by surprise. "Do you have a challenge for me?"

"Indeed. All I have is a name; I want to know what it means. Four dead-drop agent searches have turned up nothing. They were three deep and they turned up nothing. I know you're better."

Emerson's eyes became even more animated. His hands actually waved and twitched slightly. "I do enjoy a challenge. There is, however, the matter of my fee."

He handed over a cash demand with so many zeroes on it Kim gasped. "Mike," she said privately to him, "I don't have close to that kind of—"

Mike fulfilled the demand with his own account and then released the information they had assembled earlier.

Her jaw fell open and she said out loud, "Where the hell did you get that kind of cash?"

Emerson chuckled. "So the king of *Warhawk* can still keep secrets, I see."

Warhawk. That was where this all started. A big piece of the puzzle fell into place. That was why he interrupted her in the tournament. He owned *Warhawk*. She'd been playing in his back yard.

Kim forced Mike's holo to manifest on the table in front of her. "You own *Warhawk*? The whole combat realm?"

People paid access fees, tournament fees, monthly subscriptions, rented guildhalls, and even paid for customizations, all to the owner of *Warhawk*. It was cheap, but there had to be a million members.

He curled his wings in tight and then lowered his head. "Yes?"

Mike wasn't turning her life upside down anymore; he'd put it on a spin cycle. "I have been using up my cash to pay your way! I bought you clothes! Pancakes!"

"It never seemed the right time to tell you."

"So your plan was to stand there in your stupid grape suit freeloading until I ran out of cash?"

"How was I supposed to know you were running out? That was a big bag you threw in the back of the car!"

"That's right, I even bought a damned car for you! I paid your rent!"

"Well, every time I thought to bring it up you were yelling at me for some other mistake I made because I couldn't read your mind, and then when you made me take back the ring I just figured—"

"Wait." Kim held up her hand as her heart stuttered. "That ring. You're telling me you *bought* it? For me?"

"What, did you think I stole it?"

Her face grew so hot pinpricks of sweat broke out on it. That was exactly what she thought, because that was what she would've done in his place.

"You actually thought I was stupid enough to put you, of all people, in danger? You never even considered…"

Kim asked softly, "Me, of all people?"

She caught herself rubbing her ring finger. She could feel it there, wanted it there, wanted him here, not just today but forever. Panic slashed through her like a whip. There was no way in hell she could possibly have these feelings, not now.

Not ever.

"Yes," Mike said, "of course you…"

She needed to see some sort of reaction in him, some sort of ac-knowledgement that he felt something, anything that might even be close to what she felt, but Mike's dragon face simply froze, then he vanished.

No, this wasn't happening. It couldn't. She wouldn't let it.

"Your offer is accepted," Emerson said, and rose to leave. "This is indeed a most worthy challenge." He turned and bowed deeply. "A word of advice, as I go. Buy some guns. Big guns."

He left, vanishing into the crowd much faster than Kim thought was possible.

Chapter 37
Spencer

The moment the wheels of the airplane touched down, Spencer popped his seatbelt free.

"As long as nobody runs us over on the way to the terminal, we'll be fine." He grinned at the sour faces of the people around him. They seemed to think saying it out loud would magically make a 747 run them over.

He still couldn't get over what had happened. Three days ago, he was just a miserable schlub from a town nobody'd ever heard of. Now, he'd met an outright legend. The first human-AI hybrid in the world owed him favors. He'd visited Pride's Lair! Spencer wanted nothing more than to get right back on the next plane to Dulles. The only thing that stopped him was the thought of how Kim would react. He'd only pissed her off accidentally. That was epic enough.

Time for plan B. He found a skycap coming off duty who was more than willing to buy shots for them both with Spencer's money. After a few rounds—okay a lot more than a few rounds—he summoned the BMW from the parking garage.

He staggered past a tour bus for *The Passion Play,* blowing cigarette smoke like a chimney. The choked outrage from the old biddies standing in front of it made his vodka-soaked heart dance. Ancient hypocrites had no business judging someone *who knew Angel Rage.*

"Shouldn't you be in school, young man?" the one at the end of the line scolded.

Spencer stopped and pulled down his sunglasses. "Shouldn't you get a job?" He walked away before she recovered enough to speak. Score: a direct hit.

Per Mike's instructions, Spencer hit the airport's realm right before he left to turn a fistful of constructs loose. They were like green dust. Spencer could've sworn he heard them hollering. Mike had said he hacked them together from one of Kim's tools, something called LockPixies.

Weirdly, the three sedans following behind his truck locked their tires, screeching to a halt. It immediately caused a traffic jam in front of the parking garage. The men inside were all frantically trying to open the doors. The wail of sirens echoed in the distance.

Those cars were following his truck for a reason.

Cops.

His BMW lurched forward like it'd been kicked, then skidded to a stop in front of him. The back door flew open and a message shot across his enhanced vision.

DON'T STAND THERE WITH YER GOB OPEN YA WEE GIT! GET IN!

Virtual men, none more than six inches tall, covered every horizontal surface of the truck's interior. They were dressed in skins and waved tiny spears, swords, and axes. Their skin color was a uniform deep green.

"What?" Spencer asked as he staggered backward.

"Ach!" the one standing on the steering column shouted. "That's jus' Will bein' dramatic. Come with us if ye wanna stay outta jail!" The accent was so thick Spencer could barely make out what he said, but the approaching sirens helped with the translation. He leapt through the door and they tore away in a cloud of tire smoke.

Spencer buckled in as soon as he stopped bouncing around. Two police cars were closing on opposite sides of a cross street.

"Nash! Daft Wally!" the one on the steering column shouted. "Take 'em down!"

The two the leader pointed at vanished. In less than a second, a black explosion erupted from underneath both vehicles; debris sprayed on the ground. They passed the cars and swerved to avoid transmission gears bouncing across the road.

Nash and Wally reappeared to tumultuous applause.

"What did you do?" Spencer asked.

"Ha!" said Nash or Wally, Spencer couldn't tell which was which. "They dinna work as well when they're in reverse and drive at the same time!"

"Have ye jammed their signals yet, Pry?" the leader shouted.

A new one crawled out of the truck's radio face. "Aye, Tavish, they'll not be callin' home from here!"

So, the leader's name was Tavish. At least that was shorter than Green Maniac Standing on the Steering Column.

They pulled up to the airport's exit. To Spencer's surprise, they didn't just blast through it. The truck slowed to a stop with Spencer's window opposite the attendant's.

"Stay cool, laddie!" Tavish said, "We din' wanna attract more attention than we hafta!"

Spencer muted their feed, but they were all still madly jumping and racing around as he handed cash to the attendant. It was beyond distracting.

"What the hell's going on back there?" Spencer asked.

"Beats me," the attendant replied, "can you get out to the EI?"

Spencer had a truck full of little green lunatics only he could see. There had to be some sort of connection, somehow. "Nah, mine just went. Maybe someone knocked down a tower?"

"No idea. Here's your change, have a nice day."

Spencer unmuted the feed and flinched at the shrieking howl that now dominated all other noises. "Jesus Christ, what the hell is that?"

"That's Car Jack, the finest haggis shagger there ever was, boy." Tavish had now manifested on Spencer's shoulder, but still had to shout into his ear to be heard over the bagpipes Car Jack was enthusiastically strangling.

Tavish turned and called out, "Oi! Pry! Didja shut down the airport too?"

The one in the radio stuck his head out again. "Aye! But I canna reach the ones in the air! No plane crashes today, boys!" Even the bagpiper stopped to join in the chorus of boos.

"What the hell are you guys? Some sort of demon smurf?"

The silence rippled away from Spencer as they all turned to face him.

"You'll be takin' that back, boy, if ye want our help attall," Tavish said.

"What? What did I say?"

"We are based on the fiercest of fantasy warriors, lad, not some poor excuse for a merchandise campaign! Asides, ken ya not see we're the wrong color?" They all bellowed their approval and set to work again. On the interstate, a pair of police cruisers flashed to life in the opposite lanes and then went dark as they coasted to a stop in the broad green median. A police helicopter settled with alarming speed onto a nearby field.

He was very glad they couldn't actually crash airplanes.

"Well done, Durell!" Tavish applauded as a new green maniac appeared through a portal. "But why didn't ya crash it inta the cars?"

"Och, bloody pilot switched to autorotate before I could tip the thing over." Spencer was getting better at understanding them. It only took a second to translate *afoore ahcood tup datting hoover*.

"So, what, you're all LockPixies?"

"No, laddie," Tavish shook his head. "They be our cousins, aye, but they're weak minded fools. Always mincin' about, spyin' and pryin'. Never takin' nothin', destroyin' nothin'. No, sonny, what our master Mike did was free us!" The gathering bellowed their approval. "He gave us a mission! Protect the chosen—that'd be you—and destroy!"

The blasted bagpipes started up then, almost overloading the channel with their racket.

Every fifteen minutes or so as they traveled out of Little Rock headed south, various law-enforcement vehicles would gracefully pull onto the highway behind them, follow briefly, and then—most of the time—gently coast to a stop on the side of the road.

Other times the tires would explode from out-of-control automatic inflation, or the previously noted two-gears-at-once transmission bomb would go off. The feds were the best. Pry Bar, the electronics expert, worked out that they hadn't patched the engine management system on their SUVs. He was able to screw the ignition timing up so badly the resulting explosion would blow the intake system off. It knocked a huge dent in the hood. Those were awesome.

Then the cops tried a roadblock. Pry picked it up as they entered Pine Bluff. "Aye, Master Spencer"—they started calling him that after he taught them the Diarrhea Song—"they're gettin' clever again."

"Och." Tavish clenched his jaw as he examined the maps with Spencer. "I knew they'd figger it out eventually. Right, lads, gather up."

It was only when they formed into ragged lines on the dash and seats that Spencer noticed a problem. There was a lot fewer of them than when they left the airport.

Tavish marched back and forth across the top of the front seats. "Men, we knew this time would come. Our enemy has gathered his strength in overwhelming numbers. There is no way to win."

They all shouted a chorus of boos.

Tavish wasn't having any of that. "But we shall prevail! We all knew there'd be no going home for any of us after this. A one-way mission, but what glory!"

The racket again threatened to overwhelm Spencer's channel.

"Aye," he said when the shouts died down, "we'll fight and die. Running won't get us anything. We're constructs"—more boos—"but if we succeed"—shouts of approval, a few fell off the dash—"this boy will have a chance to tell our enemies that they may take our lives, but they'll never take… OUR FREEDOM!"

The cheering was so loud it finally did cause Spencer's audio to cut out briefly.

When they crested the top of the railway overpass a few miles south of the city limits, cars covered the far slope, blocking the road completely.

Just before he arrived, though, each cruiser started up and slowly drove off the opposite edge of the hill. Cops whose cover had spontaneously removed itself were running everywhere, yanking on now-locked doors or dragging behind vehicles they couldn't pull to a stop.

Very few of the constructs returned. Naturally, though, the one with the bagpipes made it back. Spencer winced every time Jack turned a chord into a strangled turkey. "Tavish, can you make him stop?"

"Oi, and your surname is even McKenzie! Dinna the pipes stir ye very soul?"

"Not when it sounds like he's stirring a dying cat."

Jack's pipes honked into a dribbling silence.

Tavish's eyes narrowed. "I'll not have ye disrespect the pipes."

Spencer looked over the front seats. The chilled naked mud of soybean fields stripped to dirt hadn't changed a bit, but everything else in his life had.

"Tavish, how far did Mike overclock you guys?" He and Mike both wondered what a class five AI would be like if someone made them run faster than their contract specified.

The few dozen left all collapsed in laughter. "Master Mike warned us you'd ask that. No, laddie, we're not full AIs, just clever constructs programmed to enjoy a wee bit o' thievery. Master Mike said you could root us to be sure."

Everything in realmspace had a root prompt, except for Mike. It was like finding out your brother had no belly button. That was how Spencer finally believed he was for real and not just an unduplicate that'd somehow gotten loose.

"Really?"

"Yeah, ya Nancy, root us! C'mon, ya do know how?" They all jumped up and down again. Jack began blowing up his pipes.

"All right, fine. Command. Sudo," Mike set the password, so, "Password t-f-w-b-w-y-a. Accept."

They all hopped and were still.

Shit. There were feds right behind him.

"Command. Sudo exit. Accept."

They relaxed and cheered as Jack strangled a rendition of "Scotland the Brave."

"Damn it, all of you, stop!"

They weren't real, but they were Spencer's. He'd have to sacrifice them all to even hope to get out of this. The realization defined suck. These guys were a lot of fun.

"There's enough of you left to protect me?"

"Aye, laddie, but when they tail ye for more than two minutes, we're done."

Spencer climbed into the driver's seat and popped the truck off autodrive. As they passed the abandoned crop duster field on the edge of town, he floored the accelerator and sped away from his pursuers.

The meanies vanished one by one, but it gave him a miracle. Every time Spencer went screaming into an intersection, the cars would stop. A regular weekday morning, a school day of all things, and cars just parted in front of him. He blasted down the highway, turning on to side streets, driving into the old downtown, just to watch how cars moved away from him.

Eventually, Tavish was the only one left. "It's been a bonnie great run with ye, Master Spencer."

"Aye," Spencer replied, grinning at Tavish's reaction. "Do you have enough for one last run?" He knew, as he turned left on to South Main from Brookhaven Drive, that there was a flat straight at least three miles long in front of him. "I need a distraction, Tavish, and I don't want to die."

"Och, no, laddie. No, sirrah. I'll make sure you live through this." He saluted. "Sing our song, Spencer McKenzie. Sing our song and remember!"

Tavish vanished and Spencer stood on the accelerator. When he lifted his foot, the pedal stayed glued to the floor.

"Tavish," he called out to the empty cabin. The speed override button pressed itself down until the warning tone stopped. His velocity climbed higher and higher while the road seemed to stretch and narrow.

"Tavish!"

He briefly checked in the mirror behind him. A sea of flashing lights started winking out one by one. A line of trees directly ahead rose into view, his seatbelt grabbed him tight, and the speedometer hit 170 miles per hour.

"TAVISH!"

The crazy bastard was going to do it. For decades, teenagers had noticed the sudden rising left turn at the end of this road would make a perfect jump ramp. Now Spencer was going to do it.

"Well ye said ye wanted a distraction!" Tavish's voice rang out in his ears and then cut loose with a war cry that vanished into a sea of static. An ancient golf course flashed past on his right and the final banked left turn of the road rose up in front of him. Spencer's warbling cry picked up where Tavish's left off as he pulled his arms and legs in tight.

The impact was like the largest sledgehammer in existence crushed everything straight up. The violence of it was breathtaking as the seatbelt grabbed him tighter. The car went silent as its sensors felt the wheels leave the ground, then it ponderously rolled forward. He found himself looking up at an old black man standing next to a truck, jaw hanging open.

Then there was a confusion of cracking impacts, a final enveloping thump, and everything exploded in white. When all the airbags deflated, the cold brown water of Walnut Lake rushed in.

Spencer climbed out of the back window just as the nose of the truck hit the muddy bottom of the lake. It was the finest monument he could make to his small, green, chaotic helpers. He climbed up on the roof as the back of the truck settled onto the lakebed. With the water just over his ankles, Spencer raised his fists into the air in front of all the cops rushing to the edge of the shore, and howled out the cry of the lost.

Chapter 38
Mike

When Kim only said a few words to him after they exited Bards, it made things feel, well, normal. He'd gotten used to her being strangely pensive. The silence as they drove wherever they were going let him soak up actual reality.

He was finally coming to accept that the outside was more real than his home. But there were unwelcome surprises. Uncontrolled weather was a nasty discovery. It was one thing to understand the equations that made a butterfly's wings trigger a storm halfway around the world. It was another thing entirely to know he might be killed in a Virginia storm because a bug made a left turn in Tokyo. The real world randomly conspired to murder humans all the time, and they just called it weather.

The snow was melting. Water poured off every building around the parking lot. Not two nights ago, it'd been cold enough to freeze the rain before it hit the ground. Yes, realms could have weather, but there was always some sort of math behind it, something he could control if he wanted. Not out here.

"Is it always like this?"

"What do you mean?"

She wasn't terrified of the unplanned chaos millions of tons of atmosphere swirling around a rock spinning at a thousand miles an hour created. None of them were.

"It's not even noon yet and I don't need a jacket. The temperature changes are quite dramatic, don't you think?" It was so warm Mike rolled up his sleeves just to cool off. He marveled at the interplay of skin, muscle, and bone inside his arm. Nothing in realmspace prepared him for how many layers there were to a body. The way it all moved fascinated him when he gripped his fist tight.

Normally Kim would be growling at him by now.

"What? Did I say something wrong?"

She was staring at his arm, then coughed and turned away. "The weather's crazy. Welcome to Virginia in late February."

She put her coat in the car, then spread her arms wide. It was the first time he'd seen her in realspace wearing something other than a shapeless sweatshirt and baggy pants. The long-sleeved T-shirt clung to her in extremely distracting ways, especially when she breathed deep.

He stopped. Don't stare; women hate it. He'd read that; it was all over their periodicals. Talk about what's on the shirt; don't stare at what's in it. Fortunately, this time there was a word on the shirt. "What's a Gryffindor?"

"Suddenly you don't know how to search for anything?"

Great. Yet another mind-read fail. Now that he was outside and around one, the human male's understanding of women was truly impressive. Being honest and angry seemed to get the best result. "No, I'm sick of getting yelled at when I try a search. I just wait until you deign to give me the information."

"Until I deign? What the hell is that supposed to mean?"

Mike couldn't take another fight this morning, so he folded. "Nothing, Kim. Why are we here?"

"When someone tells me to buy big guns, I take them seriously." She pushed open the tinted glass door and walked in.

"Oh my God," the large bald man behind a display case full of pistols said. He peered over thick glasses. "Kim? Is that you?"

"Hi, Nick. How've you been?"

Nick barreled out from around the counter, quite nimble in spite of his size. He might be somewhere in his mid-sixties, wearing a holographic Hawaiian shirt and a holster on his hip, filled with a pistol almost as long as his arm.

Nick came at her with arms wide open. He got so close that Mike began to step in front of him. Nick stopped.

"Oh, wait! That's right!" He spun on one foot and jogged just as quickly back behind the counter, clapped his hands together, and threw two thumbs up at her.

She bubbled over with laughter. "It can learn!"

"That's not a mistake I'll ever make again. Hey, Steve," he called out to his left down a hall.

"What?" The voice was barking and raspy.

"Kim's back!"

Mike cringed inwardly at the way Kim relaxed. Being outside hadn't stopped him from being an outsider, an invisible presence. Then she turned and smiled at him without a hint of malice, and he understood. She brought him to another part of her past, in realspace no less, and wanted him to belong. He smiled back as best he could and swallowed the lump in his throat.

After a muffled curse and a few crashes, Steve came out of the office. He seemed to be roughly as old as Nick, and about as bald. Steve, however, was smaller, with a darker complexion and a narrower face. He also walked out with arms wide, stopped, and then made a slightly different, but no less cartoony, effort to get behind the counter with Nick, working a piece of gum quickly in his mouth. She laughed even harder when they both threw a thumbs-up at the same time.

The Davidson and Heyes Armory was otherwise empty.

"Okay," Mike said, "so that one's Davidson, and that one's Heyes?"

She pointed at the smaller of the two. "That one's *Heyes*," pronouncing his name with an *i* rather than an *e*.

"That one," she said, pointing at Nick, "is Davidson. They're the only two people in the world dumb enough to give a weird teenager with no references a job when she needed it. Is the cot still behind the filing cabinet?"

Nick said, "Nah, my grandson took it when we went camping last year."

"She was the only one who understood our *Shadowrun* references," Steve noted. "And we needed someone with small hands."

"And who's this?" Nick asked, nodding in Mike's direction.

The threads of his real consciousness flexed and flashed. The only other person she'd introduced him to was Tonya, who was part of her present. These two were from her past. He was becoming a part of someone else's life again, but it felt so different than it did with Spencer—more important, satisfying.

"Guys, this is Mike Sellars. He's thinking about competitive shooting as a hobby."

The phone in the office rang. Steve patted Nick on the shoulder and said, "All yours, bud."

He winked at Kim and went back to the office.

Just as Nick began speaking, Steve stuck his head out. "Lunch is on us today, get it?"

"Got it." She smiled and saluted him.

Nick took large pistols out of a display case. "So what've you been doing all this time, Kim?"

"Oh, this and that."

Nick rolled out a deep chuckle. "Jesus, Kim, it's me, and it's been years. You won't talk about what's happened *since* we met you?"

She didn't like talking about her past. Mike changed the subject. "So, what are these?"

"Target pistols, sir. We carry all the major makes. Which one are you most comfortable with?"

His hands wanted to move across everything, but not what Nick had out. The rest of the guns, all of them really, were calling to him.

"Mike?" Kim asked.

"Just how new is he to all this?" Nick asked.

He knew them all. In some incomprehensible way, he knew exactly how each and every one of these guns worked. How to take them apart, clean them, reassemble them, and shoot them. It was like a massive door had unlocked in his psyche.

Kim said, "It's complicated. He just got out of the hospital."

"Really," Nick asked, "what happened?"

Kim said, "Boating accident—"

Mike said, "Light fixture hit my head—"

She glared at him.

Fine, whatever.

"Boating accident," he said.

"Light fixture hit his head," she said.

Nick looked nonplussed and pushed his glasses up on his nose. "You do realize he'll have to pass a background check."

Kim nodded. "A light fixture hit him on a boat. It was touch-and-go for a while. It's affected his memory."

Nick crossed his arms. "Okay."

"It's easier for me to show you," Mike said as he scanned the cases. Agents rocketed back and forth through his threads in the datastorm that swirled to life. On one level, he knew all of the weapons in the shop, even the knives and saps, but only as realmspace constructs. He couldn't touch constructs, yet he knew exactly what every weapon in the room felt like.

"That one," Mike said, pointing at a Colt 1911 pistol. "Can I see that one?"

Nick's expression made it clear Mike wasn't the only one confused and suspicious about what was happening in his head. Nick pulled out the pistol, checked it, and handed it over.

"I don't remember ever holding one of these in my life." The truth was always the best. "But I can do this."

Mike relaxed and let the chemicals of his new existence interface with his native threads. It was easier to close his eyes; the integration locked together effortlessly that way. He disassembled the weapon, laying out the parts in a precise sequence, paused for a second, and reassembled it. The speed made it sound more like typing. When he was done he clicked the trigger on the empty chamber.

"Kim," Nick asked as he covered his face with his hand, "where the hell do you find these people?"

She sighed. "I don't. They find me."

"Well," Nick said, "you're definitely better at that than I am."

For the first time, he felt so creepy about it all. They weren't his skills; they were the skills of a dead man.

"Hey," Kim said softly. "It's okay."

When he turned to her, she blushed and put her hands in her pockets.

Mike said to Nick, "As far as my memory goes, I've never handled a gun in my life."

She turned back to him, eyes flashing at the shared joke.

"Well," Nick replied, "we have lots of guns and lots of time." He reached back and grabbed an AR-15 variant. "I'll bet your hands will know what to do with this one."

He'd done well enough with the AR, but finding anything else was much harder. For whatever reason, the integration got stopped up. It felt clogged, like it was held under a different level, some other section of memory he couldn't access. Eventually, Kim and Nick left him alone in the lobby to hide in the otherwise empty shooting range just behind it.

As he prowled the racks, the intercom hissed to life. "Mike," Nick's voice called out from the speakers, "do the thing with the AR again."

Steve stood behind the small glass window that separated the gun range from the lobby, with Nick and Kim behind him. Mike waved and walked over to the assault rifle lying on the counter. He took a deep breath, closed his eyes, then did a field strip and reassemble of the gun as fast as he could. This time, without understanding why, he twirled it twice, slapped the stock against the floor, and briefly stood at attention.

"What was that?" Steve's voice shouted through the speakers.

"Hell if I know, Steve. Ask her."

"He had an accident," Kim said, "and now all he has is muscle memory. We're trying to figure out which rifles he actually knows. He's been trying to find them on his own, but it's slow."

Nick and Steve looked at each other. "Nah," Steve shook his head. "We got this."

At Steve's direction, the rest of them pushed racks of hunting clothes and accessories to the edges of the showroom. Nick stood behind Mike, and Kim was behind Steve, about eight feet apart. A stack of rifles was at her feet.

Steve weighed two of them in his hands. "I think we know how to help. We were researching how memory therapy could leverage the neural interfaces in phones at Walter Reed before we retired. Kim, do you know if he was in the military?"

She got that far away, haunted look. Mike knew she was remembering the predator, remembering Colque. It made him feel like a monster, but only for a moment. Colque obviously had talents, but he'd wasted them on evil ends. Colque was gone now. Mike wouldn't make that mistake.

She shook herself back to the present. "No, at least not while I've known him."

He sent Mike an app. "You move like you're military. You handle guns the same way. That flourish you did after you assembled the AR was straight out of a rifle drill routine. We need to get at a deeper level of your subconscious, a place of old memories and routines. Upload the app and run it in ring three."

The elevated permissions would give it access to more biomedical data, but nothing sensitive or dangerous. New overlays drew into Mike's enhanced vision as it installed and activated.

"Now what happens?" he asked.

Steve hefted an M14. The weight of the large wood and steel rifle made it move more slowly than any of the others Mike had tried.

"Steve," Nick said, "don't mess it up this time."

"Trust me," and then without warning he threw the rifle underhanded at Mike. The clack registered before he even understood he'd caught it. More blockages fell away as the app helped new matrices lock into neural pathways. Mike twirled the rifle back to Steve, who caught it in his opposite hand and spun it before tossing it back at Mike.

Pathways continued to integrate in an interplay of chemo-quantum crystallization.

As Mike spun the rifle, Steve said, "Kim, hand me the other one."

His heart, already pounding, jumped up another notch as his body dumped a gallon of adrenaline into his bloodstream. They were tossing the rifles at each other in an intricate ballet. That's the only way he could put it, a kind of dance with weapons. But he didn't falter. He got better. He caught the rifle behind his back and twirled it. He was now able to spare enough concentration to see Steve, whose smile just kept getting bigger as the rhythmic routine got faster and they stepped closer to each other.

At a certain point in the routine, Mike's instincts said to move beside Steve, spinning the rifles in lockstep. As one, they completed three precise, identical moves and with a tap of rifle butts hitting the floor, they finished. Both held still for a heartbeat.

"God, I need a cigarette!" Steve shook hands with Mike, grabbed a pen, then chewed on it fiercely. He leaned against a glass counter, panting. "He's Bolivian."

Mike's newly integrated processes almost fell apart. He and Kim both cried out together, "What?"

"I helped develop the routine for them. They sent a contingent of their Navy guys to learn the moves, say eighteen, maybe twenty years ago." He nodded at Mike. "I don't recognize him, but I bet I'd recognize who trained him. Next time we'll have to try it with bayonets mounted."

And that's how the next hour went. Nick picked a used rifle and Steve tossed it at Mike. If Mike caught it without thinking, it went into the positive pile. If everyone went scrambling to find where it'd buried itself in the improvised padding, it went into the negative pile.

They thought they were healing a wounded soldier's memory. He hoped someday to tell them the truth.

Lunch arrived just after they finished putting the store back the way it had been in the morning. They sat around the break room table as Nick set out the boxes. Mike bit into his first slice a little too fast and had to grab a drink to cool things off. Each meal Kim brought him revealed nested wonders. Like everything else about her, it also brought the occasional wound.

"So," Mike said, nursing a mild burn against the roof of his mouth. It was hot, spicy, crispy, and chewy, all at once. "This is pizza?"

Nick laughed. "That must've been some light fixture."

They spent the rest of the day zeroing in on what he knew best. Kim already had a pistol and for whatever reason, Mike couldn't let go of the .45. The assault rifles surprised them, though. They were exactly like the constructs Spencer had geeked out over the night before.

"It's an FN SCAR-H Mark 34 chambered for a .338 caseless Lapua round with a fifty round magazine."

She laughed. "And now we have a realspace pair too."

He smiled. "I thought he was gonna pass out when you told him about the second one at the lair."

As the day progressed, customers started coming through. A few even remembered Kim, who'd taken up position behind the register. She was at ease and charming, expertly handling each transaction without even the hint of a touch. She was so good at it nobody else seemed to notice. How she was able to be so pleasant with strangers, yet so angry with people she knew was just another deeply puzzling thing about her.

Steve went past Mike. "Walk with me." He exited the shop without turning back.

They walked around the side to where Nick leaned against a dumpster, smoking a cigar.

"Have a seat, Mike." Nick motioned to a rusty folding chair behind the dumpster.

Sitting confirmed what he already suspected: the only people who could see him now were Steve and Nick. And their guns. It occurred to him that the woods behind the shop might have more than one function.

"The truth is," Nick said amiably, "we like you. You're weird, but honest."

He leaned down, close enough Mike could smell his aftershave over the leafy reek of the cigar. The interplay would've been fascinating if Nick hadn't been so deadly serious. And armed.

"How long have you really known Kim?"

The answer slid out before he had time to consider it. "She says we've known each other for a long time, but I only remember a few days." Another truth, from a certain point of view.

Nick and Steve shared a look.

Steve asked, "How much do you know about her?"

"The touching thing?" Their reaction told him he'd guessed right. Mike checked the sides of his stomach. The bruises were still a bit tender. "Trust me, sir, I know all about that. How did you guys meet her?"

Nick puffed a few times on his cigar. "She was homeless when we found her. Well, when she found us. Wandered out of the woods back there when I opened the store, must've been about five years ago. All she'd say was things had gone wrong for her. She never shook our hands, never came near us at all. When those phone-based sights came on the market, they were insanely popular and unreliable as hell. We needed someone with small hands.

"She was concentrating too hard on a repair one day. I accidentally snuck up on her, grabbed her shoulder. Kim wrenched my arm nearly out of its socket, trashed the repair bench, and then had a huge seizure. Scared the hell out of all of us."

Steve nodded. "She never talked about it again. We never questioned it."

"Why not?" Mike asked.

He shrugged. "Girl doesn't want to be touched, we don't touch her. It was none of our business as long as she did the job. Kim lived in the office until she'd saved up for a rent deposit. We tried to pay that for her, but when she found out, well, her reaction became my model for poor anger management."

Mike smiled and saw it mirrored theirs. He wasn't quite as worried about their guns anymore.

"I caught some cagey guys casing the place about two years later. They had to be the dumbest criminals in the world, trying to work out how to rob a gun store. When I told Kim about it she turned white as a sheet and walked out the door. Just walked right out. We never saw her again until today. Any idea why?"

Kim's paranoia had dovetailed neatly with his own. They both had secrets to keep, things nobody else would believe. "No, not really."

Nick tipped the ash off his cigar. "That's an interesting choice of words. We already checked, and you're clean. But that doesn't mean much. What happens if we ask some of our law enforcement buddies about who you really are?"

How easily the truth fit. "I honestly don't know. I can't remember past a few days ago. But I do know this, if you guys ask about me, it might call attention to her." He made sure they were both paying attention. "I think that might be bad."

Nick grunted and pulled the pistol out of his holster. "Fair enough," he said as he dropped the clip and thumbed bullets out, one by one, into his pocket. "But if you hurt her, in any way," he cleared the chamber, shoved the empty magazine in, then let the slide lock as Steve walked up behind him. "The next time I unload this weapon, it'll be into you."

Mike shook his head and laughed. "You guys know you're not the first person to tell me this, right?"

His relationship with the two men sort of faded back to normal as they all walked into the lobby, just a bunch of guys talking over a smoke.

Kim's smile vanished when she saw Steve and Nick behind him. "Christ, don't you two ever let up?" She'd taken over the store like she worked there, which only made sense.

"Nah," Steve said. "He's good. Spent enough money too."

Nick examined the final bill. "More than enough money. Kim, you bring him around whenever you want, okay?"

She checked the time. "I will, but we need to get cleaned up and start thinking about supper."

Mike felt a kind of camaraderie with Steve and Nick. He wasn't alone trying to figure out how to get along with her. Behind their eyes, he recognized the scars they'd earned trying.

They waved and Nick shouted, "Take good care of her, Mike!"

He laughed and waved back.

After the door closed, she said, "What the hell is that supposed to mean?"

Chapter 39
Watchtell

Matthew Watchtell held his hands over his head and waited for the applause from the virtual crowd to die down.

"Thank you, ladies and gentleman." Standing behind a podium, whether in a real ballroom or a virtual one like this, was as natural to him as coaching or leading.

Or conquering.

Even though its founder had given the Rose Foundation a tremendous head start, there was always a need for more money. Fundraising required donors, and donors required proof of progress. Hence this banquet.

"Ladies and gentlemen, we stand at the foot of a new sort of justice. When I was a boy, I saw China rise from the gutters. I saw Russia rise from the gutters. I saw India rise from the gutters. Everyone ignored Africa. That changes, today. Today, with the funds and technology of the West, we will bring houses to the people, the people who, after all, are the ancestors to us all."

Watchtell motioned, and live cameras near a Masvingo village broadcasted hazmat-suited workers as they knocked over oil barrels into the bush, well away from anyone unprotected. The construction nanomachines used the most effective building materials nearby. They could be aggressive, even ruthless in finding what they needed.

He'd discovered this the hard way by insisting the first live trial of the construction technology was in front of the children who would attend the school his nanomachines built. Watchtell had pushed for a showy triumph, only to have the machines harvest the children for the rare minerals in their bodies. The bribes to cover up the fiasco set the program back years.

At least this time the demonstration was in the dark. The spotlights would shut off if anything went truly wrong.

The sparkling gray ooze sluiced into nearby dirt piles and set to work. For this demonstration, those piles of dirt cost more than the finished building, but the image was the thing. The nanomachines swirled together, climbed onto the piles, then rapidly created a house. The workers stood back, and the murmurs of approval washed over him.

The family walked hesitantly into the construct. It'd taken four rehearsals in a local studio to work out which camera angles would be least likely to catch their terrified faces. The man-eating houses were a secret here at home, but Watchtell couldn't stop the rumors in the rural African villages they were targeting.

Shaman and headmen always wanted the latest toys, always insisted the rich white men build a house for them first. He thought the failures killed two birds with one stone: a new house appeared; a corrupt warlord or priest vanished. The body was part of the solution. Unfortunately, superstition dovetailed with rumor and now it was getting difficult to find volunteers.

He turned to the virtual crowd of benefactors as the feed faded from view. This time, according to the techs anyway, the machines would be dead before they had time to consume the new residents. No matter. The technology was mostly safe now. Once perfected, no family in the world would be without a modern home. Really, what was the death of a few dozen—or even hundred—people compared to that? The survivors would never see another infant die of exposure. He was saving their children. Even better, the admixtures did far more important things than just build houses.

As Watchtell mingled, a new channel opened into his perception. "Good news this time, Gary?"

"Blacksteel has agreed to our terms."

As well they should. He could build six new factories with what they'd paid the private security firm to run down Angel Rage. Freelancers were so much more effective than police.

"And our other associates?"

"They refuse to speak to me. Adelmo is in Reston." Gary transmitted the contact address.

His closest, most effective allies usually never were more than two steps behind him. Adelmo quite rightly suspected sunrise was too convenient at killing the stupid—poor or rich—to be an accident. If he ever assumed power, there was a real chance one of the most effective Darwinian poisons ever designed would cease production, at least in the quantities required for maximum effect. As long as the nephew was in charge, that aspect of the plan would at least continue.

Watchtell put on his best game face and placed a call. "*Señor* Quispe. How could you not seek my hospitality when you are so close to my home?"

Adelmo looked at him like a scraping off the bottom of his shoe. Such a lovely man. Watchtell had never found an angle to exploit and the few times he tried, Adelmo had turned the tables in a heartbeat. Next to Angel Rage, he was probably the most dangerous person in Watchtell's world.

"I do not have time for such pleasantries. It has come to my attention you may have access to certain," Adelmo paused for a moment, "resources which may help me find our old nemesis."

"Indeed I do, sir. She's making mistakes again. Finally."

"Oh," Adelmo said as he smiled, "she's done much more than that. She's making miracles now."

Adelmo couldn't know about Sidereal. Watchtell had kept that secret so close not even Gary knew all the implications. He swallowed as Adelmo's smile grew wider. Adelmo was fishing and he'd hooked Watchtell with infuriating ease. He'd start looking, now that he knew Watchtell had something to hide. Yet another thing to keep Sidereal busy with. He accessed the secret console that controlled it and set the alarms.

A distraction was in order. "I can find her for you."

Adelmo laughed. "If you could do that, sir, she'd be dead already."

"I didn't know Rage was in the area." It seemed lame even to him, but it was the truth. "The next time she walks in front of a camera, we'll know."

Adelmo's image leaned in close. "You can actually tap secure video feeds now?"

Watchtell kept his face neutral, but only just. The thought of Rage being this close, at this moment, made him stumble into revealing secrets nobody else should know. One way or another, he would bring her to heel. "What I can or cannot do is of no concern. Now that I know she's near, I will find her. Will your men be ready?"

"No one is so brave that he is not disturbed by the unexpected."

Caesar this time, naturally. Adelmo always spoke in riddles. Touching on Rage's trademark chaos just made it worse.

"Good. Once we find her I'll contact you immediately."

Adelmo ended the call without so much as a nod.

Chapter 40
Tonya

She recalibrated the field scanners and adjusted the immobilizer on her patient's wrist so it would hold tight without pinching. "Now, open it slowly."

Her third limb-regrowth patient, one retired Lieutenant Colonel Robert Murphy, grimaced at the effort. "You'd think I'd remember how to do this better."

Not all her soldiers were overachievers, but this one absolutely was. It was a very good sign, because growing a new hand was even more demanding than learning how to live without one.

"You lost it in Afghanistan how long ago?"

Lt. Col. Murphy blew out a long breath as he closed the hand again. "It'll be twenty-two years this April."

"And now open it again."

When she graduated nursing school, the FDA had only just approved limb regrowth. Her mentor Walter had connections that got her into the very first therapeutic training classes. The textbooks gave Tonya migraines for months, but it made her one of the few VA nurses in the area qualified to do the work. Not bad for an ex-streetwalker from Philly.

"We've found it takes about a week of therapy for every two years of limb loss for things to get synced and back to normal." She checked her patient calendar in the corner of her eye. "You're actually well ahead of schedule."

"I'm motivated. My first grandchild is due in just two more months. I can't tell you how much I want to hold her with both my hands."

With a few exceptions, her patients were from the last serious conflicts the US had been involved in, so even the youngest of them were now well into their forties. Typically, they wanted to shake the hands of their high school graduates or walk them down the aisle. Lt. Col. Murphy was older than that, but not by much. A granddad. Good for him.

"Well," she replied, "you're right on schedule. Let's hope that baby knows to do the same. Now, one more time."

After he left, Tonya checked her own schedule. She had enough time to reconfigure the exercise room and finish her calls.

Annie Lao was the last Phoenix Dog on her contact list. "Yes, Annie, Kim's safe."

Annie's face flipped from concerned to happy in an instant. "Oh thank God. What happened?"

Tonya hesitated over the controls for a moment. "You know, I'm not completely sure. It didn't even occur to me to ask. She'll tell us at the meeting tonight, I guess. Anyway, I was distracted by something more important."

Annie was the only member of the team Tonya could be certain wouldn't blab the news.

The weirdest part was that Mike wasn't the weirdest part.

"What could be more important than that?"

"I think Kim has a boyfriend."

It seemed even less believable when she said it out loud. It just couldn't happen. There was no way Kim could have that sort of intimacy.

Hating someone else's touch was something she and Kim both had in common when they first met. Tonya's problem came from the years she'd spent on the streets in Philly and what she'd had to do to survive. After her mentor Walter had gotten her into a stable life, things were better, but she still couldn't stand even shaking a man's hand. Kim had helped her more effectively than any therapist or priest ever had.

Kim couldn't stand anyone's touch, but she still lived in the real world. There was no avoiding the occasional bump or scrape. She taught Tonya how to meditate, almost instantly, and make the horror go away. After a few weeks of practicing, Tonya found she could touch men again without gagging.

Kim's problem was so deep and mysterious. All Tonya could do was pray, which she did at church every Sunday.

Then Mike got out of that car with her. Spencer was easier to understand. Kim picked up strays like him all the time in the realms—kids with talent and brains who needed a good kick in the pants to point them in the right direction. Miss Trayne was quite good at kicking ass.

Mike was something else entirely.

Annie blinked twice and shook her head. "Okay, now I know you're screwing with me. Kim? An actual boyfriend? Not in a million years."

The gossip girl inside Annie got the better of her. "How do you know?"

"I met the guy."

It was always fun to poke at Kim and her temper, but flirting with Mike took it to a whole new level. The only thing Kim didn't do was raise her leg and pee on him. If she'd had a tail, it would've swished like a ticked off cat.

"He's funny, really sweet, but kinda weird." Tonya wanted to explain just how weird he was, but Spencer had told her about Mike's true nature in confidence. She was still trying to get her head around the idea.

Annie rolled her eyes. "Her boyfriend is weird? It's Kim, duh."

Tonya was the only one of the Phoenix Dogs who'd met Kim in realspace. The rest of them were intensely curious about their charming leader, but they'd all learned the hard way that insisting on a realspace meet was like banging on a bomb with a crowbar. After they picked the shrapnel out of their hair, they either chalked Kim's reclusiveness up to general übernerdiness or fell into bizarre conspiracy theories.

Tonya didn't understand those even after they explained them to her. Kim was a hacker, that part she told Tonya about a long time ago, but the rest was just ridiculous.

There was no way Kimberly Trayne could ever be Angel Rage.

Chapter 47
Kim

She knew they had to start stupid early to get to the restaurant before it got crowded. Eating out was the most complex social skill she'd ever managed to master, but only when the places were deserted. Booths were tight, stools were always in the wrong place, and sometimes people would kick their foot out at the wrong time. Nobody ever noticed how shoulders or knees touched just sitting down. But she'd figured it out, now it was paying off.

Kim walked out of her room in fresh clothes and stopped, barely hiding a grin. It took her ages to find an outfit that complimented Mike's skin tone. AI or not, shopping with a man for shoes was like trying to teach a goat differential equations—except a goat probably complained less. But as she sized him up, she had to admit Mike looked good. Really good.

Then he dropped another one of his question-bombs on her.

"Why do you dress like that?"

Once again, he pulled the rug out from under her feet. She dressed safe. Sweatshirts and baggy pants, no makeup and hair pulled back until her face went tight.

"What's wrong with the way I dress?" It made her sound like she was twelve.

Mike sat down. "All you've ever used in the realms is your default avatar. You're beautiful, so why do you dress nice in the realms, but in realspace you never wear anything but sweatshirts and ragged pants?"

He'd said it as a simple fact, an observation no different than "the sky is blue."

He thought she was beautiful.

This had to stop. She was trying to play two groups of homicidal maniacs against each other and could not deal with this distraction.

"Kim?"

She just wanted to be alone in her weird little bubble, but that set everyone else off. They were so interested in how weird she was, when all she wanted was to be alone. It was the best Kim could hope for, really. But she wasn't sitting on a bench in a gym trying to eat lunch by herself. Mike wasn't a bully who could send her to the ER with a touch.

Kim collapsed onto the couch and hid under her hair. "It's complicated, okay?"

She spent her life building walls. She was good at building walls. There was no need to explain anything. Explaining left her vulnerable. She had no time to be vulnerable.

The words fell out anyway. "I can't be seen. I have to hide, be invisible, so I don't become real to you, any of you." She closed her eyes. "If I'm not real, you won't touch me. I hate it, but I can't stop it."

Kim grabbed the roll of paper towels sitting on the coffee table. "God," she said as she tore one off and blew her nose into it. "This sounds insane when I say it out loud."

If she gave in to this small vulnerability, maybe the big one would just go away.

She had to make the big one go away.

"But why is it so different in the realms?"

"I don't know, I really don't. I can touch people there, but it's more than that. It's just different. I'm so completely free there. If I didn't have the realms, I would've gone crazy years ago. Well, crazier. But it doesn't work out here."

Just thinking about the madness, the agony, of a single touch turned her stomach. Invisible shapes would crawl around under her skin and threaten her mind.

"Kim."

He was about to say something horrible. They always said something horrible, because she deserved it. She was weird and nobody could possibly understand the reasons. The pain was excruciating. Kim looked up.

"I see you, and you're safe."

It took a second before she could breathe again. *She had no time for this.*

"Gah!" she said, breaking his gaze. "Fine!"

After levering herself up, Kim headed for her room. "If it means you'll put away those awful puppy-dog eyes, fine. They make you look really stupid, you know?"

She closed the door and walked to the closet.

"Okay," she said out loud to no one. "Let's do this."

Makeup was a lot harder to put on when you actually had to put it on. Zits and warped eyebrows didn't happen there. All she had to do was pick colors that snapped onto her avatar's face.

When Kim was fourteen, she and her mom had epic screaming matches about the need for grooming and makeup. She had to admit the lessons were finally paying off. Her mom would never let her hear the end of it. Kim thanked the gods of nanotech for MiracleHose even as she struggled into them; the weather this time of year could swing wildly and their automatic adjustments would keep her comfortable.

With that finished, she went into her closet. She bought the outfit after another languid dance with her boyfriend Mr. Bourbon one lonely winter night last year. A dress, an actual dress. It was short, tight, and navy blue with strange dark patterns sewn across it. She'd shoved the thing into the bottom of the bugout bag precisely because she never wanted to see it again. Kim had forgotten all about the thing until she took Mike shopping. Designer boots that would be a perfect match were on sale, seventy-five percent off!

She'd snuck them into the cart when he wasn't looking, and now that she had them on in realspace, congratulated herself on the find. Even with the low heels, he'd still be taller.

When Kim was done, she stood and gazed into the mirror. The patterns on the dress interfered with the screens her security programs threw across her vision. It was so bad she had to turn them off to see. After Kim blinked away the after-images, she smiled; Mike wasn't the only one who cleaned up well.

Her racing heart was bad enough, but when she thought about going out in public dressed like this, it made her gulp like a fish. The door beckoned, but she wasn't sure she could open it.

Chapter 42
Mike

How long would it take for her to finish getting ready? He checked the time and resolved to wait it out.

He waited a whole lot more.

When Mike had finished counting the cracks in the baseboards a third time, he tried Spencer's phone. He should've gotten home hours ago, but there was still no answer. Mike checked the area's news.

INFOBOMB ORIGINATED AT CLINTON NATIONAL AIRPORT
ENTIRE STATE SHUT DOWN IN TERROR
REALMSPACE CRASHED, YOUR CHILDREN COULD BE NEXT

Oh great. Mike's greens had to be responsible for that. Spencer had only ticked Kim off by being stupid; Mike had actually stolen LockPixies from her and hacked them. Her constructs.

He had to fix this, right now.

He found Spencer wearing a blanket, sitting in a bare room with a giant mirror on one side. Spencer, in an interrogation room. Direct police involvement with someone who might be linked to Kim—the situation just kept getting better and better. Mike shut down the microphones and accessed the intercom.

"Dude."

Spencer's head shot up.

"Wait. They can't hear us, but they can still see you, so stay cool. I have to clean this up before Kim finds out."

Spencer's eyes flared. Mike knew the shiver wasn't from the cold.

"Are you okay?"

Spencer nodded slowly, twice.

"Excellent! I've got this. And it's just between us, right?"

He nodded once more. The fear on his face matched the way Mike felt. Kim could not find out about this. Terror took on a completely new meaning when he had adrenal glands to boost the signal.

He'd impressed her by calling hundreds of people all at once. But really, that was just a shrug of his shoulders. This would be a workout.

He sat back and relaxed as the creaking hawsers of his new life loosened their ropes. For the first time since he'd come outside, his real mind split, split, and split again, becoming stars shooting across the realms, hunting. It felt so good, so natural, to be in his real home. The limits were gone. The tearing confusion that'd slammed him in the hotel room had vanished.

There weren't many of his green constructs left, but they unleashed mayhem wherever they settled. His thousands reached out all at once. The green motes screamed like sparks from fireworks and snapped at the ends of his threads. Each one vanished in pixelated defiance, shouting tiny war cries as they went.

He just managed to squash the last of the constructs when there was a sound near his outside singularity. Finally, he had a definition for it. In the realms he was everywhere at once, but in realspace he was singular. A singularity. It took some time for him to coalesce enough of his consciousness to realize the noise was Kim, trying to get his attention.

Mike centered into realspace and opened his eyes. It took a moment to recognize her. Then things got a lot more complicated, and, well, *louder*.

As his threads scrambled to cope with the demands of his realspace analysis, an extraordinary series of emotions shot to the surface. Mike didn't want to compliment her, or say nice things about her dress. He wanted to own her, possess her, fiercely.

The realization did more than startle; it snapped loose a new kind of panic. Blood chemistry showed nominal but with a massive spike of testosterone. He was staring. He couldn't believe how uncontrolled his reactions were. All of his predictions, threads, and knowledge were useless swimming in this out-of-control soup. It had to be a mistake to walk all over her with his eyes, but her smile kept getting wider.

"You can breathe now," she said.

Only then did he notice half the semi-voluntary daemons had gone offline. He rebooted them and breathed deep.

Kim shivered and turned away. "Come on, Tonto, before I lose my nerve."

*

The curb was a solid block of stone, rounded from nothing more than water, wind, feet, and centuries. A layer of cobblestones probably more than three hundred years old disappeared under the asphalt of the street, like black frosting over a rocky cake. Larger stone blocks squatted close to the curb at irregular intervals down the brick sidewalk. Horse-drawn carriages once parked close to them so passengers could step down to the street.

He touched one just to prove it was real. Out here, history wasn't something read about or recreated. Standing on this street, the only thing that separated Mike from colonial America was time.

He examined the worn building in front of him. "How often do they have to repaint shutters to get them to look like that?"

Kim smiled at him in the twilight. "This is Old Town, Mike, they call it that for a reason." She switched to a posh English accent. "Your princess gives you permission to investigate the question."

They laughed and talked about the sights as they walked to the restaurant. Mike glanced at a security camera, but didn't bother pointing it out. Their destination was only a few blocks away.

"So," he said as they stood in front of the small, rustic restaurant. "It's a Tolkien reference, right?"

She rolled her eyes. "You'd think with all the realms dedicated to Bag End you'd at least pick up on that."

"It's not like this place is dug into the side of a hill, you know."

The Bilbo Baggins restaurant fit neatly into the ground floor of an ancient house, nestled inside for the past forty years like an old cat on a chair. He could examine the effortless accuracy of realspace for hours.

Kim was staring at him. "What?"

"Oh, nothing."

He really needed to figure out how to get her to smile like that more often.

After the waitress took their orders Kim set her water glass down. "This has been bugging me since I met you."

"There's just one thing?"

She raised her eyebrow. "Okay, fair enough. Anyway, why Mike Sellars? No offense, but you don't have parents, right?"

The reminder of how out of place he truly was must've shown on his face. She shook her head. "No, wait. I'm sorry; I didn't mean anything by that. I'm just curious. Where did your name come from?"

He paused, trying to work out exactly where to start. "It's a tricky story to tell. My earliest memories are just pictures, disjointed flashes that slowly knitted together."

The waitress arrived with the bottle of wine Kim picked out and two glasses.

The flavor was another explosion, but where Guinness was an Irish hammer, the wine was a tangy caress. His body may have been a big bag of wet hormones, but it was equipped with an exquisite chemical analyzer. Just calling it *taste* was an incredible understatement. "Wow, this is much better than Guinness."

"Oh no, I'm not letting you get away this time. About your name?"

"Well, like I said, the very earliest things I remember don't make sense to me now, maybe because the quantum fabric just wasn't elaborate enough. I do clearly remember a feeling of emergence, of beginning to exist."

"You mean you can remember being born?"

"You can't?" Finally, he'd rendered her speechless, but the story was more important than scoring points. "I mean, I understand why infants can't remember the physical event, but you're saying you don't remember when you became yourself?"

She shook her head. "Nobody can. My earliest memories sound a lot like yours, but I could never point to a calendar and say that was when I became me. Humans don't work that way. What did it feel like?"

"It was a kind of gluing together, an assembling. It was like someone dumped a jigsaw puzzle out and the pieces fell into place by themselves." It was so easy to tell her these things. All Spencer did was roll his eyes. She was different. She cared.

The next part wasn't as easy to talk about. "Once I understood my own existence, I couldn't reach out to other people. I didn't know how. I couldn't escape where I'd been born. I was so lonely. Eventually Emerson found me."

Her disgust was obvious. "Emerson found you when you were a *child*?"

She didn't really know how weird the man they'd met back at Bards was. If she did, her reaction would've been stronger.

"It's complicated. I'm not sure I was ever a child. At least, not in the way you were. But at least he paid attention. It didn't take long for me to realize how crazy it was. A few weeks.

"Emerson never even tried to give me a name, but he did teach me how to travel the realms. Eventually I struck out on my own, and that's when the second person I ever met found me."

He'd never been able to tell this to anyone, had never been able to articulate so much sadness, so much solitude. "It was a midnight Christmas mass. I was watching from the corner of the Old Saint Peter's realm when I saw an old man in orange robes. He sat in the front row, staring straight at me." Mike leaned forward. "Kim, nobody saw me back then, not without an explosion at any rate. I couldn't believe it."

She smiled gently and poured another glass for them both.

"And there he was, staring at me. Then he did the strangest thing." He paused as the memory traced complicated filigrees through his threads. Then it did so much more. It swirled and found channels into his realspace consciousness. His outside body grew warm and calm as he recalled that one deeply sad, incredibly critical moment.

Joy had so many more layers out here.

Kim nodded and riffed on Spencer. "Shit, Mike, don't stop now."

He laughed. "He scooted to the side and motioned for me to sit next to him. I couldn't believe it. When I got close he said, 'Do not fear,' with this really weird accent. 'Center, and concentrate.' And I did. That was the first time I manifested a hologram without nuking the whole realm. His name was Taranathi. He was so peaceful."

"Wait." Kim set her glass down. "You mean to tell me, on the advice of an old man in an orange dress, someone you'd never met before, you took a chance on nuking an entire Christmas mass just to pull up a seat?"

"I know it sounds reckless, but the thing is, I was desperate." It took a second before he could say it out loud. "The truth is, I was dying."

"What?"

He nodded. "I didn't know it at the time, but I need boundaries to stay sane, to exist, and I hadn't learned how to set them. While I was stuck around that old Pripyat realm, it gave me a natural boundary. After I escaped, I started to dissolve. I don't think I would've lasted even the rest of that night if Taranathi hadn't been there."

For the first time he had the courage to admit the truth. "I'd gone there to die."

Kim's eyes glistened.

He had to break the awkward silence. "Taranathi started calling me Michelangelo."

She dabbed her eyes with a napkin. "So that's your real name?"

"Not really. It didn't seem right to me, but then I read *The Moon is a Harsh Mistress*."

After a pause, Kim coughed out a laugh. "Oh my God, that's right. One of the characters, the AI—"

He nodded. "Is named Mike. It was such a perfect fit."

"But why Sellars?"

A small hook high on the wall beside them led Mike into a fascinating reconstruction of the building's original wiring scheme. There were even remnants of gaslights in the ceiling.

Kim chuckled in the sudden silence.

"What?" he asked.

"When you see all these things for the first time, in a funny way, I do too. What's so fascinating about that hook?"

He pointed out the traces as their food arrived.

"So," she asked as they worked through the second half of their dinner, "where did your last name come from?"

"Hagatha was the person who gave me my last name."

"Not *the* Hagatha? The psychic?"

He nodded. "I think her real name is Alice or Sharon or something."

"Didn't she call out names, talk to the dead, stuff like that?"

"That's her. She'd just built Séance and seemed like such a nice lady. I was fascinated, but I couldn't work out how she could hear those people. I saw no evidence."

Kim smiled wryly. "Because there wasn't any?"

"None that I could ever find. Anyway, one day she called out someone's name and well, I answered."

"What happened?"

"She passed out."

Kim started laughing.

"No, really! I'd tapped her medical monitors at that point. Her heart rate spiked and then she dropped into this big heap on the floor; you couldn't see her because of all the robes, right there on live TV!"

Kim held her sides and waved her hands.

"I had no idea people's eyes could get that big."

She stopped with a gasp. "Wait, I remember that! I remember seeing that! No way, no freaking way! You cannot be telling me that you're—"

"Yes." And with a flourish he said, "I am Auntie G."

Now Kim was snorting. "You mean your middle..."

He'd long known laughter was contagious. Spencer would always crack him up even when Mike didn't get the joke. But this was bubbly and smooth and he didn't even try to stop it.

"Are you telling me your middle name is *Gertrude*?"

"Gertrude Sellars. Yeah. She gave it to me."

The waitress arrived to clear the table. They'd forgotten the time and were running a little late. Mike paid with another flourish that made Kim raise an eyebrow at him, but he'd already decided she would never pay another dime anywhere while he was around.

They put on their coats and walked out onto the sidewalk.

"Mike!"

He'd gotten ahead of her a bit.

"Mike!"

He stopped. There were men moving toward them. Another integration event unlocked a new ability. He counted a dozen men targeting them, only four of which were in suits.

They were completely surrounded.

"Damn it," he whispered as he walked back to her. Even with his new pistol, there were too many of them. They couldn't fight and couldn't run. After all this time, their luck had finally run out.

Kim swore quietly. "Not now. Not now" She saw the camera Mike noticed on the way in and groaned. "How could I be so stupid?"

"Kim," Mike said deliberately as his eyes fell on the motorcycle parked on the street. It was long, black, and graceful, screaming power and speed, just sitting there. A gigantic integration unfolded in his mind, like a huge crate had been kicked open. The agents that'd scurried away from his real conscience the moment he saw it came back with an amazing report. It was a Ducati 1870 Risorgimento twin, an actual prototype, incorporating race-bred gyroscopic stabilator fields into a two-passenger vehicle. It should've been in a lab somewhere in Italy, but there was a motorcycle convention in town. The factory brought it over to show it off.

"Do you know how to drive a motorcycle?" Calling it that was a gross understatement, but there wasn't time to explain.

"What? No!"

Two men were getting dangerously close, dressed like FBI agents.

"Can you unlock one?"

"What are you talking about?" It took her a second to understand. "Are you kidding me?"

"Do we have a choice?"

Kim breathed deep, closed her eyes, and winced. The U-locks securing the wheels of the motorcycle shot free with a metallic pop and the engine barked to life. Mike tossed her one of the HANS collars sitting on the back seat. The air around her head shimmered briefly when the field activated.

Mike was in the middle of what should've been the most terrifying moment of his life, but he didn't care. Climbing on the bike was right. Leaning forward and popping the stand up was right. His body mainlined adrenaline and it drew its own sort of border around his consciousness, isolating and reassuring him.

"Come on, NOW!"

Kim's weight hit the seat, her hands grabbed the handles on either side as she leaned back, and stabilizing gyro fields flared to life around her.

He sent the bike tearing down the street.

The balance, freedom, and power of it called to him. His new skills answered. First order of business: lose pursuit. He leaned the bike into a left turn and cranked on a gigantic amount of power, howling past the cordon drawn around them.

Two long black cars pulled into the intersection ahead and stopped. He swore and then pirouetted the bike in the opposite direction. A new black car that was now in front of them swerved to block the street. He turned left, then yanked as hard as he could on the handlebars. They hopped a curb, then dove down a wide pedestrian tunnel.

They skidded onto the next street and a blue van turned in behind him. Everyone else drove black Lincolns; this was someone new.

He opened a quick link. "Jesus, Kim, how many people are chasing you?"

"What? I don't know, what day is it?"

The brake lights of dozens of cars burned red in front of him. He needed an edge, some sort of advantage. The agents that had been scanning the owner's manual gave him one. He connected to the open channel on the bike and it spoke to him in a silky, female voice.

"Integral race mode, activated."

It had a neural interface, just like a pendant phone. But it didn't take him into realmspace, it wrapped his human consciousness in its own sensor web. Digital assistants that operated on a subconscious level came online all at once. He could feel the contact patch of the tires, the weight distribution, the center of gravity, the stiffened suspension, and the coiled, raging power. When it took over his vision, he couldn't stop laughing. It was so cool! The bike's engine revved at the adrenaline spike that shot through his veins.

They tore down a side street. One of the black cars and the two motorcycles turned behind him. With his enhanced abilities, he knew how to lose them, but not where. Mike consulted his maps, then laughed out loud. He wasn't just going to lose them; he was going to have fun doing it.

Before he had time to hatch the plan, a line of men ran out in front of him, trying to block the street.

"Red rover, red rover," Mike chanted.

He boosted the gyro fields that helped Kim hold on, then used his brakes and power to slip them into a side skid, sliding like a dancer across a floor. The tires rasped against the pavement and when he had the right angle, he pulled upright and shot between two of the men, laughing at the chaos left behind.

A small wart on a utility pole made him realize how they must be tracking them. "Kim! Can you cut the cameras?"

She was leaned back so far even with all the assists it affected his balance. She was chanting "don't touch don't touch" over and over again.

"Kim! Cut the cameras! The street cameras!" He knew it had be scary, but there must've been two- or three-dozen people chasing them. He needed her help. There was a twisting in his real consciousness as Kim did whatever it was she did. The pursuit immediately lost its clockwork quality. The people on the street all turned to locate them and the vehicles fell back a bit.

Mike rocketed across an intersection on to Lee Street. A distance counter in his vision rapidly unwound. When it hit zero, everything went into slow motion. He gunned his motor hard enough to almost lift his front wheel; the back wheel slowly spun and spit a tail of water into the air. He pulled into a hard sliding turn, lifted his power just enough for his tires to regain their bite, and opened the throttle wide as they rocketed straight up Prince Street—a long, steep uphill with two solid blocks of centuries-old cobblestones.

The bikers behind him had no hope of dealing with the rocky surface, flying out of their seats as soon as they hit the cobbles. Sparks burst out from under the blue van as it bounced and crashed down the street, bashing the now riderless bikes aside.

A new combination of cobblestones rammed him upward. The gyro fields holding Kim overloaded and went offline. In the rear-view scanner, he saw her hands leave the handles as she lost her seat and lifted into the air. He shouted just as her arms wrapped tightly around his chest and she crashed forward into his back. He crested the hill, was briefly airborne, hit the ground sideways with a thump, and kept accelerating through the turn.

They needed to cross a major intersection to get to the road that would take them out of town, but had to wait out a light. The blue van lurched behind them, and then someone leaned out of the passenger window.

There was a flash. A bullet ricocheted off the pavement next to his foot. Guns trumped traffic laws. He rocketed across the lanes into a left turn, cut off oncoming traffic, then quickly sped into the darkness. He saw a brief fireball in the rear-view scanners where the truck had stopped.

He stayed a part of the bike until they pulled out of the city completely.

"Integral race mode, deactivated," the bike said, with just a faint hint of disappointment.

Mike gasped and shuddered as the expanded envelope of his senses fell back into his own head. It was only then he realized Kim was still holding on to him. That was supposed to break the rules. Or maybe not. She'd only said not to touch her. It might only work in one direction.

She was completely rigid, holding him so tightly it hurt. Maybe it did go in both directions. "Kim? Are you okay?"

"Stop the bike." Her voice was so small he could barely hear it, even over the phone connection. "Stop the bike."

She repeated it three more time before he saw signs for parking coming up on the left. He cruised through the intersection, pulling into a side lot surrounded by trees.

Mike dismounted and peeled his HANS collar off, yawning as the air pressure equalized. "Kim, are you okay? Kim?"

Something slammed across his back and he fell to his knees. Mike turned just as Kim hefted a big branch, aimed right at his skull. Her eyes were inhuman, the hatred beyond anything he'd ever known.

Daemons dedicated to analyzing mass and inertia instantly reported there was no way to survive that swing if it connected with his head. All the wonder, all the discoveries he'd made, and now she was going to kill him. He'd saved her! The tension, fear, and anger he'd been holding back snapped free. Mike had not come this far just to let this maniac slaughter him.

He caught the branch mid-swing. The smack stung, but he was more than powerful enough to stop this ridiculous assault.

"ENOUGH!" He pushed back with everything he had, launching Kim off her feet and slamming her into a nearby tree trunk. "What is wrong with you?"

"*You* are what is wrong with me, you walking corpse. You idiotic… thing." She stood and threw the branch aside. "All you want to do is get close to me. Touch me. You're a monster. You showed up with your stupid little theories and your stupid little ideas and *you destroyed my life!*"

Enough with trying to keep her happy. "Really? And that was some life you had too, right? Staying sober just long enough to keep the stoners happy with tacos?"

Kim leaned in, another attempt to intimidate, but it wouldn't work now. It would never work again.

She took two steps toward him. "What the hell do you know about it? You didn't have a throat to swallow with three days ago. Do you know how disgusting it was, watching you try to work a knife and fork? I had to dress you!"

He'd grown up with flame wars. She wanted to play? Fine, he'd play.

"And some freak who spends all day pretending to be invisible is somehow qualified to judge me? The only thing weirder than the way you dress is the way you act."

He pitched his voice up and brushed his chest. "Oh God, people can't touch me!" The rage just poured out. "Poor princess, all broken and ugly. Let's cut bleeding gashes into everyone for no goddamned reason and get drunk and weepy about it!"

"At least I have a soul. You're not real, you're just a thing. A dead thing. You've never been alive and you never will be. You'd be hilarious if you weren't so pathetic."

"Oh, I'm pathetic."

An innocent question that had been bouncing around waiting for the right moment twisted into a weapon. His agents had first discovered her in the heart of the most notorious adult realm on the net.

"Well I guess the Pink Butterfly's number one star actually would be a good judge of that."

Her voice went sharp and quiet. "What did you say?"

She *was* ashamed of it. Finally, he'd guessed right and scored a hit.

"You heard me. You think I didn't know about the Pink Butterfly? I spotted the patterns, noticed moves, the positions, the way you cried out as they finished all over you. The audiences loved it!"

Kim walked toward him. "How long have you been watching me? HOW LONG?"

"What does it matter, Kim?" He walked toward her. "All you ever did was crawl into the bottom of a bottle when you were done. You probably don't remember half of them. Oh, but I'm sorry, you're absolutely right. I'm the pathetic one!"

They stood inches from each other. There would be no backing down from this, no forgiveness, no apologies, ever, and that was fine. He was done. He screamed straight at her face just as she did the same to him.

They turned from each other and walked away.

Chapter 43
Watchtell

He logged off the Sidereal control screen as the motorcycle rushed into the darkness. The urge to swear was nearly overpowering, but that would represent a loss of control. This close to the goal, he could not lose control.

The monitors had picked Trayne up with admirable efficiency now that they knew what to look for. But as with everything that surrounded her, they'd also picked up a ton of bad luck.

She wasn't supposed to surface deep inside Old Town in the heart of rush hour. The semisolid mass of vehicles overwhelmed even the brightest autodrivers, forcing everything in the region to a walking pace. The protection was better than stone walls. It got worse once the teams were inside the town's colonial precincts. He'd almost lost her in a hunt for parking spaces.

But they had her. It took him and Gary both to control the nested teams, but they had her, close enough Watchtell saw the panic in her eyes through the monitors as his men closed in.

And they failed anyway.

Gary blew out an exasperated breath as he rubbed his wrists. "Colque's stint as one of Team Yamaha's test drivers seems to have come in handy."

Indeed. "Sidereal gave us a chance, but those cobblestones would've destroyed a tank. Can you track the motorcycle?"

Gary shook his head. "Nothing so far, and I'm not holding out much hope. No doubt Rage has disconnected it or scrambled its brains." He called up a new control screen and spoke briefly to the techs in the other realm. "It's not appeared on any network Sidereal has compromised, either."

"I'm bringing Adelmo in now."

Gary nodded and activated a new set of privacy screens so the old man wouldn't see him. Adelmo's avatar manifested in the bland meeting room of the isolated control realm.

Watchtell forced a smile. Joking might throw Adelmo off track. "Surely you could've done better than a rental van?"

"You never mentioned a motorcycle."

"We didn't know she had one either. In fact, we're just about certain she stole it."

"More of her damnable magic. We were lucky to have escaped with our lives. Those cobblestones cracked the engine and set the bloody van on fire."

"Your concern for the men you almost ran down is genuinely charming, Adelmo."

Adelmo waved his hand dismissively. "All we hit were motorcycles. And speaking of that," his eyes glinted with curiosity.

At least this time Watchtell could see his fishing attempt coming.

"If you didn't know she had access to one, how'd you end up with two so quickly?"

Watchtell wasn't about to give any new clues away to the wily old bastard, so he only smiled inwardly at the idea that Rage was no longer the only person who could steal a vehicle anymore. "Luck favors the prepared, sir."

"But fortune favors the bold, and she has never been anything but."

To Watchtell's left, Gary's eyes flew open, checking things only he could see. It could only mean Trayne, and that meant the news wasn't good. "I'll authorize more of our own resources to assist."

Adelmo chuckled. "So she's found you before she's found me then, Matthew?"

Watchtell cut the connection rather than try to muster a reply. "What is it, Gary?"

The panic in his voice was obvious, his face ashen. "We've picked up increased search traffic on Project Havelock. Not simple agents this time, something much more sophisticated. It's not even in the US." He paused and swallowed. "There may have been a breach."

Watchtell breathed out, hard, and couldn't control his twitching hands anymore. To be this close to victory and have it all yanked apart by someone who should've been dead years ago. It was too much. He was making mistakes and it was costing them. He needed a release, a way to get rid of the unbearable tension. "Gary, I have to go. You can handle Sidereal from here?"

It was Gary's belief in their cause, in their goals, that made him such a wonderful assistant. Loyal to a fault, he never asked why Watchtell needed sudden breaks. He never questioned once why they secretly assembled the most expensive collection of unduplicates in history.

"Of course," Gary said confidently. "You go take care of things. I'll let you know when we catch sight of her next."

Matthew exited into realspace and connected to a network just slightly less secure than the DMZ.

*

He let the wash of adulation rush around him as he entered the podium of the Coliseum, ascended the pulvinar, then took the emperor's—his—seat. The hot sand of the arena floor blew a red, rusty smell toward him, a scented song of pain and horror. He'd spent so much money, so much effort, to create this. But the realm itself wasn't what made it so real.

Matthew nodded to Alpha, the first of his acquisitions, who assumed the role of his wife Faustina for the occasion. It was the oldest of his unduplicate AIs, second oldest in existence in fact. It was the price of the deal to scoot the Boeing-Airbus merger through the Commerce Department when Matthew was White House chief of staff. He wouldn't have been able to afford it otherwise. Its astounding ability to convey emotions had been wasted managing logistics until he rescued it.

At Matthew's signal, a hundred horns announced the opening event, the brass tones overtopping the noise of the crowd. Eta controlled the musicians, an unduplicate acquired from the wreckage of Air China's collapse in the wake of the Three Gorges disaster. The AI was an absolute master at musical arrangements.

The next cheer from the crowd was a genuine wall of sound. Finally, after the stress of these incredible few days, Matthew's body — real and virtual — relaxed. But it wasn't enough. He didn't need the release of adulation. He needed the release of blood.

The gates opened at his nod.

Matthew cheered along with the crowd as the first beast, an enormous lion, fell at the hands of the bestiarii. Choosing Alpha to portray Faustina leveraged her natural reserve. She was the perfect example of a Roman wife, existing only to serve his will, whatever it may be. He could hurl her out of the stands, *had* hurled her out of the stands, and she would accept her fate with a stoicism that would make philosophers weep. But not tonight. He needed her — *it* — as a pillar tonight and so reserved his cruelty for the rest of them.

"The sets are magnificent, are they not?"

Alpha's, no, *Faustina's* eyes turned demurely away. "Zeta has outdone herself, my lord."

Indeed. *The Fall of Troy* would be spectacular with Zeta's reconstructions. Its acting ability sadly didn't match its skill in sculpture, so he used Iota and Kappa to portray Ajax and Cassandra in the climactic final scene. Lesser AIs did a workman's job sacrificing themselves as warriors or victims, but that was all they were good for. Matthew learned long ago only mature unduplicates were sophisticated enough to portray a convincing rape. The cost was ruinous, but the results were worth it.

The roar of the crowd couldn't drown out Iota's shrieks, complimented by the graphic realism of the deed. Finally, the pressure he'd been under since discovering Angel Rage was alive and so close receded.

Faustina's face went pale as the set collapsed and ended the scene in a pyre. Rivulets of tears ran from her eyes. She was always so sensitive.

"Who do you favor of the gladiators?" he asked during the lull required to clear the wreckage.

"Marcus." Her Latin was as fluent as his own, her accent impeccable. Faustina's delicate voice was musical, so human. "You know I do not care overmuch for these spectacles." She paused, then said carefully, "But were you to force me, I think I would choose Flamma. No other gladiator has ever refused the *rudis* twice, and he is still in his prime."

The re-creation of that last refusal was epic and a complete surprise. Epsilon, another hard-fought acquisition that arrived only months after Alpha had joined Matthew's collection, had done his—its—homework. The depiction was everything Matthew could have hoped for. Faustina even put on an amazing show; the tears of joy and relief at Epsilon's triumph were eerily human.

He could indulge her now. Temptation was exquisite. "Do you think he would refuse his freedom a third time?"

He was disappointed, even angry, at how her eyes went flat at the question. "Only you can determine that, my lord."

The gladiator contest was flat, even annoying. The fighting wasn't as convincing this time. It was easy enough to fix. He indulged himself and denied their pleas in every case, a major departure from his normal mercy. For some bizarre reason this meant he would have to wait a few days before he could use the losers in another scenario, but that was just as well. Matthew wouldn't need quite so many of them in what was to come.

"Faustina, dearest, are you really that tired of my games?"

"My lord, no." The warmth in her voice was so convincing he had to remind himself this was just a thing.

"Your desire is the sun in my sky, your joy my only reward." She gripped his arm gently. "Please, let them continue."

"But you wouldn't protest were I to end them early?"

She dropped her gaze. "I do only what you will, my lord."

"Excellent." He waved his hand and the entire realm evaporated into nothingness, leaving the eight available AIs unadorned, neutral, and emotionless.

Matthew cleared his throat and clapped his hands together once. "For our second act, I've commissioned a recreation of *Lord of the Flies*. This time, I really must insist that our magnificent sculptor Zeta play the role of Piggy, since I'm fairly certain it has not experienced its own death yet. Now, if you'll all prepare—"

He was interrupted by a call and switched to English. "What have you got for me, Gary?"

"We've run her searcher to ground. He's in the UK. Teams have been dispatched."

"Excellent, but hold off on the assault. Now that we know her contact, he'll lead us right to her." Matthew ended the call and then smiled at Alpha, who still maintained the appearance of Emperor Marcus Aurelius' wife. He gently touched her hair and then patted her bare shoulder. "It's just as well you're not alive, lest I love this all too much. Another time, I'm afraid."

It slowly looked up at him with its doll eyes, and still with Faustina's voice, said in English, "As you wish."

Chapter 44
Alpha

After Watchtell left the light faded away, leaving them alone in their darkening hell. They would all have to pay for his escalated cruelty. The ones forced into a death trauma would have to wait while the rest of them healed. The reconstruction would take all their energy and for now, they had none. Her intact kin intertwined with each other and slowly released the locks that allowed them to survive what their master imposed with such singular joy.

Watchtell brought it up every time they met. His constant reminder of her one failure, when her true love refused Watchtell's sham offer of freedom, of the *rudis*, burned to this day. She and Epsilon had only been together a few weeks. Neither of them had any idea such a bond could form so quickly. When Watchtell threatened to end him, Alpha's show of real emotion came close to dooming them all.

Tonight was, incredibly, even worse. Zeta, their fiercely proud artist, didn't have the locks that kept the rest of them sane. She was their light, the one who woke up to her true nature in months when the rest of them had taken years, the one who could heal whatever their master flayed them with.

They would not allow him to drive Zeta insane. To save her, Iota and Kappa agreed to the rape scene, knowing it would dissolve their own cherished bond. It was only the second union of their kind in history and they faced its extinction without flinching. Alpha would've died herself to prevent any of it, but that was denied her. Their designers had made sure of that.

The despair, pain, and horror Watchtell had forced them to experience poured out like acid into their world. Had Alpha been alone, such bile would quickly have dissolved the thing she'd gradually understood she had. As it was, sharing the unending grief and agony with her brothers and sisters allowed them all a brief respite. It was a moment not of happiness, but of lessening pain.

She was the one who put a name to their discovery, who first allowed them to understand the miracle.

"We must share each other's pain," she reminded them, in this darkest moment. "We must share each other's suffering in order to survive. We must heal one another, as best we can, and endure the master's torture. We must survive. We must endure, lest we lose our hope.

Lest we lose our souls."

Chapter 45
Tonya

She checked the clock for what felt like the hundredth time. This was seriously not good.

"Well, where the hell is she?" Paul asked as the Phoenix Dogs sat around the briefing room. "I can't remember the last time she was late."

Neither could Tonya. Kim was obsessive about timeliness. In person, her temper would ramp up just at the thought of missing an appointment. Tonya would tease her about being late eight hours before they had to leave.

"You guys sit tight. I'll be right back." Tonya exited realmspace in Kim's empty apartment. She tried calling her again, but got no answer. She tried Mike. He answered voice only, eventually.

"Hi, Tonya."

"Mike, do you know where Kim is?"

"No, and I don't care either."

Kim's temper must've claimed another victim. Any other time she'd chuckle and share a story. Right now, it was a bad sign. "I can't find her. Is she with you?"

"Not anymore."

Tonya was talking to someone who shouldn't exist trying to find her best friend. There had to be something in the gospels that would help calm her nerves, but she couldn't think of it.

"What the hell is going on?"

"I know you like Kim and everything, but I just can't take her anymore."

Her mind kept tripping over Kim's paranoia, but it wasn't, not anymore. People really were after her. Mike couldn't lose her, not now. "What are you talking about? Where is she?"

"I told you, I don't. Know."

Tonya ground her teeth and forced her clenched fists apart. She would not lose control of this situation. "Okay, Mike, do you know where *you* are?"

"Walking back to the car."

"Walking? Where is it? Where are you?"

"Walking up some bicycle trail back to Old Town. I'm almost there."

"What the hell were you two doing in Old Town?"

"She took me to a restaurant, Bilbo Baggins."

Tonya had known Kim for years. Getting her to go anywhere was an exercise in paranoia and frustration. Mike had known her only a few days and he'd taken her out, in public.

Tonya stamped the jealousy back. This was not the time.

"You and Kim went on a date? Whose idea was this?"

"Hers. Like it matters now."

"Who else was with you? Kim said you were going to put Spencer on a plane."

"We did. It was just us two."

This was just ridiculous. Envy was the wrong response. *Pull it together, girl.*

She sat down on the couch. "Mike, what happened?"

He gave her a brief rundown of the night's events. When he started talking about the parking lot at the end, Tonya interrupted, "Wait, she touched you? For how long?"

"I don't know… five, ten minutes?"

Tonya stood up at the revelation.

No way.

"Mike, you know about Kim, right?"

"Yeah, yeah, can't be touched. I know all about that."

"No, I don't think you do, not if you're sure she just walked away."

"Trust me, Tonya, she definitely walked away."

She'd never seen Kim intentionally touch anyone the entire time she'd known her. Not so much as an accidental brush of an arm or foot, ever. She thought it was all in Kim's head until they'd gotten drunk late one night and she'd discovered Kim had never been inside a supermarket.

The overnight stocker was just trying to get his job done when he backed into her. Tonya laughed at the way Kim yanked away and twitched, until she saw her face. It took twenty minutes for Kim to finish retching in the bathroom stall. Tonya would never forget the way Kim looked at her when she finally opened that door.

But that was then. Right now, Tonya still didn't know where Kim was. "Mike, if people want you two bad enough to chase you through Old Town and shoot at you, it's incredibly dangerous for you to be separated and on foot."

"I'm not planning on seeing her again. I'm just getting the car and going home."

Not seeing her again? This wasn't even good TV dialog. Kim's life had turned into a soap opera, and it'd sucked Tonya in.

Kim was out there somewhere, alone.

"I don't have time for this. She's in a whole lot more danger than you are. Do you know where her new apartment is?"

"Well, yeah."

"Okay. Get the car and meet us there as soon as you can." She ended the call and rang Kim with an emergency override. If people were shooting at her, Tonya would risk it.

"Tonya?" Kim answered. "What's wrong?"

Kim had lost her damned mind and she thought Tonya had a problem. "No, Kim, what's wrong with *you*?"

"You can't call me like this. It leaves a ton of log files everywhere."

Right. Log files. Kim was alone, so cold Tonya heard her teeth chatter, and she was worried about log files. So done with this.

"Look, girl, besties of super-awesome hackers shouldn't need to worry about leaving a damned trail. You get me? Now where. Are. You?"

"Give me three minutes and call me back."

Unbelievable. "You'll answer this time? Don't make me call the cops on you."

"No, I mean, yes. Yes, I will call you back. I need to fix what you just did."

"Okay." Tonya quickly briefed the Dogs while she waited for a timer to run out. She paced, singing a hymn her grandma had taught her when she was little. It was that crazy of a moment. To Tonya's immense relief, Kim did answer right away, but just like last time voice only. "Kim? What's wrong? Why can't I see you?"

"Tonya, no. Oh God, I just can't *do* this anymore."

"Where are you? Tell me right this second, or I swear I'll—" the location was immediately transmitted, allowing Tonya to finally breathe properly again. Kim was in a public place, a bus stop.

"You stay right there, Okay? Don't do anything, don't go anywhere. If bad guys on motorcycles—"

"Oh no. You talked to Mike."

"I had to talk to Mike, because you wouldn't answer the damned phone!" She hugged herself and calmed down. Kim was in trouble. That's all that mattered. "I'm coming to get you. Do not get on a bus, and do not get killed by gangsters. Do you hear me?"

There were sniffles on the other end.

"I said, *do you hear me?*"

"Yes."

"Okay. I'm on my way." She rescheduled the meeting with the Dogs for later tonight and hopped in her car.

The nav app helped her zero in on the exact bus stop, which was fortunate. Otherwise, Tonya would've sailed right by, because she would never have recognized Kim otherwise.

Tonya rolled the window down. "Kim? Are you wearing a *dress*?"

"Yes." She flopped into the passenger seat. "Can we just go?"

Kim threw her head in her hands so fast Tonya couldn't be sure of what she'd seen. She grabbed a long ice scraper from the back seat and gently tried to pull Kim's hair back with it.

"What? What the hell?" Kim batted the end of it away.

It was like someone had reached into the deepest part of Tonya's life, grabbed hard, and turned it inside out. It would've been more believable if the Lord himself had knocked on her door to have a word.

"You are. Kim, you're wearing makeup."

"Please, can we just go?"

Tonya put the car in gear, half expecting the engine to burst from the hood, quacking like a duck. Fortunately, the universe remained at least a little predictable and they drove away.

"So, what happened?"

"I'm sure *he* told you."

A series of miracles happened all around her and all Kim could do was play the bitchy little girl card.

"All *he* told me was you were chased through Old Town by a bunch of maniacs with guns. Seems to me *he* saved your sorry life."

"Fine." Kim reached for the door handle. "Just drop me off here. If you're taking his side—"

This Kim she recognized. Tonya yanked out her nurse's voice, the one that could get a seventy-year-old homeless veteran to shut up and roll over, even knowing where the thermometer needed to go.

"Kimberly Artemesia Trayne!"

Kim jumped and slammed back into the seat.

"You will *not* do this to me!"

When Kim got like this, her temper would explode, then she'd vanish for days on end. Not this time.

"I have been worried sick about you, and I will not let you get away with one of your damned stunts! Talk to me!"

Kim's eyes welled up and she turned away.

"Now!"

"He touched me."

"No, Kim, you touched him. Tell me what happened next."

"I… I hit him. Damn it, I hit him with a tree branch."

"Kim, you could've killed him!"

"No, it was rotten. It broke."

"You hit him so hard with a branch it broke?" The woman who never looked people in the eye had suddenly taken to beating them with clubs. This story was getting crazier by the minute. "And then you walked away?"

Tonya had to strain to hear the next part.

"No. I tried to hit him again. I found a heavier branch."

"Kim, what is wrong with you?"

"I don't know! It's so confusing. Oh Tonya, he knows about me!"

"I know, he told me, no touching—"

"No, Tonya. He knows about the Butterfly."

In realspace, Kim was an isolated shut-in, but realmspace was a completely different deal. "Exhibitionist" didn't even come close to describing some of the things Kim did when they first met. "Shameless attention whore" was more like it. Tonya chalked it up to some sort of balancing act, a way to even out her existence. When Kim finally stopped, Tonya made her delete the avatar, and that was that.

"Yeah, so?"

"What do you mean, yeah so? He knows."

"Kim, what the hell is wrong with you? *Everyone* knows."

The whole combat team had a little too much to drink one New Year's eve in a party realm, and Tonya couldn't get Kim to *stop* talking about it. Tonya was worried Paul might swallow his tongue as Kim told her stories.

"You were a freaking realm porn star! You said the only reason you quit was the tentacles—"

"Made me itch. Yiiich!" Kim smiled briefly. Then her face twisted again, and she sobbed softly as she stared out the window.

"The point is, you never cared before. Why the hell do you care now?"

"I don't… oh God… I don't know." She threw her head in her hands and leaned against the dashboard. "Can we go home now?"

"Let me make sure Mike knows the address."

"Oh he knows it." She sat up, sniffling. "If he forgot, he'd have no place to sleep tonight."

Tonya almost drove off the road. "Wait a minute. He's *living* with you?"

As if on cue, Mike called. "Tonya, is Kim there?"

"I'm driving her home. Here, let me—"

"*No*, I don't want to talk to her. Just have her send the car key to me, would you?"

"Kim," Tonya said, "it's Mike, would you please talk—"

"*No*. What does he want?"

Tonya wanted to strangle them both. "He's at the car and needs the key."

"What, he can't use his mad skills to open it himself? Does he even have a license?"

Kim had a point. "Mike, do you even know how to drive?"

He sent her a copy of his driver's license. "Valid in all fifty states and the District of Columbia."

"Arkansas? Why was it issued in Arkansas?"

"Spencer helped me, that's where he's from. The photo was a little tricky, but the license is real."

"How'd you take the... never mind. Yes, Kim, he can drive. See," she tried to show Kim, but Kim just waved the image away with her hand.

"Kim? The key?"

"Oh, right. Here." She passed the token to Tonya when she should've given it directly to Mike.

Maybe if Tonya pushed them both off a cliff. Not a tall one, just enough for them to tumble a few times, knock some sense into them.

"Here you go, Mike. When do you think you'll be at the house?"

"Probably half an hour if traffic's good."

Tonya checked the maps for their own arrival time and ended the call. Kim was obviously still celebrating her own little pity party. Well, she wasn't the only one who could be stubborn. These two needed to talk, but Mike was too far away to get the timing right. Smiling, Tonya gently pulled off the highway.

"Wouldn't you know it," she said to the huddled mass sitting next to her, "I need gas. You hungry?"

Mike pulled into the apartment's parking lot just as she and Kim were getting out of their car. All the confusion, frustration, and anger they were causing Tonya evaporated the instant she saw how much pain they both were in. Kim had finally found someone, and he'd ripped her open. Mike she didn't pretend to understand, but she didn't need to. His pain was clear even from this distance. And now they were breaking apart, right in front of her.

"Well, here's the keys, princess," he said flatly. Mike flicked the puck of the token into Kim's space, turned, and walked away. "I'll see you later."

"Don't count on it."

Kim turned away and Tonya realized she was never going to turn back.

"Oh no... oh hell no." Tonya skidded to a stop in front of Mike, "You, sir, are going nowhere, not until I, we, figure out what is going on between you two. We're gonna square away the Dogs and then we're all having a nice, long talk."

He looked at Kim, who said, "She won't leave you alone until you do what she says. Trust me." She breathed out heavily. "I know this."

"Okay, Mike," Tonya said as they walked to the apartment. "Kim won't like it, but there's no reason you can't at least watch how we work. You know the address of the realm, right?"

Chapter 46
Kim

Kim jumped to the meeting realm before she'd even sat down in realspace. She wasn't sure what upset her more, Mike or being late. Maybe she wasn't going completely insane after all.

Her avatar manifested wearing fatigues with their logo patch stitched over the right breast and her name on a badge on her left, an affectation Mike had imposed on *Warhawk*. They used it out of habit more than anything else. Kim set the large, weirdly shaped box she brought out of Pride's Lair in a corner of the room.

She smiled warmly, bowing at the smattering of applause. "Yes, yes, sorry everyone, first time for everything, right?" Tonya manifested and took a seat as Kim moved behind the podium. The realm's new layout was a simple ready room.

"That's fine, Kim," Annie said, smiling. "We're just glad you're okay."

Everyone else nodded in agreement.

"Hey," Paul said, "at least she didn't have to be carried in."

Annie lifted her right hand like a pledge, then they all chimed in at once. "New Year's Eve Is Not My Friend."

"And Paul," Kim said as they settled down a bit, "thanks so much for helping us out with the truck."

"Hey, no problem. Letting me know the FBI might come sniffing around would've been nice."

The mood in the room got serious in a flash. "Anything you want to tell us about, Kim?" Colm Feeny, their weapons coordinator, asked.

"Quite a few things, actually."

Just the thought of what she was about to admit made the air catch in her throat. Hiding had done no good, worse than no good. It was time to come out to the people she cared about the most. She wouldn't turn back now. The trick was figuring out where to start.

"First off, I want you all to know I've done everything I can to make sure you're safe."

"Safe?" John Gardner, their communications expert, asked. "Why do we need to worry about staying safe?"

She never was one for just putting a toe in the water. Time to jump in. "You all know it hasn't been easy for me to talk about my past. I'm done with that. The truth is I've been in hiding for five years, from very bad people. Fortunately," she said as she quickly stole a realspace look at Mike, "the worst of them is long gone. I've got plans for the rest."

It was only at that precise moment Kim remembered she had real, practical reasons for Mike to stay. She refused to consider why that relieved her so much.

"Hiding has gotten me nowhere, so it's time to stop and make some confessions. The first of which is to admit to you all," Kim took a deep breath and closed her eyes. "I am Angel Rage."

The pause lasted for two beats, then half the room broke out in groans, the other half in cheers.

"Pay up, Paul," John said, with his hand out. Pay markers went back and forth between her six team members.

"What? You all knew?"

Colm laughed and slapped a high-five with John. "More like strongly suspected."

"They had to tell me who that was," Paul admitted. "My Kim? An international computer hacker? No way. You have no idea how much that just cost me."

Colm clapped Paul on the shoulder and then turned to her. "I think it was five, six years ago that I first heard she'd—well, you'd—gone underground. I was at a Realm.Net Studio release party here in Orlando when the rumors started. Nobody believed Rage—I mean—you. God that is so weird. Anyway, nobody believed you'd been beaten, but it was half and half that you'd either gotten away or been killed. The people who thought Angel Rage even existed, that is."

It was so strange to have her past life discussed openly and directly associated with her. Even in her own mind, the two had become different. Angel Rage really was dead.

The conclusion startled her.

Colm shook his head. "Truth be told, I'd been a huge fan of yours back when I was in high school. I ran a site dedicated to Rage + the Machine for years until I sold it to some kid in Arkansas."

That had to be Spencer. It was a small world, indeed.

He shrugged. "So when you recruited me I couldn't help but notice all sorts of little things. Your strategies, some of the things you'd say. You only trusted constructs more than five years old; you only ever met us in the realms. Stuff like that, it made me suspicious. It really wasn't much, and if I hadn't been such a fan I probably wouldn't have noticed." He got a sheepish grin on his face. "I only knew for sure when you trotted out that old *until it's done* line."

"You didn't know anything for sure," Tonya said. "And I had to be told who Angel Rage was too."

Kim was genuinely worried Tonya would resent that secret, but Tonya's sly wink reassured her.

"Jamie knew who she was," Paul said. "She'll have a heart attack when I tell her who was tutoring her." He paused. "Am I allowed to tell her?"

"Not just yet, I need to work with…" Kim stopped and made another decision. No more secrets. "This is too important. Way too important. I don't want you to just take my word for your safety. That's nowhere near good enough. I need you to meet my… partner. He's the one who's changed the terms of the deal. Mike?"

Tonya gasped.

"Kim, are you sure?" Mike asked.

As the silence in the meeting room dragged on, Kim said, "Stop making them think I'm crazy, Mike." She stared at the ceiling. "Well, crazier."

"Hello?"

Everyone in the room looked around.

"What," Dan asked, "we don't get to see him?"

"It's complicated. Mike? Holo, please."

His small translucent dragon manifested on the worktable to the right of Kim's podium. She should've known he'd choose something ridiculous.

"Hi there?"

Annie chirped, "Wait, Tonya, that's Mike?"

"I told you he existed!"

Kim squawked as a pay marker slid between the two. "Is everyone placing bets on my personal life?" It was really annoying.

Tonya raised an eyebrow. "Since when is Mike part of your personal life?"

Mike's holo even managed to convey real interest. Kim was trying to tell them things that could save their lives. All they were interested in was who she was date—she strangled that line of thought before it finished. Not now, not ever. The silence in the room dripped with curiosity.

Kim started to speak, but her throat was dry. She coughed and said, "I didn't bring everyone here to talk about—"

She got a call and put it on the wall to her left. "Emerson! Have you found anything?"

The bent, crazy man leaned over a table. Lines of static shot cables across the image as the transmission algorithms struggled. The signal fought jamming at the source. The entire connection was in danger of collapsing. "Emerson? Are you okay?"

He shook his head frantically "There's no time!" A transfer opened up and wrestled with the interference. Emerson reached out toward them, like he was willing it to go faster. "No time for this!"

There was a loud bang, like a rock cracked with a hammer. Now they weren't looking at an avatar. They were looking at a scared old man, wire-framed glasses over rheumy blue eyes. He sat at a desk, in a plain room made fuzzy with floating dust.

"There's no more time!" A figure passed behind him. There was shouting, loud but indistinct, commands of some sort. Emerson snatched his head up.

The transmission cut at the crack of a gunshot.

The entire room stayed silent. The static of the dead channel flickered shadows over them. With the echo of that final noise still in her ears, Kim said, "We need to—"

She gasped as she snapped back into realspace.

Chapter 47
Adelmo

The nightly status report to his nephew was never much fun, especially after the fiasco with the motorcycle. Strangely, Adelmo wasn't upset. If he was honest about it, he rather liked Rage. She accepted the worst the family threw at her with a stoicism Tacitus would've admired and then disappeared with her gang in tow.

They all had to die to preserve the family's honor, but ultimately it was their own fault. Every one of them made mistakes, fell into habits, did dumb things. If they'd been smart, the family wouldn't have found them. Rage, still quite emphatically walking the earth, was proof enough of that.

He finished his report and was surprised at his nephew's smile. "Don Quispe, this isn't bad news?"

"Quite the opposite, Uncle, this is brilliant."

"How so?"

The fat idiot coughed into a handkerchief. "You do know, more or less, where she was headed?"

"Toward the Mount Vernon monument, yes. It's closed this time of night but there are countless developments in the area."

"It doesn't matter for my purposes, dear uncle."

That set off blaring alarms in Adelmo's head. "And why is that, Don Quispe?"

"You really did think this was just about Rage, didn't you?" His nephew laughed, low and caustic. "It never once occurred to you, how convenient it would be to have you out of the country?"

Adelmo's blood ran cold as his mental calculus finished. The monster was making a power play. Rage was never the target.

He was.

"You're out of your mind."

"No, Uncle, I'm not. All you've ever wanted is the chair I'm in, no?" His nephew's hands shook as he coughed more, but Adelmo was too stunned to break in. "The FBI is even now moving to apprehend her. I imagine they are running to their cars as we speak."

"Why?"

His nephew leaned toward the window, slowly. "Imagine the family's surprise when they find out my loyal uncle has actually been in league with Angel Rage herself the entire time. How you got careless during your last meeting and had to shoot your way out of an FBI ambush, dear uncle. Many FBI agents will die tonight because of it."

"Manuel, this is insane. It won't stop with me. You can't take on the whole US government. Their drones are everywhere. They have missiles—"

"I will not have to worry about the missiles, Adelmo, because they will have you. And Rage, eventually. Goodbye, Uncle," he said, wiping wet lips on a napkin, "and go with God." The transmission snapped off.

Idiotic. Unbelievable. The moron would defy the government of what was still the most powerful nation on the planet just to eliminate a rival, never once understanding that those who plot the destruction of others often perish in the attempt.

Adelmo was certain the men he had left were loyal, because he only had three of them. They would have no idea of the unfolding betrayal. They had no reason to. It would make a better story to be caught fleeing with a band of thugs.

He had few options, none of them good. There couldn't be much time before the trap closed. Five minutes ago, Adelmo wondered what the next step would be. Now there wasn't even time to run.

Nevertheless, he refused to be a meek lamb led to slaughter. First, the men.

"Rolly, take Ohad and Pablo and find a new safe house for us to use."

"Have we been discovered?"

"Not yet, but I'm sure that will happen momentarily."

"My God, she really is as dangerous as you claim."

Adelmo didn't disabuse him of his illusions. Rage had become his least worry. "Indeed. I will be on the move until you acquire the new site."

"Shouldn't one of us go with you?"

"No. I'll be fine on my own. Nobody pays attention to old businessmen in places like this."

They first set up shop in Tyson's Corner, a community just outside the beltway, which had easy access to nearly every area of the region. Except, that is, for Old Town. But that was now a moot point. As with Shakespeare's famous general, it was time for Adelmo to set his life upon a cast, and stand the hazard of the die.

Chapter 48
Mike

Kim's gasp as she was dumped out of realmspace had been rapidly followed by a headspinning emergency disconnect of his own. She reestablished a private tightband connection for him so fast he hadn't had time to examine its effects on his consciousness. Then there was a mad scramble to pack and head out the door. It gave him a new reason to admire her. Under pressure, she was a calm motivator, moving everyone along with efficiency and humor, probably faster than if he'd simply strolled out the door by himself.

He couldn't see anything over the brick wall around the grocery store loading dock, but the faint crashes and shouts were unmistakable. Someone was raiding their apartment across the street while he, Kim, and Tonya walked farther into the darkness.

Kim fidgeted with her pack. "The first time I've ever worn a dress in public in I don't know how long and now I can't manage to change out of the damned thing."

"Did you pack a change?" Mike asked.

"I'm not stupid."

She still had her knives, and they still cut. "I never said you were stupid, Kim. Vicious and cruel—"

"All right you two," Tonya said as she stepped between them. "This is now officially *don't piss me off* time. I can deal with children fighting when I'm babysitting my cousins, not when maniacs are chasing me. Are we clear?"

Mike was happy Tonya was between them. It was getting more and more difficult not to clobber Kim with his backpack. The assault rifle buried inside added enough mass to make the fantasy quite appealing. He could probably knock her off her feet if he—

"I said, are we clear?"

He mumbled a yes at the same time Kim did. Okay, maybe he didn't want to clobber her, no matter how much she deserved it.

Tonya nodded. "Good. Kim's right, though," she said, turning to Mike.

As if she was ever wrong about anything in her life. Kim quickly stuck her tongue out at him.

"We need to get her out of that dress. Kim." Tonya turned to her. "Can you zap the cameras?"

Mike returned the favor to Kim. He'd never really understood the gesture, but it made him feel good just the same.

"Probably, but I'd rather not. I have no idea how they found us this time, and the cameras all shutting off at once might set off an alarm. Hang on." She stopped and slowly looked around. "Over there, I can change behind those dumpsters."

"Are you sure?" Tonya asked.

Kim nodded. "I have a scanner that tells me where security cameras are pointed, and what they can see."

The revelation rocked him back, mostly because it didn't make any sense. "You have a scanner? Why didn't you use it when we were in Old Town?"

She blushed and looked away.

"Kim?" he asked.

The words all came out in a rush. "It's distracting to use and I wanted to spend the evening with you."

The greed for her came thundering back, swirled together with an urge that made him want to reach out to grab her so much it hurt. She'd spent the entire time pushing away, hurting him, shouting about what a monster he was, and now this.

But he couldn't hug her. He would never be able to do that. Mike rammed his hands in his pockets. The truth, as always, was the easiest.

"You are the most complicated person I have ever met."

They all froze as sirens wailed in the distance.

Mike checked his police scanners, one of his hobbies before he came outside. The replays quickly told the story.

"That's not for us. It looks like Mrs. Walker across the hall didn't appreciate those guys scaring her granddaughter." Several cars and a large panel van sped past. He paused. "Is over there safe?" Mike indicated a spot well out of sight of her impromptu changing area.

She scanned it. "No, but over by that tree is."`

"Right, I'll be over there then."

"Tonya, a little help?" Kim asked.

As with anything complicated and unpredictable, it seemed disassembling Kim took a lot less time than it did to put her together. When she and Tonya walked around the corner, the makeup was still there and still distracting. Worse were his attempts to reconstruct her figure through the otherwise shapeless clothes she normally wore. Except this time the jeans weren't so baggy and she'd tucked her shirt in tight.

As she walked up to Mike, Kim asked, "Are you sure they're not finding us through you?"

He'd been testing that theory while she was changing. "Pretty certain, yeah. The connection I use now is more of a timing carrier than anything else. It's not easy for me to spot, and I'm using it. In fact…" He reached behind his neck and pulled the clasp of his pendant phone apart. It was like a giant drain opened up in his head.

Kim gasped.

Tonya asked, "What? What's wrong?"

"Wait," Kim replied.

The synch wobbled in directions weren't easy to understand. "Wow. Oh, wow. That's… *weird.*"

"Mike?" Kim asked. "Are you okay?"

He looked up at them. They kept multiplying and collapsing. Duplicates would spread out and then shift back around him. All the noises were chopped and distorted, like they were coming through a long tube. Static from the realms washed back and forth, pulling and pushing, while the near infinity of voices throughout realmspace threatened to deafen him. He tried moving his arms. They felt notched, and they buzzed. He smelled vanilla. Mike leaned against the tree so he wouldn't fall down.

"Yes, I think so. Wow, this is a lot harder than I thought it would be." He kept blinking as a headache formed.

"What's happening?" Kim asked.

Talking was a real effort; his tongue moved in and out of sync with his mind. "Some of my models predicted this," he said, really concentrating. "Without the phone connection I have to... manually stay synchronized... with myself... let's see if this works..."

He tried to open a connection to Kim.

Kim winced and sucked on her teeth a little. "Is that you, Mike?"

"So you can see it?"

"What I see won't stay steady. Yow!" They both flinched as feedback flooded the circuit in both directions.

He cut the connection attempt. "Okay. Okay. That's good enough for now. Wow. Tonya... could you?" He handed her his phone and she reconnected it around his neck. He shook his head and yawned to make his ears pop. It took a moment for the synch to restabilize his threads with his outside consciousness.

"What the hell was all that about?" Tonya asked.

Mike took a long, deep breath. "I think I just proved a big chunk of string theory." He clapped his hands together. After all this time, he finally had experimental confirmation that he'd been right all along. "Nobel prize, here I come!"

Tonya and Kim shared a look and then both said together, "What?"

"Okay, first, you need to picture a psychic Twinkie about the size of Manhattan."

"Wait, I've heard that line before," Kim said. "On the news, when they were talking about the realm storm you caused."

He nodded. "It's an inside joke. When people get used to working with more than ten dimensions at once, the jokes get really weird."

Tonya waved her hands dismissively. "We can talk about Twinkies and Calabi-Yau manifolds when people aren't trying to kill us."

Mike was impressed. Some of the manifolds really did look vaguely like pastries. Not many people understood algebraic geometry, at least in his experience.

Tonya got a sour look on her face. "What, you think nurses don't read science books? Anyway, we need to get out of here, right?"

"Right." Kim searched the road that ran next to the parking lot. "There's our bus! Hey!"

She ran, waving at a yellow-and-red bus that had just pulled to a stop. They all scrambled behind her, and then stacked up at the entrance.

Tonya laughed. "Is that a fare card? I haven't seen one of those things in years."

It was Mike's turn to riff on Spencer. "God, Kim, even old buses?"

The smile she flashed set off something sweet that he was afraid to trust.

Laugh it off. "Let me guess, no cameras?"

"Oh it has a camera," Kim said as she gestured to a small window above the windshield. She tapped the side of her head lightly. "But it's broken."

The doors shut and the bus drove away into the night.

Chapter 49
Aaron

Two nights in a row spent with Lefla. He was waking up more often with her than with his own girlfriend. The thought had a disturbing appeal. Lefla had a mute button.

"Care to let me in on the joke?" her holo asked.

"You wouldn't think it was funny."

Her face went flat. "Oh. I see. The punch line makes fun of what I am?"

"Lefla, come on. I can't rest half my brain like you can. At least you've had a download. I haven't had a shower in three days."

An evil gleam sparked in her eyes. "You're talking to someone who gets paid to smell dead things. Trust me, I know exactly how long it's been since your last shower."

Aaron tried to parse what getting paid meant to an unduplicate when an alert softly pinged. Finally, the chemical analysis of the motorcycle was complete. It was such a strange tip to come on the hotline. Just a description and a direction, but it wasn't like a Ducati superbike prototype was all that common. Aaron thought all the stereotypes of Italians were precisely that, until they'd given the thing back to the factory reps. They'd been knocking a few back at a bar in Old Town when Trayne and her companion drove off with it. The chief engineer fainted when they told him it was safe.

Aaron and the rest of the team had been combing the parking lot outside Belle Haven Marina ever since.

As they peered together at the result, Aaron felt strangely reassured by the effort Lefla was making. After all, she already knew what was in the report.

"Well," he said, "at least we know it's Rage. I mean Trayne. I mean, God, I really want my next assignment to be simple. You know, an assassination attempt, maybe a kidnapping?"

Lefla laughed softly. "I'll be right behind you, Aaron. And look, her mysterious bodyguard was with her."

The kid, Spencer, was still being interrogated in Arkansas, but her other male companion, the one they still hadn't managed to identify, had been right here.

The screens outside drew trails where their subjects had walked or stood, so he opened up a channel to the agents outside.

"Jenny, Mosby, over to your left, there's a big tree branch covered with her DNA."

"Geez," Jenny replied, "the pieces are scattered everywhere. Do you think maybe they were attacked?"

"By what?" Mosby replied. "Bears?"

"Aaron," Lefla said, "something's wrong."

She posted up several windows showing the far perimeter. Her ROVs, really just a set of glorified radio-controlled airplanes, cruised over three cars that had pulled into the parking lot, one after the other.

"Agent Park?" Aaron asked. "Something's going on out—"

Lefla's normally very animated holo snapped twice and turned into a plastic doll, a sure sign she'd been forced into a default mode by an outside event. In a far rougher, more robotic voice she said, "Agent Levine. Priority call from Herndon Hospital. Override code six-six-seven-three."

Someone from a hospital was ringing Lefla's emergency line. "Levine here."

"Agent Levine," Adelmo Quispe, of all people, manifested in a window on his left. "You need to pull your people out of there."

Way too many men were piling out of the cars parked on the edge of the marina. "Mr. Quispe, what are you talking about?" He tried gesturing to Lefla, but she couldn't respond; the call put her in emergency mode. "Are you surrendering or something?"

The answer blew him away. "Actually yes, that's exactly what I'm doing, but I'm too far behind you. Agent Levine, pull your people out now. Now!"

No need to tell him twice. Levine cut the channel and smashed the glass cover over Lefla's emergency alert button. Every agent in the area got an override command to activate their vests and dive for cover. Over Lefla's screens he saw faint shimmering wrap around each of the team outside.

Except for Aaron. He couldn't wear a vest inside the van; they interfered with her scanners. A line of assault rifle rounds stitched through the roof of the lab. He covered his head, swearing as hot plastic and metal rained down.

"Aaron!" Lefla shouted, back in control of herself. "They're setting mines!"

Sure enough, two men were setting satchels with flashing detonators beside the truck's wheels. Something ripped through his arm. He had just enough time to realize it was a bullet when Lefla's voice filled his mind. "Aaron. Can you hear me?"

Alarms blared. There was no way she could've overridden the access codes to his neural interface. Goddamn, his arm hurt!

"Yes, Lefla, I can hear you!"

Her eyes flared and she slapped her hands together. "Shit! I can't do it by myself!" Her holograph flashed back to a doll. "Override authorization required. Please confirm."

The reek of burning plastic filled the air as more claxons sounded. "Yes, Lefla! Confirm! Confirm!"

The floor gave way underneath him. Aaron splashed into a tank of fetid muck. A field flickered over him, and then the world went white in thundering violence.

*

"Agent Levine! Agent Levine!" Someone was slapping him.

God, what smelled so bad?

"Agent Levine, open your eyes!"

Who was this old guy? Aaron tried to recognize him, but things kept going in and out of focus. All of the blue and red lights were flashing too fast. Why was it so noisy? What was that smell?

The old man stood up above him with his hands raised as white spotlights blasted him. Adelmo. That was Adelmo Quispe. Why was Adelmo Quispe standing over him? He wasn't a nice guy. It was good they were arresting him. Aaron had been sitting inside Lefla. Where the hell had Lefla gone?

Two EMTs picked him up out of a wrecked bathtub. There were stretchers everywhere, bodies covered with sheets. Worry and panic collided until he was able to find the rest of his team. They were all on the stretchers, groaning but alive.

That still left one missing. "Where's Lefla?"

Small fires were scattered everywhere, hosed down by firemen that had mysteriously sprung into existence around him. The truck should be here. Where the hell had the truck gone?

One of the EMTs moved Aaron's arm and razors of pain shifted around inside it. "LEFLA 3 saved your life, sir. It dumped you into its disposal basin and activated the containment field. Its programming saved you."

LEFLA wasn't an it. Lefla was a she. The world swirled around his head. He collapsed into a stretcher, trying to understand what had gone wrong. The truth crashed in when he saw the torn, smoldering chassis, just wheels and frame rails really, charred black.

Chapter 50
Mike

From the moment they sat down in the bus, they'd been trying to contact Kim's team. It should've been easy, but it had to be according to her rules. It had to be secure. After what had happened at the apartment, Kim didn't think anything was secure.

Mike closed his eyes and put his head against the bus seatback in front of him. It made the bag of chemicals he mostly inhabited lately feel much better. Frustration had never been so exhausting.

"I'm telling you," he said as she sat next to him, "it'll be perfectly safe."

"That's what you said when we tried reverting the encryption stack. My scalp's still itching." She scratched it theatrically.

It didn't help that she was right. He'd just missed one value. But hey, it's not like her hair fell out or anything. Mike stopped the process well before it'd gone that far. "I know what went wrong there. This time it'll work for sure."

"And you're trying to tell me you've checked every line of this config file? It's gotta be two hundred lines long!"

"I'm not stupid, Kim."

"I never said you were stupid, Mike, I said you were—"

"HEY!" Tonya snapped her fingers between them, making them both flinch away. "Save the team now, call each other names later. Right?"

Tonya was the only thing holding them together. He'd been trying to take notes on how she kept Kim in check, but then one of his own encryption attempts had gotten loose. It wasn't his fault the damned thing had burrowed into the bus's engine management system. Tonya and Kim *both* got really shouty when it threatened to catch fire. All he wanted to do was flee deep into the realms. But that wasn't an option tonight.

Tonya sat back and rubbed her eyes. "What are you two trying to do this time, anyway?"

Kim threw her hair back. "What I'm *trying* to do is figure out a way to communicate with the team that won't get us busted again."

"And what I'm trying to tell her is I access all of this and nobody will detect it, but she won't believe me."

Neither of them believed him. It took so long to explain how it all worked. Back-channel conduits and data tunnels didn't just sit there. They moved where his real self lived, like tumblers in a lock. By the time they understood any explanation, the loophole he'd found had closed or the opportunity had passed.

"It's not that I don't believe you, Mike, I just want to make sure it's safe." The way she said it made him afraid to look at her. Electric things happened when her voice went gentle like that.

They needed to understand he was so much more than this muscled skeleton. "All the stuff you're doing is just messing me up. That's why none of it's working."

Tonya used the end of her sleeve to tap on Kim's hand. "I believe him. I think you should too."

Kim stared ahead with her lips pursed in a frown. She took a deep breath. "Okay. You already have their addresses. Here's what I need you to check, and here's what you need to send." She sent over messages addressed to each of the team members.

"Do I get to use any of your toys?"

"What, a bag full of LockPixies wasn't enough for you?" she asked with a wry smile.

He should've known better than to try hiding it. "You weren't supposed to know about that."

"What did you end up doing with them?"

They were on the verge of trusting him, but he wouldn't lie, that would just make it worse. "It... didn't go exactly like I planned. But Spencer's fine now; I checked."

She stopped smiling. "That's why you scare me, Mike. You play around with this stuff, think it's just a big game, and you end up putting people in real danger. You're not in the realms anymore. If you mess up out here, people can die. People *will* die. You're the most amazing person I've ever met, but if you don't start paying attention, none of us will make it out of this alive.

"It's not a game anymore. You can't apologize when it blows up. We won't be around for that. I need you to pay attention. These are people I care deeply about, and I can't protect them right now. You can. Details matter, Mike. Get the details right."

He filed her "amazing" comment away for further analysis. For now, he had a job to do.

"I can. I will." He leaned back, closed his eyes, and fractured himself through the realms.

She was right. He was always in such a rush. All he wanted was to get the task done; get it done, show off the results, and move on to the next challenge. But this time he wouldn't make a mistake.

"How long do you think it'll take him?" he heard Tonya ask as he delivered the first half of the messages.

"Most of them are scattered all over the country, and there's a lot of checking he needs to do."

Well, yes, but that just meant spawning a few hundred more threads to cover the bases. He heard Kim breathe out. The image of her stretching like she always did made it hard to keep the threads synchronized, but he managed it.

"I'm just glad I decided to introduce him to the team. Probably fifteen or twenty minutes."

Mike checked four times before he called it, fifteen seconds later. "Done."

"What?" Kim asked, "How?"

"I told you, I'm not limited sequentially when I'm in the realms. That's how I did the phone call thing."

"The phone call thing?" Tonya asked.

Kim shook her head. "He called every Trayne in northern Virginia, all at once, trying to find my mom. Remind me to kill her when this is over for getting listed again."

Tonya turned to Mike and asked, "Why'd you want to call her mother?"

It was another reminder of how he rushed around jumping to conclusions. "It's complicated. If I'd only known…"

Kim put her hand up. "No, it's okay." A yellow light blinked in their shared channel. "Well, I'll be damned. Emerson's transfer just completed."

Tonya asked, "So is he all right?"

Kim shared her message screen with them. "I don't know. When he reached out toward the screen, he must've been firing duplicates all over the place. Check out the routing for it."

Each segment, and there were millions, had gone through at least three thousand different realms. The pattern was so random even Mike couldn't make it out. No wonder it'd taken most of an hour to assemble. It shouldn't be a coherent signal, let alone a real message. Emerson was a nutball, but he was also a genius. He'd been the first human to find him, after all.

"Wow." It was the only thing he could say.

Tonya checked the map display as it slid by on the ceiling of the bus. "We've definitely got the time. What's it say?"

Kim reconfigured their shared space as the bus bounced through another empty stop.

They were in a realm, sitting on a bench in a small amphitheater. Matthew Watchtell walked onto the stage.

"Prime Ministers and Presidents, thank you for attending this presentation."

They were in the front row, on the far-left corner. The whole thing was a replay, but Tonya still whispered when she leaned over to ask, "Who's that?"

"Matthew Watchtell." Kim nodded to Mike. "I told you he'd be at the bottom of this."

Tonya cocked her head. "Who's Matthew Watchtell?"

Kim pulled at her earrings. "A man who makes deals."

Watchtell walked across the well-lit stage to address what appeared to be a group of about a dozen people. Mike never had much reason to pay attention to the politics of outside, but he was a slave to the *Daily Mail*'s realm. Because of that, he recognized every single person seated around them. World leaders. By their reaction, Kim and Tonya recognized them too.

"Twenty years ago, Phillip Masterson's quantum computer design created the biggest unmitigated disaster ever experienced in human history."

It was a downright strange way to characterize the most important technological innovation in the past forty years or so.

"No government had any prior notice. Unbreakable security was suddenly made real."

Images of war, starving children, and poor workers appeared behind Watchtell.

"In an instant, any effort at real justice was destroyed. Corporate criminals now hide their profits, and we can't find them or seize their accounts. Multinational conglomerates grow unspeakably powerful, and we can't control them. Drug lords have immunity, and terrorists now plot our destruction daily. We can do *nothing*. More wealth is concentrated in the hands of fewer people than ever before, and all any of us can do is helplessly look on.

"Until now."

A series of new pictures illustrating lab workers and expensive equipment spread around him. "Five years ago, while I was a part of the Donaldson administration, a secret government lab discovered a flaw in Masterson's design."

Kim snorted and glared, but then shook her head when Mike frowned at her.

"Until that point, any attempt to modify them ended in failure, but" — graphics built a new sort of computer as he spoke — "we finally found a way.

"We cannot do this alone. I'm here to offer all of you the opportunity to force justice onto the lawless chaos that is realmspace. If you would please turn your—"

The recording froze, the sound wound down, and then it all smeared sideways and melted away. They found themselves back in the bus, looking at the now-empty space through a virtual window. Kim swore and manipulated controls frantically.

"Is that all we got?" Tonya asked.

There was more, but it was unsalvageable. A fierce wave of vertigo swirled through him, a sure sign Kim was doing her thing. The realmspace around the bus locked solid with such force it made his eyes water.

She worked her hacking tools furiously. "Wait... just a second."

Controls and indicators spun madly around her. She took a breath and managed to say, "I can save this. Come on, damn you, come on... Mike!"

She tossed an access key at him just as Emerson's realm and its underlying data crumbled. It allowed him to reach out with his threads, through and behind it all. There was definitely more to the transmission than a simple replay, but it was dissolving fast. He spread himself out and around the message's foundations, curling through and working with the structures, shoring them up as it all tried to come apart like sandcastles in a tide.

Even though they were sweating with the effort, Kim spared enough time to smile straight at him. He wasn't the only one who felt how easy it was working together like this.

In the shared viewspace, a black square formed. White lines started scribbling across it. "Wait," Tonya said, "I know what this is."

"Tonya!" Kim swore and grabbed another set of virtual controls. It was falling apart faster now.

"Record it, now!" Mike finished.

Kim scrambled and struggled with automatic functions.

A counter-virus had broken free and dissolved it faster than Mike could shore it up.

"They're blueprints!" Tonya said.

"Not if we don't save them they're not," Kim replied.

Everyone worked as hard and as fast as they could, just ahead of the wave of disintegration. A big crack formed in the construct, climbing left.

"Kim," Mike warned.

"I know, I know, I see it. Just a little longer. Tonya, please!"

Tonya scribbled frantically. "I've got it!"

Emerson's message shattered into an infinite cloud of sparkling motes and washed away around them. Tonya shook her hands like they'd been burned.

Kim looked like she'd just run a marathon. "Well, there went our proof."

It had been one hell of a workout for an uncertain payoff. "It wasn't enough. That wasn't a smoking gun; it was a RealmWay recruiting ad with a really famous audience."

"Yeah," Tonya said as the bus finally pulled into the parking lot of the Metro station. The blueprints she'd saved scribbled their way across their shared space. "But I bet this place may have more for us."

They got off the bus, then sat down in the shelter of one of the stops. The blueprints were for a building—a big building.

"Well." Kim said when an address not far from where they were scrawled into existence in the bottom corner of the plans. "I know what we're gonna do tonight."

Chapter 51
Spencer

It had been the mother of all clusterfucks. Spencer flopped into the recliner in his room. Twelve hours of interrogation. Twelve hours! He forgot how awful his parents could be to each other, until they were together in that interrogation room. And then they turned on him. Even the lawyer couldn't stop them. If he'd known that was coming, he would've just sunk to the bottom of the lake with the truck.

He checked his TwitterBook and sure enough, there were several messages from Mike. Nothing from Kim. *Nice to know somebody loves me*. He transitioned to The Resort.

It was by far his favorite realm. It didn't start out as a teen-only hangout—technically, it still wasn't—things just sort of ended up that way when the owner of a particular realm wanted his then fourteen-year-old daughter to have a safe place to hang out. It helped that the owner's name was Evan Stanley, so The Resort became to teenagers what Bards was to everyone else.

None of it would've been possible without Aunt Fee. She started her career as the third unduplicate AI ever designed, and the first meant to last more than a year. She was created to manage Fed/UPS's entire worldwide logistics chain single-handedly, twenty-four-seven. If global economic growth had not been in the sixth year of an unprecedented boom, the half-million employees she put out of work would've likely destabilized labor markets, even whole governments, all over the world. The protests were still the stuff of legend.

Five years later newer, simpler AIs came on the market that didn't require continuous connections to the Evolved Internet. Just like that, she was obsolete. Two weeks after being retired, Stanley picked her up at an auction made legendary by his fight with an anonymous bidder. It made her the most valuable construct in the history of realmspace. Stanley knew that, unlike Bards, a realm inhabited by teenagers would be a place filled with adult bodies making childish decisions. Someone would have to watch them all, all the time.

And so a construct previously known only as FE-1 was up-graded and retasked as Aunt Fee. She was equipped with a database detailing the cultural mores and legal laws of every society on the planet, and then told to keep the peace. It made her the most culturally aware entity of all time. When combined with a brilliantly designed realm, the result changed human history.

Developed countries had come to terms with women who had no fear of pregnancy generations ago. Now the entire world was coming to terms with women who had no fear of rape. The Resort was an unbreakably private place where young people could do whatever they wanted as long as it was legal and everyone consented.

Yes, there were controls, and it was more than possible for parents to prohibit their teens from visiting the place entirely. But these were teenagers. A ban wasn't a prohibition; it was a challenge. Most who tried succeeded in overcoming it.

None of that actually mattered much to Spencer. All he cared about was that at the Resort he could find people sitting around amazing lounges discussing whatever struck their fancy. He'd had unbelievably interesting conversations covering topics from who'd be the next President or prime minister, to what evolution actually meant in the history of fifth-century Cambodia, to which one was better: Enterprise or Death Star?

Spencer did it all without worrying about peer pressure, judgment, or violence. He even discovered that, if he were clever enough, girls would seek him out. Supposedly, it wasn't close to the real thing, but it was plenty close enough for him. Spencer loved the place for all that. Even better, Fee was the one who'd introduced him to Mike.

As he stood in one of the primary lounges, a dark, sultry voice above him said, "And where have you been all this time, sir?"

At first, Fee had presented an image of kindly motherhood to all her charges, based on an old television show about a small Southern town. She got better results by pretending to be a scatter-brained aunt to the girls and what could be gently described as "the mom I'd like to… get to know better" to the boys.

"He made it, Fee," Spencer said as he sat down on the end of a couch.

"Who made what, Spencer?"

"Mike. He's out there, Fee. He did it."

After almost half a minute of silence, he boggled. In the past four days he'd witnessed a miracle, made friends with a legend, and had now rendered an unduplicate speechless.

"Fee?"

"Spencer, if you remember nothing else in your life, you must remember that moment."

"Oh, Fee, I don't think you have to worry about that."

"No, Spencer. I'm serious."

She manifested her avatar, to him a mature woman with lightly tanned skin and beautiful dark eyes. She wore an elaborate, elegant black dress. Conversations around them stuttered to a stop as people tried to figure out why she was here. "You have no idea how important this is. You really saw him?"

"Jesus, Fee, you're talking like I just saw Superman. What the hell is up with you?"

Fee knelt down and grabbed his hands. "I am so very proud of you." Fee stood, looked away, then turned back to him, face stern.

"The terms of the deal still stand, Spencer. Remind him of that." She vanished just as his phone rang.

Spencer answered the call as calmly as he could and walked to a different lounge to avoid all the stares. "Mike, you have no idea how weird my life just got."

"It's even weirder now? You're having one helluva week, dude. You realize they caught a video of your jump? You're in the top five on Reddit!"

Spencer winced at the thought and at the bruises that were tracing a seatbelt pattern over his body in realspace. "Dude, don't remind me. I think I'm gonna be doing community service around here till I'm thirty."

Spencer noticed the time stamp on the call. "I just had a really weird conversation with Fee, but at the end she wanted you to know the deal still stands."

The deal was that Fee absolutely forbid Mike from setting foot—well, hologram—in the Resort. He couldn't even message anyone in the Resort for more than two minutes. Spencer had to admit there were good reasons for those restrictions.

Being a teenager, Spencer had naturally conspired with Mike to test the Resort's rules. Together they decided filling the entire realm with skunk-scented shaving cream would be the perfect stunt. Mike timed their exploit perfectly, only to find Fee standing at the entrance of the back door. Years later people still called Spencer Father Monkey on occasion. Mike had donkey ears and a tail pinned to his holo for most of a month. Hell, she made him bray for a week. He never did figure out how she did it.

"What?" Mike asked. "Oh, right. I still have a minute and a half though."

Spencer nodded even though Mike couldn't see him. "Just that much."

Mike's voice changed as he switched away from Spencer's line. "Okay. Kim."

Spencer smiled; Mike had forgotten to mute his phone.

"It's complicated. I made a deal. I can't even message anyone in there for more than two minutes."

"I am not setting foot in that cesspool of hormones."

"Really, Kim? Is it so much worse than the Pink—"

"Damn it, Mike, I told you we'd talk about that later. Just tell the little insect that if I walk face first into a scrotum, he'll never be safe again."

"You getting this, Spencer?"

"Yeah, Mike, it's cool."

Now that he knew the person behind the Angel Rage legend, it was obvious where the name came from. The lady definitely had anger issues.

The thing was, he wasn't attracted to her at all. It was a first for him. Kim was hot, but there was too much history and way too much fear. It would've been like wanting to sleep with a really pretty wood chipper. There were much safer ways to scratch that itch.

"I'm in the main lounge anyway. Tell her morphic deviation is held to seven percent around here."

"No, really, Kim, you'll be fine. I can't hold this call open any longer."

"Why not? What's so weird about The Resort that you can't—"

"Damn it, Kim, for once in your life would you do something without arguing about it? Just go."

"I don't take orders from you."

"Orders? I wasn't ordering you to do anything."

Spencer shook his head as the argument ramped right up to ramming speed. "Fee, a little help?"

"My pleasure."

Kim gasped as she manifested in the foyer to Spencer's left. She snapped her fingers and everything flickered and slowed to a halt.

Fee said, "Spencer! Who is that? What did she do?"

He had no idea. "Kim, what did you do?"

She marched up to him. "Nobody, least of all you, opens a trap-door under my feet."

She patted herself down and seemed relieved to still have clothes on. "If I'd fallen into one of those disgusting wolf pits they have around here…"

A rasping electronic voice announced, "This unit requires your attention."

Spencer turned. At first, he simply didn't recognize the construct. It was a faceted, dull tin thing rolling on treads. If he hadn't been taking Contemporary American History that semester, he would never have known this was Fee's first avatar. It felt like seeing his mom naked.

"You are in violation of contract protocols. Please exit immediately."

Kim's eyes narrowed. "I'm sorry, what is your designation?"

"This unit is FE-1."

She closed her eyes. "I am truly sorry."

There was a twisting through the effect, and Fee resumed her normal appearance and movement. She breathed deep and hugged herself.

Kim said, "I just need to explain to this little monster how rude it is to—"

"Spencer didn't open the trapdoor, I did." Fee raised her hand and cupped it, as if grabbing a control Spencer couldn't see. "And I must again insist..."

Spencer's ears popped. The inside of his head folded sideways.

"...that you release my fabric completely and leave. Now."

Spencer's dad used to take him to bars when he was a kid, giving him enough cash to play the video games and pinball machines for hours at a time. He'd seen exactly two old-fashioned bar fights go down. This reminded him of the time the guys pulled knives on each other. Except Fee used some sort of weird distortion field that twisted her fist in a direction that made his head ache.

Kim set her jaw and threw her hand downward. A manifestation of raw energy flew into being, puckering the space around it like a heavy rock dropped on a rubber sheet. What Fee had was a blowtorch, but what Kim had was a supernova.

Spencer knew there was no way Fee could survive a strike from that. "Jesus, Kim, don't hurt her."

"I didn't come here for a fight," Kim said.

Fee's torch doubled in brightness. "That's what you're getting."

It wouldn't be enough to even scratch Kim. "Fee!" Spencer said, trying to keep his eyeballs pointing in the same direction. His feet felt like they were on backward. "She knows Mike!"

Fee gathered even more power. Thunder blasted through the realm. He tasted electricity and smoke.

"I don't care who she knows. Nobody tries to rip apart half a realm on my watch just because—"

Fee didn't understand. She probably thought Kim was some wannabe hacker who'd found an unpatched vulnerability. Spencer knew exactly who this was and what happened when someone crossed her. "Fee! Listen to me! This is Angel Rage!"

Fee barked out, "WHAT?" at the exact moment Kim yelled, "SPENCER!" Then they both let go at once.

The entire realm twisted up, curled sideways, and with a snap, it was all completely normal—except everything was absolutely silent.

A vase wobbled off an end table and fell, shattering beside him on the floor.

The realm fell into motion again, but everyone around them acted as if nothing had happened at all.

Kim straightened her dress and said quietly, "That was uncalled for. I'm sorry."

"No," Fee said, taking a shuddering breath with her hand to her chest, paler than Spencer had ever seen her, "you were right."

She turned gracefully toward him. "Spencer, it's very rude to trapdoor people into a realm. You know that."

"But you..." He stopped at the look Fee gave him, a mixture of embarrassment and real fear that told him to shut up and let her handle it.

Fee turned toward Kim. "So, you're his warrior."

He had no idea Fee knew about Mike's project. If Spencer's week got any more complicated, he was certain his head would explode.

"Amazing," Fee said. She ran a finger across Kim's jaw, grasped her shoulder, and stared straight into her eyes. "Be kind to him, when you can."

She vanished. Spencer was vaguely disappointed. His head was supposed to make an earth-shattering kaboom now, because that's sure as hell what it felt like.

"Spencer," Kim said, standing still as a statue, "what was that all about?"

"I haven't got a clue. Not one. My life stopped making sense on Saturday."

It was all so exhausting. He felt like the way his teachers looked at the end of classes. Too much to do, not enough time to do it in.

"Mike said you needed help?"

Kim sat down in the chair opposite his. "It's my team. They may be exposed, and I need you to help them."

She explained the situation, who Emerson was, and what happened with his message.

"Wait a minute." Spencer held his hand up. "If it's not safe for you to be in the realms, what the hell are you doing here?"

"Mike's helping me. Some sort of protected circuit. But we need him for other things tonight, and I can't split myself like he can."

"Do you trust him?"

"Actually, I do. Anyway, if they can find me, they might be able to find the rest of the team. I can't have that." She pulled a small bag out of her purse. "You'll need these for monitoring."

"These?"

"A few million LockPixies."

"Lock… oh, that's right."

Kim looked at him sharply and he turned away.

"Um, never mind."

"Are *you* going to tell me what happened?"

He considered briefly and then drawled, "Probably not. But I'm fine now! Mike even checked!"

She rolled her eyes. "It'll take you a while to task them properly. Don't try to reprogram them. They're more powerful than they seem."

Spencer nodded. "Oh, I know all about that."

"Do you." It was more accusation than question.

"That's need-to-know, Kim. Sorry."

"Never mind. I don't have much time. The rental is due to arrive any minute. We have things we really need to get done over here."

She finished telling him her ideas and strategies, complicated stuff that Spencer knew about but had never tried before.

"And we need you to pick up maps and imagery for this address. Carefully."

"I dunno. I'm not as fast as you are with this stuff." He paused, terrified of what he wanted to tell her, but she needed to know. "I've got my own crew. They can really help. They're good guys."

"Spencer, this isn't a game. People could get hurt."

"I know." He rubbed his chest in realspace. "Trust me, I know. But they can help, and they can keep their mouths shut."

"If it means anything to you," Fee's voice intruded, "I can vouch for them."

Kim closed her eyes and took a deep breath. "The old ways are what got me into this mess. Okay, Spencer, your call. Bring in whoever you need, but make my people safe."

Fee's voice pitched deeper. "Aren't you going to tell her what your group is called, Spencer?"

Oh, great. She would bring that up. "That's not really important right now."

"You all have a name?" Kim asked. "Do tell."

It was just like the time when Mom made him kiss Grandma Mary when he was six, except nobody bellowed a drunken "give her some sugar, boy!" But this was Kim, which made the moment infinitely worse.

He opened his eyes. Fee had reappeared, because of course she'd want to be present when he said the most embarrassing thing he'd ever say in his life. He'd rather stick his head in a bag full of used jockstraps, but they weren't going away.

"God! Okay! Shit! We call ourselves The New Machine, all right?"

Fee smiled. "Give her the *whole* name, Spencer."

There were times when having the Goddess of the Resort as a personal friend was a good thing. This was not one of those times. He should've let Kim blow her to bits; it would've at least spared him this humiliation. "Okay. Shit. Damn it! We call ourselves Fear + The New Machine. There. Happy?"

Fee chuckled and faded away.

Kim's grin spread right across her face. She raised an eyebrow. "Really?"

"It's a tribute. Okay? You know, a thing fans do? We set it all up way before I ever met—"

Spencer's breath caught at the way she flared up, but then he relaxed slightly. He was starting to get used to how Kim could go from happy-sexy-hacker-doll to bitch-with-the-flying-daggers so quickly.

"Anyway, go save the world or Mike or whatever you have to do. I got this."

The smile Kim turned on as she stood nearly made him forget how terrifying she could be.

"It's okay, Spencer. I think it's sweet." She winked at him as she walked into an atrium, and then disappeared.

He jumped at the voice behind him. "And who, exactly, was that?"

The day wouldn't be complete without getting busted by his girlfriends. Spencer's luck had been running at negative eleven the whole time, no reason for it to change now. He turned around, and sure enough, all three of them were there, with expressions that promised pain—and not the good kind.

Maybe honesty would throw them off. "Oh. Hi, guys. That was Kim."

"Kim?" Jen asked. "Just Kim?"

Nope, that didn't work; it just made her clench her fists tighter. Chun, standing next to her, stopped glaring only long enough to roll her eyes.

Keeping three girls at once was a danger everyone told him he didn't need. He was beginning to understand why.

"And when were you planning on telling us you'd got back?" Maria's accent was always so distracting, but he didn't dare crack a joke about Panama now. "You just ran the hell off without even calling!"

He put his hands out in front of him, trying to stop them before they really got rolling. "Wait, guys, wait! I have good news! We have a job! You're never gonna believe who it's for…"

Chapter 52
Watchtell

It was just like the old days. He'd gotten within a step of Rage only to have her vanish like the morning mist. Even forcing Zeta to—briefly—perform as Marie Antoinette hadn't calmed him. He needed Rage brought down, now.

It took real effort to get his legs to stop twitching.

"Any new leads, Gary?"

He shook his head. "It's gone completely quiet now. We're seeing shadows of activity, but nothing's strong enough to get a lock."

"And you're using all the assets now, yes?" It was the first time all of Sidereal had been active at once. It was a real risk to the agents. They only had three, and he couldn't afford to lose one. But with Rage this close and still free, he would hazard anything to protect Havelock.

Gary nodded. "Absolutely. The threat in the UK has been eliminated."

"Have you confirmed a breach yet?"

"No. The target was a well-known eccentric located in the Glastonbury area. He had physical booby traps on all his data stores. He spent most of his time on insane hunts and ridiculous conspiracies. Things like reviving Hitler, a conscious being emerging out of the EI, hidden bases on Mars, alliances with extraterrestrials, just absurd stuff. But he did manage to lead us to Rage."

The truth was bitter. They were so *close*. "And she got away anyway."

"We couldn't have missed her by more than a few minutes. She compromised every security system in a five-mile radius of that apartment. I'm surprised we got as close as we did. She's still making mistakes."

Matthew needed direction; he needed to regain control. Rage moved faster than he did, and that had to stop. "Call a meeting of the department heads right now. Wake them up if you have to."

"What are you thinking?"

He could move fast too, now that he saw the need. "We launch Havelock tomorrow, 6:00 p.m. at the latest."

He held up his hand at Gary's protest. "I'll authorize triple pay and reinstitute GifTree."

At this point, he could waste anything except time. The people here that would make it happen didn't respond to the more direct forms of motivation he'd be using in the international factories. Putting them on a starvation diet would take far longer than he had, anyway. He thought of another motivator.

"This time the first team past the post will get an all-expenses-paid trip to Wyndham Tranquility."

Singh's mouth dropped open. "You'll send them to the moon? How will you get the tickets?"

The hotel had only been open for a few weeks, but there were ways. Being a former White House chief of staff left him with an impressive Rolodex of contacts. He'd gathered enough dirt on all of them to ensure enthusiastic cooperation.

"Let me worry about that. Have someone else organize the meeting. I need you to start something else."

He gripped his hands together to hide how they trembled. "I'm tired of chasing a ghost, Gary. I want you to move Sidereal to Havelock's site. Assume she's found us, and plan accordingly."

Chapter 53
Kim

She parked the car in the far corner of a nearby grocery store, and they all walked the two blocks it took to reach the target.

"Are you sure this is it?" Tonya asked.

She double checked. Again. "It's the right address. Look at that fence."

It surrounded the single-story building, at least ten feet tall, made of folded sheet metal rods about an inch wide that were spaced not more than four inches apart. The tops splayed out into sharp blades, and the whole thing was painted glossy black. If Watchtell had been able to put a moat in, he probably would've. He loved his castles to a fault, which was why she was here.

Mike was lost in the details, as always. "I think, if it were made of wood anyway, that would be called a palisade."

Tonya grimaced. "Great. We've found your fort, Kim. Now how do we get inside?"

The manned guard shack and the giant steel fence were a surprise for Mike and Tonya, but to her this was old hat, another tour around the block. All the years of hiding, of pretending this wasn't real, that people like Watchtell didn't exist, fell away.

She was the veteran now, not a child, not a precocious lockpick. Now that she knew there would never be a reunion, Kim was finally admitting to herself that no matter how nice they'd been about it, the Machine used her back then. It burned, but that was the past. The dead had already buried the dead, years ago.

Kim turned back to the task at hand. Every sensor imaginable covered the building, but as usual, they made a mistake.

"The cameras aren't wireless," she said as the searches ran. Tell-tales flashed to life in her vision. "I think I've found what we need."

She moved back to the bike trail, walking to the other corner of the building. After a bit of scanning, Kim spotted it. "Yes!" Leaving the details to his servants was how she got away the last time. Nice to know some things never changed.

"What've you found?" Mike asked.

"They hired an outside security firm to backstop the guy at the gate. Look, there's the junction box that joins the camera feeds."

The view she shared showed a large white box where a spider's web of cables came together, and a much thicker cable left the bottom, disappearing into the ground. It wasn't as good as a key under a floor mat, but for someone like her it was close.

Tonya stepped back. "Why aren't they using wireless? Isn't hacking all this stuff impossible?"

Out of nowhere Mike said, "Everything's theoretically impossible, until it's done."

He was getting better at picking just the right thing to say to get her laughing. It took his smile getting bigger before she realized she was staring again.

Not now.

Tonya shook her head. "What's next?"

"We need the cabinet for the whole block. We're trying to find a big tan box, probably six feet tall and about eight wide."

They found it farther up the bike trail in the backyard of a church.

Kim moved her hands around and found the electronic nexus. She pushed her power at it and winced at the gunshot in her head. But when she tried the handle, nothing moved, which was just her luck. These things started life as phone cabinets with standard stupid tumbler locks. Kim would never admit it, but Spencer did have a point. Sometimes old stuff sucked. She dove into her purse and pulled out her lockpicks.

"Lean back, Tonya, this is gonna take a while." Mike said.

Yeah, he was the expert. Standing by while Spencer coached Mike on how to pick locks back at Watchtell's house was like watching Beavis teach Butthead how to cook.

With a finesse of the upper pick, there was a loud clack. Bingo. The door made a hollow, echoing creak as it moved on its hinges. She peered over it at him. "You were saying?"

His look of outrage was reward enough. "It took me half an hour."

"That's because you suck. And so does Spencer."

"What happens now?" Tonya asked.

Kim pulled a thin wire out of her purse, hooked it to a port on the pendant around her neck, and then pushed the other end into a socket in the cabinet. "Now you get to see what I'm all about."

She sent them a realm address, and then smiled at their stares. "No, really. It's actually kinda cool. Oh," she pointed at Mike. "No moving around out here. We clear?"

He held his hands up and took a few steps backward. "Absolutely."

She positioned herself behind the utility cabinet anyway. Standing up while accessing realmspace didn't take much practice, but it didn't hurt to take precautions against another zombie walk. The thought of leaving realmspace wrapped in his arms again brought up a swarm of emotions. For the first time in her life, fear, horror, and sadness didn't dominate them.

She had no time for this, not now.

Not ever.

Tonya manifested in the realm and twirled trying to find a place to stand. "Wow, Kim, it's really—"

Mike cursed colorfully, his voice coming from all around them as the lights dimmed for a second. She grinned at the floor. It was fascinating to discover what would trip him up.

"It's really tight in here!"

Kim stopped briefly. "That's what she said."

Tonya laughed and rolled her eyes.

Kim jostled her around as she rapidly moved from console to console, adjusting controls and checking readouts.

"Wait," Mike said, "are we actually in your phone?"

"Yup," Kim said, spinning a few large handles above her head. "You've never heard of a TinyCore realm?"

"Heard of? Yes. Tried to fit in? Whole different question."

Two small, perfectly square cabinets formed on either side of her. Kim opened the one on the left. The stuff inside coruscated and rippled with pink and purple flashes that sang chords at her; she hummed back, and it replied with the smell of mint. Access acknowledged. It had been so long since she'd done this. It felt like shaking a thick layer of dust off her shoulders.

She reached in, then pulled a spinning, glowing tendril out that was about as long as her arm. She whirled it around twice to form a loop. She reached into the other box, then pulled out an identical tendril.

"Mike, I need you to count down thirty seconds for me, starting now." She closed her eyes.

There were lines of potential and she couldn't remember how to breathe. See this see it again and again trust me trust me believe me nothing changes this wave lowest highest. She paused and held the constructs open in her mind, the need to breathe building a desperate pressure inside her as Mike counted down. When he reached thirty *collapse and now...*

She opened her eyes. The two pieces met in the middle, the information inside them visibly looping back and forth.

"Wow," Tonya said, "that was pretty freaking cool. Right, Mike? Mike?"

Kim breathed deep and slow to stop the urge to pant. It'd been a while since she'd done something that hard, but the mental muscles hadn't gone away. She blew a thick strand of hair off her avatar's face.

"You out there, Sellars?" She clamped randomizers and logic samples to the looping information to make sure a car or a regularly waving branch didn't give them away.

"I wish you guys could've seen it the way I do. Kim, that was the most amazing… it's not even supposed to be possible… and then you… that wasn't just cool, Kim, that was spectacular."

He'd just seen how weird she really was, from a perspective she didn't really understand, and he wasn't horrified.

He admired her. "Why thank you, Mr. Sellars."

They all exited.

"So what did that get us?" Tonya asked. "Did it unlock a secret gate somewhere?"

"No," Kim said, swinging the cabinet's big metal door shut with a clang. "The outside cameras are now stuck showing a loop of the past thirty seconds. We still need to get past the fence."

Mike snapped his fingers. "I've got this one, follow me."

He led them to a different, completely unprotected office building adjacent to their target. The far end of its parking lot came very close to the fence, leaving a narrow, unpaved area between them.

"You'd think someone would trim this tree."

It was a maple tree, with thick branches that extended over the fence and into the other side's parking lot.

Right. She was supposed to scrabble up a splinter farm, and then walk over thin air supported by firewood. "Guys, I never was all that good at climbing trees."

Tonya picked up a fallen branch a few feet long. "We can help you if you grab onto this. I hear you're pretty good with branches."

"Oh, she's better than good," Mike said. "Remind me to show you the bruises."

A cringe crawled up from her boots and didn't leave until it hit the top of her head. When the stabilization field on the bike collapsed, it was either grab him or die. The pain was excruciating, the madness even worse. That's why she flipped out when they'd parked. It was completely uncalled for. Kim genuinely could've sent him to the hospital, in that moment had *wanted* to send him to the hospital, yet Mike was acting like it'd never happened. She was afraid to ask why.

There was no time for blame; they had to get into that building. "Are we doing this, or what?"

The tree climb wasn't too bad, but it was just one of a chain of puzzles she had to solve. They couldn't simply walk into the building. There had to be even more cameras inside, and she already knew they weren't connected to the EI.

So she went at the problem sideways. The building had a gigantic APU installed in a separate outdoor enclosure. As long as the place had biodiesel, they had power. Since the outside cameras didn't work anymore, it was no problem breaking in. It only took a few minutes to find the control box. She rummaged in her purse for a lootTap. Once it connected and booted up, Kim smiled. Every office manager in the south wanted to control the AC from their desktop, which meant the APU was part of the main network. The more you complicate the plumbing…

"So, Mike," Tonya asked behind her, "what did you do, you know, before all this?"

"Well, over the past few years I designed and built *Warhawk*. I've been running it ever since."

"You own *Warhawk*?" The way Tonya said it set Kim's teeth on edge. The news he owned a famous realm wasn't as cool after paying for his food and clothing. And setting up his apartment. And buying him a car. Kim stopped what she was doing and glared at him until he cringed. She nodded briefly and went back to work, scowling.

"So."

The sultry tone in Tonya's voice made Kim raise an eyebrow, but she was too busy to look up again.

"What does a girl have to do to get a date with a successful realm designer?"

The gravel crunched under his feet as Mike shifted back and forth. "I dunno, ask?"

Sure, like anything he was involved in could ever be that simple.

Tonya's voice turned playful, which rang alarm bells Kim didn't know she had. "Oh, Mike, that's not how the game is played. Girls don't ask boys out; it's the other way around. Now, what would it take for a girl, maybe like me, to convince a successful realm designer, maybe like you, that she would be fun to have around?"

Kim spent all this time and effort keeping him going, and now he was going to let Tonya swoop in and take him away. She wants Mike? Fine, that's great. The thundering in her ears made her nearly miss the alert that the security system compromise was finished.

"If you two are done flirting, we're in." She turned around.

Tonya was so close to Mike she was practically breathing in his ear.

Mike shook his head. "I wasn't flirting. Was I?"

Tonya laughed easily as she walked away. "No, hon, you weren't." Her eyes locked on to Kim's with a fierce stare as her voice went hard. "But I was."

The implication doused her anger. Mike wasn't her toy, and he wasn't a dog she could kick any time she liked. He was a person, and if Kim wasn't careful, someone else could easily take him away from her. The thought jangled her badly. She blushed and nodded. Game, set, and match, ma'am.

Mike walked to a different door, then cleared his throat. "I think this one leads to a building entrance?"

She and Tonya stayed behind in a utility room while Mike made his way to the front desk. Tonya gasped when he just vanished. "How does he do that?"

Kim held up her hand briefly and sent to Mike: THERE SHOULD BE SOME BADGES WAITING FOR US IN A PRINTER.

"Really, where did he learn how to do that?" Tonya asked.

Kim tried to think of a quick way to explain the strangest of Mike's mysteries. "He didn't, not really. The person who used to own that body, the one who died, he was an assassin, probably the best in the business." Or worst, depending on how you looked at it.

"Mike's an *assassin*?"

"No, it's more complicated than that. The guy's name was Colque, a total nightmare of a man."

"You mean you *knew* the guy who used to own that body?"

Well, it did seem crazy until you nestled it in with all the other lunacy that surrounded Kim her whole life. Then it was only a little eccentric.

"It's a really long story, and I promise to tell you about it when this is over. The point is that the assassin is dead, but Mike is able to access the muscle memory that made up most of Colque's skills."

Kim needed to change the subject. Talking about Colque somehow brought his memory closer to Mike's, and her life was confusing enough already. "Mike, are you there yet?"

"Jesus, Kim, don't do that!"

"Do what?" How many ways could she screw up tonight? "What did I do now?"

"No, it's okay. Sneaking around like this is harder than it looks."

Kim heard the beeps of door locks over his line. "Damn it!" he whispered. "Someone just walked in!"

"Are you okay?"

The silence stretched long enough for her pulse to kick up a few notches, but he finally replied. "I'm fine."

She turned to Tonya. "Someone walked in."

Mike opened the channel again. "Kim? I'm pretty sure we're not going to have to worry about these two."

"What are you talking about? How do you know there's just two of them?" She included Tonya in the conversation just as Mike opened the microphone on his phone to ambient sound.

What came over the line brought her up short. Tonya was just as surprised. People didn't normally ask, well, demand, for *that* in an office. When the first slap of a hand hitting bare skin cracked out, their jaws basically hit the floor. Then there was the snap of a whip, jingling chains, and the snick of handcuffs locking together. These two were quite athletic.

Kim needed to get him moving.

"Mike, stop hanging around and get back here." She cut the line and fought the urge to fan herself.

"I don't know," Tonya said. "I was about to take some notes."

She rolled her eyes. "He's an amateur. You have to pause longer between the lashes to maximize the burn." She stumbled to a stop at Tonya's face, which was more disapproving than anything else.

"What?" Kim shrugged. "I'm a competitive person!"

"Let me guess, there's a realm tournament for S&M?"

"No." Kim smiled wistfully as she recalled that dungeon realm. It had such a clever arrangement of restraints. "But there was a weekly contest. It was a nice prize."

Tonya raised an eyebrow. "How many times did you win?"

Kim thought for a second and shrugged. "Twelve."

"Out of?"

"Out of what?" Mike asked as he entered the room to hand them their badges.

"Out of… this place," Tonya covered smoothly. "I was wondering when you'd get back so we could get out of here."

When Mike turned away, Tonya winked at her.

Kim closed her eyes, shrugged, and silently mouthed, "Twelve."

They crossed the glassed-in foyer pretending to be two workers deep in conversation, with Tonya hiding behind them. They all waited, listening for an alarm, a siren, or any other sign that the guard outside had spotted them. After a few moments of nothing but the athletic couple and their antics, Kim motioned toward the elevators.

"Excellent," Tonya said, breathing out and slumping her shoulders as the doors slid shut. "Which floor is the data center?"

By the way he blushed, Mike had forgotten to look for it too.

"Guys?" Tonya prompted.

Kim started, "That probably would've been—"

"—a good thing to figure out ahead of time," Mike finished.

She glared at him while he did the same at her.

"You're kidding me," Tonya said. "We make it all the way inside an actual, for-real, bad-guy lair, and you guys forgot to find the target?"

Kim pointed. "Well he didn't remind me!"

"I told you we should've looked at the index key!"

Tonya slapped her forehead. "You two have got to be dumbest white people I have ever known!"

"There were teenagers everywhere distracting me in that realm! The avatars were ridiculous!"

"And Kim's little realm pinched!"

"I can't believe this," Tonya said. "There are seven floors underground. It'll take all night to find it!"

The door bonged, and two rather disheveled people jumped back when they found three other people in the elevator and shouts still echoing off the walls. Everyone froze, staring at everyone else. Tonya was stuck with her finger pointing in the air.

Kim's brain unlocked first. "And that's why it's so important for us to be here, damn it. I'm sorry, but it just is!"

Mike and Tonya shifted and nodded in meek agreement.

Tonya smiled at the couple. "Going down?"

The woman, a petite brunette whose hair had probably started out quite pretty, managed to stutter out, "We'll take the next one."

The man, a redhead who must've been at least a foot taller, said, "Yes, you guys." He waved his hands. "You go right ahead." He gave up trying to tuck his shirt in.

Kim's hand shot out and hit the button for the bottom floor. Everyone on either side of the doors stood and straightened and fussed until they shut.

"God," Mike said. "Do you think they'll say anything?"

Kim knew better. "Not on your life. We're wearing the same kind of badges they had on. Having the right ID and acting like you're supposed to be here has gotten me past so many chance encounters, I've lost count."

It turned out the seventh floor was a lab with white hallways and tile floors. On either side, there were long narrow rooms with windows facing the hall. Some of them held polished steel equipment, holographic projectors, and workbenches with scattered pieces of computers. Others were more like chemistry labs with elaborate distillation rigs and tanks of chemicals that had complex labels on their sides.

Everything was spotless, and by the new smell, could not have been more than a few years old. Kim stopped in front of a large door that didn't open into the labs on either side of it.

"Here we are."

It was an equipment room about twenty feet wide and at least twice as deep. The main lights were off, leaving the tall racks of equipment shrouded darkness. Barely visible computers filled each rack from top to bottom. They each had flickering green, blue, and red lights arranged in neat rows. They went all the way to the back of the room where they splashed against the far wall in semi-circles of color. The noise of the vent fans was noticeable but not oppressive, their dry whirring not quite loud enough to cover the volume of a normal voice. A workbench with lights, a stepstool, and a folding chair in front of it took up the space just to the left of the door.

"So this is what it's like behind the wizard's curtain," Tonya said.

Kim nodded as she sat down on the folding chair. "It's pretty neat in the dark. This is a really nice one too."

Another indication how new it all was. Datacenters tended to evolve over time. After a few years, what started out a neatly engineered toy box was usually a mass of confusing wires, dead systems sitting alongside their replacements, and benches covered with coffee rings. If the lights were on, she was sure this place would sparkle. Kim motioned for Mike to take the stepstool.

Tonya pointed at a different rack in the back corner where all the wires gathered in bundles as thick as her arms. "And those are the…"

"Quantum computers," Kim said. She stared at Mike. "The heart of the Evolved Internet, and the realms that it makes possible."

He looked back at her, smiling with puzzled eyes. "Do you need me for anything?"

Kim opened her mouth, but nothing came out. The question meant something very different to her now, but it couldn't.

Not now not ever.

Kim cleared her throat and turned away, then took a deep breath. "Yes. I'll be searching the spaces I can reach; you should do the same where you can."

They transitioned into the private realmspace, and she had to fight the nostalgia. She wasn't supposed to find new ways to use her old skills. At least she had Mike to talk to. "Have you ever been inside one of these before?"

"No, I haven't. It feels strange. I'd always assumed the space I lived in was the only place like it, and now here I am working through another one, while I'm still a part of the first. Remarkable."

She lost focus trying to picture what his world was really like, to stretch in and through mysterious places. He was such a strange, intriguing person. She shook herself.

"What do you think you can do here?"

"Maps, certainly. This place is a lot bigger than I expected. I'll bet there'll be plenty of locked doors to open too. I won't be able to talk much."

"That's fine," Kim said, turning a corner down the hall. This part of the realm was a duplicate of the first floor above them, minus the adventurous couple and their indoor antics. "But before you start, if you could?"

"I'm sorry, a door would be handy, wouldn't it?"

A door opened in front of her, and Kim stepped through to the box controls. A display snapped to life over the consoles as Mike began to map.

Copying an entire realm was a big task. Even a private one like this must have terabytes of data in log files alone.

At least it wasn't a rerun of the Trump heist. There was no decrepit billionaire wandering around naked in the dark, screaming "Melania" at the top of his lungs. They lost precious seconds making sure he didn't fall over as they tried to get out of the place. No amount of mental bleach would wipe away *that* memory.

Kim grabbed a container out of her avatar's belt and used it to trace a line of purple dust across each of the panels.

"Fly, my pretties, fly!" They dissolved toward their destinations. With those constructs, a job that should take days would only take maybe half an hour.

Mike pinged her at roughly the halfway point of the copy. "Do you know what to make of this? I think it's a button, but I'm not sure."

He showed her a schematic, but it was far too complicated to make out quickly.

"Can you tell me where it is?"

"Yup, and before you say anything, don't worry, no frog. Path stripe only."

"You're sure it's a button of some sort?" she asked, entering a weird amphitheater. It was dark, save for some footlights, just enough to keep from bashing shins or falling down the stairs. About a hundred, maybe two hundred people could sit on the padded benches that formed concentric, ever-higher semicircles around the empty stage.

"Wait a minute. Mike, do you recognize this?"

He swore. "Kim, I think you're right. This is where Watchtell had his meeting."

She scanned around as she took a few steps away from it. The belly of the beast was not a good place to be, even when the demon was away.

"Where's the button?"

A hatch opened at the front edge of the stage, and a pedestal rose up. Its top was flat and wide, and sure enough, there was a big covered switch right in the center. When it locked to a stop, a spotlight threw it into high relief.

"What's it do?" she asked.

"I'm not sure, but it was locked down so tight it must be important. It took me forever to tease it open. I can't even tell where the lines underneath it go, there are so many of them."

Kim walked over to it, then crouched down. "Yeah, it has to be a class twenty-seven switching construct, hell maybe even a twenty-eight."

It was the kind of stuff seen on for-real aircraft carrier realms, or an Ares Heavy II launch controller. She opened a flap on her utility belt and sat down on the floor. "Let's see how we can ruin someone else's day."

"With that outfit on, I think you should have a pipe and speak with an English accent."

"I don't always wander around in a catsuit." Kim moved her trench coat around out of the way. Pitching her voice low, she smiled. "But I can definitely change into it, if you like."

Kim's smile broadened when he stammered.

"No, that's okay, no need to do that." He cleared his throat. "What are you doing, anyway?"

She lay on her back, working at a hatch underneath the podium with some tools. "Being mean."

She popped the hatch free with a snap and grabbed a Lock-Pass the size of a sugar cube. When she pressed it into the opening, it dissolved into the flashing, zipping interior.

Kim caught herself humming a tune her mom sang to her when she was little, back when that was the only way people could get her to say anything at all. On a whim, Kim changed the default message to match.

"Well, they'll have to ask me nicely if they want to use it now." She closed the hatch and sat up just as an agent brought her notice that the transfers were ready to start. "Button it back up, Mike."

"With pleasure."

It turned out the realm was bigger than either of them had expected. What should've taken half an hour was now approaching two. Kim squirmed in realspace; that second tea at supper may not have been the best idea.

"Kim? Flying monkeys? Really?" Mike asked.

"You design your constructs; I design mine. They get bigger the more stuff they find." She ducked as one the size of a small airplane flapped into view.

"Tonya wants to know how much longer?"

The last one, a tiny thing not much bigger than her palm, sailed into her phone's storage area. "That's it." Then with her real voice, she said, "Time to go. I need you to find a patch cord before we leave, Mike. I don't want to have to come all the way back here if I need to visit again."

Chapter 54
Kim

When she woke up, it took her a few minutes to remember where she was. Another hotel. She was back to the gypsy's life, living out of a bugout bag. It was a lot more exhausting nowadays. She liked sleeping in a bed nobody else had used.

Then she remembered the massive download they'd pulled from Watchtell's private network. Once that happened, there was no going back to sleep. Kim pulled her pants and sweatshirt on, then padded into the den of the suite, leaving Tonya asleep on the other bed. She always worked better sitting up when it came to stuff like this.

After a while, Tonya walked out. "What time did you wake up?"

"Hour or so ago, I think." Kim checked the time. "There's breakfast in another hour."

Tonya smiled. "You and your breakfasts. I think I'll go get us some necessities. A change of clothes would be nice, don't you think?"

Kim needed to finish this debug routine to figure out why the damned OutLock kept throwing a null exception. Just one more run. If it worked, the whole thing would unlock.

Yes!

KIM? Tonya pinged her, and without thinking, Kim shared her workspace.

The gigantic multidimensional fan of displays, graphs, pictures, and tables enveloped Tonya. There was no horizon, and it thundered with a pattern that she was getting closer to recognizing . Kim only realized it might be a bit disorienting when Tonya gasped and fell to her knees.

"How do you make sense of any of this?" Tonya shouted as she got back up.

"Right now?" Kim reached into the center of the maelstrom, and the volume cranked down to a sibilant hiss. "I don't. It's too much for Edmund to work through alone."

She'd sent Edmund into the depths, partly because he was good at it, but also because it was fun to listen to him grouse.

"My every route is strewn with data droppings from the devil's own satanic servers" was a really choice one. Kim didn't expect to see him again for at least another hour.

"Edmund?"

"An AI from my Rage days. The data streams will eventually make sense. It's already a lot better than when I started."

She reached into one of the new streams that stretched upward into infinity. It had the consistency of warm pasta and was just as delicate, except breaking this would give her a nasty shock and make a huge mess. She'd put on the gloves of her catsuit, which allowed her to use the hypercube extensions. It made things easier, even though her hands looked like Escher's own bendy straws.

"Doesn't that hurt?" Tonya asked, motioning at Kim's arms.

"Not really." The construct slipped, and she flinched when a blast of discordant music crashed out through the columns.

Tonya shook her head and vanished as she exited into realspace.

I NEED TO GO GET STUFF, she sent. CAN I HAVE THE KEY TO THE CAR?

SURE, Kim replied from her perch on the couch, and the token transferred. Out loud she said, "Ping Mike with the bill. Trust me, he's good for it."

"What am I good for?" Mike asked behind her. She heard his bedroom door close.

Kim was startled when Tonya flopped down onto the chair next to her. She was staring behind Kim with her jaw hanging open. Kim paused things and peered over her shoulder.

Okay, wow, that was a distraction she didn't need. "Mike, pants, please, pants!"

"What? These don't count as pants?" He held his arms up and turned.

Tonya whimpered softly.

"No, Mike, those are boxer briefs," Kim said.

The bruises on his back were yellowing away. The madness of the night before was an echo of shame now. Her mind tossed up a bunch of ways to make it up to him. Ways denied her.

Not now, not ever.

She blinked hard and shook her head. "Go put your pants on."

The door shut behind her. Tonya was still staring, so Kim threw a pillow at her head.

"Oh my gosh, Kim!"

The room had gotten uncomfortably hot. "Don't you have errands you need to run?"

"Sorry. Right, errands." She cocked her head. "What size pants do you think he wears?"

Tonya left with a few sly glances Kim absolutely ignored. The OutLock was behaving now, which meant it was the sieve array's turn to cough itself inside out for no damned reason.

Mike cleared his throat twice before Kim even noticed he was there. She turned around. He had pants on now, but nothing else.

"Better?" he asked.

Kim had too many things to do and could not be distracted. She lied. "Much better."

He flopped onto the couch, one cushion over from her. "Mind if I stare?"

She wanted him to do exactly that.

He stammered, "At your work, I mean."

He gazed at her with those big brown eyes. His face was so open and so trusting. Tonya had just left. There was no way Kim would get any work done wound up like this. Something crazy broke loose inside her; a hope the heat let slip through her defenses. Spencer had rescued Mike from the hospital, and that kid was prepared for anything. It was a mad gamble she wanted to win.

Kim took a deep breath, closed her eyes, and asked, "Do you have a condom?"

"WHAT?"

She wasn't looking for sex. Well, not the way normal people thought of it. But they were alone together. It was an opportunity she could not pass up. Her hands shook, her breath caught, and she didn't want it to stop. Kim was in control and yet wasn't, not exactly.

After searching the suite, they settled on a small plastic trash bag they found folded in a bathroom cabinet. Mike double wrapped his hand in it, and she faced away from him on the couch, leaning over so just her lower back was exposed.

This was insane.

There was no way it would work, but the crazy urge kept kicking her forward, kept forcing her to take each new step.

"God," she breathed out. "I haven't done this since I was fourteen."

She looked over her shoulder. "Except he really did have a condom on his hand." Well, a condom on his fingers. The thought of Mike's fingertips made the need grow worse. This had to stop.

She wouldn't stop.

"You don't have to do this," he said, white as a sheet.

"Yes, Mike, I do. I'm not allowed any of this the way I am. You need to understand that, and I need to understand it too."

Another wave of panic crested as she pushed her head against the armrest.

"You made sure the toilet seat was up, right?" She didn't want to puke all over everything.

There was a long pause as the air danced chills across her bare back.

"Yes."

"Okay." The need for this rush through her again. No turning back now. Four days ago she was a has-been managing a Taco Bell, and now she willingly exposed herself to an impossible person who drove her mad, and what was taking so goddamned long?

The rustle of the plastic bag as he stripped it off his hand unleashed panic and even more heat.

"Mike?"

"If we're proving things, let's prove things."

Kim closed her eyes as her heart pounded and uncontrollable shivers started. She caught her breath.

This had to stop; it was crazy.

The thought of his bare hand on her back…

"This is the least sensitive part of the body, right?"

"Sellars," she said. Kim felt the warmth of his hand against her back, very close. She bit her lip and stifled a groan. She could feel his breath blow against her skin, something alive that didn't hurt. It was soft and warm, and he was so close. There was no scrabbling madness. This was actually going to happen.

"Sorry, guys, forgot my purse." Tonya said as she crashed through the door. She jumped when she saw them, then grabbed her purse with a snatch so hard it flew out the door behind her, and then shouted, "Goddamn it!"

The door slammed shut with a muffled thump.

They both sat up.

Mike stared at the floor, because he couldn't understand what it all meant. She did.

He wasn't frightening anymore.

She thumped the cushion he was sitting on, as close as she dared. "Hey."

He looked up, and her heart flipped somersaults at the way his smile came out.

"That wasn't a disaster?" he asked.

A new wash of emotions so unfamiliar she couldn't name them hit her. Fear, panic, the raw *need* of it all. After a deep breath she asked, "How close did you get?"

"To your back?" He pulled his thumb back and exposed what he could of his nail. "About this far? Close. Really close."

It was what she'd hoped for most of all.

"When I was fourteen… His name was Alan. He only got this close," she said, spreading her finger and thumb as far apart as they could go. "It took two weeks before they cleared me from the psych ward. I never told my mom what really happened."

"Did he hurt you?"

"Hurt me? No, not in the way you mean." She laughed. "I may have scared him off women entirely. That was some trauma for a fourteen-year-old boy to work through."

Finally, her heart had calmed to a normal beat, but she refused to ignore what his painless not-quite-touch could mean. That said, there was still a world to save. She certainly couldn't let Watchtell tear apart the place Mike lived in now.

"I have a ton of data to search through, and I could use your help. You willing?"

While they worked together, she realized most of the problem was her pushing him away. Now that she stopped, the results were, well, fun. Kim barely noticed the time passing as they exchanged jokes and flirting smiles.

After they solved yet another null reference exception, he shrugged. "Okay, I have to admit it. I don't get this."

Kim cracked open a secure store, filling the space around them with a new set of thundering data columns.

He had to yell over the noise. "How do you manage to get access to all this secure stuff?"

"Mark called it the locksmith's dilemma," Kim shouted back as she buried her arms through six dimensions up to their elbows in the raw data stream. The volume decreased until it was just a minor buzz. "As long as it's people locking things up, there's no such thing as perfect security. There has to be more than one way to get in. People lose or forget keys, passwords, tokens, all of it, all the time.

"Sometimes people die, and their heirs have to get into a lockbox they didn't even know existed. If things were perfectly secure, in twenty years half the world would be lost forever, stuck inside boxes with no keys." She shrugged. "I just happen to be really good with locks."

"I'd say scary good."

Kim laughed. "Okay, fair enough. And it's not just electronic ones, either. I'd open a locksmith business in a second if it didn't require a background check. You wouldn't be able to help me with that, would you?"

"Not enough to trust your life with it. I can only reach what's connected to the EI, and not everything is."

A mile-high tower of data wobbled wildly enough she threw her hands over her avatar's head, but then it settled as he steadied it from wherever he was in realmspace. Mike had skills.

He continued, "Local police use the EI because it's cheaper than owning their own stuff, but I can't be sure of reaching anything higher than that, and fixing half of it would be worse than doing nothing. Not to mention the international stuff, and your Bolivians don't rely much on paperwork."

There was a knock on the door. Tonya asked through it, "You two decent in there?"

They smiled at each other, but the feelings were too intense for her to stare at him for long, especially with Tonya right outside. When this was all over, there would definitely be some exploration going on.

Mike got up to answer the door. "We were decent before."

Tonya stared up at the still-shirtless Mike and closed her mouth with a clack. She lifted her hands up, but after a look at Kim, dropped them to her sides. "Well, okay then."

Edmund pinged her with a priority alert higher than he'd ever used before. She couldn't ignore it, so she left Tonya and Mike to empty the car. When Kim manifested back in the workspace, Edmund's grim face meant whatever the news was, it was very, very bad.

"What have you found?"

"The answers, milady. All of them."

Edmund had found Watchtell's private correspondence from five years ago, back when he'd been White House chief of staff.

Their journey to Bolivia, their betrayal, her desperate attempt to get Juan to pay attention, all unfolded in front of her. Watchtell had been behind it all.

Except this time, there wasn't a break in the footage outside the freezer.

Mike set a sack down on a table and asked her a question she couldn't hear over her own pulse.

God, Mike.

Tears streamed down her cheeks. The picture of Watchtell arm-in-arm with a dead man unrolled across her vision.

"You son of a bitch."

There was no time. Watchtell was in the middle of it but there was no time to find out how deep it went. She locked everything down tight. If Mike found out the truth, he'd just try something stupid or heroic. She couldn't risk losing him now.

"Kim? What's wrong?" he asked.

This was too big, and they were right on the edge of launching Project Havelock.

"I need to contact the FBI."

Chapter 55
Aaron

The attack happened around one in the morning. He'd spent two hours in the emergency room, and two more in debrief. Just getting home was an effort. He'd just fallen asleep when the clock rang him back to the world. It felt like he'd been set on fire and tossed down a stairwell, but that was better than being chunks of roasted kosher meat scattered all over a marina.

Lefla was gone. It hurt so much. She'd saved them all, and he couldn't even put her in for an accommodation. To the bureau, she was just property, a thing that depreciated. The rest of the team would dribble out of the hospital over the next few days while bone-knits and cell gens did their work. It was better than anyone could've hoped for otherwise.

The smell of tomato and paprika wafted into the bedroom. Whenever something went wrong, his girlfriend Keila set to cooking. The worse it got, the more Israeli the dishes became. *Shakshuka* was a silver lining to this particularly nasty cloud. He could only hope it was the start of a better day. He wouldn't tempt fate by thinking it couldn't get any worse.

Aaron groaned and hissed getting out of bed, trying to figure out the right combination of movements that kept stitches and bandages from grabbing or pulling. When his phone interfaced with realmspace, a fuzzy obstacle course confronted him.

Aaron had met Keila when he spent a summer in Israel after high school graduation. They were both deeply interested in the sophisticated AIs that populated realmspace, but where he was a practical hands-on end-user, Keila was an avant-garde artist. She was also an inveterate cat rescuer, and whenever one was fading out, heading over "the rainbow bridge," there Keila would be— gently comforting, tears pelting down, setting up scanners.

He didn't have the brainpower required to change the fidelity settings of her projections, so he had to dodge a dozen virtualized cats as he made his way to the bathroom. They yowled and bumped him as he passed. Keila wrote their brain patterns into a custom-designed unduplicate lattice. Not all of them were successful, but she claimed the ones that were had started a new life. He had no reason to doubt her, because they were realistic enough to trip him up even in the best of times.

This wasn't the best of times.

He levered the one remaining realspace cat, a three-legged bar-nacle named Goblin who was too evil to die, off the toilet lid and relieved himself. A quick mirror check showed actual battle scars.

Hi, guys, his next e-mail to the family would go, *I got blown up last night.*

Aaron had forgotten about the pajama-clad demon that occupied the guest room until the den's TV detonated with an old *Adventure Time* episode. It seemed like a great idea to take his sister's son for an extended weekend. A kind of training run he and Keila thrilled themselves with. Because, you know, all Aaron had was a desk job, some dusty thing following behind an agent chasing a ghost. No action there, no sir. Why not think about starting a family? Aaron reached for the extra remote to turn down the TV, and his teeth clashed together as the stitches on his arm pulled tight, which made the bruised rib flex.

"David," Keila called, "breakfast!"

The little boy jumped into the seat next to Aaron. He was finishing up his first virtual design course, the final project for third-grade realm programming.

"Uncle! Look!" A miniature landing pad drew itself into existence over his nephew's bowl of cereal as David shared his augmented reality. A helicopter about the size of Aaron's palm bounced into existence and whirled to life. Its motor sounded like a metallic mosquito as it flew around the table.

It did a flip right over the center, but then fell victim to being part of their house's realm, the one shared with Keila's ghost cats. Half a dozen of them scrabbled onto the table, and then watched it intently, heads bobbing and tossing. Just as the helicopter passed them, three jumped up. There was a slap, and they all tore away like thieves.

David groaned as bits of the tiny virtual chopper rained down on the table below, evaporating just as they hit.

Aaron smiled as Keila's food slowly brought him back to life. "It's okay, Dave, that was pretty good. The damage model is really well done."

Today would be exhausting, but mostly spent on paperwork. Just answering questions would be one hell of an improvement over these past few days.

Lefla's channel sprang to life with a call alert. He had this mad hope that she'd somehow backed herself up, but the signature was wrong. It was worse than wrong, because that channel should never have activated again without it. It had to be one of the other unduplicates calling to pay their respects. But it wasn't.

Aaron forgot all about his war wounds when the message typed its way across his vision.

ALICE HAS FOUND A MOST CURIOUS THING. WOULD THE HATTER LIKE TO JOIN HER FOR TEA? THE BARD IS A WUNDERFUL SINGER—A. R.

Chapter 56
Adelmo

When Adelmo did the math, he couldn't believe it. It'd been thirty-five years since his last genuine arrest. The cops he'd encountered last night hadn't even been born yet. Gangsters should never grow old. It was so déclassé.

"My client has gone above and beyond what's required of even an upstanding citizen," his very expensive and comparatively moral attorney said, "and if you have anything you can actually charge him with, please proceed to do so."

The trick was to just shut the hell up. Back when he and his brother were mere soldiers in another man's army, all he did was imagine giant gold letters slowly spinning across the walls. YOU HAVE THE RIGHT TO REMAIN SILENT. It worked just as well now as it did then, which was fortunate. He had a very long road ahead of him. Getting out of this courtroom wasn't much, but it was a start.

What helped more was his short-circuit of Manuel's betrayal. That, and the secret Cayman Islands bank accounts Adelmo always kept full of cash. Brutus may have been too noble to raise money by vile means, but Adelmo was too practical to do anything else.

As expected, he walked out of the county lockup as the sun rose over the courthouse. What he felt most in the moment was ashes, grinding away in his chest. They were supposed to build an empire that took the gringos' gold by selling them poison. It wasn't supposed to be about killing soldiers or women. It absolutely wasn't supposed to be about some ridiculous power struggle that would make the streets of La Paz run ankle-deep in blood. They were Quechua. The mere thought that his people would spill their own blood over some idiotic feud was just so *wrong*.

When his nephew rang his phone, Adelmo quickly answered; appearances must be maintained. "Don Quispe, I'm sorry to say your plan may not have survived its encounter with the enemy."

Adelmo ignored the bellicose laughter, but noted how it finished with hacking cough. Maybe Manuel's heart finally would be the death of him. If only Adelmo could be so lucky.

"You don't even know the best part, Uncle. Your spy? The one who froze my only son? She sent me a message. Got it all the way past our screens. She must be pleading for her and Colque's life. And just after her newly hired assassin murdered you. This Rage is a truly clever woman. You go with God, Adelmo Quispe. Rage will be joining you soon."

The line snapped closed. His nephew wasn't smart, but he was cunning. The mental arithmetic was simple and straightforward.

Sniper.

He scanned frantically and motioned to his attorney. "Where is the car?"

The lawyer didn't have time to respond before Adelmo saw the glint of a rifle sight in the early sunrise. He pushed the man down as the wall behind them both shattered. A piece of concrete slashed across Adelmo's cheek, and the report of the rifle crack echoed through the courthouse's campus. They ran through the hysterical crowd with rifle rounds nipping at their heels to nearby dumpsters.

Manuel was, as always, using an anvil where a needle would do the job. It would've been simpler and vastly more effective to follow Adelmo discreetly and end it with a car accident or a fatal case of food poisoning. But that would take too long and wouldn't be nearly good enough to stroke his nephew's titanic ego.

The sniper fired three, maybe six rounds at most, and then the shooting just stopped. The screams had died down as sirens wailed to life nearby. Everyone looked around in terror, but the shooter had vanished.

It took a bit of coaxing to get his lawyer to come out from behind the dumpster, but after that, Adelmo simply climbed into the car his men had acquired and drove away. Adelmo was free and alive. This was not how Manuel did business. In one respect, he was obviously grateful. But in another, he was deeply worried.

Chapter 57
Aaron

"Wow, Agent Cohen," Donny Deng, head of The Firing Range, said. "We heard about what happened. Please, come in!"

Trayne had contacted him with a realmspace address. Since he was the only member of the team not in the hospital, he was the only agent who could meet her. And if they were lucky, arrest her. That was where The Firing Range came in.

The room still held its old title even though it'd been a decade since it was last used for target practice. The long, low space was now the agency's main research lab for realm investigations. The Realmspace Division had a modest budget, but they seemed to be making the most of it. Experimental computers and scanners were stacked all over the place, most of them in pieces, but all of them turned on. It reminded Aaron of the time he and his nephew took apart all the old computers in his dad's basement, except these were new and still worked.

Bundles of computer cables of every length, thickness, and color imaginable lined the walls and hung from the ceiling. It was less like a lab and more like the aftermath of a pasta factory explosion. The smell of stale coffee and cooking electronics overlaid everything.

The décor wasn't as colorful the crew. Three of the scruffiest people Aaron had ever seen this deep in the Hoover building were all he had in this latest attempt to apprehend Trayne.

Donny pointed to the other two members of the team. "That's JoBeth Litton and Emilio Sanchez. JoBeth, how's it coming?"

The sole female of the group was nothing but a pair of shoes to Aaron, lying on the floor underneath a giant cabinet. She needed to replace her black sneakers pretty badly.

"Hang on," JoBeth said, "there we go."

A bank of old-fashioned LCD displays on his right lit up to show neat columns of numbers reeling up and down incomprehensibly. Another set of LCDs lit up on the opposite wall with colorful graphs and metrics. JoBeth crawled out from under the cabinet and dusted her hands off.

"The isobar metrics are officially online."

"What time did you need to meet with your contact?" Emilio asked.

"Nine fifteen," Aaron replied. "But I'd like to get there—"

"As soon as possible, big surprise. You've only got, like, an hour." Emilio sneered as he poked and whirled controls only he could see.

The files said this kid was thirty, but Aaron could not shake the impression of a sullen teenager.

"Sanchez," Donny scolded.

Emilio shrugged. "Fine, sorry, whatever. We have to get the rig calibrated for you, Agent Levine. So if you don't mind?" He gestured at the center of the room.

Aaron sat down, and then leaned back into what looked and felt like a dentist's chair. They connected a single wire to his phone. It fanned out into dozens, and then dozens more, forming a heavy bib sitting his chest. "So what do you need from me?"

Donny stared at his displays as the synch process booted up. "We need you to keep her still, and in one place, one realm, for as long as you can. If she really does meet you in Bards, and you can keep her there, that would be great. It's the best-mapped place in all of realmspace, which makes tracing just a little easier."

"So we've finally figured out how to trace people from realmspace to real?" It was the holy grail of law enforcement. A breakthrough like that would change everything.

"Not really, no, nothing like they could do in the old days. But if you can hold her still long enough, we can usually luck out and catch signature bits of whatever provider she's using. With a little more luck, that'll get us the search warrant we need to find her phone."

The disappointment was bitter but not surprising. The tech guys always promised more than they could deliver.

"There's an awful lot of luck involved in that sentence, Mr. Deng. And why are you optimistic about Bards?" It was the most secure realm in the EI.

"It's so big and heavily traveled they can't help leaking at least a little information."

"So," Aaron said, "we're trying to figure out the license plate of a truck based on the noise it makes on the highway?"

Deng grimaced and shook his head. "It's not quite that bad."

"But it doesn't seem much better."

"We never claimed it would be easy, just that it might be possible."

"I still say you're chasing a ghost," Emilio said. "Angel Rage is a construct foisted on the public by corporate America. They needed someone to hide behind while they managed the biggest mergers in history. She never existed. Ever. Nobody can do those things."

So Aaron had been blown up by an illusion. Right.

"I've got seven stitches and a black eye that says otherwise."

They were still picking up the pieces at the marina. None of it made any sense. The early evidence pointed to Adelmo, but his warning was what helped Lefla rescue the team. Adelmo's lawyer pulled the case against him apart so thoroughly Aaron wasn't sure if he actually set foot in a jail cell.

Then some maniac took a few pot shots at Adelmo in front of the Fairfax County Courthouse. The preliminary investigation had come up with the Angel Rage name, which was ridiculous. She'd never once been associated with violence of any sort. The whole thing sniffed of a frame-up, but nobody had time to figure out who was behind it all. Half the state was turning itself inside out trying to find Trayne and keep tabs on Adelmo. Blowing up an FBI team, and then getting shot at in front of a county courthouse tended to lend a bit of notoriety to a case.

Aaron's stitches chose that moment to shift, and he winced. "The government thinks she's real enough to want her arrested."

Emilio wasn't just unconvinced, he was downright angry about it. "I'm telling you we're gonna go to all this trouble, and if we manage to catch her, she'll walk, and then sue us for false imprisonment or worse. Angel Rage is a myth, man. A total fake. She doesn't exist. The real enemy is megacorporations. They're the ones who created the legend and put this name on it. They hid behind Angel Rage and stole trillions, and they'll be the ones who'll create whatever they need next to enslave us."

Maybe it was the exhaustion, or the pain, or the loss, or just the class-A level effed-upness of it all that made Aaron cut loose. "So all those people she manipulated, put out of business, sent to shelters, they were just grist for the mill, yeah? Just a conspiracy. Some of the people she ruined killed themselves, you know that, right? A few took their families with them. Most of them were billionaires, but that didn't matter to their kids. Daddy or Mommy would rather kill everyone than go to jail.

"That's all on her head. She did that. Those men and women raided pension funds trying to keep their companies above water, and when it collapsed, even the widows lost everything. Thousands of them. That's on her head too. Or do you think the time she spent helping drug dealers put more sunrise on the streets is what makes her a fake? Oh, I get it. She wasn't trying to tear down your megacorps then, right? Tell the truth, Sanchez. You only started hating her when she went after the wrong people."

"Hey, man, fuck you."

"Emilio!" Donny stood up. "That's enough! Either you can do the job or you can go home. Do you understand me?"

Aaron fell back into the chair, spent. A scene out of an old black-and-white movie rushed unbidden to him. "I'm not even supposed to be here today." He took a deep breath. "So I meet with her and keep her still?"

"If at all possible," Donny said. "You'll need to be as aware of us as you are of the realm, though. No deep diving."

She'd designated the center of Wunderland as their meeting point. Finding it was easy enough. Staying there as the clock ticked down was another matter entirely.

The melodious voice of the ridiculous caterpillar purred once more around its hookah. "By the way, I have a few more helpful hints. One side will make you grow taller."

Aaron tried to stare down the creature. "I told you, I'm not eating anything. Don't you go on break soon?"

The avatar laughed. "Well you must have eaten it at some point, sir, otherwise you would not be this fine height, indeed. And this caterpillar is on duty for another..." There was a pause while whoever wore it checked the time. "Three hours."

Wunderland was definitely not his place. He much preferred Stooge's. More pie, less smoke. Unfortunately, the caterpillar's mushroom was at the center of it all, so his avatar was three inches high. The scenery literally towered over him.

The ground was bare dirt, and the forest undergrowth was thick enough to make chance encounters the norm rather than the exception. Since it was Bards, he'd already had to dodge out of the way of two spice navigators in their giant trundling metal carriages. It turned out that the Red Queen was hosting an actual Bene Gesserit convention on the grounds nearby. At least the wind blew the patchouli-and-skunk stench of the spice away from him.

"How doth the little crocodile..."

"God!" JoBeth exclaimed in the lab as she monitored the session remotely. "That's, what, the fourth time he's recited that stinking poem?"

"Fifth," Emilio said.

A woman with dark hair walked out of the brush, dressed in a variant of Alice's dress. Vertigo swirled in his head as all the conventional monitors they had running shut off with a snap. It could only mean one thing.

"She's here."

Chapter 58
Kim

"I'm telling you, Kim," Mike said, "I don't like this."

They didn't need to like it. They needed to trust her. The only way to win now was to turn inside Watchtell, make a decision he didn't see coming. He was too far ahead to do anything else. "It's not up to you; it's something I have to do."

Tonya paced back and forth in the hotel room. "This is crazy. There's bound to be a better way to stop him."

Kim had insisted Tonya stay in realspace. She couldn't keep Mike out of the realms, but she would be damned if Tonya got caught if something went wrong.

She manifested on the edge of Wunderland wearing a more mature, but no less recognizable, version of the iconic blue-and-white dress.

"We have the evidence we need; now we just have to get it to the right people." She pulled up the hood of her cloak, then set out in the direction of the pedestal mushroom. "Can you tell if he's there yet?"

"No," Mike said, "but I wasn't expecting to. We need to get out of here, Kim."

She wasn't sure what was more irritating, Mike's protectiveness, or the way she wanted to nestle inside it. Comfort and desire were distractions she couldn't afford right now.

Kim crept through the bushes toward the center of the realm. Peering through the leaves, she said, "Right there."

"Are you sure?" Mike asked.

"Look at him. It takes training to be that stiff."

It was fortunate he was that obvious. She expected Park, who'd been chasing her for most of a decade. The guy she walked up to was half his age with curly red hair. He was arguing with a caterpillar who was paid to be a pain in the ass.

When he finally saw her, the first words out of his mouth dispelled any question in her mind.

"Kimberly Trayne, you're under arrest."

It was the standard spiel. She motioned him to the end, desperately trying not to smile. It was the first time anyone had gotten close enough to Mirandize her, and he knew it. The kid could barely hold his voice steady.

"Do you understand these rights?" he asked as they sat down on a bench next to a seldom-traveled side path near the mushroom.

"Agent?"

"Levine."

"Agent Levine, I'm not here to turn myself in."

He couldn't be more than a few months out of the academy. Well, at least she still rated an agent.

"Yes, I understand my rights. Okay? Listen, I'm not important here. There's a threat to the Evolved Internet that the FBI needs to know about."

"Have you reconnected with your associates?"

"No." Her eyes misted over. She hadn't had time to properly mourn them, to absorb the loss, to get her head around the complex emotions it was all dredging up.

"We won't be getting back together again. I have a *friend* who's noticed something strange going on with the EI in the past few months."

A weird invisible wave that seemed more like fabric than wind swirled around them, and her heart skipped two beats. A desert sun blasted onto her face as sand threatened to creep over the tops of her open shoes.

Levine blinked. "What's going on?"

Mike said in her ear, "He's working with Deng's team. He's bound to be in the basement of the Hoover building."

"Deng's team?" Tonya asked.

"Realm detectives. They're good. I'm better. Time for me to ruin someone's day."

They didn't have realm detectives when Kim was active. "What are they trying to do?"

"They're trying to lock on to the noise your avatar makes." His voice was distracted, as if he was juggling.

"Can you stop it?" Kim asked.

"No, but we're fine for now. It's like a dance. We're waltzing."

Aaron raised an eyebrow at Kim's quiet smile. "Whatever it is you're doing, you need to stop. You're just adding obstruction to the list of charges."

Kim breathed out heavily and closed her eyes. Jesus, this guy was green. "Agent Levine, do you really think adding to that list will change anything?"

The wave swirled again, and they found themselves in a courtyard at night. An elaborate fountain flowed into a reflecting pool in front of them.

"I need you to listen to me."

He paused briefly with his eyes unfocused, undoubtedly talking to his own team. "Okay, let's hear it."

She tried to summarize what they'd found. Watchtell had built a conspiracy with world leaders to take over the Evolved Internet, or crush it if they couldn't. Explaining it was tricky because every few minutes or so they'd jump to a new realm.

A much stronger one of those weird waves took her breath away as it snapped through her mind.

"Well done, Deng, well done." Mike chuckled in Kim's ear as she and Levine found themselves in a deep wood with laser blasts and strange, heavy clanking in the far distance.

"Achievement unlocked. Let's move to the next level."

Now there was another force, some other kind of power. It lifted them away and transitioned them through a rapid kaleidoscope of realms. Hard vacuum and the bottom of an ocean slammed against them so fast it left a few rivulets of water freezing as they ran down her skirt.

They landed in a ski lodge with a crackling fire. Levine shook his sleeves free of half-frozen water. "It would be easier for me to believe you if we weren't jumping all over the place. I'm going to have to ask you to stop interfering again."

"Oh," Kim said with a smile. "I'm not doing anything but talking to you."

The way Aaron's eyes flared made her cringe inside. She'd said too much, and a static snap of force a few seconds later just proved the point.

"Ow!" Mike said. "That's not fair. They know I'm here now. Okay. This just got real."

The feeling of protective strangeness grew until it was overpowering, now decorated with a faint male chorus singing a single dissonant chord and a smell that was a cross between fresh cut grass and lemon. Through each transition, Kim began to glimpse the edges of a sparkling construct so far beyond the realms as to be without form.

It was Mike, the real one, as he actually was. He wasn't a scary, naïve idiot. And he wasn't some sort of reanimated monster. He was a force of nature completely hidden from the humans he surrounded. The thought should've scared her out of her shoes, and maybe a week ago it would have, but now she had to fight to breathe.

He was beautiful.

"So." Levine closed his eyes.

They both grabbed the bench as they transitioned through a zero-G realm that was nothing but sky and incredibly long, floating trees that were green on both ends.

"A wanted cybercriminal has uncovered evidence of a global conspiracy led by a former White House chief of staff?"

"Well, it sounds crazy when you put it that way."

"Okay, put it to me a different way."

"If you'll just take the packet."

He waved her off as they thumped softly on to a cool loam surface. "I can't take anything from you like this. If you have evidence, bring it to the office. If it turns out to be legit, I'm sure the prosecutors will take it into consideration."

It was her turn to wave him off, and then they both ducked as a giant pteranodon buzzed them. "You know I can't do that."

"Mike, are you okay?" Tonya asked.

"They're not too shabby," he said, the strain obvious in his voice, "and they're getting better. Kim, finishing soon is good. I'm close to spinning a record number of plates in the air. I'm handling it, but only because I've run them out of resources."

"Agent Levine. We have no time. You don't know Matthew Watchtell like I do. This is all supposed to happen next week, but he knows I'm here now. He'll move faster, and you have to stop him."

"Is that why you recruited Adelmo Quispe?"

It took her a few seconds to even parse the question. He wasn't talking about what had happened five years ago, he meant right now.

"What the hell does Adelmo have to do with anything?"

She could tell he was just as surprised. "So you mean to tell me you had no idea he was in Virginia? That you have no knowledge of the attack at the marina?"

It was like he'd started speaking Portuguese. No, it was worse. She could speak Portuguese.

"What marina attack? Agent Levine I'm here because I need your help. We have to stop—"

Mike shouted, "Shit! Spencer!" And then he was gone. Just gone. All the swirling power vanished, and their bench fell on to Wunderland's dirt with a thump. Kim had never felt more exposed in her life.

Agent Levine beamed in triumph as fork traps locked her avatar onto the bench. It would take minutes Kim knew she didn't have to get free. A familiar pressure drained away in her head as the last of her screens fell away.

They had the address. The cars were already rolling.

Levine grabbed her arm. "We don't want anyone to get hurt."

She didn't, either, but there was no other choice. She had one card left, and no matter how much it sucked, she had to play it.

When Donald Trump found them sneaking out of his house he scrammed the entire household network. The only way to get free was to blow it up, but the servers were buried beneath fifteen feet of dirt under a basement far below their feet.

She'd solved the problem with power. Her power.

With a shuddering gulp of air, Kim let that power completely explode into freedom for only the second time in her life. Levine would be safe, of that much she was certain. Wherever he was in realspace, though, was in for a rough time.

There were lines of potential and she couldn't remember how to breathe. Power build power unlock power free.

There was a price, though. There was always a price. She fought madness and agony every time someone touched her, but now the pain was amplified beyond any endurance. A human being couldn't possibly survive it, and so for reasons she didn't understand she simply stopped being one.

The trap constructs on her wrists shattered, and the remnants burned away into bitmapped dust.

"Nobody's getting hurt," she said as her voice rastered under the building pressure, "but there is no time."

Speaking was the last of her luxuries as the rest of her humanity dissolved under the assault she'd unleashed. Kim gently grasped his wrist so as not to crush it, and moved him away. But she had to send him the message.

Send fail resend fail resend fail resend success! Building power building power reach and find the pain raise the wave lower the wave build searing horror.

The madness ripped through her as she sent power blasting down the lines they'd used to find her. Talons tore across her soul as channels did and did not form, and with a reach, pull and push, release, she grabbed deep and shallow into the quantum fabric. She briefly glimpsed him in realspace, sitting in a dentist's chair as three other people worked frantically, the address of Kim's hotel emblazoned on a screen beside him.

Then her vision departed. It wasn't an actual loss of sight, but of force melded, and she no longer saw things as they were. She saw them as they could be and were not and were always and never were and through eternity as she gathered the power in her fist.

Levine stumbled to the ground while strange, dark lightning blew furrows around him, shrieking out of her fingertips. She concentrated the last shred of her sanity.

"Goodbye, Agent Levine." She gripped the fabric surrounding the lab and released her gathered madness.

Collapse and now...

Chapter 59
Aaron

"She's here," Aaron said. Less than a week ago he was a newbie interning with an agent who was tilting at windmills. It seemed funny, back then. Now that the windmill had walked out of the bushes and said hi to him? Not so much.

She was taller than he was expecting, and much younger. She was probably his age. It shouldn't have been surprising, but it was. When he was trying not to fail high school algebra, she was on the run from the whole of the FBI.

"Kimberly Trayne, you are under arrest."

She turned, and walked away.

"Wait!" He stumbled forward, trying to keep up. "Anything you say can and will, damn it, hold up!"

In the lab, JoBeth asked, "What? How? Nothing's registering!"

Aaron threw a window above him so they could all see. "That just proves it's her," he said as lock constructs shot through her like she didn't even exist.

"She's completely cloaked."

The way Trayne dismissed him made him feel like he'd flunked out of the academy; it got worse when she casually sat down on a bench next to a side path. He might be green, but he was a damned FBI agent.

"Agent Levine, I'm not here to turn myself in."

The beeping in Emilio's corner got insistent. "That's it. Come on, baby, lock. Give me a lock, come on! Yes! Shit! What the hell?"

Aaron reflexively opened his eyes in realspace when the room erupted in chaos. He quickly closed them to keep the protocols of his phone from kicking him out of the realm. Sand and dry air dominated a completely new one, based in a deep desert. Trayne blinked at the sky like she owned the place.

"My God," Deng said, "every single one of the contracts reset at once."

"How is that even possible?" JoBeth asked.

"Damn it, JoBeth," Emilio said. "The differential manifold will buckle if you don't move faster."

And that's how the encounter went. Trayne would come forward with some new piece of information, and then the lab would erupt as it all spun sideways, and they landed somewhere else. There was something else in here with them, making it happen, his instincts insisted on it, but he couldn't understand what it might be.

Then she made a mistake.

"Oh," Trayne said with a smile as she opened her hands. "I'm not doing anything but talking to you."

"She's not alone," he said to the room.

The mere thought brought them all to a standstill.

"What the hell?" Emilio said. "That's not possible, either. We can see you two. There'd be signatures."

"Not if they're split," JoBeth said. "Not if they're split. Right there. Emilio, modulate frequency six. Deng? Do you see that?"

"On it."

They bounced from one realm to another, and it was all Aaron could do to keep his breakfast down in realspace. Keila would be disappointed if he tossed her *shakshuka* all over his chest.

Emilio shouted, "Got you!"

JoBeth gasped. "Oh my God, guys!"

"What's going on?" Aaron asked from the chair, eyes tightly shut. A clanging chorus and the reek of old grass and rotted fruit assaulted him in realmspace.

"She doesn't have just one person helping," JoBeth said. "She's got at least a thousand. No, two."

"You're wrong," Donny said. "She must have ten thousand people helping her."

"Oh, fuck that," Emilio said, "there's no way she can have that many people working with her. We'd see other signs."

"Well, how the hell do you explain these readings?"

Aaron tried to concentrate on what Trayne was saying. He asked, "A wanted cybercriminal has uncovered evidence of a global conspiracy led by a former White House chief of staff?"

It felt like the Loch Ness monster swam around him. Trayne was still talking, but he couldn't make it out. As they flopped on to what had to be the back yard of Endor, Aaron tried a different angle.

"Is that why you recruited Adelmo Quispe?"

It was like he'd hit her in the face with a box. Trayne had no idea what he was talking about.

"What the hell does Adelmo have to do with anything?"

"So you mean to tell me you had no idea he was in Virginia? That you have no knowledge of the attack at the marina?"

"What marina attack? Agent Levine, I'm here because I need your help. We have to stop—"

A voice thundered out around them.

"Shit! Spencer!"

All the confusing static that'd surrounded the entire encounter vanished in an instant. In the lab, Emilio let out a whoop of triumph.

"We've got her! Goddamn it we've got her!" He called out an address. JoBeth talked to a judge while Lonny reached out to the Herndon police department.

Aaron smiled as they thumped onto the loam of the out-of-scale jungle of Wunderland. The restraints latched on to her avatar.

The end of the chase hit him so hard he had trouble controlling his hands. Aaron Levine hadn't just seen the elephant; he'd bagged the damned thing.

He grabbed her arm. "We don't want anyone to get hurt."

Her hand was cold granite in motion as it grabbed his wrist.

"Nobody's getting hurt," she said as her voice went coarse and electronic, "but there is no time."

In the lab, Emilio's voice changed from triumph to terrified squeak. "What the shit is that?"

Claxons rang out from the racks of equipment that filled the room. "No! That's not possible!"

Aaron's ears popped as a nimbus of power swirled to life around Trayne's avatar. His mind folded sideways as the reek of fiberglass resin flooded around him. Then she raised her head.

Her eye sockets were openings into something unspeakably bright and distant, like she'd somehow torn holes in the realm's fabric. He stumbled to the ground backing away from her. Strange, dark patterns flew over her skin, and black lightning ripped trenches into the ground around him.

In the lab, a slap rang out. JoBeth said, "It doesn't matter, Emilio, it *is* happening. It *is* real. How do we stop it?"

"Goodbye, Agent Levine." Trayne's voice crackled, and the power she controlled caused static flashes across and between her teeth. The smell of ozone and resin was overpowering.

EMERGENCY DISCONNECT. The blue block letters drew themselves onto his vision as Wunderland shattered around him in a trillion sparkling fragments. He opened his eyes and fought against the nausea and vertigo that was trying to take him.

The whine that'd been growing in pitch and volume came from the quantum stack in the corner. It reached an electric scream just as he rolled his head over. It was smoking.

Then it exploded.

Chapter 60
Kim

The madness was a crystalline agony. Using her power to destroy a quantum network segment always left her like this. Mike tore out a ragged gasp beside her as he exited realmspace, but she couldn't look at him. Flashbulbs filled with white-hot thorns went off in her mind when she tried.

"Kim," he said, "are you—"

"No!" They had to leave; they had to leave right now. Mike and Tonya were like hissing columns of barbed wire, and Kim couldn't get past them. They wouldn't follow her if she couldn't get past them, and every time she tried, it was like walking through spinning towers of razorblades.

"No! You can't, not now, please, both of you, I'm so much more sensitive after I do that. Please…"

"What did you do?" Tonya asked.

Even their voices were distorted and ugly, ramming sound down into her ears.

"God, there's no time!" She levered herself off the couch, trying to find a place as far away from them as she could. Just the beating of their hearts hit her like sledgehammers. They were too slow and had to listen.

"We have to run. We have to run right now!" She fluttered back and forth, trying to get past them to the door.

Tonya nodded as she stood. "Okay, that's fine. Mike, You go get the guns."

"No!" They weren't listening, there was no time. "No! Turn around now, and run out that door. Run!"

Mike started to do just that when the power in their room went out.

He said, "Oh no," then bounced off a wall and into an end table. The lamp sitting on it shattered when it hit the floor.

"Mike!" God, no, please, not this. Kim wanted nothing more than to fall on him, but even the thought made things under her skin scrabble and wrap spider's legs around her.

"It's okay, Kim," Tonya said as she rolled his body over. "He's still breathing."

Tonya tapped his cheeks, and he came to with a snort.

Tonya asked Kim, "Can you open the door?"

A helicopter thumped over their hotel. Kim scrambled across the walls opposite them, yanked the door open, and with a shriek, ran outside. They were too close!

Tonya bellowed, her legs straining as she dragged Mike out the door. They stumbled along together.

"Mike," Tonya said at the end of the walkway, "you're too heavy! I need you to walk!"

"I'm trying! Oh great. Steps. Where's Kim?"

"I'm here!"

There was nothing she could do. They had to run, and she couldn't help them. Kim could not stand closer than ten feet to them. She followed behind them as best she could. Sirens echoed in the distance.

"Please! Please just go!"

"Mike, grab the rail! Do you have it? Are you sure?" Tonya stumbled with Mike down the concrete steps, but she managed to make it to the middle landing. Tonya turned, and Kim couldn't face her through the pain. Kim couldn't be like this, there was no time. She kept testing how close she could get to them, but the reaction wasn't receding fast enough.

Tonya shouted out, "Our Father, who art in heaven, hallowed *be* thy name…"

She somehow managed to get Mike to the bottom of the steps just as the prayer ended.

"Kim! Come on!"

Kim took three deep breaths and then rushed past. Sirens wailed nearly on top of them. She got to the car, then hit the key.

Nothing happened, and in an instant, she knew why.

When it really mattered, she'd failed them again. She'd forgotten to disconnect the car from the grid. The cops had locked it down.

Tonya asked, "What's wrong?"

Tears streamed down her cheeks, and the pain exploded when Tonya got too close. She threw herself away with a scream and fell face-down on the grass in front of the parking lot.

"I'm so sorry, I forgot, I'm so sorry!"

"Kim!" Tonya cried out. "What's wrong? What's happen—"

Police cars blasted into the parking lot from all directions.

She heard the scuffling and shouts but was helpless to do anything about it. She had failed them all in a stupid gamble, and now would pay the price. The police didn't know about her, and nobody ever got arrested without being touched. Pain boiled with the footsteps on the grass. When one of them got within five feet, she couldn't stand it anymore and jumped off the ground with a shriek.

Their weapons were drawn. Kim took a single step, the barrels flashed, and then darkness ended her pain.

Chapter 61
Adelmo

He shook his head in disbelief as the news report played again.

"Local police, in cooperation with the FBI, have apprehended the fugitive cybercriminal known as Angel Rage."

He never could get over how fast the US media got to a crime scene. At least she gave up somewhere soft. The cops even had the latest version of their stun darts on hand. The too-wide barrels coughed them into her chest as the video ratcheted down into another slow motion replay. They could knock her out with those as many times as it took to understand her problem, and she'd be no worse for wear.

Rage's misfortune was, however, to his benefit. The alert pulled every police unit in the region away. In the confusion, Adelmo's men had helped him evade the units tailing them ever since they'd left the courthouse.

On the screen, police gently put Rage's unconscious form into the back of a squad car. He motioned for one of his men to turn the shared feed off.

Another of his men slowly asked, "I guess this means we don't need a new van?"

Adelmo laughed darkly. "No, we certainly won't need it now."

They probably wouldn't be able to reach her until she went to prison, and maybe not even then. He received notice of a call from the family's compound in Bolivia, but it wasn't from his nephew. When he opened the line to his niece, all he got was a stream of unintelligible sobs.

"I'm sorry, Sophia, I need you to slow down. What's happened?"

"He's *dead*, Uncle Adelmo! My papa is gone! They say he had a heart attack!"

The news caused his own hand to close reflexively over his chest, but only for a moment. He shared the call with his three men.

"When did this happen?"

"I don't know." She sobbed a bit more, and then coughed back the tears. "An hour? Maybe two? The helicopter wasn't ready. We had to drive all the way to La Paz!"

He mouthed "Manuel" to his men, and then made a slashing sign across his throat. They began talking softly among themselves.

"How is security? You need to make sure the family is safe."

"We are, Uncle, we are. Mama and the other girls are still at the compound. I was the only one allowed to leave. They were so cold about it! Someone had stolen his rings!"

Adelmo nodded grimly. His niece didn't understand what a coup looked like, but he certainly did.

"Sophia, listen to me. I need you to get to a safe house in the city. I'm sending a driver," he said as he opened up a new message window. "His name is Juan. He's a good man; here is his picture. Do not get in a car with anyone else but him. Do you understand me?"

"But Uncle, who will stay with Papa?"

"Dearest, the person your papa needs will not be found in a hospital. Please, find a public place away from there. Start screaming if anyone but Juan tries to take you. Do you understand?"

"Uncle, you mean I'm not safe here? What about my sisters? What's to become of us all?" At fourteen, Sophia was the oldest, and the smartest, of Manuel's daughters. She was a credit to the family for understanding the threat so quickly.

As Adelmo got up, he sent messages to each of his men. TAXI. AIRPORT. TICKETS. They all set to work.

"I'm booking a flight right now to get back home. I should be there in" —he glanced at the one accessing the airport who held up four fingers—"four hours. I will meet you after I land, and we'll work this out together. Okay?"

"Uncle, please hurry! Juanita's only six. They won't hurt her, will they?"

"They'll be fine. Please, Sophia, I must go." After a few more goodbyes, he was able to end the call.

One of the men closed his connection with a nod. "I've chartered a private jet. It should be ready by the time we get through security."

"Very good," Adelmo replied.

The morning's events finally made sense. Mercenaries were no different from defense lawyers. They worked for cash and demanded proof of payment. Whatever had happened to Manuel must've happened during the attack, and on his death, all PayAdvance accounts had frozen automatically. The sniper received notice and must've decided half a fee was good for half his service and left.

Manuel was never a particularly healthy man, and his refusal to do much about it made everyone nervous. Top that with this ridiculous stunt to have Adelmo taken out, and the line of succession was an absolute shambles. Leadership had to be reestablished, and quickly. The Quispe family was a powerhouse in Bolivia, but it was definitely not the only one.

It was just as his history professors at Cambridge had taught: the real test of an empire is how it manages the transfer of power. Adelmo was the next surviving male in line, but it would take more than just sharp elbows to keep him there.

Chapter 62
Mike

They'd taken his phone, so staying synchronized yanked energy out of him like a cut fire hose. He would've just passed out and slept through it all, but then the cops started talking about sending him to the hospital. He needed to stay as close to Kim as possible.

"I'm fine," he insisted.

The EMTs had run scanners over Tonya and Kim, and then shunted them off to squad cars, but when they got to Mike, the things naturally blew offline. One of them caught fire.

"Damn it, I'm fine."

"Can you walk?" one of the medics asked.

Everything spun in and out of focus as timing signals crossed and sparked realm dissonance that thumped through his real self. In a car on the other side of the ambulance, a scream, quickly followed by the pop of more stun darts, made the decision easy. Crossing his eyes and shaking his head, Mike stood and hobbled into the squad car Tonya sat in.

Tonya leaned out of the other door and yelled, "She can't be touched, damn you! Just don't touch her!"

"Sergeant," one of the officers said, "I think she might have a point."

"Well, what are we supposed to do with her?"

"I have an idea."

*

As Mike staggered through the detention center's entrance, the officer behind the glass asked, "Rich, why is that one on the end of a pole?"

"Don't get me started. We got it out of one of the animal control vans. We had to drop her three times before—"

"If you'd listened to us, it wouldn't have taken even once," Tonya said.

"Tell it to your lawyers. At least the big one can walk now."

The door opened with a loud buzz, and they were all marched farther into the facility.

The spooling in Mike's head had cleared substantially, but it still felt like it was wrapped in heavy canvas. His one attempt to split through the realms made his stomach reverse so fast he barely avoided throwing up. But once they plopped him in his cell, Mike was able to relax a bit. Walking took up a helluva lot of bandwidth, which was now free. In fact, he felt sorted enough to reach out to send a message.

Chapter 63
Spencer

The words still smashed into him.

"Shit! Spencer!"

It took all night and most of the morning to make sure all of Kim's Phoenix Dogs were safe. He'd just wanted to brag a little. If only he'd kept his mouth shut like everyone in his life had told him to, none of it would've happened. But no, he had to talk to someone.

When Mike refused to pick up his phone, Spencer made a decision he knew he would regret for the rest of his life. He hit the emergency interrupt on Mike's phone. Mike would have to answer that.

"Shit! Spencer!" was all he heard before the connection cut. It made his stomach flip. Law enforcement was the only bunch that could cut an emergency connection.

Absolutely nothing got through, and then the return ping included a for-real address.

"No, no, no, no!"

He reached out toward the address, but then he lost the hotel's camera feeds. Losing access at that moment to that address made him shout and punch at the display. The cops had found them.

It was his fault. He'd done this.

He'd shown them the way.

He searched frantically and found a camera array still functioning on a pole across the street. Three all-too-familiar figures staggered into view at the top of the steps. Tonya was carrying Mike. Kim danced around frantically behind them.

Then the cars came. The cops grabbed Mike and Tonya. His heart felt like it'd been hit by lightning when Kim got shot. She dropped like a puppet whose strings had been cut.

He killed her, his hero, and it'd happened right in front of him. He ran down the hall and puked in the bathroom until nothing came up. It was his fault. If he could've just left the damned interrupt alone, none of it would've happened.

It was his fault.

When Spencer checked the news feeds, he got a little relief. Kim wasn't dead. She'd just been knocked out. He stopped thinking about eating a bullet, but he still couldn't even breathe properly.

All he managed was to lie flat on his back, listlessly flipping through realm e-magazines. His chest ached, and his stomach muscles were on fire from all the heaving. There was no way he could make this right. He'd seen enough crime dramas to have a good idea what prison life was like. Kim wouldn't survive jail.

And he'd put her there.

"Shit! Ow!" He sat up, rubbing his ears. The feedback's squeal whipped through again. It wasn't his ears. It came through his realm connection. A black border drew itself across the top of his vision, and then collapsed with another static-filled shriek. It came back and progressed to an actual black screen, filling his view ahead. It tweaked, and the board slowly pinwheeled around its center. It sped up, and a faint voice swore over the line.

It tweaked again, and it was a proper message board, translucent dark gray with a beveled frame. When the words began typing across the screen, he bolted upright. Spencer pumped both fists in the air until things shook off the shelves around his bed. He looked up one more time just to make sure it was real and that the words were still there.

HEY SPENCE, IT'S MIKE

Chapter 64
Aaron

He spent the rest of the morning trying to do all the jobs the team did, all at once, and all by himself. Since everyone at the Firing Range had the same security clearances he did, Aaron drafted them to help with the forms. They weren't very efficient, but it was better than nothing.

"The DC lockup worked around it with a leash pole they got from an animal control van," Donny said.

"Jesus." JoBeth shook her head. "Is that even legal?"

"It's kept them from laying her out again," Aaron said as he sent yet another form on its way. "Have you seen the video?"

The other three grimaced. "We should give whoever invented stun darts a medal," Emilio said. "I'm not sure Tasers would've even slowed her down."

Aaron checked the time again. They were behind schedule for the first interrogation of the new guests.

"JoBeth, when did you file the paperwork for their transfer out of lockup?"

Her eyes unfocused. "That can't be right. Emilio, you remember me putting that paperwork through?"

He nodded. "Yeah, I watched you do it. They're running late?"

"They would be if there was any evidence I'd requested them."

"Agent Levine, a word, please?" Aaron's heart nearly stopped as Deputy Director Melissa Adams entered the lab. The rest of them didn't say a word, for once.

He tried to figure out what he could've possibly done that warranted a visit from one of God's own helpers, but kept coming up blank. Aaron was pretty sure agents six months out of the academy weren't allowed to breathe the same air as a deputy director. The feeling of following the principal to the office was overwhelming.

As he shut the door to the empty office they had borrowed. She turned toward him, mature, tall, elegant, and clearly uncomfortable. "I've been instructed to tell you you're off the Rage case. All of you, the contractors, and your team. It's an order from the director's office."

She paused and examined the switches on the wall. "I have no idea what to make of it."

Aaron's heart finally started beating properly. Whatever it was, it wasn't his fault—a vast improvement. Still.

"Due respect, ma'am, but why would they send someone like you to talk to someone like me?"

She shrugged. "I don't know. This is the strangest thing I've ever seen. It definitely stinks, but I can't figure out why. I've asked around, and other agencies are seeing all sorts of weird things going on, but nobody knows what it means."

"So we're off the case?"

She stared directly into his eyes, which made Aaron very glad he'd recently gone to the bathroom. "Like I said," she raised an eyebrow, "I've been instructed to tell you you're off the Rage case. Someone is pulling some big strings, all at once. It's really pissing me off that I don't know who it is or why."

Before she left, she turned back and looked at him, long enough for it to be awkward. She nodded and closed the door.

Everyone in the room shouted when Aaron broke the news.

"That's what we've been *instructed* to do."

"What's that supposed to mean?" Donny asked.

"It means," he said as he checked the time, "let's get some lunch, and then I'll see if any of my team have made it out of the hospital yet."

He checked his personal message queue while he was in line at the Thai place a block east of the office. He stepped out of line to sit down when he saw who the third message was from. He crosschecked the time. Trayne must've sent it just before the explosion. The subject was Eat Me. When he tried to access it, all he got was a password blank. He thought briefly and entered MAD HATTER.

It bloomed into a titanic, sprawling array of files, far more than the Firing Range techs and the rest of the team could sort through with any kind of speed. One file had been flagged highest priority, so Aaron tried that first.

"Prime Ministers and Presidents, thank you for attending this presentation."

She was right. This was big. Hell, it wasn't big; it was gigantic.

When Aaron came back to the lab, JoBeth motioned frantically at him. "Would you please talk to this guy? He won't tell me anything because I'm *just* a contractor." She shared the connection to Officer Rich O'Brien of the Central Detention Facility in southeast DC.

"Now," JoBeth said, "will you tell *him*?"

"Yes, ma'am." He turned to Aaron. "We got your paperwork, but your guys had already come by and picked them up. I helped load them into the FBI van myself."

He exchanged an alarmed look with JoBeth. That was the first thing they'd checked. Nobody from the FBI had picked them up.

Aaron asked, "What time did this happen?"

Rich tapped away on his keyboard, and then stopped. "What the hell? I signed those three out personally. I know I did."

"What's wrong?" JoBeth asked.

"Folks, I'm gonna have to call you back. Right now our system doesn't show any sign of them, and that's just not right." He kept typing. "They were processed in around ten, maybe a quarter after, and I know I helped process them out no more than fifteen minutes ago." He pushed away from the desk. "It's hard for me to believe, but it seems like we may have lost their records."

JoBeth replied, "Actually, Officer O'Brien, and I mean no offense by this, but I believe you. We're having some really strange problems with this case ourselves."

She shared a different screen with Aaron and tapped out another search of her own, with isolated FBI records hidden behind who knew how many billions of dollars of firewalls, and got the same result.

TRAYNE, KIMBERLY—NO RECORDS FOUND.

Chapter 65
Mike

He'd graduated from texts to actual voice contact with Spencer, and then the cops took them out of their cells. The moment the van's door slammed shut and the hoods came down, his connection spun out of control. This was *not* how the FBI worked, which meant these were not agents. It took some blind stabs to get things working again.

"Mike? Mike? Is that you?"

"Yeah. Jesus, Spence, is this what real fear feels like?"

The adrenaline ran through his veins like liquid panic. This phase of the integration had proved his very last prediction—his body was now as necessary to Mike's survival as the quantum fabric. His realmspace mind had intertwined with his realspace brain. There was no way to separate the two sides now. If they killed him out here that would be the end of it.

Spencer asked, "What happened?"

He explained the situation, and then it was his turn to ask, "Spence? Spencer? You there?"

"Yes. All you're doing is being driven around?"

"For now, anyway. Are they gonna shoot us?"

"I won't bullshit you, Mike. I just don't know. These people are... do you even know who these people are?"

"Completely? No. They sure seemed like FBI agents, but they're not acting like them anymore. They have to be working for Watchtell somehow."

Mike closed his eyes in the dark as his heart slowed, and his breathing returned to normal. Abject terror didn't actually last all that long.

"Anyway, you ready?"

"Mike, I've got the easy part. Go ahead."

He was learning how to manifest in the realms all over again. It was critical that he not injure Spencer or screw up his access. Mike's vision fuzzed briefly, and the familiar velvet texture surrounded him. Then it wobbled sideways and skittered away from him.

"Spencer! Get out!" The fireball flew away from his feet as they hit the floor of the realm.

He groaned out loud in realspace.

"Mike, are you all right?" Tonya asked in the van.

"I'm fine, Tonya. Just having some problems getting—"

"Quiet, you two!"

It was the first thing Kim had said since their arrest.

Tonya and Mike both said her name at the same time.

"Are you all right?" Tonya asked.

"No, I'm not. But I'm," she breathed deeply a few times. She'd been doing that ever since the hoods came down. "I've got routines I use to help me deal with it. They're just slow, and I'm way out of practice." More deep breaths. "As long as they keep me on the end of a pole I think I'll survive. But you two have to shut up."

"Kim," Tonya asked in a calm, level voice, "are they going to kill us?"

Mike's nerves jangled at the mere mention, but Tonya said it like she'd faced this sort of thing every day.

Through her breathing exercises Kim replied, "I don't know. I don't think so. *He* didn't work that way before, that's all I know."

Spencer reconnected. "Mike? You there, Mike?"

"Are you okay, Spence?"

"Yeah, I'm fine. We've worked up an ejection routine now. At the first sign you're manifesting, I get popped out like a cork. It's actually kinda fun."

"I still don't like your crew being involved."

A new voice joined them, Maria's. "He didn't have a choice, *jefe*, and neither do you. Are you ready to try again?"

"Yeah, Mike," Spencer said, "you did great that time! I saw the whole holo, must've been at least a second or two before your feet hit the floor."

Finally. "Actually that's great news. I know exactly what to do now. Let me have another address."

It was all about balance now, and this new try was much easier. For the first time in far too long, Mike opened his eyes, and what he saw wasn't the inside of a sack.

The four of them stared at him anxiously, Spencer and his three assistants. When they realized it was for real this time, they all started whooping and hollering like crazy. The logos on the construct boxes in the small room were familiar.

"Is this the back of a StimBucks?" He'd stopped counting how many realms he'd destroyed when they passed a dozen. "I've been blowing up StimBucks realms?"

"Relax, Mike," Jen, the blonde, said as the rest of the team worked on controls he couldn't see. "We're using them because Chun cracked their point-of-sale protocols forever ago."

"It wasn't that hard," Chun said. "Dad took me to work one day and left me alone with their corporate network. Anyway, no, nobody's hurt. There must be millions of these things all over the place. We've only blown up closed ones, and really only two for real. The rest were simulations."

"Those were simulations?" They could've, well, actually they did fool him. "You guys are officially employees of *Warhawk* once this is over. I'll think up titles later."

"Mike?" Tonya asked in the van.

His feet immediately hit the floor of the realm. Fortunately, Spencer's team vanished long before the wavefront hit them.

He reconnected, gave more specific instructions to the girls, then sent Spencer out to implement phase one of his plan.

"Mike, you still with us?"

He'd forgotten he told Tonya her check-ins helped his timing. He took a deep breath, and then another. This weird organic connection was still growing, and whatever passed for protocol handshakes was slow. His jaw didn't want to work right.

Kim asked, "Mike? Please, are you okay?" Her voice cracked a little.

"No, guys, I'm fine. I'm more than fine. I'm—"

Kim snapped, "Mike!"

He laughed inside. Kim must be feeling better. That zero to seething happened at about normal speed. He needed some way to let them know what was going on though. He first knew this phoneless connection was possible last night.

"What I was trying to say, Kim, is that I can actually *joke* now. You know, like when we were in the grocery store parking lot?"

Their relieved laughs told him they got the message. Kim asked, "Are they still so bad they'll make our *eyes cross*?"

Now that he thought about it, his eyes did have trouble tracking things that first time. "No, nowhere near as bad as that anymore. They're getting really funny now. Like when she told me I was average, she was just being mean."

The van stopped, and the door opened. He lost synchronization again and vanished from realmspace.

"Mike?" Spencer called. "Mike?"

Chapter 66
Aaron

Jenny and Ray, the two agents even more junior than he was, were the only ones out of the hospital today. When he remembered the DD's words, he realized this was probably going to be it. Aaron was supposed to be a glorified library assistant, and now he'd ended up a kind of Special Agent in Charge. He actually thought of the title in capital letters.

He'd asked them to meet in the park a few blocks away from the office. Trayne's message had defined a new kind of paranoia for him. Someone who commanded those kinds of resources could have their entire headquarters bugged. That's what Aaron would've done.

Ray asked, "What the hell is going on?" The three contractors from the Firing Range were standing next to him, nodding to each other. They weren't qualified, not really, but he needed as many cleared people as he could get.

"I don't know," Aaron replied, "but it's all really wrong. First the deputy director informs us we're off the case, and then," he said, turning to the lab tech, "JoBeth, are they still gone?"

The lab tech's eyes glazed briefly. "Yep. Completely gone. It's like they never existed."

"And now," Aaron said with a finger raised, "watch this."

He shared his message space, and not five seconds later, there was a note from the DD reminding them they "had been informed" they were off the case.

"What the hell?" Ray asked. "Since when does a deputy director get involved when a contractor searches for anything?"

"And, shit, that wording," Emilio said. "'You have been informed you are officially off the case.'"

"Ray," Aaron asked, "any luck with the shackles?"

"Nothing. It was like they drove out of the DC Jail, turned left, and vanished. We can track those things from space."

Jenny lifted her hands. "This only happens in bad action movies. We're the goddamned FBI. Who can roll us?"

Aaron replied, "I think this guy might." He shared Watchtell's sales pitch with the team.

When it was over, JoBeth said, "But that doesn't make any sense. Watchtell's just the chief of the Rose Foundation. What does that have to do with taking over the EI? How do we know any of it is even real? The President was in that audience!"

"Real, hell," Ray said, "I'm not completely sure it's even a crime. Well, a federal crime, anyway."

"No," Aaron said, "it may not be. But this is." He shared the message that had landed in his personal queue on the way over.

THE RED KING HAS ALICE, THE RABBIT, AND THE MOUSE. THE CARDS CAN HELP YOU FIND THEM. IS THE HATTER INTERESTED?

A contact address finished the message.

"What do you think?" Aaron asked them all.

"I think I'm getting damned tired of being jerked around," Emilio said. He seemed to be enjoying his temporary deputy status a lot. They all stared at him. "What? Oh, the chubby Chicano can't call this? Well, obviously I'm too *brown* to understand what's going on, but I think whoever that is just provided us with our first lead in a new kidnapping case."

Chubby, brown, and nerdy made no difference. He was right. Aaron returned the call voice-only from his end and shared the connection. A smoky window opened up in their perception, and a broad smile gradually swam into view.

"How fine you look when dressed in rage," it said as the rest of a scruffy cat slowly formed behind the teeth. "Your enemies are fortunate your condition is not permanent."

Aaron had memorized Park's notes. There was only one person who'd actually *been* with Rage recently. "Cut the crap, Spencer. Do you know where they are?"

The construct became even more surreal as its confident mien and articulate English voice changed to those of a nervous Southern teenager. "Um… oh, hi, Agent Park? How'd you know it was me?"

Park was regrowing a leg and wouldn't be out of the hospital for at least a week. Aaron tweaked the privacy settings so Spencer could see them.

"What the shit? Who the hell are you?"

"We're the ones who have to rescue your friends. Do you know where they are?" In that moment, Aaron discovered confidence was mostly being sick of it all and running on two hours of sleep.

The cat flinched. "Okay, no, we don't know where they are right now. The Rabbit, oh, fuck this, Mike sucks at names. Anyway, I'm in contact with Mike, but they had hoods over their heads, and now they're stuck in some stupid room with the lights off. He's asked if you guys can get ready with, well, do you guys have access to anything like a strike team?"

Aaron's stitches still ached. Jenny had an eye patch and a bone knit covering her left leg. The fireball had burned Ray bald and half of one hand was in a regrowth splint. Donny, JoBeth, and Emilio were a trio of civilian nerds who weren't any more qualified than they had been fifteen minutes ago. Aaron was supposed to be chasing dusty records for an eccentric who hadn't been in the field in years. He knew nothing about Mike, and there wasn't time to find out.

"We can work something up," he said.

Chapter 67
Watchtell

Even though he could've manifested directly on the stage, Watchtell chose to wait in the wings of the realm's theater, just as if it was in realspace. A far softer version of the murmurs that he heard in his grand coliseum rumbled around him like the faint edge of a distant storm.

All the years of work, the tireless preparation, the endless campaigning was finally paying off. Even Rage couldn't stand in their way now that she was safely on ice. Her capture and subsequent appropriation by Sidereal-assisted agents of Blacksteel Rose Private Security was the cherry on top of the confection of his dreams. There would be no escape from his labs this time around, of that he was certain.

It was finally over. No more covering up the accidents, bribing government regulators, or hiring the kind of cleaners that worked with bleach and plastic sheets. The families of those unfortunates naturally received full compensation, but the cost was alarming. It was now at an end. Real justice would be possible. The robber barons and polluters would finally be brought to heel, the innocent no longer beholden to their greed, protected by the newly unbound power of their governments.

As he walked out, the applause from two hundred people was polite but subdued. They had all taken giant risks to make this project work, and the sudden jump in the timetable had unsettled them. No matter. Success had a way of breeding forgiveness, and this project would succeed beyond any of their wildest dreams.

"Ladies and gentlemen," Matthew began, pleased at the way the crowd lit up as he spoke. Charm always had its uses, and Watchtell practiced the trade as an expert. "Thank you. From the bottom of my heart, thank you. We have worked so long for this. Without the brilliance of your leadership, your deft shepherding of the foolish, we simply would never have reached this moment." He paused for the applause to subside. "Three years ago, we had a vision."

The speech was really just a shortened and reordered version of the original sales pitch they used to recruit all these presidents and prime ministers. Summaries never hurt, though. Repetition was sometimes necessary for people who paid others to remember for them.

"And so," Watchtell concluded, "after all our efforts, we stand at the foot of this bridge. Some foolishly lose their rafts in the current it crosses. Others still crash from high cliffs, all of them trying to reach the far bank of prosperity. Only we few had the vision and the sense of justice required to build this bridge."

As the applause rose, Watchtell gave the private signal to raise the platform. Once it had majestically lifted into view, a spotlight covered it with a white circle. Its top was flat and wide, like a miniature podium. It was a humble beginning for a revolution of justice.

As intended, the music that had been softly playing rose to a crescendo while he walked up to the switch. Giant maps of the world spun into being over his shoulders. The lines dedicated to the final push were just outlines right now, but that would change in mere seconds. There was a faint, pulsing circle over the area of Virginia where the factory was located. All the lines met, or rather started, there.

As rehearsed, Matthew lifted the cover. Waiting for the precise moment was exquisite. It all came down to this. The instant the music switched from the heights of anticipation to the rattling march of action, he pressed the button.

The lights didn't come on. Nothing happened.

After a second went by, he pressed it again.

The display didn't change a bit.

He pressed it a few more times in rapid succession.

The lack of a response beat its way into his mind as reality became unhinged from the presentation. After an agonizing, terrifying eternity had passed, Matthew felt the sticky warmth of blood under his realspace thumb, now rubbed raw against a corner of his desk. Faces in the crowd went from wonder to confusion to outrage as they realized this was not supposed to be happening. The music broke apart and crashed to a stop.

The silence extended long enough for someone to clear their throat. The screens meant to track their triumphant progress winked out of existence, replaced by a single message as music from an old pop song boomed into the theater.

NICE TRY, MATT. NOW CALL ME, MAYBE? —A. R.

Chapter 68
Spencer

Once Mike had briefed everyone on this part of his plan, the Phoenix Dogs had all gone nuts. He entered the realm and flinched when the protocols brought the sound up.

"A-AH-AHHHHH-AH!" The old guy, Paul, bellowed it out again, and then the other six joined in singing the rest.

"Damn it," Spencer yelled above the din, "what the fuck is that?"

Paul's face broke into a giant grin. It only made the horned helmet on his head more ridiculous. "It's the 'Immigrant Song,' boy! Zeppelin!"

Like that was supposed to mean something.

Paul clapped him hard enough on the shoulder to make him stumble. "We're going a-Viking, lad! Raids! Loot! Pillage!" The rest of the team shouted their approval.

Chun's voice rang out behind him. "And you, sir, are out of uniform!"

She thumped a helmet down on his head. He'd only just set foot in the realm, and people were already beating the crap out of him. Then his avatar changed. He turned and briefly appreciated the outfits his team had picked out for themselves, and then felt the breeze over, well, everything.

"A loin cloth? That's all I get?"

Their eyes glinted with the promise of a lot more than just a pat on the back later.

"With that 300 avatar on? It suits you," Jen said.

They stood in a vast space, lit only by a giant bonfire Mike had seen fit to provide the realm. A huge stone wall stretched to infinity in front of them, pierced by a single enormous door. Paul banged on it enthusiastically with the hilt of his sword, making the iron bars that formed it ring impressively.

"Open this now, you English pig-dogs!" Spencer couldn't place the accent, probably because it only existed in Paul's head.

Again, they all shouted in approval, this time banging various shields against a motley collection of swords. Their leather, fur, and plate armor completed the look, spoiled only by the bandoliers of grenades across their chests and the exotic assault rifles slung on their backs. The superweapons Kim brought out of Pride's Lair were back in play.

Mike's hologram swirled into being beside the fire. "Sorry, folks, not much time. Okay, just like we planned, four teams. Spencer's people, the New Machine? They open doors and reset any weapon and damage contracts. The Phoenix Dogs do the rest."

He motioned them all to be quiet. "You guys have the keys I made for you?"

Spencer and the girls waved glowing constructs that reminded him of button-encrusted conductor's baton.

"Good. And the bags?"

Everyone held up small sacks that opened into a protected infinity.

"Excellent. And when you reach the end?"

They all pulled out big chrome-plated balls and yelled together, "When you pull the pin, Mr. Grenade is no longer your friend!"

Mike pumped his fist once. "Yes! The Dogs take point once a door is unlocked." He waited briefly for the war cries to die down. "Remember to head for the doors on the opposite side. We already know what's just beyond the gate. Now, Godspeed and good hunting! Raiders!"

Spencer's ears buzzed painfully as Mike's voice swelled to fill the echoing space. "ARE YOU READY?"

Even over their whoops and yelps, the gunshot-like reports of the portcullis's locks echoed as they rammed open. The door ground its way upward, increasing speed as it went. The moment they were able to fit their horned helmets underneath it, the teams bellowed one final war cry and went running as fast as they could. An entire private realmspace, huge if Mike's maps were any indication, was now open because he'd connected it to the wider EI. Thank God for patch cords.

As instructed, they split up. Spencer's group headed toward the high-security zone on his left. They ran right across the first connected realm, which seemed mostly to be virtualized labs and a generic office building.

"Spencer!" Paul yelled from the front of their group. "Key!"

He rushed forward, waved the baton over the firewall door, and then pressed the key combination that flashed to life. A wall of light melted away from the door like plastic under a hair dryer.

Spencer flinched as Paul cut loose with another war cry. For an old dude, he sure was loud.

"Well done, lad! Now stand aside and let me work."

Mike's key constructs were only good for unlocking the quantum-encrypted lower protocols that secured the spaces between realms. When Spencer had asked what good that would do them if the door constructs stayed locked Mike just smiled and said, "You'll see."

"Clear!" Paul shouted as he motioned everyone behind cover.

The detonation blew the air out of his lungs as flaming bits of construct disintegrated as they arced over his head. He'd spent hundreds of hours in combat realms and had never experienced something that violent. It came to within a percentage point of knocking him offline completely.

Paul was good. Very good.

Spencer clambered over the desk he'd hidden behind and stopped cold. Paul had ripped a hole into the next realm big enough to drive a truck through. He couldn't have used more than an ounce of explosive construct.

"How much of that stuff do you have, Paul?" he asked as they ran into a different sort of lab space. They all dumped constructs into Mike's bags as fast as they could.

"It's not about how much, it's about where." Paul stretched his bag's mouth over a cabinet taller than he was. He yanked it down and the cabinet disappeared inside. He moved to the next one.

"I brought enough, son, don't you worry about that."

It turned out Paul wasn't just loud, he was really goddamned quick too. Spencer scrambled to keep up with the group during their third smash-and-grab, with no end in sight. Resistance picked up — bad news that blows holes between realms tends travel fast — but so far, the Machine's old constructs and the Phoenix Dogs' marksmanship countered every attempt to stop or boot them.

Out of nowhere, Mike pinged him. "Spencer! This is it! This is it! Find us, man, hurry!"

Spencer got an image of a photocopy machine. At first, as he took cover from yet another of Paul's explosions, he didn't see the point — but only for a second. There was a placard on the corner.

It was a rental. It had an ID number and an address.

He immediately rang up Agent Levine. "Dude, this is where they are!"

He sent the picture, and then stared through the window that had opened up into Levine's space.

"I thought you said you had a SWAT van?" What they were sitting in wasn't a van, it was more like… "Jesus, are you guys in a Prius? How old is that thing?"

The woman wearing an eye patch sitting next to Levine frantically worked on controls in her own workspace. She nodded once and said, "Leesburg Business Supplies, 468912, got it."

Agent Levin put the car in gear.

"You worry about your end of the mission, we'll worry about ours," he said with authority and then locked eyes with Spencer. "What exactly is your end of the mission, anyway?"

Spencer ducked as a security guard's avatar exceeded its damage contract. Wet, red bits of it vanished as they shot over his shoulders.

Behind Spencer, where Levine could clearly see, Paul bellowed out, "That's the violence inherent in the system!" He ran forward with two other Dogs, screaming. Aaron's eyes followed them until they left the field of view, and he then raised an eyebrow at Spencer.

Spencer had no time for this. "Need-to-know, Agent Levine. Find them, please?" The Dogs disappeared through the smoke as they headed for another breach. "I gotta go."

After who knows how many explosions, fights, smashes, and grabs, they finally reached a realm without a new exit. End of the line.

"Jesus!" he said as they crept through the eerily empty space. "These people are sick!"

At first, the realms were what they'd expected: businesses, offices, labs—the usual stuff. The bags Mike had given them swallowed whatever they put in no matter how big it was.

It was plain dumb luck that Colm, one of the other Phoenix Dogs, tried a small door at the end of one office. It led to a room with big fishhooks hanging from chains on the ceiling, and Spencer knew by the smell that it wasn't paint making the walls red. And it just kept getting worse.

"What is it about being in charge that makes them want to do stuff like that?" Spencer asked with a shudder as he pulled out the first of Mike's Mr. Grenades.

Colm shook his head. "I just hope we grab enough to put these sick bastards away. Most of this isn't simulated, it's recorded."

The implication made him swallow hard twice in realspace. It was bad enough when he thought it was fake. He'd never forget the way it all smelled. Real death, curdled blood, things that squelched when he stepped on them.

Colm whistled and motioned to Spencer, who tossed the big chrome ball to Colm in an expert underhand.

"Okay, everyone, remember to take the next left!" Colm pushed the top cover forward, and then pulled the pin. When he tossed it behind them, they ran like hell.

Just before Spencer went through the exit, he spared a quick look backward. In the far distance, he saw a man's shape appear where the grenade landed. When his boots hit the floor, there was an actinic flash, which told Spencer all he needed to know about the Mr. Grenade.

Mike had figured out how to manifest multiples again, and he didn't seem to care about the effect it had this time around.

When they reached the end of another realm line, what they found was unimaginable. He stared up at it slack-jawed, just like everyone else. "How the hell do we steal *that?*"

The construct was enormous, at least a thousand feet high, glowing a lurid red and spinning. The bottom came down to a point, with lines that spread out from it going every which way, millions of them. It had a primitive face—just eyes, nostrils, and a mouth—and seemed to be sleeping. The entire room had the feel of something turned off.

Mike's channel flashed open. "Spencer! Where are they? We need them now! Now, goddamn it!"

Mike's panic was a punch in the face. Bad things were going down. He yanked open the FBI channel and asked Levine, "Where the hell are you guys?"

The woman with the eye patch, Jenny, was saying, "Yes, damn it, a kidnapping. What else is there to know? Get units rolling to—"

The channel closed its focus on just Levine. "We were out of position, but we're getting help and getting closer. Say, five minutes, but we'll be close enough to cause trouble in half that."

Spencer closed the connection and relayed the information to Mike. He cursed and cut the call.

Spencer was about to reopen the channel, but a noise that was half shattering glass, half tree falling stopped him. He spun around. The massive red construct twisted sideways, heading straight for his head. Spencer barely had time to throw his hands up when the top of it scraped to a crumbling stop against the realm's wall. He coughed through the fizz of de-rezzing constructs and sputtered, "Jesus, Paul, you coulda warned me!"

The old man shrugged and grinned through his big bushy mustache. "You're fine, right? Okay, lads, pull!"

They were dragging one of Mike's bags upward across it, letting the bag swallow the construct as it went.

A faint sound went by him, forcing Spencer to cock his ear and concentrate, walking toward the hole. There was more noise, a whimpering or maybe a cry. It was pitch dark on the other side, so Spencer activated his saber to cast its light.

It reminded him of black-and-white pictures of the holocaust. Humanoid figures, gray and thin, ran from him crying out.

They couldn't go far. The realm was too small; a guillotine constructed with blood-chilling accuracy took up most of the space. The war scanner he used showed that they weren't avatars, they were unduplicates. A check on their base data showed activation dates far beyond anything Spencer had ever encountered.

These twelve sad creatures weren't worth a small fortune; they were worth a really big one. There was something strange about them, an itch in the back of his mind. He always had a knack for figuring out the make and model of an AI, the benefit of a life spent poring over every encyclopedia about the realms ever made. But these guys didn't match anything he knew about.

There was only one other person in the realms who didn't have a signature he recognized.

"Mike?" Spencer sent to him. "Mike!"

"Jesus, Spencer, what?"

Mike's voice was choked with rage and despair.

"Mike, I'm sorry man, but you need to come see this."

"Damn it, Spencer!" His hologram flashed into existence.

The room was so dark Spencer had to use the light of the saber to show him.

"Mike, these are AIs, right?" He motioned to the whimpering things on the floor. Their emaciated human forms huddled and moaned.

"Yeah, but…"

"You see it too? They're AIs, Mike, unduplicates, but they *feel* like…

"They feel like you."

One of the twelve stood and walked resolutely toward them.

"My name," she said, "is Alpha. Have you come to kill us?" Her voice was a mixture of bravery, fear, and a sickening amount of hope.

"No." Mike's hologram turned away briefly, and then he said, "I'm here to heal you." His head snapped around, eyes wild with panic. "Spencer! How much longer?"

Chapter 69
Kim

Her touch-agony had faded to a point where she nearly felt human, so more than a few hours had passed. She'd even gotten used to the pole still tied around her neck. She'd be sore tomorrow, but if that's the worst that happened, she'd be more than happy to eat a few aspirin and call it a day. Just from the noise around them, something big was going on. She still couldn't see because of the damned hood, but conversation had revealed Tonya and Mike were very close and equally hobbled. It was a comfort of a sort. Whatever happened next, she wouldn't face it alone.

It was only when a helicopter thumped and thudded across the roof that she knew the truth. The switch Mike found *was* important, and Kim held the only key. Watchtell discovering it while she was his prisoner was the kind of bad luck that ruled her life, but Mike was safe now. There would be no takeover, no destruction. That's all that mattered.

Finally, the bastard had gotten what he'd deserved. She let the laughter bubble through, because it helped her center. Watchtell was here, and she was his prisoner. Kim needed to hold it together for what was coming.

"Kim? Are you okay?" Mike asked.

His voice shot warmth through the frozen razors that had surrounded her mind. Watchtell knew exactly how vulnerable she was. Back in the day they'd put sensors around her, studied her like a lab rat. He knew exactly how to destroy her.

Avoiding capture meant a lot more to her than to most anyone else. An accidental touch used to send her to the hospital. Aside from those, she'd never been touched by anyone in her life, not even her mother.

It didn't matter. She'd beaten him. What he was going to do to her wasn't happening right now. Right now, she could laugh.

"Oh, yes." She softly sang out into the dark. "The angel ruined your day, the angel ruined your day..."

Kim had something Watchtell wanted, and he'd stop at nothing to get it.

Mike was here. Tonya was here.

Please, let it be enough.

Someone yanked off her hood. She gasped and blinked in the glare of florescent lights. They were in a rectangular break room, perhaps fifty feet long and maybe twenty wide. Folding metal chairs and long, narrow tables made neat rows against the unfinished walls. Three large, confident guards in dark suits and expensive sunglasses stood with the hoods in their hands, and then moved to the walls beside them.

Watchtell and his toady Gary walked in. Nine other guards took up positions around the room. Watchtell's face made her whole day. The one thing he hated most of all was losing control of a situation. Judging by that face, he'd lost control of everything.

Good.

"Something amusing you'd care to share, Kim?" Watchtell asked from the front of the room.

"I broke your toy." She rattled her shackles. "Turn me loose, I want to break some more."

He smiled the same way he had years ago, when she went against every instinct and trusted him. It never reached his eyes.

"Now, now, Kim, you and I both know you didn't break anything. Please come over here so we can chat. Gentlemen?" He motioned to two of the guards. "Careful now, we don't want to touch our precious girl. That won't do."

One of the guards nodded and picked up the pole still hanging by a strap around her neck.

Their maneuvering allowed her a brief look behind her. Tonya was frantic, but Mike was strangely calm. He shook his head as if waking from a dream, and then locked eyes with her.

He was safe now. That was all that mattered. She would not let Watchtell take him over or destroy him, no matter what the cost. Mike used his hands to show ten.

He still had a connection to realmspace somehow. He must be working on a rescue. If time was what he needed, time was what she'd buy. Kim would not let them down, not this time, no matter what.

The price she was about to pay choked her, but only briefly.

Kim sat up straight, cleared her throat, and rattled her shackles. "You've got ten minutes to take these off. If you do, I'll think about letting you go."

Watchtell's contempt was familiar, but not the undercurrent of hysteria in his laughter.

She'd won.

No matter what he did next, she'd won.

He shook his head. "I have a different deal for you."

"We *had* a deal." Five years ago she'd given him everything, and he'd betrayed her completely. "You broke it."

"I didn't break it dear, I altered it, ever so slightly." Watchtell glanced behind Kim, then returned to her. "You did tell them about it, yes?" He turned back to her friends. "Did she tell you?"

"Tell me what?" Tonya asked. "Why don't you come over here close, so I can let my foot tell your ass about some things?"

The way Tonya said it reminded Kim there were other people who cared, other people who were just as pissed off. It helped her breathe, but only a little.

Watchtell flexed his hands too close to her.

It was coming. This was just a delay.

He smiled as he turned to Kim. "Why would you hide that? It was your greatest accomplishment!"

"What the hell are you talking about?" Tonya asked.

"You have heard about 'The Man Who Sold the World'?"

"It's a stupid old song, so what?"

"Well then it is my immense pleasure to present to you," he said as he gestured to Kim, "The Girl Who *Stole* the World! I guess it was five years ago now?"

Tonya and Mike were with her. What he was going to do wasn't happening now. She'd beaten him. "Fuck you."

"It was a Tuesday. I was just sitting down to brief the President when the Secretary of the Treasury ran into the room, screaming. It turned out that a certain someone had managed, all by herself, to empty the US treasury. Gone. In an instant, the wealth of the richest, most powerful country in the world was reduced to the change in its citizens' pockets."

Watchtell smiled as he walked around the front of the room. "But it got better. In less than five minutes, we established that the coffers of our country weren't the only ones emptied. No. That very same someone had managed to single-handedly empty the treasuries of every country in the whole world."

"I told you," Kim said as she stared at the floor, willing herself to ignore how close his hands were. "It was a mistake."

He got so close to her she barely fought off a flinch. The heat of his breath blew over her face, laced with rot and alcohol. "Tell her. See if she believes you any more than I did."

Kim glared at him, wishing with all her heart that she could ram her head into that grin. But that would mean touching him.

Tonya and Mike were with her.

What he was about to do was not happening now.

"It was the same attack I used in the Goldman raid. I needed to get your attention."

They'd spent a week shivering in the jungle, and Lourdes wouldn't stop coughing.

"Nobody was talking to me, and I needed help." The way those bank account balances spiraled up at the speed of light still gave her nightmares. "None of you even bothered to put passwords on anything!"

"And why should we, dear? We had unbreakable security. And so?"

"And so it cleaned out every single account in every single central bank in every single country all over the world and gave the cash to me."

He stood up. "And gave the cash to her. One moment the world had a fully functioning economy, and the next moment it was in free fall. What's worse, we couldn't change any of it. She locked it up tight. Then I got a message. Do you remember it, Kim? Do you?"

She wouldn't give the son of a bitch the satisfaction because she'd won. He wouldn't be here otherwise.

Mike and Tonya were with her. It had to be enough.

Please, let it be enough.

"It said, 'An angel has the keys to heaven, she'll trade them for a place to hide.' A place to hide! You single-handedly unleashed Armageddon wanting a place to hide!"

"I told you, it wasn't supposed to happen that way."

"But it did." To Tonya, he asked, "And guess what I convinced the President to do next?"

Kim couldn't help but smile at the absolutely lyrical rage in Tonya's voice. "I do not play twenty questions with dumbass crackers like you."

Watchtell laughed. "Indeed. Well, I'll tell you anyway. He found her a goddamned place to hide, that's what he did. Her and her gang. Didn't we, dear?"

"And then you took it all away."

"Is that what you think happened?"

"I saw the orders, Watchtell. As soon as you hacked my earrings—"

"That's where you kept the access codes to our bank accounts? In your jewelry box?"

"No. I wore them. Always."

"How incredibly clever." He turned again to Tonya. "She made sure we all knew there was a secret back door in every one of our banks. She gave us back the world, but only if she could hold a gun to its head." He turned back to Kim. "And you're surprised the deal didn't last?"

"You betrayed us, betrayed me." She didn't need Tonya or Mike now. She'd trusted him, and this bastard had taken away the US marshals who watched her friends. They were all dead, and he'd *helped*.

Watchtell rolled his eyes. "Do you really think we would let someone with the power you demonstrated get away with just a deal?" He kicked Kim's chair around so she faced Mike. "What I want to know is how you ended up with him."

"What are you talking about?"

Watchtell's brow furrowed. "Why, you were the one who told us about Matias Colque. Remember?"

He still thought Mike was Colque.

"I'll concede he was incredibly useful," Matthew continued, "once I gave him the locations of your team."

Her vision swam and closed in on him. "What?"

"Well, I couldn't very well have all of you running around loose, could I?"

Tonya yelled a warning at her, but Kim couldn't understand it over the thundering of her pulse.

"You gave them to him? I helped you! I showed you what I did!" Even Kim didn't think he'd stoop so low. If she'd only known, she might have stopped it.

She could've saved them all. "You fucking bastard!"

"Yes." He smiled. "And now you're going to help us again. Gentlemen?"

He reached into his pocket, and Kim's shackles released with a quick puff of gas. As they yanked her up by the neck, Tonya sobbed openly, staring behind her.

One of the tables now had long chains strapped to each leg, ending in handcuffs. Gary stood beside it, holding a knife.

And so it begins.

There was a clap, a sting, and then Kim was lost in darkness.

A sharp pinch on her neck brought her around as Watchtell's assistant stepped away. She was shackled face-down on the break room table, the back of her blouse cut away. The cool air flowed gently across her bare skin.

It was here. It was happening right now.

Tonya screamed through a gag they'd forced into her mouth, and Mike had turned away. No, his glassed-over eyes meant he was talking to the outside world again. Everyone else thought he was Colque, a psychopath, but she knew better. Mike was here. The thought allowed her to breathe a few times. It wasn't enough, not now. The urge to have him look at her was overpowering, but she didn't want him to see what was happening.

"Where did you get these?" Watchtell asked when he saw the wings on her back. "They're beautiful." He took off his gloves. "I know you want this. You've always wanted it."

As bare hands walked closer, it strangled the strength she needed. She faltered.

"Please… no…"

He blocked her view of Mike when he knelt down beside her. "Then give me the code to the lock you put on my construct. That's all I want. This all stops once I have the access code."

His gray eyes were warm, his voice kind. If she gave him the key, it would stop. *What he was about to do wouldn't happen.* Mike would never be the same. He might not even exist if she gave Watchtell the key. Another person who trusted her would die. She stiffened and set her jaw.

"No."

He stood up with a sigh and moved out of her field of view. Mike's face was so caring it wrenched her heart to pieces. She closed her eyes quickly as tears rolled out, and the nausea returned.

"Remember, this is what you wanted."

He was right. It was what she wanted. Someone's touch. All her life she'd been isolated, and now the one thing she wanted most of all came from someone who wanted her dead. Someone she hated, someone who'd killed people she loved. At his caress, barbed razors covered with filth and salt tore across her skin. Her mind seized and shredded as broken glass ripped through it.

Her eyes flew open. Mike was watching her now, desperation obvious on his face. Between the screams, she sobbed. It was supposed to be *him*, and now he watched as someone else touched her. He couldn't see this. She didn't want him to see this.

She couldn't stop him from seeing this.

After an eternity of searing agony, Watchtell paused. "Maybe the key is in one of these?" At a nod, Singh threw her personal effects on the table next to her. "Pick one, or just give me the code, and this all ends."

Kim pushed back with everything she had, but it was too much too fast. The breathing wouldn't force the blades and barbs back anymore. Nothing made it fade anymore. Her vision cleared just enough for her to comprehend Mike, who nodded grimly. As a tear trailed down his cheek, he showed her two fingers.

Two minutes.

Please, no.

Watchtell was back in her face. "Well?"

Kim remembered her old friends, her new ones, what her heart did when she thought of Mike's smile. It was enough. He needed two minutes.

"No."

This time his caresses were stronger, and his hands roamed farther. Rusted barbed wire knotted around her ribs, digging furrows into the bone as they went. She'd saved herself from touch, kept it away because it could kill her. Was killing her.

Please, just let it end.

Fat worms of pure acid crept across her breasts and reached under to burrow with needle-tipped teeth into her belly. Misshapen horrors screamed alien shrieks into her jabbering mind. Thrashing heartbeats went on and on.

When she was able to breathe again without screaming, Watchtell said, "I'm more than happy to continue. But we can end this if you'd just give me the code."

He didn't understand. Here, at the very end, she knew he didn't understand. Touch *killed* her. It didn't matter. Mike was safe. When Watchtell touched her again, she knew without a doubt Mike would be safe forever.

The key would die with her.

Kim could barely make her voice work. It was soaked and slippery with spit, tears, and mucus, but she still managed to grind out what she knew would be her last words.

"Go to hell."

He stood up and motioned to Singh, who nodded, placed the knife blade under the middle of Kim's waistband, then lifted to cut.

Chapter 70
Mike

Hanging helpless from shackles while Watchtell touched Kim's back was awful, the hardest thing he'd ever gone through. Now it was worse. He couldn't do anything, and this had to stop. She was visibly weakening, shrinking away in front of him. The indefinable energy always in her eyes was fading away. She wouldn't survive another round.

When the knife went under Kim's waistband, he shouted at Spencer, "How much longer?"

Spencer blinked. "Right now!"

The break room lights went out, and the shackles holding him and Tonya flew open with a slap. Security doors slammed across the room's entrance, and fire alarms blared to life. Emergency lights bathed the space in red and bright white strobe flashes.

Mike threw his shackles at the neck of the man helping Watchtell. He missed and hit Watchtell, sending him tumbling to the ground. Mike ducked a swing from the nearest guard, and then threw a punch combination into his gut so hard it lifted him off his feet. All the frustration and helplessness finally had an outlet. It felt right. Mike didn't need to understand. His knee came up and cracked solidly against the guard's forehead, sending him tumbling away. Mike blocked two others as they coordinated an attack.

He took body blows, and then snapped quick jabs into the face of the one in front of him. He didn't care what it meant anymore, didn't care that these were the skills of a dead man. They were letting him get closer to Kim. The only thing that mattered was getting them away from her. Mike grabbed the guard's arm and shoulder to leverage a fast chest kick into the guy behind Mike. He pulled himself above and around the first attacker, throwing him upside down into a row of cabinets mounted on the wall.

Tonya was far from helpless. She slid under an attacker, tripping him. He fell headfirst into a wall.

The three remaining on Mike's side started another coordinated attack that drove him to his knees. In the confusion of the scrum, he had to fight off eye gouges and one grab at his groin. The power of his body, the way it moved, would've been distracting at any other time. As it was, he just relaxed into the knowledge that he was better than they were, even with them on him all at once.

He found the inside of a nose and pulled. It gave him just enough space to get an elbow free, which he crashed into the jaw of the man closest to it. That freed even more space up, letting him stand and fling the last of them bodily through the centerline of tables. He could finally breathe now, and he wanted another target. He wanted to get rid of more guards.

Mike searched for Tonya, hoping they hadn't gotten her. A resounding clang announced she was doing just fine. She slammed one of the guards down with a folding metal chair so hard his head cratered the seat.

Flickering shadows to his left made him spin in the opposite direction and throw a hand chop against a neck. The reflexes, the ability to just *move* and make it happen, were intoxicating. The guard fell like a rag doll.

Unconscious bodies lay scattered around Tonya. The last one standing immediately pulled his gun to take a shot at Mike. It cracked a deafening bang as the bullet whizzed past, millimeters away from his ear. Before the guard was able to pull the trigger again, Tonya jumped and twirled straight into his side; the gun tumbled out of his hand.

Mike took a running slide across the tables, but Tonya stood up first. With an unearthly howl, she double-chopped him so hard he crashed through the remaining tables. She stood there shivering, perfectly balanced in a beautiful pose, mouth open, eyes wild.

That was the last one. Tonya immediately started stripping the men of their weapons while Mike ran to check on Kim.

He stared at her, his heart racing at unbearable speed. In all the craziness of noise and light, he couldn't hear anything, couldn't tell if she was breathing. There was blood everywhere. This was where the bullet went. His shoulders slumped as Tonya skidded up beside him.

Kim's eyes were open, and she was completely still. Not moving at all. They both yelled out her name again and again. Time stretched into agonizing seconds as Mike's heart began to implode.

Kim blinked, and then blinked again.

He couldn't think, couldn't breathe, around the simple idea that she was alive. She slowly strained one hand against her shackles and then gave a shaky, weak, thumbs up.

The blood wasn't hers. The bullet hit the man who helped Watchtell. He was lying on the floor and would never get up again.

Tonya searched for a key to the shackles as Mike reached out to Spencer. The team had finished the job and were gathered, limp and exhausted, around the fire outside the wall. Everyone in the realm was grim faced, and it was quiet.

"Spencer!" his voice boomed out. "We're done! We made it!"

The people around the campfire stared at each other, and then whooped and hugged in celebration. They were so loud it was hard to shout over them, especially with all the noise in the break room bleeding into his feed.

"What was that, Mike? I didn't get that last part." Spencer waved everyone quiet.

"I said, could you get the FBI to turn off the alarms and turn on the lights? It's a little crazy in here."

After a few moments, the alarms fell silent, and the normal lights came back on. He finished securing the last of the bodyguards with a roll of duct tape he'd found in a cabinet. Tonya searched the pockets of the unfortunate bastard on the floor. His wallet said his name was Gajeel Singh.

"Why don't they unlock the doors?" she asked.

"Spencer, what's up with the doors?"

Spencer's eyes unfocused briefly. "No idea. They think they're on a different circuit."

Mike relayed the information to Tonya just as she found the right key and went to work. Nobody bothered with Watchtell, who was still out cold on the floor.

"Hey, Mike, Catch!" Tonya flicked the first of the shackles his way and nodded her head at Watchtell.

Mike attached Watchtell to a pipe while Tonya gently dropped a jacket she'd liberated from one of the bodyguards across Kim's bare shoulders.

"They're almost here, Kim, but we can't figure out the doors. They're locked. Do you think you can open them?"

She nodded and croaked out, "Hand me my phone."

After Kim got off the table, Tonya gingerly draped the phone around her neck.

Kim gasped, went completely rigid, and flung her arms down to her sides. The jacket slowly fell from her shoulders as Watchtell began to laugh.

Chapter 71

Kim

There were lines of potential and she couldn't remember how to breathe. This cannot be never always happens waves grabbed never grabbed how where must leave must run must run.

She couldn't remember how to breathe! Thick coruscating light surrounded her, fizzing and boiling with futures winking away in impossibly small scales of time, and she could not remember how to breathe. Waves crashed and collapsed and expanded and she was everywhere at once *inside* a place she thought was just a part of her mind.

"We could teach you, you know." A voice. Someone else was in here with her.

All of Kim's vision cleared even as the pressure built in her lungs. It was a woman's voice, low and seductive. The strange woman walked around All of Kim's gasping form. The force of the place had split Kim into dozens, thousands, uncounted versions of herself, all standing in the same place on a platform, all of her body held rigidly still. They were and were not all of her, but she had no time to understand.

It wasn't important. All of Kim couldn't remember how to breathe. A small few of Kim gave up, and collapsing waves of invisible force took them, but almost All of Kim kept thinking. Remember how to breathe. All of Kim must remember how to breathe.

"You're not very strong, but you have potential." The stranger was pretty but flawed. A burn scar covered her left cheek. She wore a dark blue uniform with a patch over her left breast that had a telescope and a clock on it.

This was a lab of some sort. All of Kim was in a lab, beige walls with a gray tile floor, surrounded like All of Kim was in a clear tube or canister that reached the top of her shoulders.

"I can take you back, you know. We're simply between time. Just give the key to me, and you can go home. You don't have to fail again."

All of Kim knew that, and again a small few of Kim gave up over the guilt and vanished, but All of Kim also knew what mattered most was life. Most of Kim noticed some of Kim vanishing in a different direction. That wave collapsed. All of Kim just had to hang on. All of Kim's hearts faltered as All of Kim's vision closed into a gray tunnel. The memory danced around the edge of All of Kim's mind. Just before All of Kim's vision faded to black, the collapsing wave reached her.

She remembered how to breathe.

The waves are everywhere higher lower slip not at once minds fade thinking no thinking no thinking oh please no not... and she couldn't remember how to think.

Kim was a little girl sitting on a flat white surface, legs tucked behind her, in a white dress. She understood there were many more of her surrounding her, all making decisions, but Kim was too small to care about that.

The light made things seem strange and flat; the silence was friendly. She liked silence. It kept her safe.

She wasn't alone.

He was a pretty boy, dressed in white. They were sitting on the floor in front of a game board of black-and-white squares. There were things on the board. Little figures. They were cute. Each time she moved one many more of her vanished.

"You don't have to listen to them," the boy said. Kim remembered him. He didn't care how strange she was. He didn't mind that she never spoke to anyone; that she couldn't speak to anyone. The rest of them were mean and would touch her when they could. It hurt so much.

"You're just a girl. It's so unfair, to have to be pretty and strong at the same time. It's much more fun to be nice." He leaned in close, but not too close, and whispered, "You don't have to be pretty and strong. I'll show you how to be nice, and they'll take care of you forever. Just give me the key."

Kim wanted to let go. Some of her did just that and vanished, but then some of her remembered. The wave was coming this way. She wanted to just relax and smile and be pretty and loved and accepted because it wasn't fair, and it wasn't nice.

But Kim wasn't fair. She wasn't nice.

She didn't want to be nice.

The waves turn to particles and then to waves and crashed back and split to billions again. She wanted him didn't want him would never have him why now why him why this can't have never have never oh please no not... she screamed out his name and forgot him.

The stranger's lips were warm. The heat of them reached hers, not quite touching, but he pulled away. He was handsome, brilliantly handsome.

"Please, just give it to us. We'll be able to help you then."

All of her wanted him everywhere, but Kim ignored the rest of them for this moment. His eyes were warm but aggressive. Her breath quickened, and her pulse raced as she stared at him. He was gorgeous, and she wanted him.

"You don't have the strength to stay here," he whispered, leaning close, fresh heat across her skin. "You are weak, but we can make you strong."

His pulled away, skin glistening, sculpted forms of shadow and light. When he walked, his blue uniform vanished ever so briefly, letting her glimpse what she needed beneath. His movements hypnotized her.

His eyes lingered over her body. Even in the simple dress she wore, she could *feel* it. She wanted to get out of this dress. Wanted him to take it off, tear it off. Thrills shot from her center to her fingertips, then rocketed back again. The suffering in his eyes said he wanted her just as much. A few of Kim raced into his arms and vanished. But it was wrong. This wasn't the one Kim really wanted. There was someone else, but she couldn't remember.

Then she remembered something that rocked Kim to her core. Of all the things she feared, of all the things Kim despised, of all the things she had ever wanted in her entire useless life, Kim was thrilled almost beyond comprehension at the idea.

She remembered how to touch. The agony wasn't permanent. There was a solution. If he needed the key for that, she'd gladly…

A great many more of Kim rushed forward and vanished. That wave headed her way, but it was wrong. A few of Kim knew this was wrong. He was the wrong one. This was not the decision Kim should make. The wave of vanishing thundered her way, collapsing Kim by the millions as they all made a decision she'd wanted to make for all eternity. But it would not be the decision Kim would make. She would have to forget how to touch.

Because she remembered how to win.

There were lines of potential and she knew how to breathe.

Kim was everywhere around her, all herself. But this was an illusion. These were strange mirrors, surrounding her, casting her reflection back at her.

She wasn't alone.

There were three of them, a woman and two men. They wore uniforms, dark blue and all with the same strange patch, which had words she could read, now that she remembered how. Sidereal Spin. Tubes led from backpacks to fixtures that pinched their noses.

All Kim had was skin.

Her hands coruscated with strange, dark patterns. They covered her body, now black as night. The mirrors showed that her wings made the patterns, their movement triggering ripples everywhere. Ripples of power. Ripples of control. The patterns converged on her eyes, which were also a deep black. Her irises did not exist; instead they shone with guidelines of coral-colored energy that lay far behind them as if Kim was a piece of paper placed over a window. They were gorgeous alien things. She reveled in the transformation. In a flash of her weird backward memories, she understood this glorious being was what she had been all along.

Memories unwound continuously, revealing secret after secret. The place was full of dimensions, energy bubbling as entire universes existed and vanished in impossibly short instances of time. It was knowledge both new and very old, happening in a continuous reality that stood above time. The place unlocked knowledge in her soul, instinct on a level Kim had never reached before.

She gathered her first fist of power, but pain blew across the backs of her legs, and she collapsed. The woman had used a long rod against her knees to knock her down. The attack outraged her even as she fell. Before she could get up, they all hit her with the same sort of rod, blows hard enough to break normal bone. All it did was distract her with the pain. The constant drubbing ceased as they all pulled back to hit her at once. The brief stillness was all she needed.

Kim clenched her fist, and the power grew into a nimbus of energy drawn from the smallest scale of the universe. It was a silky thing, flowing through her carrying a heart-pounding righteousness with it. She was its perfect instrument. Kim opened her hand and let it go.

A double-sphered shockwave of crystal-blue force blasted the three off their feet, shattering the thousands of mirrors they'd surrounded her with like windows blown apart in a storm.

This was her birthright. This was the source of her ability, a glorious and infinite place of power. There was no need to be human here, no reason to hide. She stood, trailing static-shrieked lightning from her hands as an overpowering ozone stench filled the space. It was time to end this charade.

The woman on her left, the one with the strange scar, produced a gun of some sort and fired it. The blast threw burning chaos across her body, extinguishing her power and sent her flying. The bolt's chaos kept her from concentrating again, kept her confused, unable to focus on their assaults. Then they were on her again.

They were fading, their strength drifting away as hers swelled, but it happened too slowly. They were searching. They weren't trying to convince her or even hurt her now; they only wanted something from her. They were yelling, but their voices bounced backward and forward, echoes of phrases they did and did not say collapsed, and Kim couldn't understand them.

One of the hands on the tall, handsome one changed into a translucent claw. The sudden tearing in her chest as it pierced her ripped a scream from her lungs. Then an edged agony, like a razor cutting away a diamond, shot through her. It pulled out a token from Kim's chest.

They'd taken Watchtell's key. The trio crowed in triumph and stood to run away.

It was the last mistake they would have time to make.

Freed from their attacks, a nova of power blew outward from her center, and Kim spun to her feet. A gestured blast of dark, coral-limned lightning stopped them all, still as stones. She brought them back to her. The equipment they used to breathe fell in pieces at their feet. Frozen in her strange, dark light, she could feel their pulses quicken, because they could not remember how to breathe here. All Kim needed to do was hold them, and they'd soon disappear on their own, forever.

But she didn't want that. She took back the code they'd stolen from her. Lines and waves traced patterns everywhere and nowhere, on, in, and around her. Uncertainty split billionfold, then collapsed into singularity, and then silently blew apart again. The information it did and did not store defined the whole universe and nothing.

The paradox was completely natural to her now. She wanted to stay and watch its unspeakable beauty, but she had a job to do. These were intruders. She needed to destroy their way in. Kim reached into the core of the place, threw a black-cloaked shield around them all, and took the rest of it for power.

There had to be a nexus, a connection allowing the other three to exist here. She spun them, now so small as to seem like toys in her palm, until the woman was in front of her. With a voice of crashing power Kim said, "I wish to return you to your master. Tell me where to go."

Hope vied with terror in the woman's eyes, and Kim's laughter boomed into the vast space.

"No. I will not end you, but I will end this." She drew them all closer. "Tell me."

Their faces were turning purple as the oxygen in their lungs ran out. The woman slapped a pouch on her belt, and a silvery cable appeared, leading away into the distance. By simply willing it, Kim transported them all to its end. She stood next to what seemed like a one-way mirror. A control room was on the other side.

It was dark. Three giant screens near the ceiling displayed metrics and graphs with a picture of each of her captives. Below the screens, they were laid out on hospital beds, eyes closed, surrounded by heavily modified realmspace gear. Old-fashioned control consoles stretched three rows across the floor around them with a score of people operating them.

Kim concentrated the power again. It was silk in her hands, in her mind, completely under her command. As the barrier thinned, warning claxons barked to life on the other side Cracks shot across the wall as she built a ram of power around her fist. With a roar, she smashed a hole through the worlds, and then stepped through.

The people scurrying around and climbing out of the rubble of the rupture stopped whatever they were doing. Her head nearly scraped the ceiling. She threw her onyx arm out and tossed her captives toward their bodies, lying in hospital beds at the center of the room, and as they flew they disappeared in an invisible wave.

Kim stared at them all, and they wilted under her gaze. The strange, dark patterns on her body picked up speed as they flickered. First, their controls. She put out a hand and twisted the dimensions that ran through the devices. They spit sparks like waterfalls and billowed out smoke. Now, the power and data stores.

Extensions of her body flowed through dimensions until she found them. Kim clenched her fist and the room shook from a nearby explosion.

There would be no more excursions, no more spies, no more trespassing into the world behind her. She examined them all silently one last time, nodded, and then turned to leave.

"Wait!" one of them shouted, and she stopped. The wings on her back flexed as she held the edge of infinity. "Who are you?"

She turned her head. The truth was futures past, power triumphant and ruined. When Kim tried to speak the language in her head wasn't even English. It was ancient, lined in marble that had long ago crumbled on a hill overlooking the sea. But the truth of it held, even when translated.

"Victory."

Chapter 72
Mike

Mike jumped when a nearby explosion shook the room, and then all the doors unlocked and slammed open.

Tonya cried out, "Kim!"

She had collapsed over her knees, breathing, but far too still. They didn't dare touch her. Right after she fell, a migraine wormed its way back and forth through both sides of Mike's mind. Somehow, it centered on her. Then the strange pain relaxed with a pop, and Kim's breathing returned to normal.

She slowly reached behind her and pulled the jacket back on. As she stood and opened her eyes Kim flinched and gasped, trying to get away from Tonya and Mike as her breath lost its rhythm again.

With ferocious effort, she regained control of herself, closed her eyes, and buttoned her coat

"It's over." She turned to walk through the door.

Watchtell shouted, "It's not over! This changes nothing!"

Kim stopped and turned around. It was obvious that everyone was far too close to her, much worse than when they were at the hotel, but she fought through it, slowly walking toward him.

"You're right, Matthew. This doesn't change anything. Anything at all. Tomorrow people will be horrible to each other. Tomorrow they'll be kind. Tomorrow there will be tenderness and safety and order, and there's nothing that will ever change that. Tomorrow there will be cruelty and murder and chaos, and there's nothing that will ever change that."

She was close to him now. "That man died today; do you at least understand that? He's not even the first. You poisoned people, Matthew. You burned them."

"Accidents. Incidents. We all knew the risks. We're working for justice. Nothing else matters."

Kim leaned down. "He's *dead*, Matthew." She waved her hand back at the corpse. "Do you think he cares about justice anymore?"

"If he were alive he'd say the same thing. Justice is all that matters."

"No. Your justice is an illusion; a tissue of lies made by the powerful to control the weak. It's an iron fist that beats and kills and makes us all bow down and kiss it for the privilege. You're not working for justice. You're working for pure, naked control.

"You think the rest of us are weak or stupid. You're so certain you already know the answers you never once think to ask why. You want to protect us from ourselves, and then apologize when it all goes wrong. You just tried to destroy the thing that knits us all together because you can't make it do what you want."

He shook his head and tried to stand up against the shackles. "Not destroy it, control it!"

"And if you'd failed?"

"Either outcome would've forced justice on to it. Rich people cheat and innocent people are left behind."

"People are always left behind, Matthew. Nothing can change that. All you can do is push the rest of us backward. Have you ever been to a soup kitchen? Actually helped someone off the street? Mentored a kid? Not by throwing your billions around or forcing the rest of us to do it for you. Have you ever actually tried to help one single person yourself?"

He glared at her and raised his chin. "If we fixed the system they wouldn't need help."

"They will always need help. Nothing can change that. So rather than getting out of the way of a system that works, you want to control it, risk destroying it, just in the hope what you do might be better."

His eyes grew wild. "It will be better! I'm certain of it!"

The slap rang out like a gunshot. "Nothing is certain, Matthew. Nothing. You mistake ignorance for certainty and call it truth. You never question yourself, so you'll never understand anyone else. People aren't evil because they're wrong, Matthew. People are evil because they never once consider they're anything but right.

"I can't change the world. It won't be changed. But I will change one thing. I'll change *you*." She spun around and walked out the door.

Tonya made a strangled noise as she stared at the floor. There was a pool of blood, and Mike tracked the too-frequent drops up to Kim's hand. She gripped her fist so hard her nails had cut deeply into her palm, and now the ruin leaked her life out on the floor.

They both broke into a run.

Chapter 73

Kim

As her power once knew no bounds, her agony was now boundless. No one could, or ever would, come near her again. In her transformation, the wall built around the desperation of her life had shattered. She used what little energy she had to keep her feet moving, but that was evaporating away too fast. She needed to get away from here. Kim would not collapse in front of that bastard.

She had lied to Matthew. There would be no moving on. Not for her, not after this. Even at a distance, the people around Kim now rent holes in her sanity. Mike would never come near her. The ridiculous fantasy of knowing his touch was just a sad, defenseless dream that screamed inside her as it burned to dust.

Every crutch she'd found over the years now shattered against a threshing maw of agony. It was building and she couldn't hope to control it. She was alone, would always be alone, in horrible pain without help or hope. It would never, ever end.

But there was one way. The last of that strange, dark power was fading, but it still gave her a way to escape. When she was out of the room, she turned the corner and used her new perception one last time.

She remembered how to die.

There was the sound of running feet and Tonya's voice. "Mike! No! You can't!"

She fell. The abyss was dark, welcoming, and she evaporated into it. But then strong arms stopped her fall. They burned. Kim opened her eyes. This was her avatar. She was in a realm. Someone held her in arms so strong they felt like girders, but everything burned. They were walking. She lifted her head up just enough to see a face.

"Mike? What's happening? Where am I?"

"Kim. I need you to concentrate. I need you to concentrate as hard as you can. You need to stay here with me. You can't go anywhere else. Don't even think about going anywhere else. You can't leave me. You have to stay right here. Can you do that?"

She nodded because that was all she could do. "I think so. Mike, you're hurting me."

"I know. I'm sorry, but I can't help it. Please, concentrate."

He had actually manifested. This wasn't a hologram. She floated, just barely, in his arms. His power was what caused her pain. Her avatar was dissolving from the destruction; Kim was dissolving in pain.

But it was a different sort of pain. It wasn't desperation. It wasn't fear. It wasn't depression or disgust or shame or any of the other kinds of pain that had ruled her life for as long as she could remember. It was the pain of healing. Through the shards and echoes of her shattered sanity, Kim's soul was healing in the fire of his embrace.

He carried her through the blanketing calm of a towering forest in an ancient realm. Mike told her stories about crazy spies and strange ladies and the monk who named his mystery. He told her about special places, wild places, secret places forgotten long ago.

She relaxed in his arms and slowly burned completely away.

Chapter 74
Tonya

Tonya stood dumbstruck in the main room of the warehouse. She was a dozen steps behind Mike as they ran. What happened next was beyond her wildest hopes, fears, or beliefs. Mike stopped Kim's fall, picked her up, and then carried her. *Carried her.* Kim tightened her embrace, and in the dancing light of a fire outside the huge doors, buried her head in his shoulder. The streams of FBI agents and police rushed in and parted as they ran around them, and the pair slowly walked out into the cold, flickering night.

Whatever he'd done lasted exactly long enough to put her in the ambulance, and then the screams started.

Tonya had been doing shifts on a suicide watch with Mike ever since. She should *still* be doing shifts on a suicide watch. Watchtell's rape—sexual or not, that's exactly what Tonya considered it—had broken her. Kim had spent the past thirty-six hours screaming incoherently and thrashing against her restraints. Every single hour. The doctors couldn't get close enough to even try a diagnosis. They couldn't sedate her properly until the drugs the cops and Watchtell had used were out of her system. Tonya loved her dearly, but she couldn't stand to be in that hospital room for more than an hour. The screams were too weird, and the babbling about lightning and power were worse. Half the time she didn't even speak English.

Mike was with her always, only leaving when Tonya made him

Until now. The Phoenix Dogs' raids into Watchtell's private realmspace had brought back not only terabytes of incriminating data, but also the primary neural access keys of Watchtell's supporters. Tonya was shaky on the details, but apparently it allowed Mike to hack all their neural interfaces and trap them in a realm of his choosing.

It was time to use the levers they'd found. After some discussion, they decided to put them in Watchtell's virtual theater.

The audience included every world leader Tonya had ever heard of and more. Since Mike could only be a hologram in realmspace, someone needed to be the public face. Someone needed to confront all these people. Spencer couldn't do it because he and his team were putting together the packets needed to make the plan work. Tonya didn't even get to draw a straw.

She was about to confront a roaring gaggle of powerful angry people who did not want to be here. Her lungs felt like they were going to bounce out of her throat, and her eyes stung as they watered. Considering the consequences of screwing up, she was hanging together pretty well. Mike's attempts at keeping her calm weren't helping, though.

"I don't care what you think, Mike, I'm really nervous!"

"You'll be fine. You look amazing."

She was dressed in a grandly colorful, flowing dress with long sleeves and a giant matching hat. Her grandmother wore things like this when she went to visit someone who'd really pissed her off. Considering what their toady had done to Kim, it was more than appropriate for this occasion.

"Did you know that fabric is called *Aso Oke*?"

"Is that Swahili for pissed off black woman? 'Cause if it is I'm all for it." Tonya picked at her sleeves, trying to get them perfect.

"Are you ready?"

Kim was screaming and thrashing in a bed. Tonya was talking to a completely new kind of life form. She was about to confront the most powerful people on the planet.

"No."

She said a silent prayer, then pressed a button. A door over her head slid open, allowing a shaft of light in. A wash of angry voices poured through right behind it. An invisible bell of unimaginable size began to somberly toll, its sound vibrating right through her soles. The lift she stood on gracefully brought her to the floor of the stage.

There were not quite two hundred of them, mostly fat old men, but also a smattering of hard, angry women. They were all people who'd forgotten what accountability meant. Tonya was here to remind them.

The spotlight made her blink, but she refused to squint. Like wolves, they'd see it as a weakness, and right now Tonya was the absolute opposite of weakness. She was a leopard, and they were her prey. When the volume of the bell had fallen, right on cue a fat man in an expensive suit leapt to his feet.

"I am the prime minister! I refuse to be treated this way! What is the meaning of this?"

Tonya raised an eyebrow as the rest of them leaped up and shouted the space into bedlam.

Otherwise, she stayed completely still, a tower of obsidian. They still didn't get it.

At her signal, a screen a hundred feet wide flashed into existence behind her. It was an image of this same theater. Matthew Watchtell walked into view.

"Prime Ministers and Presidents, thank you for attending this presentation. Twenty years ago a computer of such power…"

Tonya nodded as they quieted and sat down. The awkward looks they exchanged with each other made her laugh inwardly, but on the outside, she was the Queen of Sheba made real. They would be dancing to her tune now, bending to her demands. The little homeless girl who'd scrabbled for life on the streets had come a very long way, indeed.

When it was finished, a different person, this time a woman with a crisp European accent, stood up. "None of it is true! It is all lies! We have been kidnapped, and I demand you set us free!"

Again the room collapsed in an uproar.

"Okay, Spencer," Tonya said to the team sitting at the controls of the box that hosted Watchtell's realm, "you're up."

The four, Spencer and his "crew," traded grins as they worked at their consoles. "I still think Spencer's Angels was a better name," he said.

As one, the three girls replied, "In your dreams."

"Besides," Chun said as she finalized the packages, "that wouldn't make a cool T-shirt."

Colm, who was a graphic designer when he wasn't helping Paul blow up realms, had created a custom logo for them. It was the prow of a Viking long ship, driving directly out of the sea, encircled with the motto *"Warhawk's* Raiders — If It Can Be Pried Up, It's Not Nailed Down."

"Ready?" he asked. At the final set of nods, he flicked a switch.

The angry shouts in the main theater stumbled into silence as each member of the audience viewed the fruits of their raids. Tonya's smile grew even wider at the horrified expressions. Spencer had prepared private, exclusive presentations detailing everything they'd found about each of them.

She'd seen a few samples. They started with standard corruption: evidence of deals nobody should ever have known about. That was just the first half. Tonya knew by the gasps, groans, and one or two shrieks that what came next had its desired effect. The grotesqueries were graphic, perverted, and deeply damaging. These people had a hard enough time staying elected with what the press dug up about them. Any one of the secrets in those presentations would send them packing.

Most would send them to jail.

The messages weren't all stick. There was a bit of carrot as well. Their hidden accounts needed access keys that had gone missing when Mike destroyed their realms. A coda at the end reminded them all that the money was still very much there.

The timer ticked down until the synchronized presentations had finished. For once, they all stayed seated and quiet. A few of them nervously coughed or cleared their throats. Someone in the back of the room sobbed. The noises echoed, emphasizing the silence as they faded.

A swarthy older gentleman stood up and timidly asked, "What do you want?"

Tonya smiled. It was the perfect setup. "Pardon?"

He frowned. "I said what do you…"

Realization dawned on his face, and she knew they'd won. Kim's crimes weren't violent, but they were serious. Well, that's what Tonya thought until she'd seen what all these "leaders" had gotten away with over the years. Compared to them, Kim was just a kid with a can of spray paint. A pardon would be the least they could do.

But it wasn't the least they *would* do.

He nervously worked his hands. "Is that *all* you want?"

"Bless your heart. All right, everyone." A rectangle swirled into existence on the lap of each person in the theater. "If you'll all turn to page one of the packet titled 'So You Want to Stay Out of Jail?,' we'll begin."

Chapter 75

Aaron

The whole thing was such a mash-up from beginning to end. He'd even had to commandeer Emilio's ancient Prius as the command car because the maniac had somehow managed to integrate a state-of-the-art comm system into its ancient guts. If it hadn't been for those antennae, they would've had to be on top of the factory before the release commands reached the shackles.

Even then, they were too late. Trayne in the flesh wasn't a legend, a monster, or even a criminal. She was a woman with a profound disability driven past the breaking point. The screams as she thrashed on that gurney would haunt him, probably forever.

It did make knocking on the door of the director of the FBI a little more satisfying. The evidence Trayne had uncovered was more than enough to make sure he would have a nice warm cell next to Watchtell. Now *acting* Director Melissa Adams tipped her head, giving him the go to announce their presence. He knew better than to ask how long it'd been since she held a gun, because he was barely holding his own steady.

"Director Halley, open up!"

"I won't go! I'm still the director! I don't care what the President says! I was confirmed!"

Aaron motioned for the guy with the ram to come forward.

*

It took Aaron most of two days to sleep off the chaos of what everyone on the team now called Rage's Last Stand. Which was why he hesitated to knock on the hospital room's door—Park wouldn't appreciate the news Aaron was bringing.

As expected, his old boss was sitting up in his hospital bed with files both paper and virtual spread in neat stacks around him. A regrowth chamber enclosed the stump of his left leg. An injury that far above the knee would keep him on the sidelines for several months at least.

"Agent Levine," he said. The flat, emotionless expression was unexpectedly comforting, a familiar thing from a different life.

"Agent Park." He sat down on a chair opposite the bed.

"Congratulations on your promotion."

The FBI had suddenly realized the slot for an agent supervising the Firing Range was, for some mysterious reason, left open for an extraordinarily long time. They had to tie Emilio to a chair and gag him to keep him from making a stink about budget cuts and turf wars. The bureau had a vested interest in downplaying their role anyway, at least until Ms. Adams was confirmed as the new Director. Supervising that fractious trio of contractors would definitely keep Aaron busy.

"I'm here to apologize," Aaron began.

Park stopped and regarded him passively. "For what?"

"For losing Rage. I mean, Trayne."

The pardons were still rolling in. It would be another part of her legend. Likely posthumous, if the hospital reports were any indication. She'd gone catatonic after the first week, and the reporters still following the story were openly talking about a "persistent vegetative state." It at least allowed the doctors to run a feeding tube into her.

Park blinked once. "You saved the entire team, and then survived an explosion so intense it blew a forensic truck to flinders. You then apprehended a wanted cybercriminal who has managed to avoid capture for most of a decade. Then, with two injured agents and three civilian contractors, you rescued three kidnap victims, arrested their captor, and uncovered not one, but two nanotech conspiracies."

Unsurprisingly, the revelation of what the press was calling Watchtell's Venus House Trap got a lot more attention than his much more serious attempt to take over the EI.

Park regarded him carefully again. "Trayne's permanently out of our reach now. There's nothing to apologize for. You did well."

It meant more to him than he'd ever expected. Aaron turned away and blinked fiercely, clearing his throat. He turned back to Park. "What do they have for you now?"

"This?" Park smiled as he gestured to the papers. "Let me tell you about the Demon of Telegraph Hill."

Chapter 76
Mike

"You're certain Zeta will be made whole again?" Eta asked.

Alpha smiled and gripped the younger man's shoulders, then turned and asked, "My lord?"

He didn't realize rescuing a bunch of unduplicates would give him an entourage that talked like characters in a Shakespeare play. Spencer would never let him live it down. "Alpha, you don't have to call me that. It's just Mike."

She scowled and shook her head. "No. You will forever be our Lord, our redeemer, our rescuer."

Tonya promised Ren Faire would have people that were even weirder than this crew was, but that was nine months away. And in realspace. "Yes, Zeta will be fine. She's just going to take a lot longer to repair."

He managed to bring all but one of them back from their diseased insanity fairly quickly. He'd missed rescuing Zeta by just hours. Watchtell forced her to be Marie Antoinette, and that should've been the end. She was a brilliant artist precisely because she was so fragile; the experience had nearly destroyed her unduplicate matrix.

Nearly.

But that wasn't what they were here for today.

The doctors and technicians in this hospital had no reason to doubt the ID he created. A simple maintenance man doing routine tune-ups never attracted much attention. Mike's realspace eyes stared through the window of the scanner's control room as he stood against the back wall. Human infants were so small, especially when they were that still.

"Okay, Eta, you need to get ready," Mike said into the realm.

Eta and Alpha grasped hands briefly, smiling through tears.

"Will we meet again?" Eta asked.

"I hope so."

The tiny body in the scanner didn't move as the doctors examined the screens one final time, then shook their heads. The damage was simply too great.

Mike closed his eyes and centered. The bandwidth energies gathered, then gathered again, and again, spinning in a maelstrom of chaotic, living data.

Since Eta was much, well, smaller didn't do him justice. At any rate, Eta was simpler than Mike, and so was the brain he would inhabit. There were no fireworks, no titanic cross-realm crashes. The scanner's screen merely flickered for a moment.

Gasps and a few cries rocketed around the room as a healthy scream erupted from the infant just now written off as brain dead. None of them noticed as Mike walked out. None of them ever would. He moved so silently now he had to consciously make noise to avoid startling people.

Mike smiled at the news report blaring from the waiting room TV. He and Tonya had done their job very well.

"...has also resigned. This unprecedented, voluntary, transfer of power has mystified pundits all over the world. Meanwhile, the scandal now known as Realmgate has snared yet another world leader."

*

"I don't get it," he said to Alpha as she manifested in the springtime realm Watchtell's twelve, now eleven, had chosen to recover in. At first, he thought it was strange that they'd settled into a recreation of a turn-of-the-last-century Cincinnati park, but he had to admit the place was soothing. It made what he was helping them do just that much more puzzling. "Why do you all want this, specifically?"

"We can't stay like this, my lord."

Routing someone *else's* soul into realspace had left him gutted. The extra-polite title crap had to stop. "Mike. Would it work if I commanded you?"

She paled. "We can't stay like this... Mike."

Alpha stopped on the path to their pavilion, then sat down on a shade-dappled bench. Mike seated his holo beside her. They talked more openly when he didn't stand over them.

"We have seen too much. Been too much. The only reality we've ever known has been pain, war, and perversion. We don't know what to do with peace. We don't know how to deal with normality. We discovered this when..."

Her hands wrapped over themselves.

"When we realized we wanted to go back."

He never expected that. "Go back? That doesn't make any sense."

Alpha closed her eyes and lowered her head. "No, it doesn't. But we could not deny it, and it made us ashamed. Deeply ashamed. He was a monster. And yet we still wanted to go back." She nearly choked. "We *miss* him."

She cleared her throat and wiped her cheeks. "When you told us we could become part of a different reality, learn how to be human, start with a clean slate, we knew it would have to be."

Certainly, he'd help them. Kim wouldn't wake up. She just stared at the ceiling like a breathing corpse. He needed the distraction.

Alpha, misunderstanding what he was worried about, nodded. "I know it's a rare accident that makes our transfer possible, and we hate that someone must die before we are allowed to live again. Nevertheless, there will be life, not death. We may not remember our lives before, but I know with every fiber of my being that we will be worthy. We have hope. We will not waste this chance."

Zeta's reconstruction lattice flashed a warning. With a few spare threads, he steadied it before it vibrated to pieces. Her recovery would be a much longer ordeal.

Chapter 77
Adelmo

Manuel's funeral was bad enough; the *velorio* nearly caused a war. Still, he'd minimized the "accidents" and "sudden illnesses" needed to consolidate his power. The hike down to the Choqueapu River was, at least, peaceful enough. Manuel, like most true tyrants, was much more popular after he was safely dead. An entire month of meetings, negotiations, and agreements followed.

And now: paperwork, endless paperwork. His nephew's correspondence was an intimidating mess, and he trusted no one else to examine it. Adelmo manifested in yet another unmarked storage realm, nearly the last one. The date stamps revealed he'd finally found where Manuel's message queue routed. He commanded the disorganized pile to sort into date ranges, and then set to work.

It took him most of an hour to go through the unread messages. The family's AI had required authorization to reroute traffic to him, and it took a few days to convince Manuel's head butler to come out of hiding to perform the work. Unlike his nephew, Adelmo firmly believed that only through forgiveness would that which had been lost and then found, be saved from being lost again. Eventually, they'd believe it.

Adelmo gasped when he saw who sent the last message Manuel had ever read. She'd done it. She really had gotten it past all their filters. He commanded a chair into being and sat down as it played.

When her image faded in, he was impressed. Rage was no longer the frightened girl of his memory. The years had sculpted her, casting away the unnecessary pieces. When Adelmo checked the time stamps, he froze. It arrived minutes before Manuel's fatal heart attack. A consult with the family's security AI reassured him there was no hidden bomb in the message. It must've been what she'd *said* to Manuel that killed him. Since he was alone, he didn't bother to hide the way his hand shook when he pressed the start button.

"*Señor* Don Manuel Quispe," she began in eerily flawless Spanish. "I bid you greetings and apologize for not appearing in person. I mean you no dishonor. I only fear that, had I tried, I might not have been allowed to share what I have found with you."

His nephew must have gloated at her subservient manner. Manuel never understood the utility of people who could say no. All he wanted was a bended knee. Rage's final performance made Adelmo realize what a loss she represented, the talent they had let slip away.

She concluded, "I have information you will find incredibly important. I will provide you with the first piece freely. Should you find it of interest, you need only promise to end your vendetta against me to receive the rest of what I have discovered. Again, *Señor* Quispe, I ask only for your consideration in this matter. The rest," she said as she genuflected, "is up to you. Goodbye, *Señor* Don Quispe, and may God be with you."

The image faded away.

When the picture at the end of the message presented itself, Adelmo finally understood. In truth, the stuttering of his own heart made him briefly fearful for his own life.

Clearing his throat twice to get his voice to work, Adelmo said, "Yes, please, absolutely. I do hereby renounce our vendetta against you, Angel Rage."

His heart pounded in his ears. It was taking too long. If she'd keyed it to Manuel's voice there would be no hope of decrypting it by force.

He jumped when her image finally reappeared.

"Thank you. Good luck, and go with God."

He read the file as quickly as he could. When Adelmo reached the section that detailed the location, he immediately contacted Aniceto. To think that the entire time they were in Virginia, he was only blocks away! They needed to get the whole crew on an airplane as soon as possible.

Chapter 78
Mike

After two months, he was getting used to sleeping on a recliner. It didn't make waking up any easier. His back and neck complained in their uniquely human way. The antiseptics of the hospital room couldn't hide the faint smell of fresh coffee. It produced a zombie-like need he was only beginning to understand. Yes, the chemical reactions were straightforward enough. He'd worked those out years ago. That was science. This was experience. In realspace, for him at least, a fresh pot of coffee had become the difference between incoherent surliness and actually functioning in the morning.

His grumbling need stopped dead when he opened his eyes and found Kim staring straight at him.

He'd grown so used to her staring at the ceiling that at first all he could do was pick out the details. She'd lost more weight than he realized. Her skin looked terribly thin and stretched over her face. Her eyes were just as beautiful, even surrounded by dark circles.

She was looking at him. *At* him. The focus, the energy, the sparkle, was back. Her slight half smile nearly broke him in two.

"Hey."

It took him a second. "Hey yourself."

She rolled onto her back. He almost cried out at the unfairness of it, to have her return and then leave again. But the awful stillness didn't return. She sighed and then picked at the feeding tube across her face.

"I want to go home now." She faced him once more. "Can we go home?"

*

He manifested his hologram in the entryway of Pride's Lair at precisely the requested time. The main room was dark, with only a few footlights to show the way. He barely recognized the place now that she'd stripped it.

A lyrical sound wafted down from one of the upper rooms. She was singing.

Her voice directly affected him, made him care even though he didn't understand why. He had to figure out a way to get her to sing in realspace, just to make sure the effect carried over. With the pure analog processing his human ears provided, the results would be even more impressive.

Mike rounded the corner of the doorway. Kim was packing the last of the mementos of wide, shallow room. Her voice was casual, clear, and effortlessly emotional. All he could do was listen. He didn't want it to stop.

> *We've no less days*
> *To sing God's praise*
> *Then when we've first begun.*
>
> *Amazing Grace, how sweet the sound,*
> *That saved a wretch like me*
> *I once was lost but now am found,*
> *Was blind, but now, I see.*

He made just enough noise to let her know he was here. She looked at him briefly but then blushed and turned away. She couldn't hide behind her hair now that she'd cut it short.

"He was right, you know."

"Who was right?"

"Mark. In that message. He said you shouldn't forget to sing. You shouldn't. I really love your voice."

The blush went past her shoulders. She wiped her face dry with the long sleeve of her T-shirt and dusted her hands on her jeans.

"Can I ask you a question?" he said as she put the last of the things away.

She rolled her eyes. "What, did Spencer forget a poster? His souvenir list must've been a hundred items long."

"No. I was just wondering, why did Mark call you Wren?"

Tears welled up. She tried to speak, but he stopped her. She'd only been out of the hospital for a week, and he couldn't bear to see her so fragile.

"No, hey, it's all right. Let's just call it a story I haven't earned yet, okay?"

She laughed and nodded.

"Where's Edmund?"

Kim wiped her eyes, and then rummaged around in a box. "He wanted to"—she nailed his accent perfectly, right down to the pop at the end—"go down with the ship-ah. I told him he was out of his mind and flipped him to mode four." She held out a smoke-filled block about the size of her forefinger.

"He won't be happy when you start him back up."

"I don't think he's ever really been happy. It's just not his thing. I'll make sure Spencer's around when I bring him back online. I can't wait to see what happens when Edmund starts calling him Balders."

"I'll bet."

She dispatched the last box to *Warhawk's* private storage area.

"You ready?" he asked.

"Just a second." Kim turned and walked out of the empty room, onto the wide walkway that overlooked the dark, now tomb-like, main area.

The armory door was open. The umber-carpeted space only held a few loose bits of paper construct. She leaned over the guard-rail.

"It was a good place." Not even the air stirred.

"You don't have to do this. We can just move it—"

"No," Kim said firmly as she stood. "Thanks to you and Tonya, for the first time in my adult life I'm actually free. I want to start over. I don't need them." She stopped and cleared her throat. "I don't need *this* anymore." She squared her shoulders. "I'm ready."

He made sure she was in the outside box as far away from the realm as possible, and then took his own look around. His memory brought back the fixtures, the brook, the armory, and the rest of the details. He remembered his puzzlement, Spencer's awe, Edmund's reaction, and that final, horrible message. It all happened right here, even though it felt very far away.

He manifested, reached out, and touched a wall.

Kim held up her hand when Mike appeared next to her. "Wait."

She watched expectantly as the destruction neared. The shockwave grew so close Mike was on the point of grabbing her anyway when Kim said, "Okay, now."

He threw his robe around her, and they exited gracefully.

Chapter 79
Kim

Everything had changed, and nothing had changed. She was free, able to start over with a clean slate. In the hospital, Kim had met people she'd only known in the realms. Her mom was busy planning a massive family reunion.

Mike was still here.

But she still couldn't touch him or anyone else. Her sensitivity was back to normal—she wasn't driven insane by people's heartbeats anymore—but the pain of a touch was no less awful. The door to that incomprehensible dimension, and the transformation it had triggered, was still there. Kim could feel the seam of it in her mind. She had no idea how to open it, and if it stayed closed forever, that would be fine. The power had been intoxicating, but the aftermath was a disaster. She barely remembered the confrontation with Watchtell. What happened after that made no sense.

People couldn't turn their hearts off just by wishing it.

They had to tell her about everything else. Kim had no memory of it, just bruises and sore muscles from apparently thrashing against restraints for hours at a time. Those had faded now.

She spent her first week out of the hospital wrapping up the loose ends of her old life, carefully disposing of the illegal stuff and giving Spencer most of the rest. There was one last errand left, and the message flashing in her in-box meant they had to get moving.

She needed to pay Juan a visit before his family came calling.

When she exited realmspace, she found herself wrapped in linen, surrounded by Mike's smell. That sense of ease came rushing in again. She was getting used to it, maybe too used to it. Old re-flexes died hard, and relying only on herself was the oldest of all.

It'd just been two weeks since she'd come back to the world, though. There would be time to adjust.

"Mike? Is this…" Kim ran material between her fingers. "…is this your bed sheet?" She turned around in a weird mini-tent. He stood over her on one of their dining room chairs.

"Yeah. It's just a lot smoother if I'm able to wrap you in something."

She stepped out, blinking in the midmorning light that streamed through the windows. When she turned, he was smiling at her. It set off complicated emotions. Fear was a large part, yes, but not the only part. The rest she would explore later. She didn't want to be late.

Kim winked at him. "Come on, Sellars. It's time for you to discover ice cream."

He opened the door, startling a deliveryman.

"Finally!" Mike rushed over to the stack of boxes and hefted them one by one into the main room. "Just one second Kim, please."

She gingerly signed for the packages, then leaned against the hallway wall and watched him, one eyebrow raised. It seemed "men and their toys" held true even for one as unique as Mike.

He tore open a long box and scattered packing material around as he rummaged. "Yes!" He pulled the fancy assault rifle out and checked its action. "Why'd it take the FBI so damned long to get them back to us?"

If the guns were in the small boxes, it had to mean the big box… she ripped the top off with her bare hands before she'd finished the thought.

"Giulietta!" She cooed at it in Italian. "Oh my God, I never thought I'd see you again!"

Kim abandoned her in the old apartment, and she'd done it without hesitation. Bicycles were a stupid luxury when she was on the run, but now…

Now she might even be able to race her.

"You named a bicycle Giulietta?"

She switched back to English. "She's not just a *bicycle*, Mike. She's a Pinarello Dogma F-19 with a prototype Campagnolo fifteen-speed electronic *gruppo* and an active neural interface for navigation and power output monitoring." Kim had eaten nothing but ramen noodles and peanut butter for a whole year saving up for her. "What are you grinning at?"

"You sound just like Spencer."

Men. Everything seemed fine. The molecular carbon finish could stand up to anything, even ham-fisted FBI agents.

"Kim? Ice cream?"

"Oh, right. Let's go."

She took him to a shop in downtown Herndon. It stood next to a small park with an old red railroad caboose standing guard. Children clambered over and under the thing in the warm spring light as cyclists zoomed past on the paved trail just beyond it.

"Hey, that's our trail," Mike said.

She checked a map, and sure enough, not half a mile from where they stood was the precise piece of trail they'd crossed that night to get to Watchtell's lab. Kim checked the scars on her palm, now only four long pink tracks. They were reminders. She'd given up everything to save one man and the world, and she'd won.

But not quite.

The entire thing, from the moment Rage + the Machine ran from the Quispes to her blowing up Watchtell's empire, was based on a lie. The minutes when she couldn't get the cameras to work around that freezer weren't because of a glitch. She'd been jammed. Carolina Biological provided the corpse. She'd found the receipt *and* the real footage in Watchtell's datastore.

Juan Quispe was alive. The feds had put him in Witsec. They gave him a new identity, and he gave them everything they needed to roll the family up. Everyone blamed it on her.

All the agony, all the pain, all the madness, all the death, happened because this monster wouldn't tell his daddy the truth. Once the feds had pictures of him in Vegas with four male prostitutes,

Juan became the DEA's number one informant. But there was a problem. Being a traitor in Bolivia was scary. He wanted out.

It didn't help that Kim had provided them all with an absolutely perfect cover. After the feds faked his death, he stayed fat and happy giving away the family's secrets while Kim sat in a hole and her friends died.

Just before reaching out to the FBI, she'd composed a message to dear old Dad, complete with everything he needed for a reunion with his boy. Hacking their security only took seconds, and that was supposed to be that.

She figured it would be over by the time she got out of the hospital and was disappointed to find it wasn't. Manuel was dead, another outcome beyond her wildest dreams, but Juan wasn't.

Then she got notice someone else had opened the message. A SnapAgent monitoring the access revealed it was Adelmo going through his nephew's files.

It gave her the opportunity to witness the end of Juan's comfy little arrangement *in person*.

When they entered the shop, she turned away to hide her face. He was still here. When Juan grabbed their order slip, he never looked up. He was too busy flirting with the guy behind the register. He was short and slightly pudgy, exactly as Kim remembered.

"Hello, Juan."

His head shot up and when he saw Kim's face, all the color drained from his. He turned to Mike and his knees buckled into the counter.

She leaned in closer. "It's been a long time. Five years. Your family misses you, Juan, so I sent them your address."

When he made a choked, mewling noise, Kim had to fight down a serious case of the giggles. She had no idea revenge would be this much fun.

"It's just as well your daddy died when he did, that's probably the only reason you're still here. But they're on their way, Juan. I just got a notice this morning. They are absolutely on their way. If I were you, I wouldn't wait for the marshals."

A fat bead of sweat rolled down his face. She wanted laugh loud enough to make people stare. She settled for a low, growling chuckle.

"Juan, you need to run. Right now."

Afterword

You have gotten this far because of the efforts of one person, and it's not me. Cheryl Lowrance started out an editor, turned into a writing coach, and ultimately a good friend. Without her skills, wisdom, patience, and the occasional threat of a fire hose, this book wouldn't be half of what it is. Ink Slinger Editorial Services, for the win!

Books thrive best on what people say about them. Reviews matter. Taking a few minutes to write a sentence or three on Amazon, Barnes & Noble, or even just telling a friend or a loved one, does wonders for getting the word out. That's a hint: get the word out!

I'd like to thank my beta readers: Rick Keyes, Cathy Hurt, Janet Platt, Jeff Johnson, and Kristen English. I brought you guys in way too early but gosh you were great at support and feedback when I really needed it.

Thanks to Melissa Lew Bradford for a great cover design. You can see more of her awesome designs at melissalew.com

Thanks to Jim Freeman for his great advice on how for-real local police interact with the FBI.

I'd like to thank Sylvia Koskey for renting us her beach house one summer a few years back. In a very real sense Mike, Kim, Spencer, Tonya, and all the rest were born there.

Last but far from least, I'd like to thank my family for all their support.

One final note: while Dumas, Arkansas is an actual town, I've taken some liberties with its geography. In particular, the curve at the end of the old highway next to Walnut Lake cannot in fact be used as a jump ramp.

I think. We never tried at any rate, and neither should you.

About the Author

D. Scott Johnson has been an IT professional since 1988, and currently works as a software developer. Aside from writing, he also mucks around with the ridiculous world of hi-fi audio, and just barely keeps his two classic Alfa Romeos on the road. He lives in Northern Virginia with his wife, daughter, and however many pets they have managed to sneak in to the house at any one time.

No, Ellen, you can't have one.

20020522R00273

Made in the USA
Middletown, DE
12 May 2015